September Valentine

Faye Ashley

St. Martin's Paperbacks

SEPTEMBER VALENTINE

Copyright © 1997 by Faye Ashley.

ISBN: 0-312-96279-7

Printed in the United States of America

St. Martin's Paperbacks edition/September 1997

St. Martin's Paperbacks are published by St. Martin's Press, 175 Fifth Avenue, New York, NY 10010.

10 9 8 7 6 5 4 3 2 1

This book is dedicated to my daughters:
Debbie Clayton, the nurturer;
Susan Ashley, the healer;
and my heart-daughter, Jewell Wright, whose name
says it all.

Prologue

Valentine Townsend had eyes the color and texture of woods' violets, but right now they resembled sapphires as she stared at the two white-robed Beings sitting behind their soft-as-rose-water desk. She knew the desk was soft because she had touched it. In fact, in what was probably an appalling breach of divine etiquette, both her palms were spread atop its luminous surface. Hastily she removed them.

"Is something wrong, Valentine?" the shorter Being asked.

"Well, yes, something's wrong! Good grief, you're making jokes? You're making jokes in Heaven?" she gasped. The idea of such a thing outraged the tiny orthodox part of her, even though she had rejected it years ago.

The taller Being, whose hair was a cloud wisping around his shining pate, gave her a reproving look. "A good joke is a good joke anywhere," he said.

Her eyes flashed even while her knees knocked together. "Maybe so, but I do not care to be addressed as your favorite screwup, especially in Heaven."

"Who said this was Heaven?" he inquired.

Valentine had to grab the desk again. "B-but it has to be Heaven! I'm dead, aren't I? And I know damn well this isn't ... uh, the other place," she ended weakly as the tall Being frowned. Now she was cursing!

Valentine drew herself up to her full height of five foot, three and one half inches, and eyed him defiantly despite his air of

*brisk, pompous authority. Let him spend some time walking in
her shoes, see if he'd be all sweetness and light!*

The bracing flare of defiance fizzled out as the Being's full
magnificence struck her senses. He glowed with light. Brilliant
light, pure white light imbued with a golden hue. An incredible
light that radiated outward and shone through every pore of
his skin, every strand of hair, every thread of his long robe.

His eyes, however, were piercingly brown. His regard was
unsmiling, his countenance stern, and Valentine had to admit
to a knee-weakening quiver of fear. He resembled her fearful
childhood image of God The Father Almighty, Maker of Hell
as well as Heaven.

"Don't be afraid," the shorter Being, with hair like sun-
beams, said gently.

"I'm not afraid," Valentine replied, smiling back at him.
He was composed of the same brilliant light. It was brighter
than sunlight, she realized, yet looking at him did not hurt her
eyes, nor did it fill her with dread. Just intense awe, and a
quick, singing joy at the wonder of it all. "I'm just a little
nervous," she explained, suddenly shy.

"No reason to be nervous," he chided lovingly. "There are
many other places you could have gone, but you requested
this one . . . although if you disagree, I can double-check my
facts easily enough."

He looked upward. Valentine followed his gaze and gasped
again. Above his head, written in superb penmanship, were
the last words she had spoken on earth. "Oh God, please! I
wasn't a bad person—pleaseohplease let me find bliss—"

"That dash is when the plane crashed," he said.

The writing disappeared. Valentine's gaze shot to the one
with clouds for hair. "How did you do that?"

"The Akashic Records, of course." His smile turned quizzical. "Why so surprised, Valentine? Weren't you taught that
everything you say and do will be written in the Book of Life?
It's the same thing, just a matter of semantics."

"Well, yes, but . . ." Valentine's voice rose to a new high
of incredulous dismay. "Everything?"

"Everything."

"Oh, but . . . I mean, when you're young, just a child, really, an adolescent at the most, surely you can't be held accountable—''

"Everything."

"Ohmigod." She needed to sit down, but there were no chairs, just this gauzy stuff swirling everywhere, and she really did need to sit down. She no sooner thought it than a big, comfy, overstuffed chair appeared behind her. She dropped into it. "How . . . ?"

"Ask and you shall receive," replied the Being she mentally called Sunbeam. "Only here, unlike Earth, you don't have to wait or work for it. You create it, just like you created this place."

When Valentine opened her mouth, nothing came out but a squeak. She cleared her throat. A question finally untangled itself from the writhing mass in her mind and emerged in a husky, "And this place is?"

"The southeast quadrant of the sixth plane of the tenth realm. Oh, in the state of Bliss, of course, just as you requested. And you may indeed call me Sunbeam. I rather like it."

"My name is Bradley," the other Being said curtly. "Now, if there are no more comments"—he directed a sour look at Sunbeam—"or questions," he continued, glancing pointedly at Valentine, "perhaps we can get down to basics. Valentine, how do you feel right now?"

Surprised by his question, she examined herself. "I feel . . . oh dear God, I feel wonderful! So peaceful, so happy! And light as a feather, so light I could float on a breeze . . . oh, jeez!" Her shriek coincided with the lazy, circling, upward drift her body was taking. She was floating? "No, wait, I didn't mean—" With a smothered cry she plopped straight back down into the chair.

The two Beings exchanged knowing looks. "Enough gymnastics," Bradley said. "Suffice it to say that you feel wonderful and you want to stay here."

"Oh, yes, God, yes!" Wondering if she could actually fly, Valentine spread her arms as if they were wings—and sailed *into the celestial blue sky like a balloon freed of its restraints.*

"A bit too fast, but I'll soon get the hang of it," she said breathlessly when she touched down again. She whirled around in a blaze of rapture. She felt so cherished, so loved! She felt absolutely consumed with this total, boundless, utterly inexpressible love! "Oh, yes, I do want to stay here!" she exulted.

"Well, you can't."

She blinked. "I beg your pardon?"

"I said, you can't," Bradley repeated. "Did you think our calling you a screwup just idle words? We never speak idly, even in jest."

"But why can't I stay? What have I done that's so terrible?" she protested. "Okay, I admit that once or twice I might have gotten a little carried away—like that time I snuck a horse into the mayor's office—but for Pete's sake, I was just a kid. A teenager having a bit of high-spirited fun, that's all. The mayor was a pretentious ass, you know that. Besides, he's my uncle, so I wasn't in any danger." She sent Sunbeam a limpid glance. "How was I to know he'd make such a mess on the carpet? The horse, I mean. Anyway, everyone but the mayor thought it was hilarious."

"I certainly did," Sunbeam said. "And finding a horse at that hour of night was certainly commendable."

"It was a police horse," she told him. "My cousin Ned is a cop and he—"

"That's quite enough about mayors and horses," Whitecloud thundered. His brows shot together. "My name, young lady, is Bradley. I would appreciate being thought of as that."

Valentine apologized, even though she did admire her play on words.

"We do love a good sense of humor," Sunbeam reminded him. "And she surely has that."

"Granted, she does have an essentially merry nature. But it's buried under all that fear and caution. Look what she has done with her precious gift of time on Earth. Wasted it, just frittered it away."

"Oh, now, Bradley," Sunbeam tut-tutted. "Not everyone

wants to be Mother Teresa." He smiled at Valentine. *"Love one another, live life to the fullest and in a way that does no harm; that's all the One asks of you."*

"My point exactly." Bradley's brown eyes nailed her to the spot. *"Have you lived life to the fullest? Have you gladly taken risks, welcomed challenges, grabbed every opportunity that came along?"* His voice softened to molten steel. *"Have you loved, Valentine? I mean real love, pure love."*

Suddenly uneasy, Valentine chose her words with care. *"Well, sure I've loved. I love lots of people. Like my cousin Samantha. You must know her—everyone knows Sam!"* she said, her gaze suddenly as soft as her laughter. *"We have a bond of love and loyalty that goes all the way back to my childhood."*

"Actually your bond goes back thousands of years," Sunbeam said.

Her eyes rounded. *"It does?"*

"Oh, yes. In fact, you've been mother and child many times, including the last two lifetimes."

"Which you also screwed up." Bradley transfixed her with his stern stare. *"To proceed; and love between a man and a woman? Have you experienced that?"*

Tension sculpted her cheekbones. *"No, I can't say that I have. I want to,"* she hastily assured him. *"I want it all, love, marriage, children. It just hasn't happened. But that's surely not an offense; lots of women forego love and marriage. Take Mother Teresa, for instance—"*

"There's a tad difference between you and Mother Teresa," Bradley cut in with withering irony.

"I know that, I was just making a point," Valentine responded with gratifying dignity. *"My point being that I haven't been fortunate enough to find my true love, that's all. But I'm only twenty-three, I have loads of time yet. At least I . . . I thought I did."*

"We always think that," Sunbeam said sadly. *"But your time is up, Valentine. Life on Earth is a school, and you've failed it once again."*

"But what did I do?" she asked, clearly bewildered.

"It's not what you did, it's what you didn't do," Whitecloud answered her. *"Life is for being, for doing, loving, living! With gusto, yes, with vibrant excitement and joy."* His voice soared. *"Life is for gaining experience, for feeling, with every sense you possess, the wonderful adventure you've undertaken! It's for diving into with headlong enthusiasm, secure in the knowledge that nothing in the whole of Creation can harm the essential Valentine. What's the use of living if you don't live?"*

"You knew all this when you first came to the Earth plane," Sunbeam said. *"But then you grew up, and the knowledge slipped away. Now, instead of living, you simply exist. You skim the surface, afraid to risk, afraid you'll get hurt. You can't trust, you can't give trust. You can't let yourself be vulnerable because you're afraid of the potential for pain. Always so afraid."* He sighed.

"You haven't even experienced passion," Bradley said. *"The most Divine pleasure possible between a man and woman, and you missed it."*

Valentine's head reeled from all these accusations. The shock of knowing they were irrefutable had the effect of a slap in the face. *"Well, that's not my fault,"* she snapped, outraged at the last one. *"I want to know what passion is like, every woman does. But I . . . I'm chaste, you see, I'm a chaste person, dammit! I thought that was considered a good thing to be?"*

"Chastity is beautiful," Bradley affirmed. *"If it's a heartfelt decision and not a knee-jerk reaction to fear."*

"Huh. Damned if I do and damned if I don't," she murmured wryly.

"Oh, nonsense, no one's damning anyone," Sunbeam said, gently smiling.

"Of course not. Impossible," Bradley harrumphed. *"We're simply trying to help you realize where you went wrong. Not an easy task in itself, I might add."*

"Well, at least I lived my life in a way that did no harm," Valentine said with a relieved sigh.

"Wrong," Bradley promptly refuted. *"You have never*

learned to take responsibility for yourself. Thus someone else must make your decisions and bear the consequences of what should be your actions.''

He stopped as a shimmering apparition appeared beside him.

''Oh, quit badgering her, Bradley,'' a sweet voice chided.

To Valentine it sounded like music. Her mouth went dry as she watched the beautiful woman assume form and substance. Although a Being of the same light that haloed Sunbeam and Bradley, she seemed less ethereal. She wore a long, white, full-sleeved gown, gathered and sashed just beneath her breasts. Pearly pink toes in silver sandals peeked from under the ribboned hem. Her glowing hair, soft as thistledown, was piled atop her head, completing her Grecian look.

''Hello, Valentine,'' she said like a warm, loving hug. She smiled, and flowers sprang up around her pretty feet.

Trying desperately to scare up a drop of spit, Valentine croaked, ''Uh, hi.''

''Valentine, this is Elisse, your guardian angel.'' Sunbeam beamed.

''My angel? But she has no wings—you have no wings!'' Valentine said, then flushed as Elisse chuckled at her childish outburst.

''Do you need wings, Valentine?''

This time her voice was a gentle chime of temple bells.

Valentine swallowed. ''No, of course not. But all the angels in books and paintings have wings, so naturally I thought . . .''

''Artistic license,'' Sunbeam explained. ''You two have been together for a long time, Valentine, so Elisse should feel very familiar to you.''

''Or would, had you paid her any attention,'' Bradley said. ''I'm sorry, Elisse, but the matter is settled. She has to do it over. How else is she to learn these particular lessons?''

''All right, Bradley, but does she have to start as an infant again? She has so much potential in this current life!''

''Now, Elisse, you know the importance of childhood. It's the only time she gives free rein to her basic nature; eager, joyous, inquisitive—''

"Merry and mischievous," Sunbeam finished for him. *"I love that mind-set, that 'let's try it and see what happens' attitude! Like the horse in the mayor's office! If you could have seen his face, Bradley!"*

"I did see his face," Bradley reminded his associate. *"While I don't approve of the horse incident, the underlying motivation was quite courageous and daring. In my opinion, she needs to reexperience that feeling. Maybe the next time it will stick with her. Yes, I definitely think it best that she return to Earth as a newborn."*

"Oh, now, wait a minute!" the subject of their conversation leaped in. *"It's bad enough that I have to go back, but go back as a baby?"* Valentine's stomach lurched as she thought of being trapped in an infant's helpless body. *"And then to go through puberty again? Oh, no, no, no! Oh, please, help me?"* she appealed to her angel.

"Perhaps she could return as she is now, simply take up her life again," Elisse suggested. *"What time is it on Earth?"*

A row of lighted letters obligingly appeared to answer her question: 2:16 . . . February 4.

"Oh, good, it's just been a few minutes," she said. *"The pilot is still unconscious, so no one will notice her absence. And this time, knowing I'm there to help her, I'm sure she'll do a much better job."*

"She wouldn't know you were there," Bradley reminded the angel. *"It's not permitted; she has to sense your presence and then follow your guidance. Though when has she ever given the slightest sign of that? If following her intuition involves doing something spontaneous or unpredictable or even just a little out of the ordinary, she blocks it."*

Elisse sighed, her eyes darkening to the color of fine brandy. *"No one's more aware of that than I, Bradley. On the other hand, this near-death experience always has a strong impact on human character, so perhaps she might begin to embrace change instead of fearing it. But it's your decision,"* she yielded. *"Good-bye, Valentine. Whatever the verdict, I'll be with you, darling, remember that. Oh, you won't consciously know it; as Bradley said, it's not permitted. But if you look deep inside, listen with your heart instead of your ears—"*

"Elisse," Bradley murmured.

Her mouth quirked in acceptance of his just reproof. She nodded, blew Valentine a kiss, and vanished.

The brilliantly colored flowers vanished, too. Valentine groped for her chair. It obligingly slid into position. She sat down and crossed her legs. To her astonishment, she had to pee.

"We'll be through in just a minute," Sunbeam promised. "Speed it up, Bradley?"

"Yes, of course. Where were we? Ah, yes," Bradley muttered as that eerie writing appeared above his head, chronicling his previous words as well as Valentine's last plea. He turned to Sunbeam and inquired testily, "You do agree that she cannot stay here?"

Sunbeam nodded.

Her face fell like a wilted flower.

He sighed, his beautiful, hound-dog eyes liquid with regret. "I'm sorry, Valentine. I did so hope you would learn your lessons this time around. But you didn't, and now it's too late . . . isn't it?" he checked with his companion.

Glancing at the young woman huddled in her chair, Bradley hesitated. Such guileless appeal, he thought. A real heartbreaker, this one. Her eyes were as innocent as the flowers they resembled. And Earth was the hardest school in the Universe.

"Drat it all," he muttered. He scowled at Sunbeam, who smiled with radiant sweetness. "Oh, all right," Bradley yielded. "Keeping in mind that we are her Counselors, a heavy, heavy responsibility," he reminded his associate, "let's reconsider our options. There are only two: returning as an infant—after a little R and R, of course—or continuing with her current life."

"I vote she takes up her current life," Sunbeam promptly decided.

Bradley cast him a pained look. "Why? Why heal her just so she can go back to doing exactly what she was doing before, just muddling through?"

"She won't," said Sunbeam. "Will you?"

"Absolutely not," Valentine said. "No more muddling, I promise."

"Her solemn promise, Bradley. That's good enough for me," Sunbeam said with a dazzling smile.

"Humph." Bradley worked up another scowl at being so grievously manipulated. "She's not there just to learn, she's supposed to teach, too."

"Which she will," Sunbeam swiftly asserted. "There are so many people farther along her path, waiting for her love and assistance. Their growth will be altered, too. Perhaps even delayed."

Bradley sighed and looked Heavenward. "All right, it's agreed: She gets a second chance. But it's conditional," he warned, forestalling her effusive outburst. "Do you accept that?"

"Yes, sir," she said meekly.

"Very well. Condition number one: You will cease being so fearful—"

"This is not to say you will not feel afraid," Sunbeam cut in. "Of course you will—that's just a natural part of living on the Earth plane."

"True," Bradley agreed. "But it's something you can, and will, overcome."

"Just remember that you are a Spiritual Being inhabiting a physical body," Sunbeam went on. "The body eventually dies, but you go on forever. So lighten up, Valentine. When you make a mistake, just laugh at yourself and get on with it."

"Condition number two: You will take control of your life and accept responsibility for your decisions," Bradley said.

"Stand on your own two feet, in other words," Sunbeam helped.

"Precisely. Number three: You will embrace life's challenges with anticipation rather than apprehension. Indeed, you will joyously risk everything and anything to attain a worthy goal. Number four: You will love wholeheartedly and without reservations. At the same time, you will wisely refrain from going overboard.''

''Don't get too reckless, he means. Take care of your precious Self, Valentine,'' Sunbeam said tenderly.

''Really, Sunbeam, I do think I am making myself clear,'' Bradley harrumphed. He turned back to Valentine, his gaze cool and steady, and filled with boundless love.

''Condition number five is a time limit, Valentine.''

''What do you mean, a time limit?'' she asked warily.

''I mean,'' said the Being with clouds for hair, ''that you have exactly one Earth-year in which to fulfill the other four conditions.''

Chapter 1

Valentine Townsend came awake with the words of her silent cry still ringing in her ears. *Please let me stay—don't make me go back!*

She had no idea where she had been in that dream, or why she had wanted so much to remain. Impressions floated through her mind like snippets of long-forgotten music, maddeningly evasive, just out of reach. Lingering sensations of something that transcended time, space and logic clogged her throat with longing. A great, soul-deep longing. For what?

Anguished by her haunting sense of loss, she stared at the ceiling, straining to see beyond its pale substance. Where had she been? And what had she lost? Her memory supplied no details save for a swirling white haze and the sweet scent of flowers.

Eerily, the evocative fragrance seemed to mist the air around her. Seeking reality, Valentine found it in the cold February dawn streaking the windows.

In the distance she could see Cincinnati National's big neon sign flashing the temperature, date and time. "Eight degrees!" she whispered. God, she hated February, hated being cold, hated the whirling arabesque of wind and snow!

Her inner turmoil eased as a soft snore from the other side of the bed anchored her even more firmly in place. It was her cousin Samantha's bed.

Nicknamed Sam as a precocious tot, Samantha was three

years older. And by far the prettiest Townsend, Valentine thought fondly. In the misty glow of a street lamp, Sam's oval face took on an ethereal beauty that belied the redhead's crisp, feisty manner. Impulsively Valentine leaned over and kissed her smooth cheek. They were closer than friends, closer than sisters. It was always Sam she turned to when life became too onerous.

Aglow with light and welcoming smiles, Sam's childhood home was similar to hers in age and design. But similarity ended at the front door, Valentine thought morosely. Her impression of her own home was one of chill, dimly lit rooms, her mother working the night shift, her stepfather slumped in front of the TV in a beery stupor.

Angry and frustrated, she'd come here again last night to seek comfort in the warm normality of her closest and dearest confidante. Sam always had both feet on the ground.

Which is more than I can say for myself, Valentine reflected. Sighing, she doubled the pillow under her head and tried to analyze her disturbingly intense dream. For of course it was a dream! Very likely it had something to do with her gnawing discontent. But what?

And what the hell can I do about it? she thought irritably.

Leave.

The word fell across her mind like a pristine snowflake.

Valentine smiled, bleak humored. Leave? She could just imagine her family's reaction to that! Just run away and leave your poor mother to cope alone, Valentine?

Not only would such behavior be totally out of character, it wouldn't be right—

Right according to whom?

Valentine stilled at the question. She tried to brush it away, but it simply slid in from the other side, as persistent as a bedroom mosquito. Confused at this unasked-for advice from what must be an overworked conscience, she shook Sam's shoulder.

Sam stirred, then opened her eyes. "What's the matter, can't you sleep? Are you okay?" she asked, turning on the light. Anxiety darkened her green eyes.

"Sam, will you stop worrying about me?" Valentine chided. "I slept, but a dream woke me up." She sighed. "A dream I can't remember, yet it feels so terribly real."

"Oh, honey, that's natural enough," Sam soothed, patting her arm. "You've been through a lot, Val. A plane crash isn't something you can easily forget."

"It's been three weeks, Sam, and I walked away from it with only a concussion," Valentine reproved. It felt silly blaming her mysterious malaise on the plane crash.

And yet something had changed her. Nothing fit anymore, not her lifestyle, not this city she loved so much, not even the cherished network of family and friends. She felt suffocated by the very things that were once synonymous with vitally needed security. Which was shameful, she brooded. Only the rankest sort of ingrate would forget for even one second how very lucky—how enormously *blessed*, to quote sundry aunts— September Valentine Townsend was.

"God, I feel so mixed up inside," she whispered. Tears flooded her eyes. "Sam, I don't know what's happening to me, everything's so different lately!" she blurted. "It's all changed, my perspectives, my beliefs—nothing's solid anymore. Sometimes I think I'm crazy!"

"You are not crazy!" Sam said, wonderfully indignant. "Good grief, you looked death in the face, Valentine. Of course it changed you!"

"I haven't told you all of it," Valentine said, wiping her eyes. "These changes in me go really deep, Sam. I walk around practically drenched in emotion! And I'm so much more intuitive now." She hesitated, wondering how far to go. "There's something else that's kind of disturbing. I . . . I know things about people, things I don't think I should be knowing."

Sam propped herself up against the quilted headboard. "I don't understand. What kind of things?"

"Things like . . . like what sort of person they are, if they're happy or sad, whether they're generally decent or something totally opposite. I can't tell why they're any of these things, just that they are. And not everyone. It either has to be very strong, or else I must really want to know.''

Sam arched one eyebrow, a trick Valentine had always envied. ''Excuse me? You're saying you know what kind of person someone is just from . . . from what, looking at them?''

''That's sort of what I mean. I look at someone—like that intern I wouldn't allow in my hospital room, remember? I looked at him and saw all those shades of darkness.'' She grimaced. ''I didn't want him near me, near my bed or even in my room, for that matter.''

''On the surface that does seem odd,'' Sam granted. ''But we all meet people we dislike for no reason. Jeez, Val, if you really could see those kind of things, it would be invasive. An infringement of my privacy.''

Trouble. The warning floated across Valentine's mind like a wisp of fog. But she caught its meaning. ''Your privacy? Oh, Sam! Darlin', you don't have any privacy! You're an open book to me, don't you know that?'' she teased. ''Haven't I always been able to tell when you're sad or happy or mad as a wet hen? And can't you tell the same about me?''

Relieved, Sam nodded. ''You've always been sensitive, so I suppose it's possible that you're even more so since the plane crash. Trauma can do that, I hear.'' She grinned. ''Any other explanation gets into the twilight zone, babe!'' She hummed a few bars of the TV show theme song, making them both laugh. Sobering, she asked gently, ''Val, you want to try talking about the crash? Sweetie, I know it was terrifying; just tell me what you can bear to remember.''

''That's just it, Sam, I don't remember much about it,'' Valentine confessed. ''Weird, huh? The biggest experience of my life and it's a hazy void!'' She paused, then burst out, ''But there are things in that haze, words and voices and . . . and even reprimands. Somebody was bawling me out for wasting my time or my life or something like that. And someone else was defending me. And even more absurd, I have this freaky memory of someone asking me if I needed wings!''

She stopped to catch her breath. ''Well, obviously I was hallucinating, but even the hallucinations were weird. Eerie, actually. Scares heck out of me that I keep trying to make sense of it. Doesn't say much for my mental balance, does it!'' she finished with a shaky laugh.

"Oh, stop that,'' Sam commanded. "What else do you remember?''

"Like I said, the crash itself is kind of a blank. I woke up in a snowbank, saw Jack in the plane, unconscious and bleeding. I checked him out, discovered the blood was coming from a gash on his forehead, not his mouth, thank God.''

"Good lord, Val! Weren't you hysterical?''

"No, I wasn't. Another astonishment—why wasn't I crying and screaming and carrying on like I usually do in emergencies? I was upset, sure, but mostly I was so darn cold. Cold from the inside out, Sam. I now know exactly what being trapped inside an icicle would feel like!''

Sam shuddered, too. "I can imagine!''

"But the cold must have helped, because I kept acting in such a rational manner,'' Valentine continued. "We'd gone down in the wilds of Montana. Jack had sent out a Mayday, but who knew how far we'd traveled since? And then, like magic, I remembered him saying that the ELT was in the tail of the plane. The Emergency Locator Transmitter,'' she explained. "It's supposed to trigger automatically in a crash, but Jack said he would never leave that to chance, he'd make sure it was working. So I found it and flipped on the manual switch.''

Sam's eyes widened. "You knew what an ELT was? And how to work it?''

"Well, sure. Flying in that tiny little plane was absolutely *terr*ifying, Sam. I kept asking questions to keep from screaming. Luckily I remembered the answers. Amazing, isn't it, that I could be so cool in such dire circumstances?'' Valentine marveled.

"God, yes! I doubt I'd have had the wits to even climb out of that snowbank.''

"Oh, you would have. You've never lacked for courage or daring,'' Valentine said, her tone wistful, bittersweet.

"Neither have you, babe. If that wasn't pure, raw courage,

I don't know what is.'' Sam's jaw clenched as she glanced at her cousin's tear-streaked face. To her, Valentine was just plain adorable, as soft and cuddly as a spring lamb. She was heart-catchingly pretty with her drooping mouth, little tipped nose and that cloud of midnight black hair. Her impact upon men was sometimes amusing, sometimes puzzling, but always intense. They might yearn to pet her, bed her or marry her. But whatever their needs, one look into those big eyes the color of wildwood violets and just as innocent, and men were absolutely driven with the urge to take up cudgels and defend.

She, too, was hung up on the compelling need to take care of Valentine, Sam admitted, when she knew better than anyone that her dewy young cousin was as helpless as a barracuda. A glance at Valentine's hunched shoulders intensified the urge to hold and soothe and fix-it, whatever *it* was. Instead, she leaned forward, her manner conspiratorial.

"So tell me about the ski trip itself, Mouse,'' she said, using her old nickname for this petite cousin. "Did *it* happen?''

"What? Oh!'' Comprehending her cousin's meaning, Valentine flushed. "No, I'm still pure as the driven snow.''

"You're kidding! You fly all the way to Montana to spend a weekend in an erotic ski shack with Studly Jack Jackson— and nothing happens?'' Sam studied her virginal cousin with amused disbelief. "How on earth did that come about?''

Valentine's flush deepened. Sam had already been married and divorced by the time she was twenty-three; at twenty-six, she wore her slick gloss of sophistication like a hand-tailored garment. *What would she say if I told her I went skiing with Jack just to prove something to another man? Valentine wondered.* In retrospect, her motive seemed so puerile it made her wince.

She gave an elaborate shrug. "Well, we were getting around to it—we were both in our robes. Then he started untying his sash, his hypnotizing gaze supposedly holding me entranced, but I . . .'' Valentine bit her lip. "Oh, Sam, all I could think of was, 'Okay, now he shows me his pee-pee and I show him mine.' I started laughing, couldn't stop, couldn't tell him what was so funny, couldn't act like I was on fire with passion when I was howling like an idiot.''

Sam grinned. "Ah, so. And how did ole Studly react?''

"Traumatized, of course. After all, he's been deflowering maidens since he was old enough to walk. He accused me of being frigid.'' Valentine sighed. "Well, maybe I am, who knows?''

"Oh, honey, that's just a masculine trick to save face; if he can't turn you on, then you must be a popsicle! Just chalk it up to experience and forget it,'' Sam advised. Bristling at Valentine's downcast expression, she asked bluntly, "Hey, you're not still hung up on Bill the Jerk, are you?''

Smiling at Sam's penchant for pinning tags on men she disapproved of, Valentine shook her head. "No, I'm over that lunacy. And that's really what it was, Sam, lunacy. It's a little scary—I mean, you know how I rail about Ed,'' she said, grimacing. Ed Brady was her stepfather. "And yet I seem to attract the very same kind of men; handsome rogues, charming as hell, oh, yes, but without a responsible bone in their body! God spare me from irresponsible males,'' she said with a dramatic sigh. "Sometimes I wonder if they aren't all like that.''

Although Sam wondered the same thing, she said gamely, "Val, you're only twenty-three, you'll find someone. Sooner or later.''

"Yeah.'' Falling silent, Valentine turned her brooding gaze to the ice-rimmed window. Longing gripped her—God, how she hungered for sunshine! In the same instant a sweet fragrance suddenly filled her nostrils. Flowers, she realized. Perplexed, she glanced at Sam's bedside bouquet. But this wasn't the musky scent of chrysanthemums. No, this was an exquisite blend of spring flowers: hyacinths, irises and freesias, a cool lacing of arbutus. It was as if something or someone knew how much she loved and needed flowers, and offered them to her.

As though sentient, the fragrance spun a silken mist around her face, soothed and caressed her skin with a softness that approached touch. Valentine gasped at the very real sensation. It swirled around her and through her like a warm hug.

Then, as swiftly as it came, it vanished.

Imagination, she told herself. Noting Sam's concerned gaze, she said quickly, "It's okay, Sam. I was just . . . just thinking."

"Thinking about what?"

Valentine nibbled her lip. "Procrustes."

"Pro . . . who?"

"In Greek myth, Procrustes invited strangers to sleep on his bed and made them fit by either shortening their limbs or stretching their bodies."

"Where do you come up with this stuff?" Sam asked incredulously. "And what's it got to do with you?"

"That mythology course I took last year," Valentine hurriedly explained. "And it has to do with me because I think that's what I've done for most of my life, making myself fit, chopping off bits and pieces of Valentine until I conform to the image others hold of me. And that, as you well know, is a prim and proper poop. Certainly not someone who gets up one morning and decides to light out for . . ." She hesitated, then the words just popped out. "For Texas."

"Texas!" Sam sat up. "What on earth are you talking about?"

"I . . . I'm talking about leaving Cincinnati and striking out on my own!" Valentine replied, stunning herself.

Abruptly, propelled by an inner urgency, she threw back the covers, slid out of bed and walked to the window to gaze out upon the frigid night. Another shiver raked her spine. The long icicles adorning the eaves were sculptured statements of winter's intent, as sharp and impaling as the weather itself. She turned to face Sam, who was clearly at a loss for words.

"I have to go, Sam. I *have* to." She caught her breath, startled at the literal truth of that. Words spilled from her lips with fiery intensity. "Because I can't stand it anymore. There's an empty place inside me and I feel such longing."

"Longing for what?" Sam asked, still perplexed.

"I don't know. Maybe just excitement. Adventure. Love and romance, happy ever after," Valentine replied slowly. "You know, the magic."

Sam's voice thinned. "I seriously doubt that so-called magic even exists outside of books, Val."

Disturbed, Valentine studied her cousin. Sam was a knockout with that mass of red hair and willowy figure. Her dimpled smile compelled attention, but it was her eyes people noticed first. Those clear green eyes could flash anger, sensuality or iciness with equal intensity. At the moment, however, Sam's eyes were clouded and world-weary.

Gripped by sadness, Valentine replied, "Maybe not, but I intend to find out. There's such an urgency in me, such a need to go and do! Too live, Sam! To live life to the fullest!" she cried, desperate to explain something she didn't understand herself. She spread her hands in surrender to that forceful need. "So I'm going. To Texas."

Sam shook her head. "Texas!" she repeated as if she'd never heard of it.

"Texas." Valentine sucked in a breath as the absolute rightness of it struck home. "That's exactly where I'm meant to go, Sam, I know it is!"

"Val . . ." Sam cleared her throat. "Honey, you're going off the deep end here!"

"Could be," Valentine agreed wryly. Gazing beyond the blackness shrouding the window, she felt a sudden keening cry well up in her throat. How could she go into that dark unknown without Sam?

She shivered. "I wonder what's out there, Sam," she whispered. "What's waiting for me in Texas?"

Houston, Texas

"This is lunacy," Jordan Wyatt declared in his deceptively lazy drawl. The caravan of cars, pickup trucks, limousines and sleek travel vans had stalled again. Its objective, the huge white dome approximately three-quarters of a mile distant, shimmered like a mirage in the afternoon sunlight.

The car he drove was equipped with every possible luxury, but it was still a velvet-padded cell with locked doors. A cell to which he had voluntarily committed himself and three other supposedly intelligent adults. "Sheer and utter lunacy," he repeated.

As expected, none of his passengers paid the slightest attention to Jordan's opinion. It was that time of year again, when lunacy became the norm rather than the exception. He, his friends and half a million other people were on their way to the Astrodome to see the Houston Livestock Show and Rodeo.

Jordan threaded both hands through his dark, perennially tousled hair, an irritated gesture that caught his companion's attention. When she looked up from her magazine, he gave her a quick, rueful smile. Gaby's strong desire to see the rodeo for the fifth time in as many years was the only reason he was trapped in a traffic jam that seemingly had no beginning or end.

Gaby Selles was a classy blonde, an accomplished equestrian who excelled in the art of dressage. A high-maintenance woman, he suspected. But one of exquisite beauty, and Jordan was a man who loved beauty in any form: in timeworn stone, in a windflower, in the architectural absolutes of a blueprint.

And, too, above the waist, he knew she wore only a green satin shirt and diamond earrings.

Jordan's ironic sense of humor erupted in a muffled sound. When he mauled his hair again, the thick chestnut locks simply sprang back into the tumbled, wavy mess that drew feminine fingers like bees to pollen. Astonishing what women found attractive, he thought, bemused as ever by the unfathomable mysteries of the opposite sex.

Shifting position, he glanced into the rearview mirror. Clay Tremayne and a tawny-skinned brunette named Leia occupied the backseat. Meeting Clay's gray eyes, Jordan shrugged sympathetically, knowing his friend's discomfort equaled his own.

Clay hated wasting time. There was never enough of it, in his opinion.

Jordan shifted again. His long, lean frame was a mass of knotted muscles that desperately needed stretching.

"Oh, Jordan, will you please stop squirming?" Gaby chided.

He gave her a level look. "There is only one thing in the world that can make me squirm and that is being stalled in a car in a traffic jam," he exploded mildly. Penitent, he touched her hand. "Hey, gorgeous, where are we eating tonight? A nice, home-cooked meal would be nice. Yeah, silly idea," he agreed as she shot him a look.

His tone was warmly indulgent, for Jordan genuinely liked women. A natural affliction that came from having four younger sisters, he thought, chuckling. That she neither fascinated nor intrigued him once they became intimate saddened him, but his big, generous, stubbornly resistive heart forgave her this flaw. It wasn't her fault; that's just the way it was with women, he thought sadly. At least all the women he knew . . .

For an instant Jordan's charitable acceptance hung up on an old and unresolved wonder. What was the source of his inevitable disappointment in relationships? Love? Some people thought so, but he doubted it. He'd been in love a few times and hadn't found it all that consuming. Or even all that painful when it ended: a few, almost pleasantly sharp pangs, some soulful melancholy, a period of longing that made sunsets and sad songs wonderfully effective.

True, love made a man feel good. But it didn't do much to fulfill a man's deeper needs. It didn't erase the strange, inflexible loneliness that gripped his heart at times, usually when he was the least equipped to deal with it.

Startled by the intensity of his thoughts, Jordan gave a deliberate shrug. Loneliness was merely part of being a man. A trait, just like any other. Nothing to get into a stew about, he chided himself. Soft-spoken and congenial, he was essentially straight-arrow, and comfortably aware that he, like Clay, possessed the financial means and rugged good looks befitting the world's image of a Texas male.

Maybe too aware; his ego was certainly healthy enough, Jordan conceded with a quick, lopsided grin. But hell, women had always showered him with affection. In return he held and comforted them, bedded them, loaned them money, fixed their leaky faucets and listened to their problems with immense tenderness and patience. The latter was probably another trait derived from his role of big brother, he reflected. Whatever the cause, most of his old flames considered him not only a marvelous lover, but a very good friend as well.

Amused by his thoughts, he nuzzled Gaby's ear to make up for his inattentiveness. Gaby had one more sterling quality that set her apart from the other women he'd known. She didn't try to change him, she took him on his own terms; no demands either way, nothing that entailed responsibility. Which was why their pleasurable, on-and-off relationship had lasted so long, he acknowledged, kissing her neck.

"When you two have a moment to spare," Clay Tremayne drawled, "I'd like my magazine back."

Gaby tossed it over the seat.

"Thanks, Gaby," he said dryly. Quickly he thumbed through its glossy pages. "I saved this article for you," he told Leia. "Thought it might give you some idea of what rodeo-mania is about. I'll read it to you, give us both something to do beside sit here and listen to Jordan cuss the traffic."

"Yes, read, please," she said. She touched his hand for an instant, her cool, clever fingers weightless on his skin. Clay felt a wistful pang as she turned her face. Her profile could have been sculpted from marble. That's what had first caught his attention, in fact. He had mistaken its purity for soulful innocence. Their month-long relationship had been based on that hope, but he could not deny his growing conviction that he was building on sand. And as one of Montgomery County's premier home builders, he knew the disaster inherent in that.

Well, hell, he'd just turned forty. Middle-aged crazies, he supposed. Clearing his throat, Clay focused his attention on the magazine. "It's a great piece of satire," he told her.

She smiled her cool little smile. Deciding to take it as enthusiasm, he settled back and began to read.

" 'Anyplace but Texas, the Houston Livestock Show and Rodeo would be a rodeo, but is instead a *rodeo*, a mad extravaganza requiring a glorious round of parties for the entertainment of out-of-town guests all simply agog with the spectacle of Going Texan. During this rapturous interlude the population of Texas is indeed a little addled, but nobody minds. Portly bankers strut around in Stetson hats, satin shirts, western-style trousers and crocodile boots, and no one blinks an eye. Impeccably coifed wives stuff themselves into the same stylish getup and perform any number of charitable acts, which are then dutifully reported to the public, who simply eat it up.

"'A strong preference for, indeed, an adoration of, the honeysuckle-sweet smell of horse shit is an absolute requirement. The evening news lovingly follows the progress of trail riders who are converging on the city from all directions, in covered wagons, on weary saddle horses, on foot; thrillingly stalwart souls, animals and riders alike. The spirit of the Old West moves in mysterious ways and newly arrived Northerners speak Texese so fluently that even God is confused.

"'It's all such grand fun that everyone who is anyone wants to participate. At parade time, parking facilities near the center of town run as high as fifty dollars for the duration, the Astrodome is splitting its majestic seams, and the spectacular traffic jams, a thrilling part of Rodeo Mania, are taken in stride with the help of brotherly love, six-packs of icy longnecks, and the shotguns that frame every pickup truck's back window.'"

Jordan snorted. "I for one am not particularly thrilled, nor do I have a shotgun in my pickup."

"Me, either," Clay said. Chuckling, he glanced at Leia and saw nothing but polite interest. He wondered suddenly if she even had any feelings. Chagrined at his harsh judgment, he leaned over and kissed her. It was a dead-fire kiss. No emotion, no arousal, he acknowledged with melancholy honesty.

"Here, you can read the rest," he said, handing her the magazine. "Jordan's right, this really is insane, sitting here like a turtle trapped in its shell."

"Hang in there, Clay," Jordan drawled. "In no time at all we'll be sitting in old Deke's sky-box propping our feet up and sipping twenty-year-old Scotch."

Deke Salander was a mutual friend.

"I'll do some Scotch sipping, but you're the designated driver," Clay growled, but inside himself he grinned. Jordan Wyatt was the closest thing to a brother that he would ever have.

Clay had an ex-wife, but no children. Jordan's mother had raised six kids by herself, which meant that each child had grubbed for his daily bread. As Deke Salander so succinctly put it, they'd all three had piss-pot poor childhoods. At least Jordan had family to wrap around himself like a warm blanket. In sad contrast, he and Deke were a couple of "good ole boys" who had nothing but money to show for their lives. Well, money could heal a helluva lot of wounds, Clay concluded a little grimly.

"Hey, we're moving!" Jordan exclaimed.

"Yeah, a good ten feet that time," Clay said.

Jordan chuckled, amused by his friend's sardonic humor. An excellent architect, he worked with Clay in Destiny, a small, affluent city north of Houston.

Traffic inched forward, then lurched to a halt. Accepting the inevitable, Jordan Wyatt leaned his head back against the seat and idly wondered what he'd be doing this time next year, when the friggin' fabulous Houston Livestock Show and Rodeo came to town again.

Chapter 2

The big clock at Destiny Savings and Loan flashed its message with delightful insistence: 3:38 . . . 72°.

"You beautiful sign, you!" Valentine murmured, gazing over the dusty red hood of Sam's Blazer. *Texas*! The word was vibrant with promise. Her heart turned handsprings every time it collided with the fact that she was actually here.

And that Sam was here with her was pure wish fulfillment, Valentine thought joyously. She hadn't dared ask her to come; back home Sam was one of the Beautiful People, much too busy and important to follow someone else's impractical dream.

Yet here she was, green eyes sparkling as she took in this pretty Texas town. Even now Valentine had to pinch herself to make sure she wasn't dreaming.

"Oh, look, Sam!" she exclaimed, "There's another poster for the Houston Livestock Show and Rodeo. It's over now, darn it. I wish we'd gotten here in time to see it."

"Next year for certain," Sam promised.

Next year.

Suddenly chilled, Valentine touched the Celtic pendant inherited from her grandmother. "I wonder what we'll be doing this time next year?"

"Living high on the hog, I hope," Sam muttered. Although she'd been as excited as Valentine by the tantalizing promise of a new and different tomorrow, doubts still plagued her.

Valentine had no qualms about leaving her job as a glorified gofer for her uncle, a television evangelist. But Sam had been head designer for prestigious Halliday Interiors, Cincinnati's answer to lack of taste among the wealthy.

A hard-earned position, yet she'd tossed it aside on what could be termed a mad whim! "Don't worry, it'll be fine, Mouse," she said, reassuring them both.

Valentine nodded. "Destiny; that's an intriguing name for a town, don't you think? I like it. I like the town, too. Small, but nice." She stretched, then propped her bare feet on the dashboard with voluptuous pleasure. "I can't believe this is only the first week of March—just feel that sunshine. Oh, Sam, isn't this great!"

Sam agreed it was, although her enthusiasm was worn a little thin from so much agreeing. They had explored the Dallas-Ft. Worth area, were now en route to Houston, and possibly Corpus Christi. A helluva lot of driving, Sam conceded, but they had not found The Place yet.

Valentine had named it; The Place, where they would stop roaming, settle down and make a wonderful new life. To her surprise, Sam found herself thinking of it in the same way.

Traffic snarled ahead of them. Braking, she swore and shifted position. They had been on the road for a solid week now. There wasn't a spot on her body that didn't ache and she had never felt so good.

Valentine rolled down her window. "Umm, smell that air! I think that's jasmine, don't you?"

"All I smell are gas fumes," Sam said, stubbornly averse to liking anything about a traffic jam. "If we had stayed on the Interstate we'd be in Houston by now. As it is, it could be next week before we ever get out of this town."

Her grumble raised Valentine's hackles. It had been her idea to detour to Destiny, seeking out a restaurant touted by a gas station attendant. It seemed very important at the time. She'd been wrong, though; the food was too greasy for their tastes.

"You don't have to get snotty about it, Sam," she huffed.

"I'm not being snotty about it," Sam snapped, then gave her cousin a rueful smile. "I'm being bitchy about it. Sorry.

Damn, we're stalled again. What is this holdup, you reckon?''
she asked, exasperated at their stop-and-go progress.

"Who knows?" Valentine shrugged. "And who cares?
We're not tied to the hands of a clock. This must be what it's
like to be filthy rich," she said dreamily. "No worries, no
oughts and musts and shoulds, just doing exactly what we
want without care for what anyone else thinks. I've never
known such luxury, Sam."

"Neither have I. And it is nice. But it's short-lived," Sam
warned. "The real world will come crashing in soon enough."

"Oh, for goodness sake, don't be such a pessimist," Valentine chided. The sense of urgency that was her companion
of late had abated, and she relished her lucent sense of freedom. Without actually defining it, she knew they were on the
right track.

"Wish we could get out from behind that truck," Sam
grumbled.

"Hang a right down this side street," Valentine said.

Sam responded almost reflexively. "God only knows where
this will take us," she said. She winced as a guitar loudly
twanged its repetitive chords. "Will you please turn off that
radio? Or at least change the station. I'm sick of that music."

"Oh, now, Sam, you have to learn to like country music.
It's all they play in Texas and if we're to be Texans, then we
have to like their music."

"I doubt country music is all they play in Texas," Sam
said, amused. "It's a fairly big place."

"I'm just quoting the mailman, from his trip to Texas,"
Valentine retorted. "Oh, look at that pretty little park!" she
enthused, headily responsive to the greening view outside her
window. From the snow and ice of winter to this enchantment
of flowers and misty-hued trees was very nearly intoxicating.

"Oh, Sam, I can't wait!" she sang out.

"Can't wait for what?"

"For our new life to start. Really start, Sam. It's going to
be so different! Because *I'm* going to be so different," Valentine said fiercely. "You remember what the cousins used to
call me? Fraidy Cat Val. Well, why not? It fit. But that was

then, this is now. And now I'm recreating Val, changing her into someone brave and daring. And madcap. Yes, a bit outrageous, a bit racy. Saucy. Sexy. Scintillating. Spunky, spirited, sagacious. All those lovely *S* words. What do you think?''

"I think I'm going to be stunned," Sam said dryly. "But you know, I kind of like the old Val. She has many good qualities, too. Discarding her would be an awful waste, don't you think?"

"Maybe you're right. She wasn't all that bad," Valentine said reflectively. "So, instead of discarding her, I'll improve her. Like a diamond with many unpolished facets. The question is, do I need a polish cloth, or a chisel?"

"Oh, Val, you nut!" Sam said, chuckling. She made another turn and suddenly the dreary commercialism of gas stations and convenience stores vanished. The narrow street wound through a section of older homes intermingled with tiny shops and enormous old trees.

"Goodness, this is . . ." Valentine caught her breath as she realized what she saw and felt. Here it was, just as she had dreamed of, yearned for, drove thousands of miles to find! Heavenly hot sunshine, robin's-egg blue sky stretching out forever; green, green grass and air rich with promises sweet enough to taste.

Here were the flowers so vital to her being.

Here, she thought with breathtaking certainty, was home.

"Oh, my God," she whispered, clutching her suddenly hollow stomach.

"Val? What's wrong?"

"Oh, Sam, this is it! This is The Place!" Valentine cried.

Startled, Sam said, "Oh, come on, Val! *This* burg? What on earth gives you that idea?"

"I just . . . just feel it," Valentine floundered, taken aback by her cousin's cheerful disdain for this beckoning town. "I can't explain it, Sam, it's just a . . . a knowing."

"Well, believe me, honey, you got your signals crossed on this one! There's nothing for us here, we're city girls. We just haven't found the right city yet, that's all."

"Maybe not," Valentine agreed, tucking her nugget of awareness away for now. Sam was eager to see Houston, so they would. "But this is where I'd want to live if we did live here."

"We probably couldn't afford it, at least not for a while. Oh, great, we're back at the intersection again. I'm going to ask one of those cops what's going on."

"Ask the shorter one," Valentine said without thinking. *Late thirties, unmarried.* The information was just simply there.

"Tall or short, what does it matter?" Sam grumbled.

"Because he'll be more sympathetic to our situation. I just think he will, that's all, okay?" Valentine forestalled her cousin's question.

"Ooh, touchy," Sam teased. Pulling abreast of the two local policemen, she asked the shorter one, "What's going on? Why this traffic jam?"

The policeman's attractively weathered face cracked into a smile as her silky voice pleasured his ears. Sharp blue eyes checked out the Blazer before settling on her face.

"Rodeo, ma'am," he said.

Valentine straightened with a snap of excitement. "Sam, another rodeo! Let's go? I've never been to a rodeo," she confided to the policeman. "Is this one as good as Houston's?"

"Better!" he declared. "Y'all go and see the rodeo, it's a fine one, finest in the state, bar none." Noting Sam's unimpressed mein, he added, "And there's a dance afterward."

Sam perked up. "A dance, huh? Well, maybe . . . but we'd need to clean up a little. What say we hit a motel, Val? Stay the night if you want. My backside feels like I've been riding one of those broncs," she told the policeman.

He blushed. "There's a nice little inn, called Mom's Place, three blocks ahead and hang a left, go another two blocks. And look up Deke Salander when you get to the rodeo. Tell him Dan Marshall sent you, get you good seats and right fine treatment."

Grinning, he stepped back and waved them on. "I'll be

there myself at that dance," he called as Sam shifted gears.

"Nice guy," Valentine said, flirtatiously blowing him a kiss. Just then a dark green pickup started across the intersection and she screamed. "Watch out, Sam!"

Brakes squealed; Sam swerved; the other driver managed to stop with less than an inch between their vehicles.

Valentine let out a shaky breath. "Whew, that was close," she said as he pulled around them and went on his way. Although she had caught only a glimpse of the other driver, her impression was favorable. Tousled dark hair, and blue eyes glaring at them beneath a glowering brow.

"Along came a stranger, reeking of danger," she murmured, giggling at Sam's fierce scowl.

"Reeking of danger is right! That idiot nearly creamed us!" Sam exploded. "Dammit, are you all right?"

"Well, sure. Just shook up a bit. No big deal. Lighten up, Sam," Valentine advised her set-faced cousin.

"No big deal, my foot!" Sam clawed back her hair. "Don't tell me to lighten up! If it hadn't been for my quick reflexes, we'd have been squashed like bugs!"

"We were in no danger whatsoever of being squashed," Valentine reproved. "So lighten up, darling Sam. Umm, I feel uncommonly good! I wonder what this 'Mom's Place' is like?"

"Cheap, I hope," Sam said.

It was small but not cheap, charmingly well-ordered and run by Mom at the moment. When she learned Dan Marshall sent them, "Mom" became mommish to an absurd degree. Clucking like a hen with her chicks, she ushered them to a large, airy room, showed them all the wonders contained therein and, after warning them to beware the evils of the bar down the street, left them in peace.

"Do we look like babes in the woods or something?" Valentine asked, flopping down on one of the twin beds.

"It's you," Sam accused. "Every time they see you they want to hitch up your drawers and wipe your little nose." She slung her tote on the other bed. "I get the shower first, I'm bigger."

"Not to mention older," Valentine murmured.
Sam threw a pillow at her.

The dark green pickup moved up another space, but a policeman's outstretched arm stilled its progress. Fuming at this delay, Jordan Wyatt drummed a staccato rhythm on the steering wheel. Once again he was caught in a traffic jam caused by a rodeo, Destiny's, this time. Which he was not attending; he was merely trying to get back to his friggin' office.

Checking his watch, he swore with satisfying venom. No way could he make his four o'clock appointment. To top off his day, some idiot woman in a red Blazer had nearly smashed up his truck. His heart was still pounding from that overcharge of adrenaline!

Thank God he always kept a cool head in a crisis. Only his quick reflexes had prevented a collision.

"Careless idiots," he muttered, rumpling his chestnut hair unmercifully. Well, there were two females in the Blazer, so what could you expect? Put two women in the front seat of a car and what did you have? Half a driver.

A laugh rumbled through his chest as Jordan imagined his sisters' reactions to his thoughts. Many a time he had been pummeled by feminine outrage for voicing such biased—and ridiculous—opinions. Which was why he'd done it, of course!

Recalling the Blazer's Ohio license plates, he wondered what two young women were doing so far from home. Were they chasing a dream? he wondered with unseemly tenderness. But he knew all about dreams. He had chased one most of his life.

He knew the odds against them, too. When his father walked out on his family, twelve-year-old Jordan had been forced to step into his shoes. Shoes that were far too big for a skinny boy, and crushingly small for a dream, he reflected, his face somber as memories scratched at the doors of his mind. Though still very much a child, suddenly he'd been responsible for the welfare of his whole family.

Five people, looking to him for sustenance. His mother, a frail, lovely flower, had needed a strong comforter-protector-provider. His siblings needed a father figure, a disciplinarian and decision-maker, a steady source of hope and security—God, so many things! And Jordan had needed . . . what? Just relief.

Relief that was a long time coming, he thought, startled, as always, by the abrupt resurfacing of old pain and anger. The shame of his father's desertion was compounded by the financial mess he'd left behind. They were poor. Not picturesque-poor, but bitterly poor. No-food, no-shoes poor. His job at a local grocery had been but a drop in the bucket. He'd had no choice but to put his family on welfare.

That was the bitterest blow of all. The prideful Jordan Wyatt, forced to use food stamps at the store that employed him.

He had loved playing football; suddenly there was no more time for playing. His high school days became a grind of keeping up his grades while keeping his family fed. So many times he'd been tempted to quit. But he wanted to go to college, and a scholarship was his only hope.

So he persevered. And he'd done it, Jordan reminded himself with a warming smile. He had caught his dream and made it a reality. He had his education, his degree, a successful career. His siblings had grown to more or less satisfactory adulthood; his mother, ever the fragile flower, had lived in an expensive, assisted-living condo until her death two years ago.

The home he planned to build was another facet of that childhood dream; a small estate complete with a pool, rose gardens, an orchard. A smile softened his mouth. Musing on this future *magnum opus* was immensely enjoyable. It would have a library, for his interests in a wide range of subjects had inspired the collection of more than a thousand books, far too many for his present home, so most were in boxes. Good food was another passion. He loved to cook. So the kitchen would be first-rate, geared to both food preparation and kibitzing guests.

He had no desire to share his dream house with anyone. Raising four sisters and a brother had cured him of any desire for domesticity. His personal life was as smooth as a symphony and he had every reason to expect it to stay that way.

Relaxing into the velvety seat, Jordan Wyatt mentally tipped his hat to the two women in the Blazer, and wished them luck. Whatever they were searching for, he sincerely hoped they would find it.

Sam emerged from the bathroom to discover Valentine curled up in a chair feasting on beer and pretzels. "Want a longneck, Sam?" she asked, holding up another tall bottle of beer.

"Lord, yes, I want one. Where did you get them?" Sam asked, uncapping hers with lusty pleasure.

"That bar down the street, just a couple of blocks from here. Nice, friendly people there. I liked them. They liked me, too."

"I'll bet they did."

"You have a dirty mind, Sam," Valentine proclaimed as she headed for the bathroom.

A few minutes later she came out feeling fresh and clean, her entire body invigorated by the cool-water rinse that always followed her showers.

Sam, dressed in fitted slacks and a silk shirt, fastened a belt around her slim waist. Her hair hung loose around her shoulders. She shook it back with narcissistic approval. "I feel like a hungry tigress," she said, catching Valentine's gaze.

"You look like one, too," Valentine said. "I wish I did."

Sam was immediately pierced with a devastating pang of love. "Honey, believe me, there's nothing wrong with the way you look. Although I would wear something besides that towel, were I you."

That throaty laugh rang out again as Valentine discarded her towel and hurried to the closet. Sam laughed, too, even though she felt a twinge of unease. Valentine had indeed changed since the plane crash. The reckless confidence racing like some rare wine through her blood was very nearly visible to Sam. She knew from personal experience how delicious it was. But could her young cousin handle it?

Valentine emerged in tight white jeans and a scooped-neck, pink cotton T-shirt. "We need boots, Sam. And hats," she fretted, checking out her backside in the mirror. "I bet everyone's wearing them."

"All in good time." Sam brushed back the curl caught in her cousin's lashes, touching her piquant face because she herself needed the caress. "Valentine, I love you," she said quietly.

"I love you, too, darlin'. You ready?"

Sam sighed again. "Ready as I'll ever be."

Deke Salander carried himself with all the courtly arrogance of a Spanish conquistador. Five feet nine, lean and fit, he projected the impression of a much bigger man. His bronzed skin, glossy black hair and high cheekbones were hints of a mixed heritage. His silvered temples enhanced his mystique rather than aged him. He wasn't a handsome man. Even so, his quick, sardonic smile, rakish mustache and the mystery gleaned from the scars on his face, made him magnetically attractive to the opposite sex.

Deke knew there was nothing romantic or mysterious about those scars. He had acquired them in the lettuce fields of the Rio Grand Valley during a bitter struggle for nothing less than survival. However, since the ladies found them intriguing, he did not disillusion them.

His background was shrouded in mists of speculation. Even those who considered themselves his closest friends found Deke something of an enigma. That he had somehow reached the age of forty-five without having been married was, in this fertile land of Community Property, not only high treason, but vastly unfair.

Women were particularly outraged—a man of his means walking around single? Deke good-naturedly accepted their matchmaking efforts, but he was a loner, and the pattern was too ingrained to change at this late date. Besides, the mistresses he kept here and there around the state served his needs too well to meddle with the system.

If it ain't broke, don't fix it, was his motto. And it sure wasn't broke, Deke mused. His gaze wandered over the crowd with a tinge of patriarchal affection. He was one of three sponsors who guaranteed the purse for Destiny's annual Festival and Rodeo. Although he maintained residences in two other cities, Destiny was home, second only to the rock-strewn land he owned in the Hill country.

Along with Deke, several more men lounged at the base of the grandstand, laughing and talking in well-oiled camaraderie. The two politicians he owned outright. The rest owed him favors extended at one time or another. None of them were fooled by Deke's "good ole boy" air. He'd take your hide if he thought it was owed him.

Deke looked at his watch, wishing he could head out for his ranch. But civic duty held him here.

"Pardon me, where is Deke Salander?" a feminine voice inquired behind him.

Turning in response to the hand tugging at his sleeve, Deke's eyes widened as he took in the lovely redhead who was, happily enough, accosting him. He shoved back his fawn-colored Stetson, black eyes boldly assessing as he asked, "Well now, little lady, who wants to know?"

Sam eyed him appraisingly. "Well now, little man, *I* want to know," she mimicked his drawl.

"Sam, be nice," Valentine scolded. "Excuse me, sir, do you know Mr. Salander?" she asked sweetly.

Deke meant to answer her; he'd just forgotten how to speak. But then, he had never addressed an angel before.

"Well now, Deke, own up, boy!" called a man on the stage. He wore a pale gray suit with a decided western flair. He looked oily, Valentine thought.

She switched her attention back to Deke. "You're Deke Salander?"

Deke's eyes narrowed. Then he laughed, swept off his hat and bowed. "Deke Salander at your service, ma'am!"

"Valentine Townsend, sir, from Cincinnati, Ohio," she said, bowing in return. She was instantly at ease with the flamboyant man. "This is my cousin, Sam, and we're delighted to meet you, Mr. Salander. A charming policeman by the name of Dan Marshall told us to look you up."

As she spoke, Valentine's gaze moved down Deke's bright red western shirt and superbly tailored black trousers to the high-gloss shine of expensive boots, and back up again. "My goodness, are all Texans this gorgeous?'' she asked with bowled-over awe.

"Naw,'' Deke admitted, falling easily into his backwoods manner. He was damn glad that his first impression had been wrong; Valentine Townsend was the sweetest thing since spun sugar, but that impish grin fell far short of angelic. "Now, what can I do for you two ladies?''

"According to Dan Marshall, you can find us a good seat,'' Valentine replied. "You look just like Sam Elliot with that mustache,'' she added breathlessly. "I loved him in that movie where he played a forest ranger!'' Enjoying Deke's startled laugh, she cast a wistful eye on his hat. "Darn, everyone does have a cowboy hat but us, Sam.''

Deke's laughter enveloped them again. Grandly he offered an arm to each woman and escorted them up the rough wood steps to the grandstand. As they accepted a seat on one of the bleachers that backed it, the other man came bustling over.

"Reed Ballinster, ladies. Welcome to Texas,'' he said.

The warmth in Valentine's smile dimmed slightly. He repelled her much like a snake would have, had she touched it. This quick, instinctive judgment saddened her; on the surface he appeared to be a likeable man. But in some unfathomable way, she could sense what lay beneath the surface. Grays and blacks. Although by now she had become used to this strange sense of knowing, it was still unsettling, and often disappointing.

Always well mannered, she smiled and said, "Thank you, Mr. Ballinster. Are you by any chance a Texas ranger? I've always wanted to meet one.''

"Reed's a trifle short of being a ranger,'' Deke answered her question. "Would a Texas senator do?''

"Well, it comes close,'' Valentine decided. "And what are you, Mr. Salander?''

"Intriguing question,'' the politician murmured.

Deke shot him an oblique glance before saying, "I'm just a country boy. Hey, Bubba, come here a minute,'' he called to a portly lad at the edge of the platform. "Here, run down to Andy's booth and get these ladies a cowboy hat.'' He rammed a hand into his pocket and pulled out a money clip. Peeling off several bills, he handed them to the boy with an admonition to hurry it up.

Valentine's mouth dropped open and Sam looked downright uncomfortable. "Hey, we don't need cowboy hats," she said.

"Yes you do." Although he spoke to Sam, Deke's gaze was on Valentine. His mouth yielded to a smile. "Permit me my pleasure, Sam. Lord knows I get little enough of it."

Startled by his soft request, Sam wondered if it was genuine.

Valentine didn't wonder; she knew it was, knew it better than Deke did, in fact. His words came from the deep, inner space where self-truths lay waiting for acknowledgment.

In the same mystifying way, she could sense the darkness in Deke Salander, the traits he had discarded and the ones he had kept. He didn't give, he took. He didn't love, he possessed. He didn't forgive, he avenged, and because of buried childhood terrors, he would strike swiftly at any threat to his carefully structured defenses.

Yet she was not intimidated by him. Quite the contrary, she felt a strong liking for this powerful man, for she could also sense his loneliness and pain. He still possessed integrity, encapsuled in fear and almost out of reach, but viable.

He's been hurt so badly. He cannot find his way back alone. He needs help. . . .

Valentine caught her breath—where on earth were these odd thoughts coming from?

Before she could decide how to respond, the rodeo began with a roar of applause that canceled any further conversation.

Sam found it extremely boring, but Valentine was fascinated. Deke watched her reaction with mingled emotions. When Bubba came back with the hats, he scowled at the boy.

"They didn't have any hats left at Andy's booth, so I went to town and got 'em," Bubba explained.

"Town done moved to Houston, has it?" Deke mildly inquired. He took the tan hat and set it on Sam's head, then placed the white one atop Valentine's raven curls. "There you go, ladies," he said, displaying immense satisfaction.

"Oh, hush, Sam," Valentine said before Sam could voice

her opinion of the hat he'd practically rammed on her head. "You look gorgeous, like one to the ranch house born!"

"I think that's 'one to the *manor* born,'" Sam replied stiffly. Meeting Valentine's sparkling gaze, she added a conciliatory, "Although I don't suppose one wears a cowboy hat in the manor. Thank you, Deke."

"Yes, thank you, Deke." Valentine stretched up and kissed his cheek. "You're a nice man," she said.

Deke looked nonplussed and a small silence ensued.

Abruptly Sam stood up. "I smell food."

"Oh, lord, me, too," Valentine moaned. She caught Deke's arm as if they'd been friends forever. "Take us there at once!"

Her mouth watered as they joined the line for barbecue. She was ravenous and the smell of hot bread and the rich, brown, dripping-with-sauce ribs were unbelievable torment. A few minutes later, carrying heaping plates of food, they found a table and dug in with gusto.

After their appetites were satiated, they watched the rest of the rodeo, then moved on to a big, crowded barn of a room with a battered wood floor. Magically, Deke secured a table.

Hank The Grand Champion Cowboy joined them, along with the senator and fat Bubba. In no time at all their table for twelve held sixteen. It was like being with the most popular crowd in high school, Valentine mused; Deke's presence caused a parade of comings and goings, and just-stopping-by.

Music played; dancers thronged the reserved patch of floor. Doors and windows were opened to the breeze, doing their best to lower the room's temperature, which Sam estimated at a hundred and twelve degrees. By the time Valentine had downed her third longneck, she was enthralled with Texas and its marvelous hospitality and wonderful, fantastic people.

Since they were in total agreement, naturally they loved her.

Some would like to turn that into physical affection, but Deke had taken both women under his wing, and nobody messed with Deke. "You having fun, Valentine?" he asked.

"Super fun, thanks to you!" Valentine lilted. She felt wonderful, all warm and at ease inside. Patting his hand, she sat back to watch, in openmouthed amazement, a peculiar dance that got wilder by the minute. At the end of each reel, a concerted shout went up in ludicrous accord. When she finally interpreted that boisterous roar, she whispered to Sam, "Are they saying what I think they're saying?"

"Yes, I believe they are, Cousin," Sam replied, and winced as the joyous opinion was voiced again.

"BULLSHIT!" the dancers roared as one.

"Come on, Sam, let's give that a try," Deke proposed as Valentine danced off with Cowboy Hank.

"I don't even know what that *is*," she retorted.

"That's the Cotton-Eyed Joe," Deke explained. "Anyone can do it." He grabbed her hand and towed Sam to the dance floor despite her vocal disinterest in going there. Making a foursome with Valentine and her cowboy, they entwined arms to circle the floor and shout it to the heavens.

Sam loved to dance and was next swept off in Hank's strong arms. Valentine, content to sit with Deke and watch her cousin's enjoyment, had another beer.

And another, and who was counting? She felt perfectly safe with her new friend. The rapport that had sprung up between them was too warm and natural to question. As she watched his eyes crinkle and listened to his rough voice, she experienced a surge of affection for Deke Salander. He really is a charming man, she thought fondly, and such a nice one, too.

And so friendly. His big hand moved over her head like he was petting a puppy. Although not quite, Valentine thought puckishly. He didn't seem to know what to do with her.

As the night grew bleary, a fuzzy camaraderie sprang up among the survivors who lingered on. There were now ten people at their table for twelve. Instead of relaxing, Deke doubled his guard. Sam's hair glowed ripe apricot and she was altogether delicious. But Valentine he would kill for.

He didn't object when Dan Marshall joined their group and promptly claimed Sam for a chain-dance. "A fine man, Dan Marshall," he told Valentine. "Born and raised in Peoria, until he had the good sense to move to Texas."

Her giggle melted ancient ice.

"How about you and Sam?" he asked. "Think you'll stick around for a while?"

Her smile pensive, Valentine glanced toward the dance floor. "I don't know, Deke," she said.

The next morning Valentine awakened just as sunlight reached her side of the room. Despite a mild hangover, she felt extraordinarily good. She stretched like a cat, slow and deliberate, while memories of last night danced in and out of her mind. Finally she stilled them and freed the decision that clung like a burr of awareness even when she closed it out.

Destiny was home.

But Sam thought differently.

Signing, Valentine got up, shrugged into a robe, and quietly let herself out into the morning.

Their room opened onto a central courtyard. The day was cool and breezy, and birdsong filled the lambent air. Vivid pink azaleas bloomed at the feet of flowering dogwoods, and God, it was all so beautiful! Especially when her mother's words came to mind, Valentine thought softly.

"We're buried under a foot of snow, darling. Pick a blade of grass for me."

Guilt invaded Valentine's lovely sense of well-being as she recalled their last morning together. She and her mother in the cluttered kitchen, teapot steaming on the yellow Formica-and-chrome table, the cat asleep at their feet. With her petite stature, raven hair and tired blue eyes, Julia Townsend Brady's appearance was that of a gentle-breasted dove battered by life's storms. She was forty-four, and at that moment she had looked it, her face downcast, her shoulders hunched in conflict as the pragmatic logic of a Frenchwoman warred with the poetic dreaminess of her Celtic genes.

"If you feel that strongly about it, of course you must go," she'd told her daughter, marvelously matter-of-fact.

But Valentine had felt her mother's anguish.

Remembering it, she blinked at tears. "Please, please be all right," she implored the beloved image filling her mind's eye.

She's fine, darling, just fine, a soft inner voice responded.

Startled, Valentine lifted her head and stood as if listening. For what, she didn't know. Just my own wishful thinking, she decided. But she did feel better.

"Hey, what are you doing up so early?" Sam's query brought her back to this tiny patch of lawn. "Couldn't sleep?"

She shrugged. "Just woke early. Excitement, I guess. Last night was so much fun. How are you feeling?"

Sam made a face. "My head and feet are screaming bloody murder, but I'll live. How about you?"

"I'm fine." Valentine stroked the dogwood's rough trunk. "Sam, I like this town. I like its people, at least those I've met. I even like its name, Destiny. It seems so significant."

"Do you have a point or are you just making conversation? I haven't had any coffee yet," Sam said. Her watchful green eyes were at odds with her drowsy voice.

"Yes, I have a point." Valentine cleared her throat. "I haven't changed my mind, Sam, I still think Destiny is The Place. And after last night, I'm even surer. I want to stay here." She hesitated, uneasy with her arbitrary decision. "I know you disagree. But I really feel strongly about this, Sam."

Sam shook her head. "I should have known you wouldn't give up so easily. Any logical reasons for this strong feeling?"

"Well, the people, as I said. Last night we met some of the common folk, like ourselves, and then we met some others, too: rich and powerful, community leaders. Movers and shakers, Sam. It can't hurt knowing such people when you're newcomers."

"We are nothing like those 'common people' and the others don't matter diddly-squat. We're not taking favors from anyone," Sam said flatly.

"Well, pardon me!" Valentine huffed. "I fail to see how knowing the upper echelon of society falls under that category. In fact, I think it'd be considered a helping hand."

"We don't need a helping hand, we can do this on our own. Dammit, Mouse, I've had enough trouble with 'helping hands' in my life! That's how I met my ex. And then old man Halliday gave me another 'helping hand' by letting me work my tail off for him, then he put me through the wringer when I turned in my resignation. He said he owned me, that he had made me.'' Sam lifted an azalea blossom to her face as if to find comfort in its silken petals. ''No letter of recommendation, Val,'' she confessed, husky voiced. ''Not even a civil good-bye after years spent working in his firm and practically idolizing him as a designer icon.''

''You didn't tell me that! That pusillanimous old . . . old polecat!'' Valentine swore. ''But don't worry, we don't need any old letter, we'll do just fine without it!'' Her head drooped like a flower after a heavy rain. ''But I know he hurt you and I hate that. I'm sorry you went through more disillusionment, Sam.''

Sam shrugged. ''Men are such bastards, what can you expect? I'll survive. So, give me some other reasons why this would be a good place to live.''

''It's an affluent area with a high standard of living,'' Valentine said promptly. ''Good schools, lots of culture; a thriving town, Deke said. There's a big shopping center a few miles farther on, near another monied town. A lovely lake north of here with more big developments—all potential clients, Sam.''

''It does sound promising, I admit,'' Sam said, her tone neutral. ''Anything else?''

''Yeah, there is. It feels good to me, Sam. It feels right. I know that may sound silly, but it does. I want to stay here, live here, make a life here.''

Sam regarded the younger woman for a moment, then smiled. ''Well then, darlin', I reckon we've come home,'' she said.

Chapter 3

Six weeks later Valentine sat hunched on the steps of Brighton Apartments, watching the lively couples go in and out of Redd's Bar and Grill located directly across the street. Music and laughter drifting on the balmy air filled her with wistful longing. She was scared and lonely and homesick. The lump in her throat literally ballooned whenever she thought of family and friends left behind.

Sam didn't seem to need this support system. But Valentine did. It was an intrinsic part of her nature.

She wiped away tears. Even her initial excitement had dissipated. She missed its warmth, too. It was as if a bright, glowing light had been turned off inside her. She wanted so much to turn it back on; but she didn't know how, which added frustration to her emotional stew.

Living here in these shabby, impersonal surroundings didn't help, she thought glumly. But Sam said it made good financial sense to take this one room efficiency until they got on their feet. Valentine had gone along with the idea. Why? she wondered irritably. Why, when she hated it so, had she stifled her feelings and agreed with her cousin's decision?

Because it was a good idea, dammit, she reminded herself. Sam knew what was best for them. Although leaving Mom's Place had been a wrench, the Brighton was much cheaper. And like Sam said, they needed every cent they could save to fulfill their dream. The apartment's tiny kitchenette would cut their food bill in half, she predicted.

Which it did, Valentine thought loyally. The effect of that dark little flat on her spirit was not important in the long run.

"Sensible, economical—and temporary, remember that," she advised herself whenever the walls closed in on her. She was lucky that the front door opened onto these shielded steps. It gave her a good place to sit and dream. Or cry.

Her shoulders slumped again. She missed her cat. Why hadn't they brought Snowball with them? She missed Sweet Cherry, too, her dear little red car. They had sold it and used the money to finance their trip. She'd agreed that keeping Sam's Blazer was far more practical. Now, however, Sam had to use the Blazer to get back and forth from her job, which left Valentine without transportation. And being carless in Texas was the absolute pits. But the longer they could put off buying another vehicle, the better, Sam said.

Valentine had found employment within walking distance. Clerking in a bakery was a dead-end job, but five bucks an hour was better than no bucks an hour, she'd told Sam.

For her part, Sam had secured a position with a design firm in Houston. On the lowest rung, of course; years of experience in Ohio counted for naught in Texas, she'd said, humorously, but with enough bitterness to pierce an anxious heart.

Filled with guilt and misgivings, Valentine wrapped her arms tightly around her knees and held herself in the makeshift embrace. Maybe she really had made a bad decision, dragging them off to Texas on what could be said—and *was* said—to be a foolish impulse. Maybe there really was nothing here for them.

She shoved the thought away as if it had physical substance. She hated these doubts! And she still loved Texas. Leaving here would be incredibly painful. Even so, true to Sam's predictions, reality had soon shorn her of her blind adoration for this mystical land. Texas tantalized and promised, but it didn't just hand it to you on a platter. You had to go and take it. *How* was up to you.

She didn't know how to do that either, Valentine admitted.

This outraged her. She was intelligent and strong—a *woman*, dammit, absolutely filled with woman-power, a power so intense at times that she seemed to pulsate with the universe.

But it was undirected power. Or maybe just *mis*directed, she amended, drying tears with her shirtsleeve. That odd sense of urgency was plaguing her again, telling her without words that she'd taken a wrong turn. She had to change things. But how?

Since Sam's opinion of Deke Salander's "helping hand" hadn't changed, even that avenue was blocked. Deke didn't accept that, of course. He kept track of them through his own private means, and their current residence aggravated him immensely.

They hadn't seen much of him since the rodeo. This, too, was Sam's decision; and Valentine, respecting her cousin's complexity of reasons, had gone along with it. Although not entirely, she thought with a tiny grin. Last night, in desperate need of laughter and stimulating company, she had defiantly accepted his invitation to dinner. Where upon Sam had agreed that eating out might just be a welcome change after all.

And old Mother Hen, Valentine thought, smiling at her cousin's protective bent, *had a wonderful time*. They had met Deke at the restaurant, and shortly afterward, Senator Ballinster materialized beside their table. Naturally such a personage was invited to join them. In deference to the others, Valentine had put aside her dislike for the man, a gracious gesture that was amply rewarded with several hours of absolutely fascinating conversation. His intimate knowledge of Texas politics, both past and current, had sparked the evening. She and Sam listened enthralled as the two attractive males embellished their stories with laughter and some very fine wine.

In a private moment, his black eyes glinting, Deke had demanded, "Why can't you two admit that you're having a tough time and accept some help? At least get out of that dump you're living in!"

"Thank you, Deke, but we're doing fine," came Sam's firm response. "I know the Brighton isn't too impressive, but it suits our purpose right now."

"Yes, we just love our little cottage," Valentine had murmured.

Later she and Sam had exchanged heated words on the subject.

"There's nothing wrong with accepting help from a friend, especially when we could use that help. That's what friends do, Sam. They help each other."

"We don't need help and he isn't a friend, he's an acquaintance. And probably just as corrupt as those politicians he hangs around with," Sam sniffed. "Ballinster's married, but that didn't stop him from trying to grope me tonight under the table. As for Deke, I don't trust him, either."

"You don't trust any man," Valentine had countered. "Granted, Ballinster's a pig so we'll simply avoid him from now on. But Deke's different. He may be shrewd and even ruthless in his dealings, but he's not corrupt," she went on with a certainty she could not explain, even to herself. She simply knew it.

Besides, she liked Deke. And when Valentine Townsend liked a person, that person was considered worthy of her loyalty and trust. "At least until proven otherwise," she muttered, her voice barely audible above the wailing music.

Jerked back to the present by a movement near her foot, she shied from it. Another one of those damned things casually referred to as tree roaches was investigating her shoe with possible ideas of having it for dinner. Their first morning at the Brighton Apartments, they were greeted by a horde of small brown insects playing around the sink. When, later in the day, a monster at least three inches long chased her from the bathroom, Valentine had flown on wings of shrill disbelief to the manager's office, where a chinless little man listened to her complaint with nodding indulgence.

"Just a tree roach," he said, shifting his unlit cigar. "They won't hurt you. They're just lookin' for water. You live in this part of Texas, you got roaches," he continued chattily. "Nobody pays any attention to 'em. Just squash 'em."

"Good grief, Sam, *squash 'em?*" Valentine moaned. "Oh,

my God, what if one of those horrid things crawls in bed with me!''

She was a nervous wreck that first week. Sam, though, took the manager's advice; she squashed 'em, then daintily disposed of the remains. By the second week Valentine, too, had found a way to cope with their unwelcome guests. She simply closed her eyes and hit out wildly in the direction where a monstrous insect should be. Sometimes she actually got one, which was even worse.

Sam worked late; Valentine was usually home by four. During those long evenings by herself, she often fled the apartment for the gregarious atmosphere of Redd's Bar. She was on first name basis with the clientele. But while it was a lovely bar, it was still a bar.

A *den of iniquity; the Devil's playground; a pit of lost souls enslaved by Old Demon Rum* . . . She smiled, recalling the names the Reverend Uncle George had given these infamous places. In actuality, Redd's was a comfortable meeting place for Destiny's young career people.

"Of which I am one," she stated. But she couldn't keep up even this little pretense. The sad, secret truth was, Valentine Townsend did not want a career. To her, work was what you did to pay the bills. Since that was heresy, at least as far as Sam and her sisterhood were concerned, she kept it to herself.

Valentine slapped at a mosquito with true Texan forbearance. She burned to do something. Something other than sit here and watch night fall, she thought sourly. The sound of the Blazer was deeply welcome. She breathed easier as Sam, slim, expensive chic in a pin-striped suit and heels, mounted the steps.

"Hey, Mouse, why're you sitting out here? The mosquitoes are gonna carry you off," Sam teased.

"I'd rather battle mosquitoes than stay in that room any longer."

"Can't say I blame you." Sitting down beside her, Sam curved an arm around her shoulders.

"I got fired today, Sam."

"I see. What happened?"

"I just got sick and tired of that chowderhead rubbing up against me every time he edged by—and taking longer and longer to edge by!" Valentine blurted.

Sam stilled. "Sonofabitch!" she swore. "If you want to file suit for sexual harassment, I'm behind you all the way."

"No, too much hassle," Valentine sighed. "Besides, I never should've taken that job."

She didn't mention the voice screaming NO in her mind all during the interview. Sam balked at discussing her cousin's unnervingly strong hunches.

"Don't worry, Sam. I took care of it."

Suddenly wary, Sam asked, "What did you do?"

"I told him how much I hated being rubbed up against," Valentine replied reasonably. "Then I decked him."

"Good lord!"

"Well, you said go with your feelings. So I did." Valentine hugged her knees again. "Sam, is this why we left Cincinnati? To live in a one-room flat and work in a bakery and get fired just because you don't desire touchie-feelies on your backside?"

"No, of course not, but this is only temporary—"

"Only temporary? Just how long is temporary, anyway?"

Sam tucked a stray tress behind her ear. "Oh, honey, come on, it's only been six weeks. That's not such a long time."

"Six weeks is a very long time when you only have a year!" Startled by her outburst, Valentine quickly lowered her gaze.

"What do you mean, you only have a year?" Sam asked, puzzled.

Valentine just shook her head. She had no idea what she'd meant.

To her relief, Sam instantly applied logic to the oddly intense statement. "Oh, Val, is that all the time you've given yourself to create a brand-new life?" she chided gently. "One year? That's putting a lot of unnecessary pressure on yourself, don't you think? What's the big hurry, sweetie?"

"I don't know. There's just this impatience in me, like I need to get going somewhere and instead I'm just spinning

my wheels and going nowhere." Sighing, Valentine added
ruefully, "I'm sorry, I didn't mean to jump all over you the
minute you came in from work. I'm just feeling really down.
Guilty, too."

"Guilty? What on earth for?"

"Lots of things. Leaving Mom so sad and weary—"

"You can't help your mother, Val. She'll stick with Ed
through thick and thin. Bounden duty and all that rot."

"I guess. But I feel guilty about you, too, Sam. Bringing
you down to a lousy job of playing third fiddle to someone
with less than a quarter of your talent."

"Val, I came with you of my own free will. I wasn't all
that happy with Halliday Interiors, honey," Sam reminded.

"Maybe not, but you were sure as hell happier than this.
And I . . . I feel like I didn't level with you, Sam. You trusted
that my decision to leave was based on something solid. But
it wasn't. The night before you decided to come with me, I
had another dream, about Grandma Fiona, this time. She was
with an angel and they were smiling and waving good-bye to
me. Taken together, it felt like an omen to me, sort of a celestial go-ahead to my scary decision."

Glancing at Sam's impassive mein, she rushed on, "I mean,
even your mom told us to always pay heed to dreams,'cause
they bring messages from far places. Anyway, that's what really solidified my decision. Well, and the horse. That helped,
too."

"Horse? What horse? Helped you how?" Sam shook her
head in mock despair. "Connect the dots, Valentine."

"Helped me realize I wasn't always such a mouse. Remember the time I sneaked the horse into the mayor's office. How
scandalized everyone was? Jeez, the uproar it created! I was
even on television the next morning, remember?"

"Oh, *that* horse. Sure, I remember." Sam chuckled. "A
catastrophic event!"

"Well, it was, kind of. Of course I apologized and professed
my shame, but secretly, I was proud of myself. To be frank,
some part of me still is. Enough to 'aid and abet,' anyway,"
Valentine said with a shaky laugh. "I didn't mention any of

this because I was afraid you'd change your mind if you knew my thinking was so illogical." She dried her wet eyes. "I should have told you, Sam. You deserved to know all the factors in our decision to leave Ohio. I'm sorry."

Sam regarded her, amused and perplexed. "Valentine the paragon," she said, shaking her head. "Stop with the guilt, Cousin; I came because *I* wanted to come. Your reasons had nothing to do with it. Enough said," she said briskly. "You're right about one thing, though, I do detest this bitching job. On the other hand, it does pay the bills. God, I wish I hadn't been such a spendthrift." Her clasp tightened to a squeeze, then loosened. "Mouse, I have to do what's best for both of us. To get started in any business is tough, but starting without adequate capital or the help of a backer is almost impossible. Even a shoestring start-up is beyond us right now."

Valentine nodded. She had no savings; her past salary had barely covered living expenses. Sam's excellent salary had been consumed by financial help to her parents as well as expensive tastes in clothes and cars.

"Right off the bat we'd need to make major outlays of cash; a car for you, a decent home, furniture," Sam continued. "We need so damn much." She stood up. "But you're right again, it's time to change this abominable situation."

Opening the door, she recoiled. "Whew, that stinks!"

"Exterminators came today." Valentine followed her inside.

"Oh, great. Well, make some coffee while I get out of this suit." Sam undressed, then put on a navy robe and pinned up her hair. "Geez, I am beat." She sighed, massaging an aching foot.

"Oh, your poor little feet!" Valentine crooned. "Here, sit down at the table. I'll fetch a pan of warm water and you can have a soak."

Gratefully Sam accepted this bit of pampering. She turned on a lamp and the shabby room took on a warm glow. Soon the good smell of coffee filled the air. Relaxed, ankle deep in warm, herbal water, she sighed deeply. "Ah, that's much better. Okay, honey, let's start making a list. First thing is another vehicle. Next, a house to live in.''

"Yes, a house," Valentine echoed eagerly. Her face lit up as she spoke. "A pretty house, with a yard and trees and a place to grow flowers. I'll get another job right away, Sam."

"No, you won't."

"I won't? But you said we had to conserve our money."

"Yes I did and yes we do. But this mucking around with petty little jobs . . . I'm an interior designer and a damned good one. So why the devil am I working for someone else?" Sam's fingers began pacing in lieu of her feet. "The problem is that we're coming in cold and it's a highly competitive field. We need connections, a foot in the door."

"Deke."

"I said connections, not charity," Sam retorted. "There's a fine line there, which obviously you're missing. You've got to take every break you can get, but you don't give those bastards the advantage in any way, shape or form."

Valentine laughed aloud, her spirits lifting as a spot of light began to glow at the back of her mind. Rising, she poured two mugs of coffee, spooned in sugar and cream and handed one to Sam. "Deke is not a bastard."

Sam stuck out her chin. "All men are bastards."

"They are not," Valentine countered, eyes twinkling. "Well, some are. Aristotle was. Or maybe not. More like a male chauvinist oink."

Sam gave her a pained look. "Now how do you know that?"

"Elementary, my dear Sam," Valentine said airily. "Aristotle believed the male form was the norm. When this sublime form was distorted with female matter, it produced an inferior species; women. Deficient physically, morally and mentally."

Sam stared, her mouth working. "What the hell has Aristotle got to do with . . . with whatever the hell we were discussing? Damnation, Val, get serious!" she snapped.

"But that's just it! We don't have to take it seriously, don't you see?" Valentine exclaimed. "That's the beauty of . . . of . . ." She faltered. The thought that had lit up her mind like a strobe light vanished before she could capture all of it. "Okay," she said ruefully. "Seriously, Samantha, Deke is a kind, decent man."

Sam rallied. "Deke's rich. You don't get rich by being a kind, decent man."

"You don't get rich by being stupidly stubborn, either," Valentine shot back. "I wish you weren't so cynical and distrustful."

"And I wish you weren't so trustful and naive. But we are what we are." Sam paused for a sip of coffee. "Okay, as I see it, we have two problems. The first is how to get started. That's a big one! We need—what? And don't say Deke Salander," she warned.

"I don't state the obvious," Valentine stated. "Hey, how about builders?"

"Builders?" Sam's green eyes rounded. "Builders! Ohmigod, yes, yes, *yes!*" She began laughing. "Val, you are a bleeping genius, darlin! Builders! This place is crawling with them. Those new subdivisions west of town; two hundred thousand and up if they're a penny. And then there's The Woodlands, lots of new-home construction going on there, too. Builders must have a coordinator for their homes and I have experience—I was damn good at handling them, too! How could I have overlooked that?" she marveled. "We really aren't in a position to set up shop and launch out, but this would cost nothing! And we'd make enough contacts to lead to bigger things eventually, just by word of mouth if nothing else. All we need is one dissatisfied builder who knows class when he sees it."

"Amen!" Valentine refilled their coffee cups. "What's problem number two?"

"We can't run a quality design firm from a shabby apartment, not even for such an admittedly limited clientele."

"But we're getting a house," Valentine reminded her.

"Honey, we've got to be realistic about that," Sam backtracked. "Just thinking what a dent it'll put in our savings makes me shudder! It's an expense we could avoid if we stayed on here, at least for a while."

"This place kills the spirit, Sam, don't you feel it?" Valentine asked softly. When her cousin looked puzzled, she sighed and said, "But I see your point. Okay, so we stay, so what then?"

"I don't know." Sam's fingers resumed pacing. "I need an idea, an idea . . . Of course! A cellular phone!" she crowed. "Not a perfect solution, but as a compromise, it'll do. So that's it, Valentine, we're off and running. We can endure this sad excuse for a home a while longer, can't we, sweetie?"

"I guess so." Valentine donned a smile. "Sure we can."

"You bet we can! So. First we find you a car, then a car phone, then business cards with that phone number. And then, darling Val, while I drive off to my Houston job, you, your car, your telephone and my portfolio are going out there and interview every premier builder in the county!"

"Me?" Valentine squealed, appalled at such a prospect. "Oh, no, Sam, I couldn't ! I've never done anything like that. You'll have to handle something that important."

"Let me put it this way; you *have* to handle it," Sam said tartly. "It's your job, babe."

"But I don't know how to talk to builders!" Valentine's throat tightened in the grip of an old, familiar fear. "I'll make a mess of it, you know I will," she said dully.

No you won't. You can do it, Valentine. You can do anything.

The assurance washed across her mind like sunlight. Fear simply melted in its mellow warmth. Ambushed by wonder, she stopped mangling her bottom lip and looked at Sam. "But if that's my job, then we'd best get on with the training program, Cousin. I've got an awful lot to learn."

Valentine's days took on a dark-edged repetition as she began the search. After much consideration, Sam had decided they would have a better chance with small builders. Blissfully ignorant of what lay ahead of her, Valentine tucked Sam's portfolio under her arm and jauntily set out for her first appointment.

Rejection also became a routine part of her routine, but

oddly enough, her self-confidence grew stronger. Or at least, I can take it in stride, Valentine thought rather proudly.

Several days later, while scrambling eggs for Sam's supper, she summed up her experience with satiric amusement. Builders, she declared, were never content to remain in one spot for longer than ten seconds; one must track them down with skill and stealth lest they slip right by you. And builders, she accused with a despairing sigh, were notoriously prone to looking a person everywhere but in the face, and spitting streams of tobacco juice with such ferocity that she was continuously leaping aside to escape the splat. "Undaunted, our brave little heroine has logged wearying miles of sometimes polite, sometimes crude turndowns," she intoned, adding toast to Sam's meal. "The crudest was a jerk named Arnie Peershaw. Said he hated to turn me down, but he had this witch-wife who would figure us out—*us* meaning him and me—before we even got going good. When I realized what he meant, I started to pin his ears back, but he simply wasn't worth it."

She spooned homemade raspberry preserves onto Sam's plate. "I mean, there was just so little *substance* to the man, Sam! So I turned and walked away."

"My God," Sam whispered disgustedly.

Defining the cause of her cousin's distress, Valentine replied, "Hey, come on, Sam, I'm a big girl now, so let me be one, huh? Besides, I was exaggerating. Well, not about Peershaw, but the rest of it. Just trying to give failure a humorous spin!"

"I see nothing humorous about it. Besides you having to deal with creeps, we're no further ahead than when we started."

Valentine tried not to be invasive with her heightened sensitivities. Yet she could not help but sense Sam's deep discouragement. "We need that sense of humor. Sometimes it's the only thing that keeps my ship afloat!" she teased, a futile effort. "Ah, Sam, don't be disheartened. Things will change, truly they will. You just have to have faith, that's all."

Sam killed a large roach with a vicious swat of newspaper, then watched incredulously as the insect got up and staggered down a crack in the floor. *"Sonofabitch!"* she swore, and hurled the rolled paper at the crack. Then she burst into tears.

Astonished, for Sam rarely ever cried, Valentine flung her arms around her cousin's quivering shoulders. "Oh, Sam, don't cry, darling, please don't cry!" she pleaded. "It will die—I'm sure you injured it badly. It'll die! Later on, just not now," she babbled, too upset by Sam's weeping to realize what she was saying.

"Oh, for pete's sake!" Sam choked. "It's not the damn roach, it's you! You and your *don't get discouraged, Sam, have faith, Sam!*" she mimicked savagely. "We've been rejected by every builder you've contacted—we have a right to be disheartened! In fact, we'd be idiots *not* to get disheartened! Dammit, Val, you don't have a clue what it's all about, you've had everything handed to you from the day you were born! Even your job was a gimme! But I've scratched and struggled for every blasted thing I've ever gotten! So don't you tell *me* . . ." Her voice choked off as she glimpsed Valentine's face.

"I'm sorry. I didn't realize you felt that way," Valentine said painfully. Dropping her arms, she stepped back.

"Oh God." Ashamed of her outburst, Sam sighed, wiping tears like a child. "No, I'm the one who should be sorry, and I am," she said tiredly. "Ordinarily I love your sunny optimism—I do, darling. But I . . ." She paused, choosing her words with care. She knew that she was a source of security for her cousin. There was no reason for Val to know that big cousin Sam was just as lonely, just as scared, just as anxious about the future. "Don't look so stricken, Mouse," she chided, raking up a laugh. "I'm just tired and cranky."

She pushed at the auburn tendrils that crying had loosened. "You're right about this place; it does kill the spirit. I didn't realize that until I was walking up the steps tonight. If you hadn't been here, I'd have turned right around and left. So I'm taking your advice, Val. I'm getting us out of here and into a decent home," she said fiercely. "I don't know how or when, but I promise you, from now on that goes to the top of our list."

*   *   *

Monday morning Valentine resumed what looked to be her life's profession; hot on the trail of another builder who might or might not require a decorator, but who must be approached. In person, not by telephone.

True, the first week had been unfruitful. Nonetheless, she started this one just filled with hope; that lovely light at the back of her mind glowed steadily now.

She dressed in tan slacks, a white shirt, and a classic gold blazer. With her hair neatly coiled at the base of her neck, she looked and felt stylishly competent. Portfolio in hand, she sallied forth.

The day soon turned overcast and windy. By the time she had tracked down—and been turned down—by her quarry, her sleek hairdo had disintegrated and her shoes were resoled with mud. As she plodded back to her car, Valentine was in a bit of a temper. "Damned horny toads," she muttered.

After restoring order to her hair, she doggedly set off on the trail of another one, a Mr. Clay Tremayne.

He was not, of course, in his office. "Try again tomorrow," suggested the gum-chewing girl sitting behind her shiny desk.

"But I had an appointment," Valentine pointed out.

The girl waved her outlandishly long, red, acrylic nails. "Well, you know how busy these guys are. But he'll probably come back in a little while. Wish I could hang around, but I have a nail appointment. You can wait in his office if you want. Just make yourself to home," she said, and tootled out the door.

Disconcerted, Valentine stared at the closing door. Annoyance made heavy inroads on her determination. The devil with C. Tremayne, she decided. Why should she sit around here and wait for him? Wasn't her time just as valuable as his? Damn right it was! She stood up, grabbed the portfolio, and started for the outer door.

Something stopped her.

Something, a feeling, a momentary wonder, or perhaps just plain old doubt, turned her toward the desk again. What if this C. Tremayne person turned out to be pivotal to Sam's career?

"Oh, nonsense, he's just another builder," she said crisply.

But she sat back down—and jumped right back up again. She couldn't just sit here! Defiantly, she strode into Tremayne's private office. Unlike the formulaic outer office, his was luxuriously furnished in leathers and tweeds. Several awards for excellence hung on the wall, she noted. Her quarry was growing more impressive by the minute. She searched for a photograph, but this horny toad provided no clues to his appearance.

After another ten minutes, she called Sam and reported in.

Sam commanded her to wait there; she would be at Tremayne's office in twenty minutes. Sam was also unemployed as of two o'clock that afternoon.

One block over, Clay Tremayne and his partner, Jordan Wyatt, stood on the sidewalk listening to another builder sing a chorus of The Builder's Blues.

"You try paying a decent wage, Arnie, you might keep your crews," Jordan said mildly.

Arnie Peershaw shrugged, unimpressed by his advice. "Listen, boy scout, I pay 'em enough." He turned to Clay. "Hey, I done you a big favor last week," he said with a broad grin.

Clay grunted. "How much is it gonna cost me?"

Arnie guffawed and shot a stream of tobacco juice a scant inch from Clay's foot. "Don't cost you nothing, on the house this time. I had a little gal come around lookin' for work, a interior dec-o-rator, hottest little thing you ever seen! And she needs work in the worst way. Or maybe the best, dependin' on which side you're lookin' at. Damn, I got a hard-on just talkin' to her." He sighed. "Anyway, I sent her round to see you. And I'm tellin' you, buddy, she's ripe for the pluckin', so hot for a job she's willin' to trade off."

"And you passed it up, hum?" Clay asked with amused disgust.

Arnie scratched through his sparse brown hair. "Had to. My ole lady would strip me right down to my jockeys if I screwed around with something so obvious," he said ruefully.

"So I passed her along to you. In fact, I saw her goin' into your office just a little while ago."

"Oh, hell, *she's* my four o'clock appointment?" Grimacing, Clay turned to Jordan. "You want to come back to the office and see this fine favor Arnie did me?" he asked sourly.

"I think I'll pass," Jordan said. "Knowing Arnie's taste in women, she probably looks like a cross between a lady wrestler and an orangutan. I'll come by a little later, after you've gotten rid of her." Ignoring Arnie's bombastic protests, he strode across the muddy lawn to his dusty green pickup.

Clay felt a glow of pleasure; it would not occur to Jordan that his partner might take advantage of the situation. Mutual respect played a big role in their friendship.

"See you around, Arnie," Clay said, and crossed the sad little lawn to his own truck. He wasn't looking for a decorator. He already had one, a fussy little man with a vitriolic temper and a penchant for the exotic. Still, once Clay got him calmed down, he did a pretty good job. But a builder had enough problems without having to ride shotgun on his crew. . . .

Clay's mood curdled as his thoughts ran ahead to the woman waiting in his office. He'd had a run-in with her kind just last week and it left a bad taste in his mouth. That one's proposition had demeaned her, which was bad enough, but what it inferred about him was a face-slapping insult.

That infuriated him; he'd had a helluva time keeping his honor unsullied by all the crap he had waded through to reach this level of success. Doubtless women had to do some wading, too, he conceded, but that was no excuse for all this goddamn hanky-panky! And then to have that weasel Peershaw think he was doing him a *favor*? Clay wheeled into his parking lot mad enough to chew nails.

Thinking only of getting rid of her as fast as possible, he strode into his office and stopped dead as the petite brunette on his couch sprang to her feet. The wide violet eyes that swung up to meet his startled gaze skewered him, not with lust, although he certainly appreciated her appeal, but with disappointment. He took another step, then stopped again, dis-

tracted anew by her tentative smile. The impact she had on
him was downright astonishing.

Eerie, even, Clay thought, eyeing her warily. Her character—or lack of it—was none of his business and he had no
intention of making it his business. Yet all these urges
chomped at his innards. He wanted to yell at her, grab her
shoulders and shake some sense into her! And by God if he
didn't want to take her home and feed her milk and cookies.
Crazy!

Shoving back his Stetson, he said carefully, "Evening,
ma'am. What can I do for you?"

"Good evening," Valentine returned, eyeing him with feminine pleasure. Clay Tremayne fit none of the categories she
had allotted to builders; everything she intuited about him told
her he was in a class by himself. "I was wondering if you
required the services of a very good interior designer," she
added.

Clay honestly meant to boot her out of his office, but her
diffident smile rattled him even more. Removing his hat, he
sat down at his desk and frowned at her.

"You look awfully young for this line of work."

"Oh, it's my partner, Sam, who's the decorator," Valentine
replied. "I'm merely a junior associate out beating the bushes
for jobs. We just moved here from Ohio and it's always tough
to come in cold," she said knowingly.

Clay's stomach clenched. She was shilling for a man?

"Everyone has to start somewhere," he said tersely. Feeling
confused and strangely disillusioned, he wadded up a memo
and shot it forcefully into the wastebasket, a perfect hit. He
flicked her a glance. "Are you at all familiar with our work?"

No immediate rejection, no summary dismissal! Elated, Valentine cleared her throat. "Yes, sir. We went through a couple
of your beautiful homes in Candlechase."

"You checked out Candlechase?" Clay asked, maintaining
his brusque manner despite an almost automatic buzz of excitement. Candlechase, a new subdivision he and his partner,
along with several other builders, were developing on Lake
Conroe was his finest endeavor yet.

"Oh, yes, Sam and I drove through it this weekend," Valentine said excitedly. She was nearly breathless; this was so wonderful! Not only had she liked him immediately, but to come upon this juicy prospect after days spent plowing through seared wastelands—her heart leaped like a bird in her chest.

"Mr. Tremayne, if you decide to use our services, you won't be sorry, I promise you," she said fervently. "Sam's the best, in every way. And I'm certainly not lacking in my own talents," she added, thinking happily of working with her supremely gifted cousin. "Although I don't have formal training, I'd throw my heart and soul into whatever I'd be called upon to do."

"You really do want this job, don't you," Clay remarked.

"More than want it, Mr. Tremayne; we need it," Valentine said, deciding to trust her first impression of an innately nice, albeit disgruntled man. "Even more important, Sam needs it, and I'd do anything to make Sam happy. *Anything*," she repeated with a sudden ache of desperation as the memory of Sam's tears washed across her heart. What a thrill it would be to tell her, casually, of course, just toss it out—*oh, by the way, Sam, we have our first job. I told him we'd start tomorrow morning, if that's all right with you . . .*

Oh God, she just had to make this man see what a valuable addition two such hardworking people would be to his staff!

Unwaveringly she met his daunting gray stare. "There's no job too small or difficult for me, not if it means fulfilling our dream. What I don't know, I can most surely learn." She laid the portfolio on his desk. "This is Sam's portfolio. I know you can't help but be impressed."

Stepping back, Valentine waited with ill-concealed eagerness while he scanned Sam's work. Would he like it? Would he think her work better than anyone else's? How could he help it? It *was* better, she thought loyally. Just the same, she sent up a quick little prayer.

When she raised her head, Clay Tremayne was standing in front of her, his expression grim. "You're right, I am impressed. Your partner's work could sell itself without your

favors thrown in as a bonus." His lip curled. "Sam's got
talent, no doubt about that, but you're wasting your time with.
me. Talented as you both might be, I just plain despise dealing
with unprincipled people." His eyes were hard as slate as he
concluded, "You're also wasting my time and that I don't
tolerate."

Clay's control snapped as those lovely eyes widened with
dismay. "Now please get out of my office," he growled.

Too stunned to react immediately, Valentine froze in hot
confusion. Outrage hit her; questions bounced off its fiery surface. *He thinks I'm offering my favors as a bonus? Sex? In
return for a job? No! He can't think that! Because if he did
that means I read him wrong.*

That thought shook her even more. Making quick, instinctive judgments of the people she met had almost become second nature by now. The depth of her knowing depended on
her degree of interest, and certainly she was interested in *this*
person. He couldn't really think that she was . . .

But he could. And obviously did. In swift succession she
felt a stinging shock of disbelief and hurt, then the first hot
slash of anger. *The job*, she thought dazedly. There was no
job. Disappointment caught her by the throat and choked her.
She had built up such high hopes!

Her breath escaped in a hiss as the second part of his insult
struck her. She was already fed up to *here* with builders, and
that this one had the nerve, the sheer and utter *gall* to attack
Sam! Sam, the most scrupulous, most principled, most decent
person he would ever have the good fortune to meet . . .

Valentine's anger reached flashpoint in a matter of seconds.
She could take it for herself, but not for Sam! Blindly she
reacted. She pulled back her arm, clenched her fist, and swung
wildly to connect most solidly with his chin, a beautiful left
hook if she did say so herself.

Clay stumbled backward with a startled oath. His scowl became positively ferocious as Jordan Wyatt entered the room
just when that small fist found its mark.

Having spent much of his adolescence dodging the flying
fists of a fiery little sister named Jacey, Jordan took in the

scene with one quick, skilled glance, judged it harmless, and thus entertaining. Clay was in no serious danger and his enchanting opponent was in no danger at all.

Jordan burst out laughing.

Valentine jerked around to locate the source of that deep, husky laughter. Feathery lacings of a curious bent coiled through her belly as she glimpsed the tall, dark-haired man with crinkly blue eyes leaning against the door frame. Before she had time to investigate this phenomenon, Clay touched her arm and she hissed at him.

She was far too distracted to notice Sam coming up the walk.

"Dammit, Jordan," Clay growled. "This is not amusing."

Jordan. A lovely name. The wisp of thought vanished as Valentine looked wildly from one man to the other. Her hair had fallen around her face. She clawed it back but there were simply too many things demanding her attention. For one thing she was so disappointed that she could burst out bawling at any second. For another, her cheeks flamed with chagrin at her actions. No wonder Jordan with the beautiful crooked grin found this amusing. Shaken inside and out, she tried to gather her scattered wits.

Clay made a stab at taking charge again. "Look, Ms. Townsend, maybe I was a little too quick on the trigger—"

"No maybe about it," she snapped, rounding on him. "What on earth made you think such a thing about me?"

"Ah, well, Arnie told me that you . . . That is, he said that you . . . ah, hell," Clay said as those flowerlike eyes narrowed to slits.

"Aha!" Jordan said knowingly.

Clay glared at him.

Valentine gave him a lingering glance before repinning Clay with her gaze. "Arnie? You mean Arnie Peershaw? That nasty little puffball of a man told you I was . . . was available and you believed him?" Her voice rose to unnerving heights. "You actually believed I'd let that lecherous billy goat lay so much as a *finger* on me for anything short of *dismemberment*?"

"Well, I . . . I certainly didn't want to believe it," Clay floundered.

"But you did," Jordan Wyatt leaped into the fray. "Tsk, tsk, shame on you, Tremayne, questioning the honor of such an honorable young lady," he chided.

Valentine caught his gaze and then her breath as something punched her in the solar plexus. Those heavenly blue eyes twinkled with boyish devilry. She wanted so much to hug him.

"Thank you," she said primly.

"Yeah, thanks Jordan, that was real helpful," Clay said. "However, I take blame when blame is due."

"And it is due," Jordan helped.

Valentine's mouth twitched as his eyes connected with hers again. He winked, and sweet tinglings happened inside her. Her interest in him, already avid, was suddenly unwieldy. She wondered what kind of man he was—and realized she hadn't a clue to his deeper nature! Any opinion she had formed of him was from such superficial sources as appearance and reactions.

She couldn't read Jordan Wyatt!

Valentine was so surprised that she clutched the desk to ensure her upright position. What blocked her perceptive skills?

Clay Tremayne moved into view, commanding her attention. And what, she wondered nervously, was she to do about him? Give up or persevere? Apologize or wrap herself in hauteur and not budge an inch? "Mr. Tremayne—"

"Ms. Townsend," Clay said simultaneously. He stopped.

Graciously she motioned for him to continue.

"If I misjudged you, I'm truly sorry and I apolo—" The rest of Clay's statement dried in his throat as a redheaded whirlwind blew in the door and singed his very soul with her blazing emerald eyes.

Chapter 4

S am had heard Valentine's screech just as she started up the walk to C. Tremayne's office. Her already foul mood rapidly escalated to a need to maim. She hit the door running and skidded to a halt in front of the astounded builder, who hastily backed up a step.

She wheeled to Valentine. "Are you all right? Just what the hell is going on here? Are you the lecherous billy goat?" Arms akimbo, she flung her icy hiss at the man by the door.

"No, ma'am, he is," Jordan said, pointing at Clay. He bit his lip as hot green eyes fried C. Tremayne to a crisp.

"Why you scuzzy bastard!" Sam spat, advancing another step. She still had no idea what he had done, but he'd done something.

"Well, damn!" Clay said in a strangled voice.

Jordan had the temerity to laugh. Sam flung him a look mean enough to stop it or at least muffle it.

"What did he do to you, Val?" she asked menacingly.

Realizing that unless she intervened, Tremayne was going to find himself scattered all over his office, Valentine stepped between them. She'd been doing some fast thinking, and in hindsight she could see that perhaps she had caused part of this uproar. Her words hadn't been all that well chosen, and, coupled with her eagerness to impress him, might well have conveyed the wrong impression.

"It's all right, Sam," she said forcefully.

"The hell it is! I heard you yell, I heard you say—"

"Yes, okay, I did yell, I did lose my cool, but it's over now and I'm fine."

Clay decided to intervene. "Look, we had a little misunderstanding—"

"Did I ask you to speak?" Sam inquired acidly.

"Now, Sam, just calm down," Valentine urged. "It's not what you think, honey, I'm the one who—"

"Sam?" exclaimed the bedeviled Clay Tremayne. "*This* is your partner? This is *Sam?*"

Valentine gave him a quizzical look. "Certainly this is Sam. Who did you think . . . Oh my gosh! So that's why!" she said, flinging out her hands. "Sam, when I told him about us, I guess I left you ungendered and he thought . . . well, who knows what he thought, but I'm sure that explains everything."

"Yes," Clay said brokenly.

"It's okay, anybody can make a mistake," Valentine soothed him. "Sam, this is Clay Tremayne, owner of this office." She broke off with a horrified gasp. "Oh, Mr. Tremayne, your cheek is bleeding! I'm so sorry—it must have been my ring! Sam, do you have a tissue? Wait, I think I have some." She rummaged through her jacket pockets and pulled out a wad of tissues. "Ah, here we go! Now just let me—"

"I'll do it," Clay said, dodging her reach. He took the tissues, his expression dazed as he looked at Sam.

"Valentine, why is he . . ." Sam stopped and shook her head. "Why are you sorry he's bleeding? And why would your ring . . . Oh, my God, you hit him!" Her voice went up three full octaves. "You had to *hit* him?"

"A misunderstanding, like he said," Valentine replied hastily. "He, uh, mistook me for a woman of easy virtue and I had to dissuade him of such a notion!" she explained with an amused smile.

Sam was not amused. "And why should you have to dissuade him of such a notion? Did he touch you?"

"No, no, I was upset so I . . . belted him. Before that, however, we were discussing possible employment since he's dissatisfied with his current decorator.'' Valentine turned to Clay. ''Mr. Tremayne, as you've guessed by now, this is Samantha Townsend, my partner and the best decorator this side of the Ohio River. Sam, meet Clay Tremayne, builder extraordinaire.''

Sam nodded coolly. She still harbored a suspicion that Valentine was glossing over something unpleasant—like an unwanted advance—and if so, he was not only a miserable bastard, but lucky to be alive. She resented his sweet smile, too, and the dents it put in her armor. ''Thank you, Mr. Tremayne, but we don't need this job. Come along, Valentine.''

Wheeling, Sam strode to the door. Jordan could have been a handsome painting on the wall for all the notice she gave him.

Valentine stayed in place. Inwardly she was elated; she hadn't read Clay wrong after all! The steel gray eyes held a humorous glint whenever they caught hers.

''Oh, come back here, Sam, and stop making all those threatening noises,'' she chided. ''We're not going anywhere until I say so.''

Sam's mouth fell open. ''Well, damn, Val, who put you in charge?'' she asked peevishly.

Valentine smiled. ''You did. When you stuck your portfolio under my arm and ordered me to go forth and interview builders, remember?'' She let her eyes delight in Jordan for a few seconds before she continued, ''So let's not get turned crossways here, darlin' Sam. I've already handled the matter; Mr. Tremayne is very sorry and he apologizes, don't you, Mr. Tremayne? And he promises to keep in mind at all times, unless of course you desire to change the rules, that should we agree to work for him, it will be strictly business. And the sad truth is, we do need this job,'' she concluded on a sigh.

She spared another look at the captivating stranger leaning against the wall, his arms still folded on his chest, face alight with humor. As her gaze connected with his, she blushed at the surge of something warm and marvelously good feeling.

He threw back his head and laughed, compelling her to laugh with him. Joyous laughter, straight from the heart. It was communication without words, she thought wonderingly. It was "hello again" to an old friend, sweet with pleasure, warm with memories . . .

"Valentine!" Sam snapped. "We do not need a job this bad." Following her cousin's point of focus, she frowned at the other man. "Who are you?" she asked crossly.

"Jordan Wyatt, innocent bystander." He left his lazy lean on the wall to join them. "Are the fireworks over?"

His bedeviling grin shook Valentine anew. Her chin lifted. "Yes, they're over. Nice to meet you, Mr. Wyatt."

Graciously she extended her hand. It was promptly swallowed up in a firm clasp that explored each dainty digit from fingernail to palm. Her eyes rounded in startled surprise; there were so many sparks between them! Like a Fourth of July sparkler, she thought, warily meeting his gaze. Her silent gasp sufficed for words. Seen close up, his eyes, half-concealed beneath thick, dark lashes, had a strange effect on her. She seemed to float into them and land gently somewhere in their azure depths.

Sexy eyes. And a sexy smile, framing perfect white teeth, in a mouth that was in turn framed by two deep, curving lines that just begged to be explored by a woman's fingertips. *And then by her lips, and then her tongue* . . .

Her brief fantasy brought a sensual, kiss-shaped smile to Valentine's lips. Of its own volition, Jordan's entire being swayed toward her. He blinked and quickly dropped her smooth, indescribably delicate, strong little hand. Recovering swiftly, he switched his attention to Sam.

"A pleasure to meet you, Sam. I feel like I know you already," he said, a trace of mischief in his voice. "Are you two sisters?"

"Cousins," Sam said, yielding nothing.

"Almost sisters, though. Her father and my father were brothers, and her mother and my mother were sisters, so we're very close," Valentine said.

She turned her limpid gaze on Jordan again. He had an arrogant nose and a noble brow. He was speaking again, but she liked his slow, deep, river-bottom voice too much to pay attention to mere words.

Sam was eyeing Jordan, too, but with another slant. Valentine gave herself a shake and plunged back into the conversation. "Are you a builder, too?" she asked cautiously.

Jordan's laugh played up the knobs of her spine in a symphony of tingling pleasure. He was not a builder, he asserted, although he was in partnership with Clay. His firm, Wyatt Architectural Designs, handled all the plans for Tremayne Enterprises, both private and spec homes, as well as their other projects.

Valentine stroked her grandmother's Celtic pendant, experiencing its warmth as an inward blush. "Well, thank heavens you're not another builder!"

Thank heaven he wasn't, Jordan agreed, letting his gaze map her piquant face.

Clay took offense at this, but Sam said most builders she knew deserved the description. Chuckling, Jordan pointed out how erroneous her opinion was. Valentine's merry laugh bestowed approval on the verbal duel.

Scanning first one pleasing face and then the other, Sam used the moment to get a grip on herself. Perhaps she had been a trifle hasty in her judgment; Valentine could confuse a saint at times. And they did need this job. Clay's black hair was curly and she'd always had a weakness for curly haired men. Not that this had a thing to do with changing her mind. A person had to look at all the angles.

"Strictly business," she said coldly.

Clay looked surprised. "Certainly. Didn't I just promise to keep that in mind at all times? Unless, of course, you desire to change the rules."

"Trust me, I won't."

"Well then, we don't have a problem, do we?"

Watching them thrust and parry, Valentine laughed to herself. The lightning flickering between them was very evident, at least to her. She was pleased, for she felt fully satisfied as to Clay's character.

Jordan's, however, was another matter. His mystique, while

alluring, formed an impenetrable wall around the inner man.

Putting her speculative wonder aside for the moment, she looked up to meet Clay Tremayne's measuring gaze.

His appraisal—or reappraisal—of the woman who had left her mark on his cheek, took only an instant. Relaxing, he stuck out his hand to Sam. "Apologies all around, and welcome to Destiny. Sam—may I call you Sam?" he stopped to check.

She didn't reply, just gave him an emerald look, which he decided to take for assent. He glanced at Valentine, who nodded.

"Valentine showed me your portfolio. Damned fine presentation," he said, all business. "If you're half this good, I'll be pleasantly surprised."

"You mean we're really hired? Oh, Sam!" Valentine exclaimed softly. Relief hollowed out her bones. This felt so right. She drew a steadying breath. "We have our first job, Sam!"

"Why?" Sam asked, leveling her gaze at Clay.

"I just told you why." Clay moved behind his desk and unrolled a heavy sheet of paper, his manner terse, his words clipped as he continued, "Candlechase; artist's conception. A gated community. This section here . . . and here, are ours."

"What's the price range?" Sam asked briskly.

"This section begins at one sixty. The other, lakefront property, mainly, begins at two hundred. That's spec. Custom homes go for whatever the owners can afford, of course. Whirlpool, game rooms, upper and lower decks, top of the line built-ins, all standard." A long finger stabbed the paper. "These three houses are near enough to completion to require your services, beginning next week." He eyed Sam keenly. "Jordan's in the process of drawing up plans for this house, a four hundred and fifty thousand dollar contemporary."

Sam's expression matched her voice. "I recently completed a half-million dollar home for the Burl Shepherds of Cincinnati. Architect: Grayson Tyce. Builder: Carl V. Andersol. There are letters of reference from both gentlemen. If you wish to verify this information, there are telephone numbers included."

Startled, Valentine said, "I thought you said we didn't have any letters of reference."

"I said my last employer refused to give me a letter of reference," Sam corrected, flashing her cousin a will-you-please-shut-*up* look. To Clay, she said coolly, "Mr. Halliday and I had differences of opinion about my leaving his firm."

Clay grunted. "I'm not questioning your word or your competence, Sam. It's just that I'm a businessman first and a lecherous billy goat second." He scowled at Valentine, who had the grace to blush. "Tomorrow we'll tour these developments. But for now—well, it's been a long day and I'm hungry. What say we go get some barbecue, forge solid ties." His gaze flickered to Valentine again. "Professionally speaking, of course. Jordan, you in?"

Jordan's assessment of Valentine Townsend was a lightning quick no-brainer. About as big as a twig, but nice. Exceedingly nice. He was suddenly very glad that Gaby, for business reasons, had canceled their date tonight. "I'm in," he said.

Sam stiffened. "I don't think that's wise. Besides, I'll have to mull over your job offer before I—"

"Oh, Sam, come down off your high horse!" Valentine said explosively. Her nerves were electric with tension—she absolutely could not bear it if Sam let her pride screw up this splendid opportunity! "Give the man a chance, huh?"

Taken aback, Sam looked at Clay, her expression both proud and stubborn. "I am not accustomed to doing business like this," she stated. "It's unorthodox, to say the least."

"What's wrong about being unorthodox?" Valentine asked. "You see anything wrong with it, Mr. Tremayne? You, Mr . . . ah . . ."

Jordan's mouth quirked. "Wyatt."

"Wyatt," she echoed with a quick, sparkling smile. One hand waved airily. "Orthodox, nonorthodox, it's not important. We need to stop wasting precious time and get on with the stuff that really matters."

Sam stared at her. Then, inevitably, her gaze returned to Clay Trermayne. He was a big, rumpled man with rough-hewn features. Definitely not handsome. Just very appealing. Incredibly so. There's no way I can work for this man, she thought wildly.

"Valentine, may I speak with you in private? Excuse us, please," she said to the two men and started toward the door.

Making a moue, Valentine followed her to the outer office.

Sam wheeled around. "Dammit, Val, what are you trying to do? This is important. There's a personal element here I don't like. We can't place our trust in complete strangers. We don't know what sort of people we're dealing with."

"Yes, we do," Valentine said in gentle reproof.

"Now don't start that again!" Sam inhaled. Exhaled. Moderated her voice. "You haven't had any real experience in this matter, so maybe you don't realize that this just isn't the way people conduct business. At least it's not the way I do."

"Well then, Sam, darlin', it's time to try something new!" Valentine responded breezily.

Sam threw up her hands. "Did it ever occur to you that there might be a *Mrs.* Tremayne waiting for him at home?"

"There isn't."

"How do you know that?"

"I just know. So there's no reason not to become better acquainted."

Saying something under her breath, Sam straightened her dress. It was green, a perfect shade darker than her eyes. Secretly glad that she'd worn these leg-enhancing pumps, she fluffed her silken bell of hair. "Well, I guess we *could* talk terms over dinner as well as in an office," she muttered.

"Of course we can. People do it all the time, I'm told." Valentine strolled back into C. Tremayne's private office. "Gentlemen, you may pick us up at seven," she said. "We're at Brighton's, apartment number two."

As they drove home, Sam's responses to her cousin's excited chatter were terse and brief. At length Valentine gave up the one-sided conversation and withdrew into her thoughts, which centered mainly around twinkling blue eyes and a sweet, crooked grin. Once out of his presence she could tell herself that meeting him was not a profound experience, nor were her feelings about him all that unique. Just because she had never before felt such a deep-seated response to a man did not rule out its commonality. Other women, she concluded, were probably very familiar with the exquisite sensations aroused by the mere thought of seeing him again.

She tried to be amused—silly little Valentine—but it rang hollow. She was simply very glad that she would see him again.

As they dressed for dinner, she waited for her cousin's explosion. Finally she asked, "Okay, Sam, what is it? What's stuck in your craw, hmm? Better spit it out before you choke."

"Cute, Valentine," Sam bit off. "As a matter of fact, it's you I want to choke. What the devil got into you back there? Since when are you making the decisions?"

"Well, someone had to handle the situation."

"I was trying to handle it, but you kept butting in!"

"You just kept going around in circles. Orthodox, for god-sakes!"

"There's a right way and a wrong way to do something," Sam retorted, fastening diamond studs to her earlobes.

"Oh, pooh." Valentine slithered into a black satin slip. "Where's the merit in bulling through obstacles when you can go around or beneath or over them, and in half the time? Have you seen my black patent sandals?"

"They're under the coffee table. What's this obsession with time, anyway? You're always in such a rush."

"I don't know. I just get so impatient to get on with life, you know? And yet . . . Well, the roses."

Sam sighed. "What about the roses?"

"Stopping to smell them. It's important to." Picking up her dress, Valentine carried it into the bathroom. "Were you really mad, Sam?" she called.

"Yes, I was. And confused. The whole situation was confusing, if you want the truth."

"To me, too. The only thing I could think to do was follow my instincts." Valentine misted the air with perfume and stepped into it. "You about ready? They'll be here any minute."

"Nearly ready." Sam drew on a fluidly soft silk dress and zipped it, then sat on the bed to slip on strappy pumps. Her generous mouth curved into a smile as Valentine came floating up for inspection. "I think you ought to wear your hair up with that dress. Here, sit down . . . lordy, I do hate for them to see this place," she sighed.

"They know what Brighton's is like, you saw Clay's eyes when I said the name," Valentine replied matter-of-factly.

"Did I ever. If he only knew how much we need him!"

"Oh, I think he's well aware of that," Valentine murmured.

"Thanks, Val, that helped just oodles." Drawing up Valentine's unruly hair, she fashioned a soft chignon, leaving wispy little tendrils to dance at her nape and temples. "Perfect, sweetie, just perfect. As will be your behavior tonight, I trust?" Her eyes narrowed. "No more decisions without consulting me first?"

"Yes, Samantha."

"Good. Just let me handle any and all negotiations, and we'll do fine."

"Yes, Samantha," Valentine intoned.

A sharp rap came at the door. She rushed to answer it.

"Valentine, remember, this isn't a date," Sam hissed.

"Right." Laughing to herself, Valentine opened the door. "Hello, Clay. Hi, Jordan."

"Hello, Valentine. You look lovely," Jordan said.

"Thank you!" She pirouetted, sending a swirl of filmy black pleats around her legs. "You like it?" she asked artlessly.

"Yes, I like it," Jordan replied. He coughed to clear the frog in his throat. Feeling oddly breathless, he stepped inside, then just stood there like a gangly lump. Incredible that he, Jordan Winslow Wyatt, suave, thirty-three-year-old bachelor, could feel this clumsy; legs too long, feet too big, hands that had nowhere to go! He knew he was staring, but didn't know how to stop it. Innocence in a heart-shaped face: a sweet, faintly challenging smile, eyes clear and guileless, yet simultaneously so mysterious. Fascinating! He looked at her and saw a sprite, a gamine, a sexy, sensuous woman . . .

And a grown man standing here like an addlepated idiot, he thought sardonically, but it didn't have the desired effect. Thank God Clay broke the awkward moment.

"Tell me, is the impertinent infant going to engage in fist-icuffs tonight?" he asked Sam. "I brought a spare handker-chief just in case."

"I happen to be twenty-three years old, Clay," Valentine sniffed.

"In places, yes," Clay said.

They swept out the door on a wave of laughter. Jordan was immensely grateful to regain his habitual composure. But he was still having breathing problems. Valentine fairly radiated excitement. He wasn't at all sure that her dainty feet ever touched the ground. This nettled him; she seemed more like some fairy-tale creature than a real woman. So ethereal, he fumed. Yet so earthy. He'd never met anyone so utterly, im-possibly . . .

All right, Wyatt, say it, he prodded himself. Enchanting.

The admission made his insides wobble. He was not accus-tomed to using words like *enchanting*. But there she was, in the glorious flesh, drifting along beside him like a handful of thistledown.

Deciding they would forego the delights of barbecue, Clay chauffeured them to his club, which boasted dim lighting, pink napery, and a postage-sized dance floor. When they were seated, glasses of wine in hand, he proposed a toast.

"To your success," he said, touching Sam's glass.

"And to yours," Sam said tightly.

"Here's to friendship," Valentine chimed in. Her lashes lifted on a puckish grin as she clicked Jordan's glass. "May it live long and prosper."

"Hear! Hear!" Jordan said. *Oh, good comeback, Wyatt*! He hid his usually unflappable self behind the menu. He had nearly made a dinner choice when another thought struck him like a blunt object. "That red Blazer parked in front of your apartment—Ohio license plate—good God, that was you!"

A trace of amusement defrosted Sam's gaze as she eyed him. "Connect the dots, Jordan?"

Valentine giggled deliciously. He stared at her, then at Sam. "My green truck—you nearly hit me! The week of the rodeo, in the center of town?" he prompted. "Green pickup?"

"Oh my goodness, that was you?" Valentine asked, eyes rounding. "Remember, Sam? We had just arrived in Destiny. Well, it really is a small world! Imagine!"

"Yes, I remember, and what do you mean, we nearly ran you down?" Sam demanded. "The only reason we're all still alive is due to my quick reaction to your reckless driving!"

"Your reaction?" Jordan retorted. "If it hadn't been for *my* quick reflexes—"

Under cover of a smile, Valentine tuned out the debate to ponder the string of coincidences that had brought the four of them together. "Awesome," she murmured before rejoining the lively discussion.

Time unwound, bright ribbons of moments shimmering with magic. The food was fabulous, the wine like a tawny autumn day on the tongue. After dinner, no one wanted to leave, so they moved to the piano lounge.

Valentine's gestures grew ever more languid and graceful as the evening flowed on. Jordan caught one of the small hands flying about her face and drew it under the table, enfolded in his. He smiled over the rim of his glass as her eyes widened.

Valentine left it that way for a while, then laced her fingers through his. Curiously, she felt no sense of strangeness with him. She thought; I've known him forever and was astonished that this was so.

Yet she still could not glimpse the inner man. He was a complete mystery to her.

In comparison, Clay Tremayne was an open book. But it wasn't Clay she wanted to know with such compelling intensity.

Covertly she studied Jordan Wyatt. Who was he? What was he? Besides the most mesmerizing man I've ever met, she added wryly. Looking up to encounter his alert blue gaze, she licked her lips.

"Shall we dance?" she asked lightly.

Jordan rose immediately. Preceding him to the floor, Valentine was acutely aware of her lissome movements. It was as if her body with its strange pulsations and odd little rushings of warmth, belonged to someone else.

She turned and came into his embrace. With beguiling naturalness, he drew her closer. She closed her eyes as he touched his lips to her cheek. She felt weightless, untethered to earth. Sheer pleasure. Cool it, Valentine, she warned herself, alarmed at her capricious romp of desires.

"You feel incredibly good in my arms," he murmured.

"Well, I try, Jordan," Valentine said, wrinkling her nose.

He laughed, his mouth hovering just a kiss above hers.

She fought a fierce urge to take it, just melt into him and brand that warm, laughing mouth with blazing ardor. She concentrated on the pattern of his handsome silk tie.

The dance ended all too soon. Flushed and breathless, she led the way back to their banquette. As they passed the curving mahogany bar, a statuesque blonde stood up and caught his arm.

"Jordan! What luck to find you here!"

Jordan looked surprised. "Gaby, hello! What are you doing here? Thought you had a meeting tonight."

"I did, but I got through much earlier than expected," she explained. "I called you, but ..." Her sherry brown eyes flickered over Valentine. "Anyway, I thought I'd have a drink and relax a bit before heading out."

"You deserve one," Jordan said with an easy smile. Quickly he introduced the two women.

"Glad to meet you, Gaby," Valentine said. *Gaby.* The name tasted sour on her tongue. Covertly she eyed the long, red-nailed fingers clasping his arm. Jordan might be an unreadable mystery, but this woman wasn't. She wanted Jordan and didn't care who knew it.

Well, that's not so surprising, Valentine thought, her smile firmly in place as they parted. Any woman would want Jordan.

He's with you tonight, not her.

The silken curl of thought brought a real smile to her face. Tossing her head in symbolic dismissal, Valentine preceded him back to their table.

Sam and Clay were still engaged in what appeared to be relaxed conversation. Seated again, Valentine took a cooling draught of wine. Casually, Jordan recaptured her hand and she stole a glance at him. Those magnificent dark brows gave an imperious air to a face made all the more attractive by his sculpted mouth and strong jaw. As he smiled into her now open regard, a deep indention plumbed one cheek. She felt a wild urge to kiss it. Awash in rose-tinted warmth, she withdrew her hand and tuned into Clay and Sam's conversation.

"My first priority is finding us suitable living quarters," Sam said. "Preferably a house—"

"With a garden for me," Valentine leaped in.

"A garden for Val," Sam agreed, her gaze softening. "And room for a shop as well."

Clay looked thoughtful. "I've just gotten a house as partial down payment on one of our new homes. It's an old, two-story dwelling, but it's in good condition," he assured Sam. "The former owners modified the outdated heating and cooling system, and I've done some work, too, with intentions of selling. But old frame houses aren't easy to sell in today's classless society. Fifteen-foot ceilings, shiny wood floors; no one seems to appreciate them anymore," he lamented. "And, too, it's in a less than grand section of town. So I guess I'm going to have to rent it."

Sam contested his opinion of shiny wood floors, pointing out that someone had to expend a great deal of time and energy to keep them shining.

"Oh, hush, Sam, I'll polish the darn floors with my hair if need be!" Valentine said. She turned to Clay. "When can we see this house? Tonight? Okay, *o-kay*," she said as Sam rolled her eyes. "Tomorrow morning, then."

Clad in panties and a T-shirt, Valentine helped make up the sofa bed with little regard to neatness. She was exhilarated, but exhausted. "I sure will be glad to get into a real bed again. Sleeping on this thing is just one step above sleeping on the floor," she grumbled.

"I'm not even sure it's better than the floor." Straightening,

Sam fluffed her pillow, smiling as her cousin tumbled bone-lessly into bed and pulled the covers up to her chin. "What happened to your promise of good behavior tonight?"

"I just said we'd go look at the house, Sam. I didn't buy it, for goodness sake."

"Thank Heaven for small favors," Sam groused, but she let it go. "You okay, kiddo?"

"Oh, yes, I'm fine." Valentine fiddled with the covers. "He's really some kind of wonderful, Sam."

Sam took a closer look at those shining eyes. "Huh. Stirred up a few things, did he?"

Valentine's soft laugh was admission enough. "Oh God, Sam!" she breathed.

"Oh God, Val," Sam mimicked gently. "Just be careful, babe. That's a pretty strong dose of poison there." She climbed into bed and turned out the light. "Mouse, I'm due two licks with a wet noodle for fussing at you today. I know I gave you a difficult task, but you did very well for us. Thanks to you, we have a job, and a start on the future."

"Thank you, Sam. You don't know how much that means to me," Valentine replied. "Anything else?"

Sam sighed loudly. "Okay, your ability to read people still spooks me, but, tell me about Clay, what qualities you sense in him. Business-wise, it would be helpful if I know him better."

Valentine laughed to herself. This was the first time Sam had openly acknowledged her heightened intuition. "Just what you're hoping he is, Sam. Honest, kind, fair. Can't hardly find anyone better than that. To work for, I mean."

"Good," Sam grunted. Another heavy sigh. "I know I've been reluctant to talk about your new, uh, talent, but it's just been real hard for me to admit that you possess ESP or what-ever you call it. I mean, even you have to admit it's kind of . . ."

"Eerie?" Valentine supplied with laughter in her voice.

"Well, at least strange. And how can you laugh about it?"

"I was laughing at your reaction. You're spooked by the

ESP or whatever you call it,'' Valentine mocked gently. ''But at the same time you're fascinated by it.''

''I'd hardly say fascinated. I've read about this sort of thing, so it's not wholly new to me. But this is *you*, not some kook in a magazine. That puts an entirely different perspective on it. It's still weird, though,'' Sam insisted. ''What's it like to look inside a person? Do you read his mind or what?''

Instantly alert, Valentine replied, ''Goodness no, I don't read minds! It's just an intuitive feeling I get about a person. I don't know its basis, but still, I trust it. I admit I found it a little scary at first, but now I'm just grateful. Mystified, but grateful. It's a gift from out of the blue. I mean that literally, because it started after my plane crash.''

''Weird,'' Sam repeated. ''What about Jordan? What's he like?''

''Jordan?'' Valentine hesitated, wondering how to explain her lack of insight into Jordan Wyatt's character. *How can I explain something I don't understand myself?* ''He's what he appears to be, Sam, a decent guy,'' she said, yawning. ''Now let's get some sleep, I'm beat.''

Valentine was up at seven the next morning. By nine she was pacing the floor. The eagerness mingled with her impatience was normal enough, but beneath it, like a gossamer lining, lay that odd sense of urgency. Although she had come to accept it as just another part of the puzzle that made up Valentine Townsend, she still wondered at it. Why this keen awareness of the passage of time? She knew when it had started, but not the reason for it.

If there even was a reason.

Around ten Sam emerged from the bathroom wearing plaid slacks and a light cotton sweater in shades of her favorite color, green. ''What?'' she asked, questioning her cousin's grin.

''No wonder poor Clay's walking around in a daze,'' Valentine said. ''You look terrific!''

Sam flushed. ''Oh, nonsense!''

''You don't look terrific?''

"I was referring to Clay's mental condition," Sam replied frostily. "Val, about this house of his. Honey, it sounds most unsuitable. When I said we'd get a house, I was thinking more on the lines of a modest, partially furnished, two bedroom with a formal dining room we could use as an office. Not some big old, completely empty, four-bedroom and parlor-sun-living— and God knows what else—room."

"Oh. I thought . . ." Valentine's hands rose up in fluttery confusion. "Well, I guess I didn't think. I mean, I saw nothing wrong with having a big old house. I kind of like the idea, actually. But if you don't . . ."

Glancing at her crestfallen face, Sam sighed. "Well, let's wait and see what we're talking about before I say more."

Valentine turned away. "Okay, sure."

When Clay finally arrived, he was alone. Valentine's heart sank; she had hoped Jordan Wyatt would accompany him. But that was silly, of course; Jordan had more important things to do than look at an old rental house.

Clay was nervous; Sam, prickly and still resistive to accepting even the appearance of a favor from him. Valentine chose to sit in the backseat of his big sedan.

"What's the address of this place?" she asked.

He checked his notes. "It's 35610 Rosehill Lane."

"Pretty address," she said. After that, subdued by Sam's silence, she lapsed into moody contemplation of the view.

The homes on Rosehill Lane were spaced far apart, their long driveways often screened by dense hedges. Some were in disrepair, but the over-all area had a well-kept look. Most of the intermingling businesses were family owned establishments.

"This is kind of like that area we saw the first day we came to town," she roused herself to remark. "Remember, Sam? You said we probably couldn't afford it."

"I remember," Sam said shortly.

Sensing that her remark had affronted Sam's pride again, Valentine shut up. She paid little heed to front-seat conversation until Clay said, "Jordan might drop by later."

Her spirits immediately soared aloft on tornadic winds of

anticipation. *Might* come by, she repeated, trying to get a grip on herself. *Might,* Valentine. Even her passionate interest in seeing the house revived, and with it, her sharp, deep yearning.

She wanted a home. She needed a home.

Well then, go get it, Valentine! Don't just sit around waiting for it to come to you, a soft, melodic voice admonished from some far part of her mind.

"If I knew how, I would," Valentine began indignantly, then stopped as she realized no one had spoken to her. "Just arguing with myself," she answered Sam's inquiring look.

You know how.

I don't, she answered the chiding voice, then shook her head in exasperation. Okay, okay, I know; *take charge of your life, Valentine,* she parroted her thoughts, then stopped short again. Who told me that? she wondered.

From somewhere came a ruffle of the softest, sweetest laughter. Relaxing, Valentine let herself drift into its warm approval. Not only did she argue with herself, she also gave herself a cozy mental hug! "Weird, Valentine," she murmured.

She sat up, eyes widening as Clay made a sharp right into a stone-embedded driveway that ran between tall, stone pillars. The high fence that concealed the house from the street was itself nearly hidden by huge crepe myrtles with sculptural trunks, interplanted with mounded, pink-flowering shrubs. Although she thought the enormous azalea with its glowing coral blossoms absolutely breathtaking, she managed to keep her opinion to herself. But the beauty of the next breath-stealers, an allée of camellia trees—not shrubs, but *trees,* for God's sake, their glossy green leaves studded with lush pink, red and white blossoms—could not be borne in silence.

"We'll take it, Clay," she said.

"Shut up, Valentine," Sam suggested.

Charitably, Valentine ignored this. Sam was deaf to the old house's whispering, rustling welcome. Before she ever stepped foot inside the door, Valentine loved it. She'd come home again.

Yessss . . . The thought floated away like a soap bubble.

"Feel it, Sam?" she asked as they traversed the cracked walk. "The same aura as grandmother's old house, remember?"

"Similar," Sam conceded. "But this is much bigger."

A wide veranda encircled three sides of the house. "A lemonade porch, Sam! I love this house, Clay," she declared.

"You haven't even seen this house," Sam pointed out, but no one was listening.

Splintery steps led to double doors weathered a dull gray. When Clay opened them, Valentine darted inside and stopped with a gasp. High above their head, a curving staircase was shadowed with blue, green and lavender prisms of light funneling through a round, leaded-glass window like a blessing.

Directly across was a small, paneled study. "That's bleached maple burl on the walls, Sam," she said reverently. Catching Clay's glance, she explained, "Uncle Jim's in the wood business, so I know wood."

"I thought I did, too," Clay said, "but this slipped by me. Nice. Real nice."

More than nice, Valentine thought. The house was a dowager queen. She knelt and touched the floor. A sensation of warmth, not unlike a gentle caress, transmitted through her fingertips.

She stood up. "We'll take it," she informed Clay.

Sam hissed and flashed her a look that clearly said, *You're doing it again!*

Making a face, Valentine led the way to the big kitchen. A vine completely covered the tall, narrow windows. The end result was a pale, watery light reminiscent of an underwater cave.

"A little paint would fix this," Clay said.

"New vinyl floors would help an awful lot, too," Sam retorted. "And what's that blocking the windows?"

"I'll hack down the vine," Valentine said. Avoiding Sam's gaze, she escaped to the backyard. A moment later she came tearing back inside to inform Sam of an orchard, an abandoned garden where tomato plants had become weeds, and a red rose rambler growing over a little ramshackle outbuilding. "It's everything we wanted and more, Sam!"

"We? Valentine, did you notice that the kitchen is devoid of appliances?" Sam inquired. "And one usually asks the rent before running around shouting, 'We'll take it!' "

Valentine kissed her cheek. "Lighten up, Sam, all is well," she whispered, and raced upstairs to choose her bedroom.

"This one," she decided as she stood before the white-shuttered window now unveiled to her eager gaze. The entire backyard lay open to view. More roses. Blossoming peach trees. Purple violets spangling the grass. The gnarled branches of an oak tree nearly touched the windowsill. At the rear of the lot lay a jungle of weeds and shrubs choked with black-berry vines. God only knew what treasures it concealed, she thought excitedly.

Raising the window, she inhaled deeply. The smell of flowers gave her intense pleasure, pleasure based on a sense of well-being, of security and radiant joy. Questions teased her mind. Never before had she been so responsive to nature. Of course she had noticed her mother's flowers, but not like this, not with this soulful intimacy. Now she saw the abiding strength of an ancient oak, the elegant curve of a lily, the intricate tracery of leaves against the color-wash of clear blue sky.

There was a mystical essence in this garden, in this house. Someone wonderful had once lived here, someone beautiful, with sweet, musical laughter . . .

She lost the thought in a sudden riotous swirl of emotions. Her entire awareness veered to the man walking up behind her. Jordan Wyatt stood so close, his breath stirred her hair.

"Hi, Jordan," she said without turning. "What are you do-ing here? I figured you'd be in your office drawing up blue-prints for fabulous houses."

"Hello, Valentine," he replied lazily. "I decided I had to see Clay's treasure for myself."

"It is a treasure, don't you think? A little paint, some re-pairs—"

"It's a dilapidated old house. But it does have possibilities," he added as she faced him.

"It has great possibilities," she asserted. "So it's not as fancy as those expensive homes you build, so what? What were you raised in, a mansion?"

Jordan was a long time answering. When he did, his harsh reply startled them both. "A fifty-foot trailer in a seedy trailer park."

She stared at him. "Oh. That's nothing to be ashamed of, Jordan. People do the best they can and that's that."

Shrugging, Jordan drawled, "I didn't say I was ashamed of it, I simply said I lived in it."

He may not be ashamed, but he sure sounds sensitive about it, Valentine thought. "I grew up in a little frame house in a blue-collar neighborhood. I loved that house. It was home."

"But it's not home now?"

"To the child in me, yes. But to Valentine the woman, no. She's temporarily homeless." Valentine laughed. "Which is the reason I'm so enthusiastic about this place. One reason, anyway. Wouldn't this make a fine bedroom?"

"A fine bedroom," he replied gruffly.

"Well, it will be, as soon as I get that turtle green paint off the walls. I think perhaps an off-white, with a deep blue, fluffy . . . carpet . . ." Her voice fell away as her gaze locked with his in deep, intense communion.

The moment stretched out to infinity. She closed her eyes when his mouth lightly touched hers, the merest brush of lips, but it still took her breath away.

"Oh, Valentine, I have so wanted to do this," Jordan said huskily. The murmur warmed her lips before he sweetly, gently tasted them again.

His arms encircled her in mind-hazing warmth. Valentine closed her eyes and just savored the sensations velvetizing her being. With the sweet slowness of the seasons, he trailed his lips from her hair to her face, feathery touches, while she smiled in anticipatory delight. Then his mouth took full possession in a kiss that literally spun her head.

Valentine swayed on the wave of warmth coursing through

her body. Last night she had imagined how it would be to kiss Jordan Wyatt, and fantasy hadn't come close to the real thing.

The kiss deepened as his arms curved around her, embracing her, gathering her in, a heavenly sensation, she thought giddily. Very slowly, his mouth trailed up her cheek into her hair, nipping her earlobe before invading the sensitive flesh behind it. His gusty breaths quivered her body. Then came a stirring of hummingbird wings in her midriff as he whispered, "Valentine . . . sweet, sweet Valentine . . ."

She loved the sound of her name on his mouth, that hot, seeking mouth that captured hers again with resistance-melting ardor. His hands slid down her back and drew her closer. Her breasts were crushed against his chest and she felt his heart thudding even as hers hammered into a wild new rhythm.

Time passed and left no imprint. Forgotten were the two people waiting downstairs, forgotten was the startling fact that this man was still very much a stranger. In the cloistered intimacy of this empty room, they were shut off from the world for long, fiery moments of the most delicious pleasure she had ever known.

When Jordan abruptly released her, she made a muffled sound. She didn't understand why he had let go of her.

Neither did Jordan, and his taut body echoed her puzzled protest. His arms didn't want to let her go—*he* didn't want to let her go. Yet he had. She stepped back and regarded him with mingled emotions darkening her eyes. So lovely, he thought with a peculiar inner ache. Her head just topped his heart.

Feeling adrift upon an unfamiliar and possibly dangerous sea, he forced a smile.

She turned on her heel and left the room.

More disturbed than he wanted to admit, Jordan swiftly followed. "Valentine," he began urgently. "Hey, honey, it was just a kiss."

His only answer was the rhythmic sway of her hips.

"Valentine, wait! Are you angry? Why are you angry?"

She stopped. "What makes you think I'm angry?"

"Well, you . . . I . . . the kiss," he explained.

Her lashes fluttered. "You're imagining things, Jordan. It was just a kiss, you said so yourself. Just like this is *just* a kiss." She grabbed his shirtfront and kissed him, hard and quick and most thoroughly, then released him and stepped away.

Jordan had momentarily lost the power of speech—her move was totally unexpected! Even though he was stunned, the quality of her smile did not escape him. It provoked, demanded and surrendered, all at the same time. A smile, he eventually decided, designed solely for the purpose of driving a man crazy.

"And your response to my kiss? Was that my imagination, too?" he asked roughly. And then she did the impossible. She blushed and made him feel ashamed of himself.

Jordan bridled as masculine outrage added its din to the chaos that was, just a few minutes ago, a fine, disciplined mind. The reproach glimmering in her big violet eyes was damned unfair—he had no earthly reason to feel ashamed! He had been dying to kiss her and had done so the first chance he got. Perfectly natural, he assured himself.

But he'd stopped. He had it all going for him; they were alone, she'd responded with more ardor than he'd dared hope for—and he pulled away. Just brought it to a skidding halt when he could have . . .

Ah, hell, no, he couldn't have. Hadn't he been on the verge of apologizing when she grabbed his head and kissed him and utterly ruined the fit of his pants?

"Well?" he demanded.

She did that thing with the lashes again, the lacy fringes lifting and lowering like the flutter of butterfly wings. "No, that wasn't imagination. Just something you must be terribly, tiresomely familiar with," she said quietly.

Now what did that mean? Jordan stared at her with a kind of baffled wonder. He was aware of several strong urges, some of them blazing hot and some of them incredibly tender, and all of them congregating in the area of his groin. At least that's what he chose to believe. Anything more profound than the way of a man with a maid was quickly discarded.

"Val, I'm sorry," he heard himself saying humbly.

"Don't be. I admire your confidence, Jordan. Now me, I'm confident of the sun's rising and setting, and a few other things, but the rest is a vast fog of uncertainty," she said with a droll smile. Turning, she started downstairs again. "If it's all right with you, I think I'll ask Sam and Clay to join us for dinner tonight. After all, it's her celebration, too."

"Perfectly all right with me," Jordan asserted manfully. He was right behind her. "What's the celebration?"

"Why, finding our new home, of course."

"Your new home? But you haven't settled anything yet!" He was talking to empty space. Valentine was already downstairs.

Bedeviled, he could only follow her. What had happened here? Why was he so rattled by something as ordinary as a kiss? And when had he asked her to dinner?

Chapter 5

Clay and Sam were still in the kitchen. Before entering, Valentine paused to gather her scattered wits. Jordan was right; she was angry. She was also elated and slightly terrified by this swift introduction to her own passionate self. She wished she had time to hide somewhere and ponder her feelings. Maybe then she'd learn how she could meet a man one day, and kiss him so passionately the next; why she felt all aglow inside; what had passed from her to him during that brief, disturbing contact of bodies and souls. But she didn't have that luxury.

Shoving it to the back of her mind, she promptly slammed into the blizzardlike swirl of doubt and indecision that took its place. She really hated incurring Sam's anger, but the compelling urge to take charge again was irresistible.

Sam might not like it right away, but perhaps later . . .

Deciding to act on this green-light thought, Valentine stepped inside the kitchen.

Sam took one look at her heightened color and opened her mouth to release a flock of questions. Valentine headed her off with a bright, "We'll take it, Clay. How much are you asking?"

"A very reasonable—"

"Reasonable, my foot!" Sam retorted. "Val, the man says six seventy-five, which is far too much for this musty old ruin, not to mention being well beyond our means. And if you say we'll take it one more time . . ." She thrust both hands into her hair and plowed its silky sward. "Valentine, there's no refrigerator; we'd have to buy one. And no dishwasher, and I'll be damned if I'll work all day and wash dishes to boot. We haven't so much as a stick of even the most basic furniture, no laundry facilities . . ." She vented a sigh as Valentine listened to her valid objections, then, with a lift of shoulders, sweetly discarded them as irrelevant.

For a seemingly careless moment Valentine studied Clay Tremayne. She knew he considered her an airhead. It stung, but in good time he would change his mind about her. But he couldn't change his mind about Sam. "No matter, Sam, we'll take it."

"Goddammit, Val!" Sam exploded. A glance at Clay brought her up short. For an instant she aimed her anger at him—who gave a damn what Clay Tremayne thought of her! With effort, she calmed herself. "Valentine, I just gave you several good reasons why we *won't* take it."

"Won't, or can't?" Valentine asked gently.

"Well, can't, I guess," Sam said, flustered. "I told you why, outlined the situation—"

"I know you did, but the situation can change, Sam," Valentine reasoned, holding tight to her composure. She didn't need to turn around to know that Jordan had entered the room. She could actually feel his presence! After an almost imperceptible pause, she continued, "Nowadays all houses are equipped with dishwashers and stoves, so naturally these will be provided by our landlord. And the wall separating those two little rooms there, the dining room and whatever that thing is—will have to be removed. It'll make you a fine office, Sam. We'll want the rear veranda glassed in before cold weather. October at the latest. Is that when it gets cold, Jordan?"

Jordan's mouth twitched as he looked at his best friend. "Cold weather usually starts a month or so later, but October would be a good time."

"Thank you," Valentine said. "This kitchen does indeed cry out for paint and new flooring; Sam has a point there. The bedrooms all need painting as well, and the front door will

have to be sanded and repainted, which is a bitch of a job."
She glanced at Clay's face to gauge her timing. Perfect. "But
Sam and I are capable painters and flooring installers. All you
need do is buy the materials."

"Are you out of your mind?" Sam cried.

Clay coughed. "Valentine, I think—"

"However," Valentine sailed on, "since we're doing so
much to improve your property, naturally the rent must come
down. What do you think, Sam? Five-fifty?"

Giving Sam no time to answer and ignoring Clay's croak,
she continued thoughtfully, "Utilities are bound to be high
with a house this size; maybe we'd better lower that another
fifty dollars. So, okay, four seventy-five a month and the
above-mentioned improvements. Oh, and a garbage disposal,
of course. Is that acceptable, Sam?"

"Well, I . . . yes, I guess so," Sam floundered.

"Oh, good. Write him a check, then."

"But . . ." Sam threw up her hands in lieu of words.

"I know, it's chancy," Valentine blandly agreed. "We'll
just have to accept his word of honor that these conditions will
be met within a reasonable time. By the end of this week
sounds pretty reasonable to me."

Her gaze flickered to Clay's mottled face. "I assume you'll
be wanting a month's rent in advance? No deposit is required,
however. As you can see, Sam and I aren't going to be dam-
aging your property. Well, write him a check, Sam," she
urged as Sam just stood there gaping instead of writing.

Clay gaped, too, but only briefly. "Well, damn! Hell no, I
won't—yes, a month in advance and a deposit as well! Four
seventy-five? You're crazy if you think—I am not knocking
out any walls! A dishwasher and a stove? Well, damn!" he
sputtered in a voice that cracked badly.

Valentine eyed him with indulgent affection. Sam began
making muffled noises. Jordan's grin didn't give him much
solace, either.

Valentine sighed. "When he calms down, Sam, write him
a check and we'll get on with this. Now I'm going outside to
check possibilities for a rose garden. On the house, Mr. Tre-

mayne; I shall bear the cost of my rose garden even though it does enhance your property. Oh, and if I were you, I'd start thinking twice about jumping to conclusions about me," she said gently, and slammed the screen-door behind her.

Jordan immediately followed her. "Hey, lady, that was one fine performance!" he said, chuckling. "You caught Clay flat-footed. He wasn't expecting anything like that from you."

"Well, he'd better get used to it," she said crisply.

"Me, too, hmm?" he said, smiling.

She shrugged, her gaze evasive.

Deciding to put an end to the awkwardness between them, Jordan eased a finger under her chin and tipped her face to his. "Valentine, I'm truly sorry if you were offended. But to be honest, that's all I'm sorry about," he said softly. "I'd be lying if I said I was sorry I kissed you." His mouth tilted awry. "After all, I spent a great deal of last night thinking about it."

Her eyes searched his, then she smiled, and it was sunshine breaking through the clouds, Jordan thought. Turning, she raised her arms to pick a spray of bridal wreath. In that pose, her hair reached to her hips. She wore a navy blue dress trimmed with white buttons and crisp white piping, very neat, very ladylike. And she radiated such sensuality she made him ache.

Annoyed at his quick response, he prompted, "Valentine?"

"All right, Jordan. Shall we go back inside and see if Clay has calmed down?"

"Sure." He grinned. "By the way, your math was wrong."

She tilted her head. "Darn! And here I thought it was exactly right for the occasion."

"You did?" He frowned, seeking the logic in that. The light dawned. "Well, I'll be sheep-dipped," he marveled. "You knew exactly what you were doing in there, didn't you? It wasn't just some feminine whimsy, you knew precisely how far you could go with Clay." He began to laugh. "Poor son-ofagun never had a chance, did he? Women!"

Valentine lifted her shoulders in a delicate shrug. He shook his head wonderingly.

"I think it'll be just you and me for dinner, though," she remarked. "Sam's still not too keen about this job. Knowing her, she'll spend the evening analyzing every pro and con."

"Fine with me," Jordan said. He felt cool and confident again, quite capable of acknowledging that he liked her, a feat accomplished by repairing the breech in his self-preserving walls. A minor breech, he assured himself.

She started back across the lawn. He walked beside her to the house, where Clay Tremayne had indeed recovered.

"Five hundred a month, firm! No dishwasher and no walls knocked out!" he greeted her with a fine, indignant roar.

"Nonsense," said Valentine, and the battle carried through every room of their new home.

Already certain of the outcome, Jordan soon left for an appointment. Sam, tight-lipped, deigned to participate in the skirmish Clay and her cousin so obviously enjoyed.

After they'd settled it, he invited them to lunch. Sam courteously but firmly refused the invitation. "Just drop us off at the apartment, please," she requested, flashing Valentine a warning glance.

Subdued, Valentine followed her to the car. She knew that look—Sam was simmering! Conversation was kept to a minimum and mostly between Clay and Valentine. If a response was absolutely necessary, Sam gave it with celery-crisp politeness.

When they reached the apartment the smoldering redhead thanked their new landlord, then strode up the sidewalk.

"What's she so riled up about?" Clay asked, puzzled and not a little anxious himself.

"It's nothing to do with you," Valentine assured him. "This is strictly my problem." Exiting the car, she held open the door long enough to say, "Thank you so much, Clay, for everything." Then, girding herself, she went to confront her bristling cousin.

Sam immediately sat down at the table with her notebook.

"What're you doing?" Valentine asked, her tone neutral.

"I'm trying to make out a work schedule."

Valentine busied herself at the sink for a few minutes, then peered over her shoulder. "That looks like it's all for you. What about me?"

"You wanted that house, you got it. There are utilities to turn on, telephones to connect, furniture to buy. That's your job. Mine's bringing in some money."

Valentine sighed. "You're really sore, aren't you? I didn't think the rent was too bad for a place that size. Or is it something else? Like me butting in, for instance."

"That chapped me a little." Meeting Valentine's quizzical gaze, she burst out, "All right, a lot! What gives you the right to decide where *I'm* going to live? Dammit, Val, I take care of you, not the other way around! Decisions like that are my responsibility, not yours! What's happened to you, anyway? You weren't like this before, you didn't override my wishes or second-guess me! I just don't understand you!"

"Sam, believe me, I'm sorry if I hurt you. I didn't deliberately set out to usurp your responsibility. But you've been doing everything in your power to get us settled, and I just wanted to do my part. And last, but not least, I really want this house. I want it very much."

"Why?" Sam asked, bewildered by her intensity.

Valentine turned away. "It's just very important to me. But you know if you say no to the house, then that will be that," she added, her habitual response to Sam's displeasure. She brushed away the tinge of resentment. Sam knew best.

"Well," Sam stalled, still indignant. "You know your opinion's important to me. Just let me think on it, okay?"

Jordan, happily restored to his habitual, easygoing, urbane self, whistled as he drove to Brighton Apartments that evening. During the afternoon he had found a niche for Valentine Townsend. She was simply a challenge to his masculinity. A particularly *challenging* challenge, true, but nothing he couldn't handle.

For the most part, this rationale cleared away the cobwebs of doubt that had temporarily clouded his reasoning. His heart still skipped a beat or two when she opened the door to him, but a peppery sense of youthful anticipation could be termed a bonus, he reflected in the few seconds required to reassert his authority.

"The restaurant I chose has a piano player. Good food and good music. Sound okay?" he asked, escorting her out the door with a peculiar sense of lightness.

"Sounds wonderful!" Valentine said. She shivered as the wind touched her bare neck. He promptly unfurled her shawl and draped it around her. She thanked him, chattering like a wren as they settled into his car. "No wonder Texans are so engrossed with the weather," she exclaimed. "It was a balmy seventy-five this afternoon! And then a blue norther comes in and lowers the temperature thirty degrees in an hour's time. Now that's preposterous, Jordan!"

His laugh rewarded her efforts.

Despite her tension, conversation was lively on the drive. Social chatter, Valentine admitted, but she really didn't want anything more right now. She still hadn't formed any solid conclusions about their kiss, and there was a tropical storm brewing in her stomach.

The hours stretching out before her suddenly seemed fraught with peril. What on earth would they talk about? True, she'd had no trouble talking with Studly Jack during those interminable hours aloft in his small plane. But Jack didn't reek of sex appeal, she thought with face-saving humor, while Jordan's natural scent seemed composed of pure pheromones, doing exactly what pheromones were meant to do, attract the opposite sex. She wrapped herself in another layer of deflective armor.

Jordan carried the conversation with annoying ease. He drove to an upscale restaurant fronted by four large palm trees and aptly named the Four Palms. Seated at a white-linened table, they had dinner, although she couldn't have said what she ate had her life depended on it. She hated being so nervous, but he was such an enigma to her! Why can't I read him? she wondered for the umpteenth time.

"Jordan, tell me about yourself," she suggested, settling

back with an insouciant air. "Where did you get your degree? In Texas?"

"Yes. I'm that rarity of rarities, a natural born Texan." He sipped brandy. "What about you? Don't I detect a bit of boarding-school primness now and then?"

"Yeah, you do. I spent my elementary and junior high years in a private Catholic school, courtesy of my grandmother. I wasn't Catholic, but she was, and not too many people said no to Grandma Fiona! She really had a way with people, especially men. Even when she was seventy, they found it hard to resist her."

"And you, of course, are her spitting image."

Enormously pleased, Valentine replied, "Don't I wish! She scandalized the whole family by dating a man twenty years younger. Said she'd probably have married him had he not died of a heart attack. Mother nearly croaked, herself, whenever Grandma said things like that."

"And you? Would you have risked scandalizing the whole family?" he asked, eyes twinkling.

"I doubt it. I'm not a brave person, Jordan. Heading out for Texas is the boldest thing I've ever done. And I probably wouldn't have done that had it not been for the plane crash."

"What plane crash?" he asked sharply.

"A friend and I were flying home from a ski trip in his small plane. We went down in the wilds of Montana..." Quickly Valentine related the pertinent details. "It changed me, made me really look at my life. Sam, too, in a way. She was very firmly established in her career, you know. But she chucked it all to come with me."

Jordan's gaze lowered. "Ski trip, hum? Must have been a pretty special guy. But you left him behind, too."

It was a question hidden in a comment. Her mouth curved. "Not that special. How about you? Has there been anyone special?"

"Sure. Texas abounds in special women," he tossed off.

"And you've loved them all, huh?" she copied his tone.

"I've been too busy getting a degree and earning a living,

among other things, to love them all. Anyway, love . . .'' He shrugged.

"Love?" she prompted.

"Is the stuff fairy tales are made of."

"You don't believe love exists?" she asked softly.

"Certainly it exists. Ask any lawyer." Jordan drained his glass. "I hate to end this, but my day starts early tomorrow, and I imagine yours does, too."

"Oh, yes," Valentine quickly agreed. She even managed a gay laugh. "Sam finally decided we'd take the house, so I've got a home to furnish on the proverbial shoestring. She's too busy. Funny, huh? She's the designer, but I'll be the one making us a liveable home."

Her nerve-induced chatter spilled from her lips unabated, but Jordan didn't seem to mind. Casually he draped an arm around her shoulders as they waited for the valet to bring his car. Suddenly rosy with warmth, Valentine appreciated the screening darkness. *Pure pheromones,* she thought, inhaling deeply.

The car finally came. When they were seated inside, he buckled his seat belt, lifted his hand to the valet, and drove smoothly onto the street. Only the purr of the engine filled the silence. The tension was electric. Valentine's stemmed from a vibrant wonder; would he kiss her again? Her entire body responded to the question. Wonderful! Scary, but wonderful. She felt a sudden, acute urge to skip right over social conventions and get to the heart of the matter. Her normal curiosity had expanded to a virulent form of interest in everything he had ever done.

"Do you have family nearby, Jordan?" She loved saying his name.

"Not nearby, no. Well, in Brenham, but none here in town."

Silence again. "Jordan, do I have to pry it out of you word by word?" she asked, exasperated by his stone-man act. "Who's in Brenham? And who's elsewhere? And how many?"

"I have four sisters. Susan is with the World Health Organization. Last time I heard from her she was headed for the Ukraine to work with the children who've survived Chernobyl.''

"Oh, my goodness, that's a tremendous thing, Jordan! And the others?''

"Glory lives in Brenham with her two kids. She's divorced. Jacey's in California with her third spouse, a film producer. Debralee just married an Oklahoma oilman.''

"Money?''

"Tons of it. She says it's a love match.''

"But of course we cynics aren't falling for that old line!''

"Unfair,'' Jordan decreed. "I'm just quoting my sister. Who, by the way, I want very much to be happy.''

"Of course you do,'' Valentine agreed warmly. "You're very lucky to have so much family around you. No brothers?''

"One. He died young.''

"And your parents?''

"Dead.''

"When did they die?'' she asked with dogged persistence.

"A while ago. You about through with the inquisition?'' he asked dryly.

"Displaying interest in your family is hardly an inquisition. But yes, I'm through.'' Folding her arms across her chest, Valentine stared straight ahead. Since she had practically grilled the man, he had a valid point. But that didn't lessen its sting.

Jordan glanced at her from the corner of his eye. She was miffed and he regretted that. But he didn't want to talk about his background. He was afraid he'd tell her too much. Get started and can't stop, he acknowledged his keen desire to unload the entire story of his life. It made him edgy. His private life was just that, private.

When he parked in front of her apartment he was pleased that she expected his gentlemanly gesture of opening her car door for her. Her thank-you was starchy. Oh, great, she was still ticked off. To his consternation, his annoyance was directed more at himself than her.

At her doorstep, concealed by tall shrubbery, he had no

choice but to kiss her. He wanted it, and so did she. One quick kiss, he promised himself. Then he'd go.

Holding her soft, curvy form in his arms was a singular pleasure. He had to savor this lovely feeling before going on to the next. She smelled delicious and tasted even better. The winey sweetness of her mouth sent its feminine message all the way down to his toes.

She whimpered, and his pulses thickened. The alarm he'd set earlier went off in his brain—things were rapidly getting out of hand. Time to end this. But then she wound her silken arms around his neck and opened her lips for the rough thrust of his tongue. He drew her close . . . closer. She responded with guileless ardor. Her soft little belly felt the power of him, rubbed against the tantalized heft of him, cuddled his arousal with an intimacy that set his heart to a hammering beat. A moan raked his throat. When his hands plunged into the glory of her hair, she stayed where he had placed her.

Emotions, undefined but very powerful, glossed his excitement. Jordan stopped functioning as a thinking being. He was drowning in perfumed flesh and honeyed lips, and he simply meant to go on kissing her forever.

When she drew back and buried her face in his shoulder, he felt the lovely tremor rushing through her body. She gave a heart-touching little sigh and he ached all over with the need to keep her right here, safe in his protecting arms.

His ego insisted she wanted it, too, and certainly her response was gratifying enough to encourage any man. Yet, instead of following up on his knowledgeable urges, he dropped his arms and stepped away from her.

Jordan's reaction caught him totally unprepared. Never, not once in his adult life had he harbored reservations about a budding sexual relationship with a pretty woman. But he'd never felt with such intensity, either, and not all of it was physical.

All right, it scares me, Jordan admitted, mauling his hair. Not the normal, run-of-the-mill fear, like fighting a tiger bare-handed. The danger was emotional. And all things considered, he concluded ironically, he'd rather take on the tiger.

He inhaled, exhaled forcefully. "I hear there's a pretty good play at the Crighton Theater. You want to go see it tomorrow night?"

Even as he asked it, Jordan marveled at the question. It had come out of nowhere, on its own. Yet he was boyishly happy when she said yes.

He drove back to his apartment deep in thought. Her soft words nagged at him. *You're very lucky to have so much family, Jordan.* . . . He shook his head. When his sisters came to mind, so did years of worry and desperate attempts to do and be what they needed.

Mommy's sick again, Jordan, she needs her medicine refilled . . . I'm crying 'cause I'm afraid my mommy's gonna die, Jordan . . . When's Daddy coming home, Jordan? . . . Will you sign my paper for my field trip, Jordan? If I go I have to wear jeans, the teacher says, and I don't have any . . . Did Daddy die, Jordan? . . . I hate peanut butter, I hate these ugly shoes— I hate you, Jordan! . . . My throat hurts. Will you stay with me at the hospital? I'm scared, Jordan, I'm scared . . . Jordan, I need a prom dress . . . Momma's throwing up again, Jordan . . . One week before graduation, and he dumps me, Jordan! I'll die, I'll just die . . . Jordan, I'm pregnant! What'll I do! What'll I do, Jordan? . . . Hey, big brother, I'm dropping out of school. There's no reason to hang around this burg . . . Jordan, Jacey's gone, but she left you this note. Where's California, Jordan? . . . Jordan, I want to be a doctor, but I know there's no way we can afford it. Is there? . . . Jordan, I'm getting married . . . Jordan, I need a car . . . Jordan, I need . . .

For an instant the pleas and cries and demands swirled around his mind in overwhelming discord. He gave himself a sharp shake to dislodge the guilt of resenting the clamorous past and its immense cost. It was ridiculous to feel guilty about the value he placed on the peace and quiet of his current lifestyle. He'd earned it. Still, he could see that the enormous task of raising four little girls to lovely young womanhood had blurred his image of them. He'd almost lost sight of the fact that they were his family.

His new awareness did not, in any way, alter his determination never to repeat the experience. But it was nice feeling this way, viewing it from a new perspective. Thanks to Valentine.

"Nosy little thing," he muttered sourly. But his mouth stretched around a smile. He hoped she liked live theater as much as he did.

Valentine discovered that she loved live theater. "It's so intimate," she told Jordan as the curtain came down on Act One.

Sitting beside him in the small theater, laughing with him during the wickedly comical scenes, filled her heart with pleasure. Dangerous pleasure, perhaps, if last night's fiery embrace was any indication. Feeling vulnerable to a man was too new an experience to judge with any degree of accuracy.

To add to her uncertainty, she had not, for the first time in her life, confided her feelings to Sam. Instead she had hugged them to her like a treasure too precious to expose to the harsh light of logic. She had even tried to downplay them as she dressed for the evening. Sam was curious enough as it was.

"Two dates in two days, Valentine?" she had asked, slanting an eyebrow.

"I want to see a real play in a real theater," Valentine had replied with pleasing dignity. Then she'd added, "Don't worry, Sam, I'll keep my head straight and my legs crossed, I promise!"

Well, at least I made Sam laugh, Valentine reflected, momentarily saddened. There was still a tiny rent in the fabric of their relationship. Sam didn't understand her. But then, Valentine didn't understand herself.

Just then Jordan leaned to her ear to murmur something. His comment went unheard. The sensation of his warm breath brushing hyper-sensitive skin packed an amazing wallop. Luckily the small sound she made sufficed for a response.

At intermission, they walked out to the tiny lobby so Jordan could stretch his legs. With a mixture of relief and delight, Valentine spotted Deke Salander in the crowd. The wickedly sweet thought just *slithered* across her mind; *it wouldn't hurt to let Jordan know he's not the only man in your life!* She waved and called Deke's name.

"Well, hello, Valentine," Deke drawled, his black gaze taking in her tailored red suit and the strip of lace that bridged its lapels. She wore a camisole beneath the jacket. He grinned.

"Hello, Deke, you nice man!" Valentine replied. Flooded with affection for this complex person, she stretched up to kiss his cheek. "What rascally deeds have you done since we last met?"

After a sharp look at her impish expression, Deke laughed and hugged her. "Nary a one, honey. Been good as gold." He kept an arm around her shoulders as he greeted Jordan. "Haven't seen you in a while, Wyatt. What's been keeping you so busy?"

"Same old, same old," Jordan said, shrugging. "I didn't know you two were acquainted."

"Oh, yes! Deke was practically the first person we met when we first arrived. We went to the rodeo with him. In fact, he bought me my first cowboy hat!" Valentine said, sparkling up at Deke. She had seen the glint in Jordan's eye, heard the edge in Deke's voice. One didn't have to be a mind-reader to realize, with a purely feminine thrill, that she was the cause of it.

"You were at the rodeo?" Jordan asked.

"Yep. I even got to dance with the Champeen Cowboy! Thank goodness Deke saw us back to the hotel—both Sam and I had a little too much to drink," she confided, her merry gaze on Deke.

"It was my pleasure," Deke informed her.

"And mine." She took his big hand in both of hers with genuine emotion tremoring her voice. "Meeting Deke feels far more purposeful than coincidental," she said softly. "He's the one who helped make up my mind about settling here. It's like our paths were destined to cross. Doesn't that kind of give you goose bumps? I mean, there's the future stretching out ahead of you like some vast, featureless plain and yet there are certain people out there, complete strangers, waiting to meet you for reasons you may . . . may never know."

Valentine flushed and dropped Deke's hand. She had both men's rapt attention and she wasn't even sure what she was talking about. Lamely, she laughed. "Well, anyway, we're good friends now, and I'm glad."

"So am I." Deke grinned again and twirled his mustache. His black gaze flickered to Jordan as he addressed Valentine. "Didn't I promise to show you Galveston? Seems to me I did, albeit through a drunken stupor."

"Yes, you did, but not because you were intoxicated," Valentine said, prettily indignant.

"Huh. Well, whatever the reason, I always keep my promises. What about Friday? Less crowded during a weekday. It's still a little too cool to swim, but we could do the tourist bit."

"I'd love to!" Valentine said. "But I'd have to be back early. Deke, I've so much to tell you! We have a house now! We'll probably be moving within the next few days. It's gorgeous—needs a little work, but you'll love it. Oh, and Sam has her first job, with Clay and Jordan, can you believe it? I'm sorry I neglected calling you with all this news, but it's been hectic, to say the least!"

"Intermission's about over," Jordan said. Taking her arm, he nodded at Deke. "Deke."

"Jordan. See you Friday, Valentine. About ten," Deke called as they walked away.

She blew him a kiss over Jordan's arm.

"Watch your step or you'll stumble," he warned.

A grin tucked into her lips as Valentine preceded him to their seats. "I'm really enjoying this, Jordan," she murmured.

"I'm so glad, Valentine. Do you know anything at all about Deke Salander?" he asked irritably.

"I know all I need to know about my good friend Deke."

"Like what?"

"Like, he's sweet and kind, decent, basically good-hearted, and trustworthy to the core. He's also lonely, and needful, a little lost, but aren't we all," she added wryly.

"I don't know how you formed *that* opinion, but it certainly doesn't jibe with mine. I see much different character traits."

"Like what?"

Jordan sighed. "Deke is my friend, too, and I like him. I also trust him, to a certain degree. But he's not America's sweetheart, Val, especially when it comes to the ladies."

"I know. But that's irrelevant. We're just good friends. Right now, anyway."

Jordan drew back and folded his arms across his chest.

Valentine's hand clenched. She'd give anything to know what he was thinking!

Sam and Valentine went back to work the next day, Sam in a tailored suit and hose, briefcase in hand; Valentine in jeans and a cotton shirt, arms filled with cleaning equipment. She didn't mind. In fact, she wouldn't have traded jobs with Sam. She felt as eager as a child as she walked out into the cool, wet morning.

She carefully did not think of her evening with Jordan. He hadn't mentioned Deke's name during the drive home, nor even alluded to the date she'd made with him. All she had to work with was conjecture and wishful imagination, so why drive herself crazy trying to ascertain his true feelings? However, on the plus side, he hadn't even tried to kiss her good night, a possible sign of anger . . .

"Good God, Val, you're back in grade school again! He likes me, he likes me not," she mimicked, pulling imaginary petals off an imaginary daisy. Deriding her angst, she wheeled into heavy morning traffic and headed downtown.

Before she could work on the house, the utilities had to be transferred to her name. For a hefty sum, of course, Valentine fumed, writing checks at the various offices she visited.

Next on her tidy list was a stop at a paint store to select her colors for the house, mainly a warm, creamy white, except for her bedroom. "Charge it to Tremayne's account," she said blithely.

The clerk had to call him, of course. She could hear Clay grumble as he okayed the charges. Taking the receiver, she thanked him nicely, then asked, "When will the painters arrive?"

Lord, that man could growl!

She took the paint with her. It was still raining, so she went upstairs and painted her bedroom a soft, mellow apricot. Afterward she pulled up a section of worn carpet and discovered scarred oak flooring. Delighted, she spit-rubbed the small spot until it shone with a warm, golden glow, as though it appreciated her attention. "Which you do, don't you?" she murmured. "My lovely, mystical house."

She went from room to room, checking floors. Solid oak! She wanted all of them refinished, of course. But she would settle for her bedroom, Sam's office and the living room.

The rain let up around noon. After lunch she went outside to cut back the wisteria strangling her jasmine arbor, but soon had to run for shelter as raindrops spattered the ground. Then, with shocking ferocity, the skies opened in a deluge that drowned out every noise but its own.

Marveling at the sheer volume of water, Valentine retreated to the kitchen. She fetched her tool kit from the garage and began taking up the ugly linoleum, a tedious job, for it came up in bits and pieces. For several hours she worked to the heavy drumbeat of rain. At length, tiring, she returned to the veranda.

The sensation of cool, fresh air on her hot skin was exquisite pleasure. Valentine sheltered against the wall and gave her mind free rein. Her body tightened as she imagined Jordan here with her. *Wrapped in his arms, becoming one with the elements, souls soaring on love's wild, sweet winds—*

"Valentine! Where are you?"

The irritable male voice penetrated her bemusement and became part of it for an instant. Jordan's tall form materialized out of the torrential downpour as if by magic. Valentine gave herself a hard shake and tried to get a grip on reality. Fantasies did not come clad in yellow slickers, nor did they glare at her. "Jordan?" she asked incredulously.

"You're still here. Thank God for small favors." He shoved back his hood. "Get your jacket, I'll drive you home."

Raindrops bedewed the lustrous dark hair tumbling over his forehead. Her fingers rose to brush back the damp locks. He moved aside. Lowering her hand, she said, "I am home. But what are you doing here?"

He shrugged. "The rain canceled my afternoon appointments so I decided to leave."

"You live clear across town, Jordan. Were you worried about me?"

"I was concerned about the weather," he said testily. "A heavy downpour calls for caution—the streets are flooded and some underpasses are downright dangerous. You wouldn't be safe in that little car of yours."

Valentine stared up at him. His eyes glinted in the gray light and his jaw was clenched. The man and the storm hammered at her senses. She needed to be held. She needed to cradle his face in her hands and soften that hard mouth with a kiss. On the practical side she needed some hot food and cooling wine, and him sitting across from her in a cozy restaurant.

She almost asked him, but all this neediness disturbed her. Her chin came up in automatic defiance. "I'm sure I'd be fine in my little car. But if it makes you feel any better, I won't leave here until the streets are dry."

"You promise? I'm not joking around, Val. It's crazy out there and I don't want you driving in it. If you do need to leave, call Sam; her Blazer should make it all right. You're not afraid, here alone in a storm?"

Her mouth curved sweetly. "No, I'm not afraid. I love storms. They excite me."

Jordan grunted. "At least go inside away from the lightning."

"There's very little lightning."

"It only takes one bolt." Looking as annoyed as he sounded, he checked his watch. "Well, I'm meeting someone for dinner so I'd better run along."

Her heart sank somewhere around her knees. "Yes, I guess you'd better. Thank you for coming by, Jordan. I appreciate it. Take care now."

"You, too. I still wish you'd let me drop you off at the apartment, but short of dragging you to my truck, I can't see a way to change your mind." One long, tanned finger tipped her chin up for a suspenseful breath or two. "Remember your promise, Valentine; no driving until street conditions clear up. Now go inside, we're under a severe thunderstorm warning." He disappeared into the sluicing rain.

"What the heck was *that* all about?" Valentine wondered aloud. "And why was he so cranky?"

Because he cares for you and he doesn't want to.

The mind-whisper provoked a wry smile. "Don't you wish," Valentine chided her whimsy. But it felt good to think he was concerned about her. And by coming here, he had revealed a tiny segment of his personality. Jordan was a caretaker. A nurturer, she thought with tender pleasure.

Noting that the sky still looked bruised and swollen, she went inside and tackled the linoleum again. Her thoughts ranged far and wide, yet she was always aware of the question crouching at the back of her mind. Who was he meeting tonight? Firmly she told herself it was none of her business. But she still wondered.

Hail suddenly pelted the windows, shattering her reverie. A cannonade of thunder rolled overhead with a reverberating *clap!* that made her ears ring. Jordan's predicted thunderstorm had arrived. Eyes shining, Valentine ran out the front door into a cacophony of sound. Earsplitting thunder, the slashing whips of lightning, an avalanche of wind, rain and flying leaves! It was wonderful! A thunderstorm *royale,* Grandma Fiona used to call these elemental tempests. She had loved them, too.

Leaning against a pillar, Valentine became lost in the inexplicable beauty of the storm. She savored its delicious peril, a shivery sensation tightening her skin as she rode its volatile energy. The ions in the air stood her neck hairs on end. She closed her eyes and felt simple enjoyment metamorphose into something resembling an exquisite, unearthly bliss. . . .

The storm withdrew. Valentine clutched the railing as raindrops pattered, kitten soft, on the veranda roof. She had no idea what or where her thoughts had been during that brief time-out. Stretching, she realized she felt drained of energy, and contrarily, filled with radiance.

Aimlessly she wandered through the house, and, as if following a beaten path, upstairs to the attic. It was dark, musty and faintly sinister with the indistinct outlines of discarded furniture. She pulled the string on the naked bulb hanging from the ceiling, and light flooded the room, revealing nothing more sinister than two broken chairs and stacks of yellowed newspapers. Some ancient Christmas wrap, a battered old trunk, disappointingly empty, and an antique dressmaker's form with an impossibly tiny waist were all she turned up in her explorations.

Matter-of-factly, she began gathering the flotsam of someone else's past life. The plain wooden chairs had the simplicity of Shaker furniture and looked repairable, so she set them in the hallway. Next she tried moving the trunk. It was surprisingly light; cardboard, she bet. When she shifted it, a piece of paper floated down from the raised lid.

Startled, Valentine gently unfolded the dry, brittle, water-damaged paper. It was a newspaper clipping of a wedding announcement. Only a few of the words were legible. She read them, and then reread them, with the same prickly feeling of familiarity.

"Elisse . . . something something of something Manor, will wed . . . wed who, I wonder?" Valentine murmured. The picture was blurred, yet she had an impression of a beautiful young woman with fair hair piled high in a pompadour, a tall, wasp-waisted figure and a beguiling hint of a smile. She wore a simple, ankle-length dress, circa 1900. A cameo centered the black velvet ribbon encircling her elegant neck.

Studying the picture, Valentine felt a sudden, shivery thrill run from her hands up her arms. The woman reminded her of someone. That made no sense; she had never seen this lovely being before. Yet, in the far reaches of her mind, she promptly began seeking an illusive image. Nothing. Just this tantalizing sense of deja vu.

"Elisse. Who were you?" she whispered. "Am I living in your house, Elisse?"

Valentine tilted her head as if expecting an answer from the time-worn picture. For an instant she thought she heard soft laughter. . . . But it was probably just the wind soughing through the ancient tree just outside her window.

Chapter 6

Removing the fragile newspaper clipping from the house where it had lain all these years felt wrong to Valentine. As she lifted the yellowed paper, her skin prickled with an awareness that stole her breath. She held it gently, and with a deep sense of reverence, for the atmosphere had become pervaded with something very similar to holiness.

Then the sensation moved on like a passing cloud, and the attic was just dim space again. Yet the sublime peace that had pervaded her heart still lingered, as tangible as perfume.

Profoundly stirred, Valentine replaced the clipping back in its original resting place. How odd that she had overlooked it when first opening the old trunk. The satin-lined lid had no secret compartments that she could find. She decided to call it a mystery, for she loved mysterious happenings.

Regrettably, the source of the velvety stillness that surrounded her had a ready explanation. It was the hush that comes immediately after a storm, she realized with a twinge of disappointment. The soft *patter-patter* of rain on the roof had stopped and nothing yet filled its void.

A shaft of sunlight came through the attic's octagonal window, haloing her face in its golden light. She felt so warm, so contented here in this house. Closing the trunk, she sat back on her haunches and thought of other hands touching this scuffed surface. Soft hands, pretty hands . . .

Unbidden images of the empty bedroom just below came

to mind, filled with this same golden light, waiting with infinite patience for the time she would arrive and stamp her own unique imprint upon its living walls. With a sweet, internal ache she thought of Jordan in that bedroom with her. In hindsight, his kiss seemed to put a sanction on her presence in this house.

She surfaced from the cozy depths of reverie without warning. Like cat claws, thoughts of Jordan shredded her serenity and she was thrown back into the murk of frustration.

A sibilant breath echoed her heart's lament. While her ability to read people had sharpened considerably, she hadn't a clue to his feelings. The person she wanted most to know and understand—the only man who could delight every cell of her body with just his grin—was still an enigma to her.

As for his kisses . . . she shivered deliciously. Desire and passion became more than words when Jordan Wyatt touched her. She'd often wondered, a little cynically, what all the fuss was about. She had a gorgeous feeling that he could answer that question, magnificently.

She literally ached to find out, Valentine admitted with another long, sensuous shiver. But she didn't want to rush it. No, no, she yearned to savor every step of the experience, from courtship to fulfillment. To take her time, make sure this was right for her—

Make sure there's no emotional risk involved, no possibility of getting hurt.

Valentine jerked, surprised by the gentle mockery originating from deep within her mind. Without thinking, she responded, ''That's not true! I just like to think things through, that's all. Besides, no one enjoys being hurt!''

Her defensive voice rang inordinately loud in the stillness. Abashed, Valentine looked around the dim room. The sunlight had shifted away from the window, leaving her in semidusk. Suddenly chilled, she hugged her arms. There was nothing wrong with taking it slow, she thought defiantly. That Jordan wanted her was thrillingly obvious, but in what way? As a means of satisfying sexual curiosity? Or genuine interest in the woman herself and not just her attributes? Oh, yes, she concluded with a sizzling edge of resentment, sometimes a little caution paid big dividends.

A sense of disappointment as faint and untraceable as an air current wisped through her mind. Annoyed, she sat erect. The tiny attic window was completely dark now. How long had she been sitting here, brooding over Jordan Wyatt and thoughts of sex, passion and love?

"Jeez, Valentine!" she muttered, chagrined at her excessive absorption in what to others must be commonplace. None of this heated supposition could be deemed a matter of life and death, so why this primordial urge for haste?

The telephone rang. It was Sam, bidding her come home.

"I am home," Valentine replied. But she obediently packed up her tools and left the house sitting empty and dark in the gathering dusk.

"I'll be back," she promised as she drove away.

At the apartment, the appetizing smell of pizza greeted her. "Oh, bless you, Sam!" she moaned as its ravishing odors flooded her nostrils. "I'm famished!"

"I'll consider myself blessed," Sam replied with a quick hug. "Sit down and let me pamper you for a change. You looked worn to a bone. I just got off the phone with Mom; all's well at home. They're having chicken and dumplings for supper, so I ordered pizza the second I hung up." She frowned at Valentine's blistered hands. "Oh, Val, you and that damn house!" she said, sighing. "I'm free tomorrow morning so I'll come help you."

"Great!" Valentine said, tackling an aromatic slice of pizza. "The faster we move out of here, the better."

"Hurry, hurry, hurry," chided Sam. "But I'll be glad to get out, too." She opened two icy beers and sat down at the table. "Here you go. So, tell me about your day."

"Well, Jordan came by and ordered me not to drive on flooded streets," Valentine replied, chuckling. Then she told of exploring the attic and finding the newspaper clipping, deciding at the last second to edit her narration. Sam didn't like mysteries.

"The clipping goes in my bedroom when we move in,"

Valentine chattered on. "And that old dressmaker's form, too.
I think it might have been Elisse's! Isn't Elisse a pretty name?
Doesn't it make you wonder what she was like? What dreams
she dreamed, what made her laugh and cry, who she loved,
was she happy here?"

"September Valentine, the eternal romantic," Sam teased.

"That's me!" Valentine agreed. "And underneath that
hard-as-nails veneer of yours, so are you, Samantha Louise."

Sam's snort conveyed her opinion of *that* misconception.

The next day the two women worked together on the house,
which brought them closer to getting into their new home in
more ways than one. Appalled at the thought of Sam indulging
in heavy physical labor, Clay Tremayne sent over a crew of
workmen.

He came with them. Later Valentine spotted him down on
his knees, helping Sam lever up bits of bathroom tile.

"Isn't he a sweetheart!" Valentine enthused as she and Sam
made take-home salads from a supermarket deli that night.

Sam shrugged. "I suppose everyone has their good points.
You still going to Galveston with Deke tomorrow?"

"I probably shouldn't—we're so busy right now. But yeah,
I'm going."

The following morning Valentine still felt ambivalent about
taking the day off. But Deke's affectionate hug soothed her
conscience. She was becoming more and more aware of how
much she needed family around her. Lacking this vital emotional support, she was instinctively gathering friends to create
a similar environment. Deke, she thought happily, was one of
those friends, whether Sam liked it or not. Or Jordan either,
she gave fleeting acknowledgment to part of the reason she
had made this date in the first place.

"It's so good to see you again, Deke. I'm really looking
forward to this!" she told him—and herself—firmly.

"So am I." Deke opened the car door and handed her inside, then settled himself behind the steering wheel. "Usually
I prefer a chauffeur, but I thought I'd do the honors this time."

"I'm suitably honored," she said.

"You should be. Good God, what've you been doing?" he growled, inspecting her hands.

"Working on the house," she replied, wincing as he touched a broken blister.

"Did you ever hear of wearing gloves?"

"I wear gloves, but they're always getting lost or misplaced. Oh, Deke, I can't wait for you to see the house! It's going to be so beautiful!" she exulted.

Deke shrugged. "I've seen the place; it's just an old, run-down house. Structurally sound, I assume, since Tremayne's your landlord, but still just an old house."

"It's not either, it's a lovely, magical place," she rebuked. "And it welcomes me, Deke. The first time I walked inside it greeted me with open arms. Houses are living things, you know."

He looked amused. "How do you figure that?"

She eyed him, so colorful and attractive in his western shirt and jeans, with that wonderfully battered Stetson shoved back on his head. It was battered just *so,* not an iota too much or too little. His handsome, weathered face and powerful body were the stuff of feminine dreams. Not to mention all that money, she thought puckishly. So why wasn't she looking at him from that sensible perspective? *Maybe I should.* Letting the thought drift where it would, she answered his question.

"I read something once that said everything on this earth and even the earth itself—the entire universe, for that matter—is created from the same building material. It's like if you had a handful of living clay and you created trees, people, stars, toads and so on ad infinitum, then colored them, characterized them, whatever made them different," she said, hands flying. "Well, they'd be different in appearance, texture and form. But basically, they would still all be made from the same substance. Atoms, molecules, cells; whatever you name the clay, it's still clay." She beamed at him. "Doesn't that make a kind of beautiful sense?"

"No, I can't say that it does." A smile twitched his mustache. "Maybe because I don't go in for deep thinking."

"Well you should. As Shakespeare so succinctly put it,

'There are more things in heaven and earth, Horatio, Than are dreamed of in your philosophy.' ''

"He's probably right," Deke remarked. "You're very knowledgeable, aren't you?"

"Why, yes, I am," she said as if just realizing it. "Well, I read a lot."

"And that explains it, hmm?" He glanced at her, sidelong. "I've been wondering what you'd say if I suggested we hop on the Concorde and weekend in Paris? My treat, of course."

Valentine stilled, momentarily speechless. Did he mean it?

"Good grief, Deke," she sputtered, "you trying to give me a heart attack? I'm just a small-town girl, not at all accustomed to that kind of invitation. You're not serious, surely!"

"Dead serious." Cynicism tinged Deke's amusement as he drawled, "So, small-town girl, what would your answer be?"

Composing herself, Valentine stared at him for the few seconds necessary to analyze his reaction. She rather liked the uncertainty lapping around the edges of his arrogant male confidence. "I'd say, thank you, that truly sounds lovely. But regrettably, I must decline. It's not seemly."

Deke gave a startled laugh. "Now *that's* an original rejection! Why isn't it seemly?"

"Because we're just starting, Deke, still building a friendship," she said earnestly. "It takes time to do a good job of it, and we haven't had that time yet."

He looked astonished. "Christ, Valentine! Who worries about being *seemly* in this day and age? Instant gratification is the name of the game. People get an itch, they jump in the sack and scratch it. No big deal."

"That may be so for some people, but not for me. For me, it is a very big deal. I couldn't be intimate with someone just because I'm attracted to him. Especially if he considers it no big deal," she added dryly. "I'd have to care for him, and the caring must be mutual."

Deke's smile softened. "Ah, Valentine, you're a breath of fresh air," he said wonderingly. "You almost make this weary old cynic believe in romantic notions like idealism and honor, not to mention good old-fashioned *seemliness!*"

"They're not romantic notions, you're not old, and if you're weary, it's your own fault," she reproved. " 'What you think about, you bring about.' I also read that, and I think it makes sense, too. So hush that kind of talk."

For a reflective moment Deke was silent. Then he asked, "What's going on between you and Jordan Wyatt?"

"We've dated a few times," Valentine answered carefully. "He's my friend, too, Deke."

"Yeah, I noticed how friendly he was." Deke tugged at his mustache. "Jordan's also my friend, and I don't bad-mouth friends. But I tell you this, Valentine; he's a real ladies' man. Love 'em and leave 'em is his motto, or at least that's been his way since I've known him. He avoids commitment like the plague. Don't get me wrong—he's a straight arrow in his own way. But marriage and home and children are not part of his plans, however much you might hope otherwise. When the fun's over, he moves on."

Valentine concealed her quick, reactive hurt. She told herself that this was only Deke's opinion. He resented Jordan's importance in her life, so naturally he'd be biased. "I don't notice a wife and kiddies hanging onto your shirttails, Deke Salander!" she huffed. "Is it possible you could be tarred with the same brush?"

"Hell no, I never made any plans in that direction. It just hasn't come up, you might say." Deke grinned. "Or maybe I just haven't met the right woman yet. Isn't that in your books? Right woman, right man, happy ever after?"

"It is, and it applies to everyone," Valentine said in a tone that brooked no argument. Why did everyone find her reading habits so amusing? "So stop your mockery. And stop judging Jordan. And me, too. I do have a mind of my own, you know."

"I've never questioned that," Deke muttered.

Valentine laughed and poked his arm. She stared out the window, wishing with all her heart that it was Jordan sitting beside her. But Deke was fun, and she did love to have fun, she reminded herself. "Tell me about Galveston. Wasn't it wiped out by a bad storm in the early part of the century?"

"Very nearly. And it wasn't just a bad storm, it was the biggest, most destructive hurricane in history." With a natural bent for storytelling, Deke told her about the great hurricane that destroyed a gracious seaside city and thousands of its inhabitants that terrible night. "They didn't have the hurricane warning system we have now, so it seemed like the storm just suddenly showed up. The sea got rougher, of course, and the wind increased, streets flooded. But one woman was quoted as saying they still didn't realize what was happening until someone tasted the water and found it salty."

"My God, the Gulf of Mexico running through the streets of town!" Valentine shuddered. "That must have been terrifying! I've never seen the ocean, so I can't really—"

"You're kidding! You've never seen an ocean?"

"Well, no. We don't have many oceans in Ohio, Deke."

Deke grinned at her acerbic tone. They had entered Galveston and were driving toward the seawall. "I suppose you'll want to go shopping on the Strand," he said, sighing as he parked the car.

"Of course." She jumped out and waited impatiently for him to join her. "What's the Strand?"

"It's where they hold festivals like the Mardi Gras."

"The Mardi Gras is in New Orleans."

"Not this one. It's the Texas Mardi Gras," Deke answered buoyantly. He felt wonderful.

Valentine felt pretty good, too.

Her first look at the sea's endless horizon, dotted with silhouettes of oil tankers and other enormous ships left her wordless. The sights and sounds of Galveston, the delicious seafood they consumed in a restaurant perched on a long pier overlooking the Gulf, the wind in her hair and the invigorating smell of sea-rinsed air, were sensuous pleasures.

Later they walked the beach. Children played in the sand, and gulls wheeled overhead. Their perpetual cry blended in with nature's song of wind and waves. The powerful ambience held her entranced. And aching. Aching for another man's presence, she admitted. As much as she liked Deke, she couldn't help wishing she was sharing this with Jordan.

She wondered what he was doing. And how did he feel about her trip to Galveston? She knew how she wanted him to feel, but that didn't count for much, Valentine conceded ruefully. Still, she could dream . . .

Her quick smile was meant as atonement when Deke presented her with a souvenir of her trip, as well as a delicious lemon ice. Licking the tangy sweet, Valentine vowed not to allow Jordan Wyatt to spoil so much as a second of this lovely day.

It was late afternoon when she and Deke returned to Destiny. Although she enjoyed her day, Valentine could hardly wait to get home. "Just drop me off here in front," she said when they reached her apartment.

Deke insisted on walking her to her door.

"Such a gentleman," she said, kissing his cheek. "Thank you, my friend, for a lovely day."

As soon as he drove away, she ponytailed her windblown hair, grabbed the keys to her car and headed for her house.

The work crew had already left. Sam and Clay were sitting on the floor enjoying a beer. Three was definitely a crowd, Valentine decided. She took herself back outside.

Rounding the corner of the house, she was surprised to see a shirtless Jordan Wyatt whacking at omnipresent trumpet vines and ivy still clinging to the window frames. She stopped, suddenly wary. Why was he here? From his reaction at the theater, she expected—or maybe just hoped—that he would be angry because she'd spent the day with Deke. At least a little irritated, she thought, suddenly furious at this maddeningly elusive male. Once again he refused to respond the way she thought he would.

And once again she wished she could sense what he was thinking, what he felt. She could read Deke all day long. Sam and Clay were open books. But Jordan was a blank page. Damn!

Thanks to Deke, she wasn't sure of anything. More than likely Jordan's testiness at the theater was just ego reflex.

He looked up and saw her. "Hey, Valentine!"

"Hey, Jordan!" she caroled. Just that offhand greeting was enough to curl her fingers, and she positively loathed his knee-weakening grin. Weightless again, she drifted toward him. She would be flip and casual with him if it killed her! "I really appreciate your doing this."

"Clay asked me to help out, so . . ." *Snap* went a woody section of vine. He threw it onto the pile. "How was your Galveston adventure?"

Hoping she'd heard a hint of jealousy in his voice, she laughed. "It was great! We even rode the ferry. And look at these little shells I found, pink and yellow and blue, all sorts of pastel colors." Standing, she dug into her jeans' pocket and withdrew a handful of tiny, fan-shaped shells. "See? Aren't they pretty?"

"Those are Cochinas. Quite common along the coast."

"I like them, common or not. But I have a basket of big, fancy shells at the apartment. Deke got them for me as a memento of our day."

"Very nice of Deke." *Snap* went another brittle vine.

Well, at least he's feeling something, she thought, heartened by the sharp sound. Tilting her head, she regarded his lean, spare features. "Jordan, that crooked way you grin—"

"Something wrong with my grin?"

"No, not a thing. As you well know," she sniffed, chuckling. The little rise she'd gotten out of him was enough for today. "I just find it interesting, the way one side of your mouth tilts up and creases your cheek while the other side stays put. How do you do that?"

"I don't do that, it does itself," he said, doing it again. "In high school I differed with some guys and we got in a brawl. Left me with some muscle damage on this side." He touched his mouth. "Ergo, crooked grin."

"You fought with them? Why?"

"Because of a female, of course," Jordan replied, sardonic. "My sister Jacey, in this case." He paused, distracted by Valentine's sudden, radiant smile. "By the time she was eleven," he continued, "Jacey was, uh, built, as we callous youths termed it. Anyway, some high school Neanderthals got her alone one day and began baiting her. Made her cry. Lord, I hate being around weeping females.''

''So you rescued her. You jumped those creeps without a thought for yourself, or for being so outnumbered. Why, you're a hero, Jordan!''

Jordan ducked his head, his tone dry as alum. ''Oh, sure I am. If a teacher hadn't stepped in I'd have been pounded to mush. That's stupid, not heroic. Instead of calling for help, I went flailing in alone. Cost me a week off work and a lot of pain.''

''A hero,'' Valentine reiterated, her heart warmed by this peek into his personal life. Ignoring his mocking smile, she gathered up ivy clippings.

''Get some gloves on if you're going to help,'' he commanded.

''Oh. Okay.'' Holding back a grin, she found a mismatched pair on a nearby bench and resumed helping him. ''You have nice muscles,'' she said primly. ''Do you work out? Is it hard?''

''Yeah, I belong to a gym. It's not hard, but it's not a matter of raising a weight up and down, either.''

His voice grew beguilingly warm and light as he got into the subject. She listened, asked questions, piled ivy. All was exactly as it should be, she thought wonderingly. There was no erotic pressure to disrupt the pleasure of a budding friendship. It was as if they had moved to a dimension above physical attraction for the moment. Basking in the glow of this precious new camaraderie, she laughed easily, unguarded, unafraid.

''This is nice, Valentine,'' he said. ''Nice enough to nurture, in my opinion. What would you say to starting all over again?''

She stiffened. ''How do we do that?''

''By me apologizing,'' he said gruffly. ''I shouldn't have kissed you like that, right off the bat. Doing so made friendship impossible. I hadn't realized that. But sharing this small task with you, being able to laugh and talk without sex messing up the vibes has been fun. I enjoyed it.''

"So did I. Not enough to regret the kisses, however!" she said with a shaky laugh.

"Umm, well, they were nice, but this is nicer."

She bit her lip. Didn't he realize they could have both?

Removing her gloves, she flexed her fingers. "We made a good start, anyway." she said, sizing up their progress.

"Yes, we did make a good start." Jordan's smile told her he wasn't referring to removing ivy. "Let's go wash up and drag Clay and Sam out to eat. You like Italian?"

"I love Italian," she said throatily.

"Val?" Sam stepped out the back door holding a box. "This just came for you. It's from Deke."

"What on earth?" Opening it, Valentine examined its contents, then let out a whoop of laughter. The box contained three dozen pairs of gardening gloves.

"What the devil is that all about?" Jordan asked.

Valentine grinned. "You had to be there, Jordan," she said.

The last week of April broke out in a rash of hot, muggy days. What happened to spring, Sam wondered? Wiping her brow with the back of her hand, she hurried up the cracked walk and into the blessed coolness of the house on Rosehill Lane.

The apartment was history, thank God. "I'm home, Val," she called, pausing in the handsome foyer.

"Back here, in your room," Valentine yodeled.

Sam stopped in the first of the two small rooms that formed her office, and picked up her mail. Then she hastened on down the hallway to the first-floor bedroom she had chosen. "Hey, Mouse! What are you up to?"

"Fresh flowers," Valentine said, pointing to the vase of purple irises on Sam's desk. She smiled as the willowy red-head kicked off her shoes with a sigh of relief. That her darling Sam could end a long, exhausting day in the luxury of a white-on-white bedroom furnished with a handsome bed, dresser, desk, chair and a small nightstand centered with a leaf-green ginger jar lamp, was due to Valentine. From thrift shops and garage sales she had furnished two bedrooms at a cost about equal to the designer suit Sam wore.

That she and Sam could walk into a shining kitchen awash
in mellow sunlight was partially due to their landlord, Valentine readily admitted. His crew had painted walls, laid new
vinyl flooring, sanded and varnished the door. A new range
had been placed in its allocated spot; a dishwasher and disposal nestled under the counter. The laundry room held a
washer and dryer, but these had been hunted down and paid
for by Valentine, as was their refrigerator. Enough was
enough, Clay said.

Valentine knew that his grumbling masked a deep enjoyment. The house was technically his and its mistress a very
special person who was, in some alchemic way, also his. Helping Sam establish a home was very satisfying to Clay Tremayne.

Sam refused to listen to such talk. Her relationship with
Clay was business oriented, just as it should be. On the job
she was cool, professional, briskly competent, and very good
at holding everyone in the firm at arm's length.

And yet, and yet . . .

Valentine sensed that for the first time in her life, Sam was
having very strong feelings for a man. They were yet hazy,
but they were definitely there.

Sam kicked off her shoes and gave a luxurious stretch.
"Umm, this feels good. I love coming home at night, Val."

Valentine grinned. Sam's resentment of her high-
handedness in renting this house had dissipated as it began to
take shape, until, to hear her tell it, *she'd* made the decision.

"Ah, letters from home," Sam said, rifling through her
mail. "Did you get any?"

"One from Mom. She's fine, but Ed's had a stomach vi-
rus—"

"Hangover," Sam grunted.

Valentine had no handy response. She checked her list. "I
picked up your new business cards, returned the faulty message machine and got another one. No charge. And this item
here is a bill from our dear neighbor, Gladys Belton. It's for
our half of the cost of a buffer she was forced to erect between
her golf course quality lawn, and the patch of nut grass that

constitutes our pitiful excuse for a lawn. Any suggestions?"

"Yeah, but they're all illegal," Sam said, sighing. Mrs. Belton, a blue-haired widow of indeterminate age, had come calling when they were still in the process of getting the house ready for occupancy, and left with the expression of one who has just bitten into a luscious apple and found half a worm. Now she just left little notes on their door. "Pay the darn thing. Then maybe the wicked witch of the West will stop griping about our yard." Sam shed her jacket. "What else?"

"I also had those new tires put on your van."

"Great. Did you get the good ones?"

Valentine scowled. "No, Sam, I got the cheapest, rattiest tires I could find, guaranteed to wear out within a year."

Sam made a face back at her. "Sorry. Force of habit, I guess. Oh, super; chilled wine! From our personal stock?"

"Of course," Valentine said. Deke's housewarming gift of wine racks complete with a handsome supply of bottled nectars from his Texas winery had delighted her. "Now that's class, Sam!" she'd said with such satisfaction that Sam laughed aloud.

The lovely, long-stemmed crystal glasses she filled were part of Jordan's housewarming gift. Although she pronounced it "very nice," Valentine was secretly thrilled; Baccarat was a name she knew only from books.

"Join me?" Sam asked, bottle poised to pour a second glass.

"Just one. For medicinal purposes," Valentine said primly. "Oh, Dan Marshall called. He wants to take us to the Texas Crawfish Festival this weekend in Old Town Spring. I said yes."

"Yuck. In Ohio we fish with crawfish, we don't eat them."

"I know, but Dan says they're delicious. Would a policeman lie? Besides, there'll be all sorts of Cajun food: funnel cakes, boudin sausages, jambalaya, seafood gumbo, even fried alligator."

Sam made a face. "That doesn't sound too tempting. You go if you want."

"Coward." Valentine handed her their business ledger.

"I'm still kind of bothered by our partnership. You're working, bringing home the bacon, so to speak, but I'm not contributing anything." Her dimple flashed. "Except for maid service. Maybe I should get a job—"

"You *have* a job," Sam cut in. "You do the books, take care of taxes, mess with insurance, social security and all that stuff that leaves my brain numb. As for maid service, well, darlin', don't you know that every working woman's secret desire is a wife of her very own?" Green eyes twinkled. "You know how it is with housework and me, I'm fatally allergic to it. Making up my bed is the absolute limit of my tolerance."

"Well, thanks, but I still feel like I'm doing nothing except having a wonderful time. And we still need so much stuff, Sam. Hey, Texas has a lottery—maybe I ought to buy a few tickets."

"Forget it. I don't hold with playing the lottery, it's a waste of good money," Sam said dismissively. "We're doing fine."

"Yes, of course we are. But we still need things, a living and dining room set, me a better car. A pickup would really be more practical. Then I wouldn't have to keep paying Bubba to haul my stuff," she fretted.

"All in good time," Sam soothed, opening the ledger.

"In good time," Valentine mimicked under her breath. Everyone was so complacent about time!

Still grumbling, she went upstairs. Her own bedroom was lushly feminine because she was lushly feminine. It was similar to walking into the heart of a rose, Sam had teased.

Valentine didn't care. She loved the soft, radiant pinks and corals, the saffron pillows, the simple cotton draperies. She drifted over to the small, muslin-swathed table that held her collection of photographs. She had framed the newspaper clipping and added the mysterious Elisse to these visible bits and pieces of her heart. She fit in perfectly.

Sam had teased her about that, too. "What'd you do, Mouse, adopt her?"

"I like her. She goes with the house," Valentine had replied. Holding the picture to her chest, she looked around the airy room. She couldn't imagine living anywhere else. Which brought up another nagging concern. She had asked Sam about buying the house, just in case Clay decided to sell it.

But that was the last thing on Sam's busy mind. She had looked amused and sang, "With what shall we buy it, dear Mousie, dear Mousie?" Then Sam had called her a worrywart.

"And maybe, she's right," Valentine conceded. Replacing the picture, she wandered to her dresser. She was tired and a few places ached, one of them centrally located and fiercely insistent. Grabbing her hairbrush, she raked it through her raven mane as though it alone were to blame for her edginess.

It was Jordan, of course. Valentine appreciated the rapport that had sprung up between them—truly she did, she assured herself. But friendship, for all its beauty, did not assuage the hunger he had ignited in her. Admittedly she didn't know how to deal with passion. On the one hand its intensity frightened her; on the other, it challenged every muscle and sinew of her femininity. She was dancing to two different drummers, which required a skill and courage she wasn't sure she possessed.

Maybe that's why he had taken to treating her like a little sister, Valentine mused. Maybe he could sense her anxiety and wanted to put her at ease. If so, she really ought to be grateful. Although she'd managed to shrug off Deke's assessment of Jordan, it had left a tarry stain of unease in her mind. Sexual involvement was scary enough without the added requirements—her requirements—of trust and reliability.

"Ah well, what will be, will be." She sighed. But she didn't completely believe that, either. It was the decisions and choices one made that determined what would be. Even inertia had an impact. So maybe she should take the initiative—

A swift shake of head rejected that notion before it was even completed. Oh, sure, he desired her. But that was no big deal, men always found nubile young women desirable. Elemental chemistry between male and female, often defined and accurately so, as *lust,* she reminded herself.

The word had a sour taste on her tongue. She replaced it with passion . . . which tasted like wild honey.

Rejection was another odious word, one that could cut to the quick. But she'd managed to survive it without too many scars. Her ironic smile withered as Jordan's image filled her mind. His rejection would ravage far more than mere ego. It would cut to the heart. Valentine hugged herself against the fear that swept up from stygian depths. Surely it was foolish to take such a chance again when the outcome was so uncertain—

Take that chance, Valentine! Dare to soar with the eagles!

"Oh, sure, and fall and break my neck? Do I look like an idiot?" Valentine chided her free-spirited inner voice. Obviously it wasn't earthbound, she thought, exasperated at the challenge. To block this mental interference, she began stripping the bed. But even her vigorous labors could not clear her mind; eerily, the words were just there, pouring in like water through a hole in whatever dam she flung up against it.

Change it. Do it. Try it. Living is acting, not thinking.

"That's easy for you to say—you're not the one living it," she retorted, angered at being thrown on the defensive by something she couldn't explain. She'd given her trust once before, and been hurt and shamed. Not deeply, for she hadn't given deeply. Still, she had adored the dark-eyed engineer whom Sam so aptly tagged Bill the Jerk. To confidently let herself into his apartment with her prized key and catch him with another woman had been a searing shock to every aspect of her femininity.

"A valuable lesson and one I'm not dumb enough to forget," she muttered. She wondered if Sam ever felt this conflicted and confused. She doubted it. Sam had become so cynical after her bitter marital experience. "Hard as nails," she claimed.

But Valentine knew that if a man could penetrate Sam's armor, he'd find a stunningly soft, giving woman.

And if a man got past your armor, what would he find?

Frowning at yet another pop-up question, her inner turmoil increased as Valentine realized she had no ready answer. She didn't know what kind of woman she was.

Chapter 7

$\mathcal{A}$ few days later Valentine wandered around her empty living room in a state of raw frustration. Yesterday she'd bought a lovely sofa and loveseat, used, but in excellent condition, for a price that absolutely thrilled her French-Celtic-English soul. But since Sam had the van and Bubba had gone fishing, she'd have to wait until tonight to pick up her furniture. Blast! Waiting was akin to ants in her pants and no way to shake them out.

Stalemated, she went back upstairs. Sam hadn't seen the living room furniture, but she trusted Valentine's taste, or so she said. In truth, she thought sadly, Sam wasn't all that caught up in homemaking. Was she abnormal?

"Or maybe I am." Valentine sighed. "Am I, Elisse?"

Hearing her question, Valentine smiled at this bit of whimsy. She had started talking to the woman's picture as if to a flesh and blood friend. This embarrassed her a little. Then again, maybe it just pointed up how much she needed friends, she thought wistfully.

The house was always so quiet. After their day in Galveston, Deke had disappeared back into the hill country, keeping in touch via brief telephone calls hedged with a faint awkwardness she found endearing. Sam was always gone, happily, but so much absence left a hole in the fabric of Valentine's day.

Jordan, too, seemed to be very busy lately. As another favor to Clay, he'd come by one evening to fix the library's wobbly ceiling fan. He was a handy man to have around, and she'd *like* to, Valentine fumed. But his mission took all of ten minutes. Then he'd ruffled her hair and hurried off to some more important task.

"Blast!" she muttered again. That insouciant male air that surrounded him like armor annoyed the hell out of her. Well, sometimes it did, she amended, impaled on self-honesty. At other times, it bent low and whispered sweet nothings between her legs.

Valentine expelled a hard breath. In her most secret heart she held such hopes for the future, fragile hopes that required patience and timing to bring to fulfillment. But intimate thoughts of Jordan could shred even the staunchest resolve into confetti. That was wickedly vexing; she had a timetable, dammit! But it was taking too long—everything was taking too long!

Baffled by her raging urgency, Valentine surged to her feet. Why was she always in such a hurry? No longer merely rhetorical, the question suddenly sprouted tentacles that held her there, caught in the spotlight of startling new clarity. Until now, she hadn't realized how much impatience had influenced her actions.

She had wanted to savor every mile of the trip west, yet she couldn't wait to get here.

She had wanted to tour the Lone Star State's varied terrain and see its fabled cities. Instead she had persuaded Sam to settle here without further exploration.

It could be argued that she then precipitously thrust them into jobs they disliked and a lifestyle neither wanted. All because she was in a hurry.

Even the costly move to this big, empty house was driven by her peculiar sense of urgency. Then, instead of taking her time turning it into a home, she itched to get it done *now*.

Why?

Stopping before the mirror, she held back her raven hair and tilted her head searchingly. Sometimes, when she came face-to-face with herself, she felt as though she were meeting a stranger.

No more muddling, I promise. . . .

The echoing words spiraled down like windblown leaves. She shivered. Blown from where? On what wind?

It made no sense. Quixotic thoughts, cosmic questions, she concluded half-humorously. Still edgy, she paced to the window, and gave a little start of surprise. There had been no sign of life from the house next door, but apparently its owners had returned from vacation or whatever, for a bronze pickup truck stood in the adjacent driveway.

Valentine sighed. What she wouldn't give for that truck! If she could borrow it . . . But what if these neighbors turned out to be sourpusses like Mrs. Belton? Then again, they could be perfectly lovely people, future friends just waiting to be made.

Toying with a strand of hair, she hesitated a moment longer. Then with a snap of fingers, she turned from the window. For better or worse, it was time to meet these neighbors, too.

Valentine instantly felt the rightness of her decision as a buoyant lift of spirits. Even the tree seemed to agree, brushing its leaves against the windowpane as if applauding. She felt a prickle of excitement as the sure sense of knowing surged within her mind. It was meant to be.

Tossing a kiss to her photographs, she ran downstairs again, past the dazzling points of amethyst and sapphire light streaming from the blue leaded window set high above the landing, and out a side door to the yard. Her feet arbitrarily stopped under the white-flowering jasmine ennobling this scruffy patch of grass. Catching her breath, she stepped over a low brick wall mellowed to ruddy disrepair and waded through a sea of bluebonnets to the hedge that separated the two properties. Such freely given beauty sent Valentine's spirits soaring. "Thank you, Elisse," she whispered.

You're welcome!

Chuckling at the fancied response, Valentine made her way through the hedge and into the neighboring yard,

A man of indeterminate age was watering the red geraniums flanking his front steps. His receding hairline receded all the

way to the back of his head, and from three sides of this bald
oval flowed rivulets of thin, black, frizzy hair. A wispy beard
and mustache completed the concealment of his face except
for a rather large nose and shy brown eyes.

Swiftly Valentine assessed him. Good-hearted. Gentle. And
closed up tighter than a clam. Smiling, she introduced herself.

The man grunted.

Courteously she explained her furniture-hauling problem.
"I'd be very careful with your truck," she assured him. "And
of course I'd refill the gas tank when I'm finished."

The man grunted. So far that was all he'd done. She shifted
stance and stubbornly waited. Deep brown eyes studying her,
he aimed a splat of tobacco juice in the only clear spot in his
flower bed.

While she was awed at his accuracy, it hardly helped matters. "Well, I . . . I'm sorry to bother you," Valentine said,
bewildered by his lack of civility. He was nice; she could feel
his niceness. He was also wary of her, and she didn't know
why. "It's just that I'm from Ohio and back there, any time
a neighbor needs help, everyone pitches in. I thought Texans
were the same way, but I guess I'm mistaken."

He didn't reply. Valentine bit her lip. What now?

"Ozell Loving, what the hell's wrong with you?" came a
sharp feminine voice, and around the corner walked a thin slat
of a woman who greeted Valentine with a smile as bright as
sunflowers. "Hello, honey, glad to meetcha! My name's Vera.
Vera Loving."

Sheer relief blazed in Valentine's answering smile. She introduced herself and shook hands. The woman's long, blond
ponytail swung as she in turn swung on the taciturn Ozell. In
shrill voice she berated his rudeness.

Ozell grunted and spat, then shifted his cud. He said something that could have been "hi." Or not.

Vera turned back to her guest with that beautiful smile
breaking up her face again. She had a little pot belly and
fabulous breasts. She must be near forty, Valentine decided.
The luxuriant mane was such a contradiction to her weathered
face that Valentine was forced to swallow a giggle. Vera wore

short shorts and a halter, and her pipestem limbs added to the total picture of absurd contrasts. But her warm smile and those guileless, cornflower blue eyes offset any scorn Vera Loving's appearance might engender.

Vera's gravelly voice boomed out again. "You one of the girls next door, huh? Renting the old Manning house—it's a beauty, ain't it!" She beamed. "I been dyin' to meetcha, caught glimpses of you, but I didn't want to intrude. Besides, we been gone a lot lately. Now and then Ozell gets the wanderlust," she confided. "I swear, that redheaded gal's a doozy! You all settled in now? That your little black car in the drive? How much is that sweet rascal Tremayne charging you? You need a truck, you say?"

She flung the questions out like bullets. "Yes," was all Valentine managed to say. Another raucous laugh smote her ears.

"No problem there, honey," Vera assured her. "The truck's mine, that ole coot's got nothing to say about it. Think I'd let him drive it? Hah! Fat chance," she caroled, turning merry eyes on her husband. He grunted. "Ozell, you turn off that water right now and come on, we'll need muscles. And lose that tobacco. And put on your shirt."

Taking his own sweet time about it, Ozell obeyed. His grunts all sounded like guttural "haans!" to Valentine, but apparently Vera could interpret them. "You met your other neighbor yet?" she asked with a touch of slyness.

"Mrs. Belton? Yes, she came over once. She seemed almost appalled at having Sam and me for neighbors," Valentine said.

"Well, she appalls easy. Figures you and Sam to be sex-crazed female libbers," Vera explained. "That's scary to a woman like Miz Belton. She's from the old, *old* South, where they don't have women libbers. Or sex, either, apparently. I mean, can you imagine?"

"Uh, no, I can't," Valentine said faintly. Noting the playground equipment in their backyard, she asked, "Do you have children?"

"A girl, eighteen. She's away at school right now."

"Eighteen? Goodness, you must have married young!"

"Sixteen. Ozell wasn't too much older. For crying out loud, Ozell, Valentine ain't got all day," Vera chided. Turning, she led the way to the truck.

Its spacious cab accommodated three comfortably. Vera drove, Valentine sat in the middle, and Ozell by the window. Vera carried on without letup. When she paused to catch her breath, Valentine asked, "How long have you lived here, Vera? In your house, I mean."

"Close to fourteen years now, huh, Ozell? Got it for a song when it went on the auction block. A real fixer-upper, but Ozell did most of the repair work himself."

"Wow, that's great!" Valentine said. "Do you know anything about our house? I'd love to learn its history."

"Well, didn't you come to the right person, then!" Vera crowed. "A friend of ours belongs to the Historical Society. She knows everything about these old houses. Has it all written down. I'll get you a copy of yours, okay?"

"Oh, thank you, I'd really appreciate that!"

Vera flushed. "My pleasure. You like to garden, honey? Got lots of space out there to do it, and soil's rich, too. Ozell here, he's the gardener at our house—grows the prettiest tomaters you ever seen! He's got this secret," she confided. "Lots and lots of goat and chicken manure. Horse, too, when the rodeo's in town. And once he went all the way into Houston to the circus grounds to get a load of elephant doo. Don't that beat all? He just—*watch out there, you idiot!*" she broke off to shout at another car. "Sumbitches don't know how to drive in this town. You notice it was a man driver?" Vera snorted as she wandered back across the yellow line into her own lane.

Valentine's strangled breath reaped a benign smile. "Ozell'll get you a couple loads if you like," Vera sailed on.

"I'm sure I'd love some." Smiling, Valentine looked into Ozell Loving's eyes, the sweetest, most bashful brown eyes she had ever seen. They crinkled. Delightedly she laughed. She liked these people and the liking was mutual, which pleased her immensely.

Thus far, just being with them had kept her too busy to

analyze the deeper impression they'd made on her senses. Stealing a moment for reflection, she turned her intuitive antenna on them and felt a searing jab of empathetic pain. Sadness lay beneath their unified contentment like dark seams in a white dress.

Ozell carried the worst wounds. Vera's had nearly healed, but his were still raw under their scabs. What terrible thing had happened to this dear couple? Valentine wondered. Her heart clinched as she mentally explored the deep vein of sorrow. . . .

Children. Something about children. Questions swarmed her mind. She swallowed every intrusive one.

Tuning into the conversation, she listened with interest as Vera related the town's history. Ozell added an occasional grunt. As Valentine suspected, he was an amiable man. Under his wife's supervision he handled the transfer of furniture with muscular ease.

Returning to Valentine's house, they helped her situate the living room set and its bonus floor lamp, Vera tossing out suggestions and Ozell trying his best to satisfy her.

He escaped as quickly as possible. Vera, however, lingered on. "Now that looks grand, just grand," she said, surveying the comfortable living room.

"It really does, thanks to your help," Valentine replied, her voice rich with the same feminine pleasure. "With these white plantation shutters, it resembles an airy garden room. . . . Is something wrong, Vera?" she asked, nothing the woman's perplexed expression.

"No, nothin' wrong. I just—Valentine, I feel like we've known each other for ages!" Vera blurted. "Gracious, ain't that funny, though!"

"Funny, but true," Valentine agreed warmly. "Sometimes it's like that between two people, no rhyme or reason for it." Inviting her new friend to the kitchen table, she fetched two glasses of iced tea and a bowl of sliced limes. "A new addiction," she confided. "I rarely drank tea at home."

"Can't live without ice tea in Texas," Vera declared, nearly draining the glass. "I swear, my eyes nearly popped outta my head when I seen what you've done with this old place. And in such a short time, too!"

"Well, I was highly motivated; I needed a home and this place needed someone to love it again." Valentine took the other folding chair. She was burning with curiosity. "Is Ozell retired?"

"Sort of. Partial disability. His brother Cecil is a big shot down at one of the TV stations and Ozell works nights there. Saves him from having to interact with the public. He ain't too good at that, as you might've noticed," she added, beautifully ironic. "Although he sure took to you in a hurry."

Valentine's eyes widened. "He did? Oh! Well, I took to him, too." Still hesitant to pry, she took another sip of tea. "Do you want any more children? I'm thinking of having three or four myself, but that's my own particular brand of insanity," she remarked, chuckling. "Is one all you planned to have?"

"Goodness no, we planned to have a dozen of 'em," Vera replied with a sudden soft, pensive smile. "We've had five, honey. But four are in the cemetery."

"Jesus, Vera!" Valentine blurted, looking as appalled as she felt.

Vera slapped her forehead with the heel of her hand. "Oh, hell, where's my brain at—just blurtin' out something like that! You're just too durned easy to talk to, Valentine. But I'm real sorry I was so blunt."

"No, that's okay. I was just taken by surprise, that's all." Composing herself, Valentine invited gently, "I'd be honored to listen if you want to talk about it."

"Well, usually I don't. But like I said, you're such a good listener . . ." Vera fiddled with a teaspoon. "Ozell and I really did want more children, but I guess it just wasn't meant to be. First we lost stillborn twins, then a five-month miscarriage; and then a little boy just two days old."

Valentine froze, mute with horror as a devastating vision swamped her sensitive mind. *Four tiny white tombstones on a plot of lush, green grass.* A shudder crawled down her back. Stark with meaning, those minuscule monuments to unfinished lives pierced the sky like desolate cries for answers, she thought, flooded with their sorrow. In her heart she could hear Vera's agonized weeping; Ozell's raging grief. Eyes blurring, she gazed inward, marveling at the clarity of this strange divination. Each tiny marker was inscribed with a name in the sheltering wings of an angel . . .

Valentine's skin prickled as realization crashed in. *This was Vera's vision. Taken directly from Vera's mind.*

Instantly the images vanished, the mental linkage shattered by her stunned recognition. Valentine released a shuddering breath, suddenly boneless with relief as her own mind cleared.

Becoming aware of the other woman's concerned gaze, she collected her badly shaken wits. "But you . . ." Swallowing, she tried again. "You do have a girl."

Vera nodded. "Yes, we do, and we're thankful. This child is the sweetest human being I've ever met, Valentine, not a mean bone in her body. True, she has problems, but she's been worth every tear we've ever shed."

Seized with apprehension, Valentine asked, "What kind of problems?"

"Shanna has Down's syndrome," Vera said with heart-breaking simplicity.

Staggered, Valentine fought to control her reaction. No tears, she warned herself. Forcing her gaze to Vera's, she said, "Shanna. My, that's a lovely name."

"We think so. Like I said, she's away at a special school right now. They don't have nothin' suitable for her here. The damn fools didn't consider her capable of learnin', can you beat that? But I knew my baby could learn," she said fiercely. "Next time she comes home, I'll let you meet her. We don't do that often. People tend to look sideways at her; embarrassed, you know? Don't know what to say. So we just avoid all that by keepin' to ourselves."

"I'd love to meet her. And so would Sam. I . . . oh, Vera, I'm so sorry," she burst out, too deeply affected by this woman's courage to hold it in any longer.

"Oh, honey, nothin' to be sorry about. You just gotta take things as they come and hang on to each other." Vera tucked a bra strap back in place under her chartreuse tank top. ''Me and Ozell have gotten pretty good at that. But he still has trouble. When it gets too much for him, he gets that wanderlust I spoke of. We just take off and drive until his soul is calmed.''

Valentine, beyond both wonder and words, simply nodded. She touched Vera's hand. ''You have a beautiful way of speaking,'' she said softly.

''Me?'' Vera snorted. ''I'm just an old country girl, honey, dumb as hell, never got past the eighth grade.'' She stood up. ''Well, I hear Ozell callin' my name—durned fool can't do anything unless I'm there to help!''

Valentine rose, too. ''He's a dear and you know it. Thank you, Vera, for confiding in me.''

Vera's sallow cheeks pinkened. ''I think I'm the one owin' here, the way I went on and on. Ozell says I talk too much, and I reckon I do, but never about private stuff,'' she said shyly. ''Well, I better get. Remember, if you need us, just holler.''

''I will.'' Valentine held her smile until the other woman disappeared from view, then slipped to the floor in a turmoil of emotional reaction. Hunched into a ball, her head buried in her arms, she wept for Vera and Ozell Loving.

Then she wept for herself. She had always assumed her children would be perfect. What woman didn't? How could you even dare have a child if there was the slightest suspicion otherwise? God, how did people endure such tragedy!

''How could I endure it?'' Valentine whispered. She didn't possess that kind of courage.

Would she even have time to bear a child?

The question struck with the swiftness of a viper. She shuddered. ''That's silly, Valentine, you're only twenty-three,'' she derided her runaway imagination.

But it didn't feel silly.

It didn't feel silly at all.

Chapter 8

There was a storm cloud in the celestial blue sky of the southeast quadrant of the sixth plane of the tenth realm. Trying to ignore it, the Being called Sunbeam plucked a tiny feather from the hem of his immaculate white robe. "Probably from a cherub's wing." He chuckled.

The taller Being, who had created this rare disturbance in the first place, scowled at him. He preferred the name Bradley, but Sunbeam, with his puckish sense of humor, secretly thought of him as Clouds-For-Hair. At the moment the wispy white nimbus encircling Bradley's bald pate was practically standing on end.

"Where is she?" he fumed. "Surely it's reasonable to expect an angel to be punctual?"

"Oh, now, Bradley, give her some leeway. After all, Elisse is operating on Earth time. And so are we, for the moment," Sunbeam reminded him. Turning, he smiled at the sweet-faced woman standing off to one side. "When you deal with Earth matters, you have to deal with time and space as well," he explained.

Bradley included both his associate and the woman in his regal glare. "I hardly need a lecture on the qualities peculiar to Earth," he harrumphed. "I've been dealing with that particular planet for centuries now."

"I was speaking to Miriam," Sunbeam reproved gently.

A fragile woman of indeterminate age, Miriam was newly

arrived in the tenth realm, and would soon be given her first earthly charge. Before that, however, she would apprentice here, for Earth was a most difficult assignment, no matter in what form a soul chose to experience its emotional vibrations.

Bradley very nearly acted upon his impulse to bestow an encouraging smile upon the nervous neophyte. But just then a glorious young woman materialized from the mists, and he reverted to his habitual bulldog jaw-lock.

The scent of flowers filled his nostrils with sublime pleasure. Doggedly he held on to his stern expression as Elisse assumed full form and substance. She wore a simple gown the color of forget-me-nots, and a rainbow adorned her fair hair. When she spoke, music filtered through his soul.

"Hello, again," she said like a warm, loving hug. Everyone felt it, whether they wanted to or not.

Bradley bristled. He had always been business-oriented, and this, in his opinion, was serious business indeed. "Good of you to come, Elisse," he said with just the tiniest touch of sarcasm. "Shall we get on with this?"

Her topaz eyes twinkled. "Of course, Bradley," she said, properly contrite. "How are you, darling?" she asked Miriam.

"A little intimidated. I've never been a guardian angel before."

"You'll learn," Bradley said. "That's what you're here for." He snapped his fingers and a file folder leaped from his shining desk into his hand. Opening it, he cleared his throat. "Case in review; Valentine Townsend. Secondary review; her guardian angel."

"Me!" Elisse exclaimed. "What in Heaven are you going on about, Bradley? I don't understand why we're reviewing Valentine's progress, much less my own. It's only been a few months since she and I returned to Earth. And she's done so well. Don't you think she's done well?" she appealed to Sunbeam.

"Oh, yes, very well. But . . ."

"But what?" Elisse interrupted, indignant. "Good Lord, just look what she's accomplished in three months' time! She

left her familiar home for a faraway city in another state,
settled down, got a job, found a house—"

"And whose house did she find?" Bradley asked with the
smoothness of a surgeon's scalpel.

"Why, mine, but—"

"Aha!"

"Aha?" Perplexed, Elisse stated, "I see no reason for
ahas, Bradley. I loved that house, and I remember that lifetime
with great affection. So I led her there. For her benefit, Bradley, not mine. Guidance is my job—it's what I do," she
pointed out, tenderly exasperated with this dear but pontifical
soul. He'd assumed quite a few earth qualities himself, she
thought, amused.

"I don't question that," Bradley said. "But I do question
how much influence you've exerted on her progress."

Startled by his accusation, Miriam piped up, "But that's
absurd! Only rank beginners interfere with another soul's progress. Or so I've been told," she hurriedly added. "Surely
Elisse is far too enlightened to make that mistake."

"It is very, very easy to become caught up in earthly affairs
and emotions, even in spirit form," Sunbeam told Miriam. "In
fact, it can be as difficult to rise above terrestrial matters when
incorporeal as it is in a physical body. Especially if you've
sown Earth's reflective fields with love time and time again.
The vibrations are tremendously powerful, inducing a particularly poignant sense of longing. That's if the lifetime memory
was a happy experience, of course. If not, well, on Earth even
sorrow exerts an attraction."

"Sunbeam, I know you must teach," Bradley interposed,
casting him a pained look, "but must you do it right now?"

"Yes, I must. Sorry," Sunbeam answered. He turned to
Elisse. "Dearest Elisse, regretfully I, too, have questions con-
cerning Valentine's progress and your part in it."

Surprised, Elisse flung up her hands. "But there's nothing
to question! Valentine has found herself a new home, a pleasing new lifestyle, supportive new friends. She has also fallen
in love," she informed him.

"And has done nothing about it. Loving from a safe distance isn't all that constructive," Bradley contended dryly. "Granted, the man involved is adverse to serious involvement, but has she tried to change his mind by showing her own willingness to love despite the danger?"

"He's a good soul with problems to work out," Miriam said.

"But has she even touched upon the source of those problems?" Sunbeam put in. "We gave her the gift of expanded insight. Why isn't she using it? One of her objectives is to help others through her own good fortune. Who has she helped, besides herself, that is?"

"And even there she's had to have celestial encouragement before she acts," Bradley took charge again. "Her grandmother took time off her own projects to appear to her in a dream," he explained in an aside to Miriam. "Valentine dithered this way and that before deciding not to share this vital event with her cousin. What was the risk? That Sam would laugh at her?"

Positioning the hem of her gown, Elisse sat down on a cushion of air and regarded him with sweet reproach. "It is far more than that, Bradley. It's Sam's disapproval. It's the threat of scorn, anger, embarrassment, rejection, humiliation. On Earth, those are potent consequences for failure. Maybe you've forgotten, dear one, just how painful negative emotions can be," she said quietly. "Why this early review, anyway? We gave her a year to achieve her goals."

"I know, but something's come up that may change that," Bradley replied, very nearly excited. "A female infant's form will be fully created in exactly three months, six days, two hours and fourteen minutes, that is perfect for Valentine."

"That would only be October, earth time," Elisse objected.

"Yes, I know that," Bradley said impatiently. "But family circumstances are ideal, and the potential for accelerated growth is outstanding. It could be an excellent learning experience, excellent! Exhilarating, actually, if one opens fully to its opportunities. We haven't assigned it to anyone as yet, and we thought we might give her first choice. As her Counselors, we are just as concerned as you are with her spiritual *journey,"* he reminded Elisse with touching pomposity.

She smiled, and hyacinths surrounded her bare feet. *"That's so sweet of you, Bradley. You, too, Sunbeam. I know how much you both adore Valentine. But I really think she can do this. The goals she set for herself are well within her reach."*

Sunbeam shook his head. *"Since Jordan is one of my charges, it's unpleasant to make a negative prediction, but the odds are against a successful relationship. In the first place, there was no soul recognition when they met."*

"You're wrong, Sunbeam, you're wrong!" Elisse cried joyously. *"I was with her, remember? There was instant recognition! Not consciously, I'll grant you, but the cosmic winds of that meeting actually gave me goose bumps!"*

Springing to her feet, she switched her focus to Bradley. *"Jordan is constantly plagued by her intrusion into his snug little world and he can't figure out why. Oh, I love it!"* she caroled, performing a graceful pirouette. *"You had to be there, Bradley,"* she said, laughing at his uncomprehending frown.

"Perhaps their souls did touch, but their hearts didn't," Sunbeam went on without missing a beat. *"Oh, they like each other, but they've always liked each other."*

"They love each other," Elisse corrected softly.

"I agree," Bradley said. *"Jordan wouldn't be half so miserable if it was only liking."*

His heavy-handed jest elicited a chuckle from Sunbeam. *"True. So he loves her, Elisse. But sharing his present journey with her is quite a different matter. He's had his fill of responsibility. Even worse, he's had what he considers more than his fair share of caring for others. He sincerely thinks he has nothing left to give, and he doesn't care to put that rationale to the test."*

"You can't blame him for feeling like that," Miriam said fiercely.

"Of course not!" Elisse agreed. *"No one's placing blame."*

"Could we stick to the main issue?" Bradley asked.

"Sorry," said Miriam, Sunbeam and Elisse simultaneously.

"Valentine will find the way to climb over those obstacles," Elisse assured Bradley.

"I doubt that," he countered, truly regretful. "She's still such a fearful person. Look at her right now, hunched up on the floor, crying—"

"From the infinite goodness and compassion of her heart—"

"And from being scared to death that Vera's misfortunes might happen to her—"

"Of course she's scared!" Elisse continued this ping-pong conversation. "Bradley, you've been male too many times in a row if you can't understand this most intimate, feminine fear. There's not a woman alive who doesn't have it. But the thing is, they go right on bearing children despite their fear, which is a darned good thing because otherwise the population of Earth would come to a roaring halt!"

"Touché, Bradley," Sunbeam murmured. "I've advised him to take another stab at being physical again," he told Miriam.

Bradley's face mottled. "May I remind you, Sunbeam—ridiculous name, I don't see how he tolerates it," he confided to Miriam—"that this is Valentine's review, not mine?" His voice softened as he glanced at Elisse's lovely face. They had walked together through several lifetimes: on Atlantis; in ancient Egypt; on Sagiii, the twelfth planet. He hadn't forgotten the beauty of Earth-love.

"All right, for once I must bow to superior advice," he harrumphed. "To sum up, Valentine has to overcome her pleasurable inertia and start moving again. One can also hope she'll have the courage and grit to implement any other painful growth experiences she takes on, but I—"

"Why painful?" Elisse broke in. "Why can't she take the joy-and-happiness-route to enlightenment instead of pain and struggle? It's just as sure, and certainly faster."

"For some souls, joy is the best way to learn and evolve," Bradley agreed. "Unfortunately Valentine is not among that group. She's certainly spiritual enough, but her mind is still cluttered with the negative dogma that shaped her childhood. It's strictly a personal choice, but until she cleanses herself of

*everything but love and its unjudging compassion, she'll
choose the hard way again."* He slapped the folder between
his palms, a revealingly sharp sound in the tranquil hush.
*"Because 'they' say it's the only true way to grow! Because
she hasn't bothered to question the omnipotent 'they'! She just
takes their word for it. But so many do,"* he subsided with a
hard sigh.

"It's Earth, Bradley," Sunbeam reminded gently. *"Progress is rarely straightforward."*

"Be that as it may, it still saddens us." Bradley replaced
the folder in its former spot on his desk and tarried a moment
to straighten its perfectly straight edges. *"As for your own
personal growth, Elisse, I must caution you against getting
too closely involved with Valentine's life,"* he said heavily.
*"You know the rules; you guide, you don't take by the hand
and lead."*

"But I haven't," Elisse protested.

*"Maybe not yet, not entirely, but I feel the danger is defi-
nitely there."*

*"I disagree, but knowing that it is always a possibility, I,
too, yield to superior advice,"* Elisse replied, her eyes darkening to the color of fine brandy. *"Therefore I request another
review in four months."*

Sunbeam answered. *"Request granted. Oh, now, Bradley,
we can give her that much."* He beamed her a smile of radiant
sweetness. *"Another review in four Earth months."*

Bradley looked suitably severe. After all, it was part of his
job as Counselor to these valiant Souls. *"Very well, I concur.
But please keep in mind, Elisse, this review will be as much
for you as for Valentine."*

Chapter 9

Jordan Wyatt anchored his handsome pontoon boat at his private dock on Lake Conroe. He was waiting for his two young nephews to join him for an afternoon of fishing while their mother shopped.

Jordan whistled as he checked out the supply of life jackets and iced-down colas. On this bright, hot Sunday in early May, the hedge of pink Carefree roses he'd planted along one boundary line filled the air with heady perfume. Sunlight danced on the water. Behind him, tall pines fringed the shore. He owned five acres of this valuable land, which was immensely satisfying to the young boy who had once been tagged "trailer-park trash."

So why wasn't he happy? His life was Everyman's Dream, Jordan asserted with an angering touch of defiance. He was free of entanglements. He had money, good friends, a satisfying career. He should be awash in happiness. Instead he felt so uptight that the knots in his muscles had knots of their own.

Jordan plowed a hand through his hair. He could handle feeling strung out by sexual frustration. Now and then it did happen, he admitted sardonically. It was this additional tension, this strange, disturbing sense of missing something that made him so edgy. Because what he missed was the pleasure of being with a woman.

Such an ordinary pleasure, he reflected, pulling off his shirt. Not ordinary in a demeaning way, for Jordan genuinely liked women. Too much, in his opinion. His sisters had been capable of bringing him to the point of simpleminded adoration merely by running to him with outstretched arms and tear-streaked faces. He was rendered weak by their need for his protection, and made fiercely strong by his own need to protect.

Once they became independent young women, however, both needs had diminished. At least enough to deal with sensibly, Jordan thought irritably. Up until now, this flaw in his character had been confined to family. Outside his private circle, he was authoritative, discriminating and accustomed to running things, including his life, with a tight rein.

Then along came a sorceress by the improbable name of September Valentine.

"Valentine!" Jordan sent the lovely name across the water on a puff of outrage and the wind promptly brought it back. Damn! He couldn't get away from the wench. Even at night she haunted him. He lay in bed and had fantasies of holding her against him, under him, on top of him, all over him. Sleep, of course, was hopeless, and he didn't know how he was going to survive many more of that kind of night. Missing sleep was hard on a working man.

To admit he desired a woman with such fevered intensity discomfited him. Hell, it was downright embarrassing; rather like regressing to a super-horny teenager again, he acknowledged with strained humor. She looked at him and smiled, and he wanted her. She wrinkled her nose and hissed at him, and he felt exactly the same way. The less time he spent thinking of her, the more she drove him crazy. She fired his very blood with that delicious softness, and this was no play on words. He could take an icy shower right now and still be warmed inside just by thinking.

"Lord!" he muttered, indignant at the indescribable impact she'd had on him from the instant he gazed into those truly beautiful eyes.

He popped a Sprite, sat down in the captain's chair, propped up his feet and stared unseeingly across the water. Something else weighed heavily on his shoulders. *Celibacy.* The very

word appalled him with its ghastly connotations. Yet he had
not been intimate with a woman for weeks now.

Another puzzle. He was a lusty man with lusty appetites.
Suppressed appetites, all balled up in his stomach, very likely
ruining his health, he thought darkly.

Why he liked her so much was a mystery. She gave him a
headache. She made his blood pressure shoot sky-high. She
robbed him of rest, and even interfered with his work. Why
would any sane man even want to be around such a woman?
Yet he still liked—all right, dammit, craved—to be near her.
Even when he knew he was letting himself in for more of that
preposterous, exquisite torment, he went to see her on the flim-
siest excuse. Why? He was a disciplined man. A man of steel,
actually.

Derisively, he snorted. "Oh, hell, Wyatt, you're an addict,
pure and simple. A Valentine addict," he muttered, and swore
at the aggravating grain of truth in this. If he didn't get a
Valentine-fix pretty soon, there was a good chance he'd go
howlingly mad right in the middle of Lake Conroe. . . .

"Uncle Jordan! Unca Jordan!" Childish voices snapped
him out of his brown study. Jumping to his feet, he laughed
aloud as two redheaded little boys ran wildly toward him.

As usual, the four-year-old worked mightily to keep up with
his brother, who at six was a natural-born sprinter. Behind
them came their mother, Glory, her foxy little face nearly concealed by wraparound glasses. Jordan's mouth tightened as he
watched his baby sister's plodding progress. He'd tried his
damnedest to ease her misery, and scored a big fat zero for
his efforts. God, he hated feeling responsible for another's
happiness! But when do you get beyond it? he wondered. And
how the hell do you stop?

His resentment evaporated as he held out a hand to each
little boy. They swirled up his tall frame like agile monkeys.
Cradling their small bodies against his strong shoulders, Jordan was nearly overwhelmed with emotion. He accepted it,
because he knew why loving them was almost painful. They
were the sons he would very likely never have.

*   *   *

Late that afternoon, Samantha Townsend paused at the door to Clay's office, her heart turning a disconcerting somersault as he looked up at her. He was on the telephone with Jordan. She waited, using the moment to study him. He had such craggy features, she thought. Nothing matched. Yet it all came together like a fine spring day.

Replacing the receiver, he stood up. Eyes the sweet, calm gray of dawn crinkled with his greeting. "Need something?"

"The specs of the Morgan house."

Clay considered her request. "Nope. You've worked long enough today, it's time to play a while. Jordan's out at the lake with his boat, and he's invited me—and any friends I care to bring along—to join him. Naturally I thought of you. We'll take a sunset cruise, have dinner at a seafood shack with loud music and fantastic food, then a moonlight cruise back to the pier."

He paused to assess her reaction to his take-charge manner. Tolerant amusement. "How does that strike you?" he charged on.

Sam lowered her gaze. "It sounds like a lot of fun," she said. Her cool voice betrayed none of the tumultuous excitement fizzing through her veins. Thus far their socializing had been limited to a working lunch in his office now and then. Still, they'd found moments to share bits of their personal lives: backgrounds, marital statistics, superficial likes and dislikes.

Covering her pause with a cough, she continued, "But Valentine and I are planning on dinner and a movie tonight."

Clay grinned. "Sam, you know good and well this invitation includes Valentine. Jordan would probably push me overboard if I turned up sans our sassy Ms. Townsend. That little woman's got him so wound up, it's a wonder he can still walk!"

"Do I detect a note of censure in that?" Sam inquired.

"Oh, come on, you know that little act she puts on!"

"What little act is that?"

Green eyes froze his smile into a rictus. Wishing he'd kept his mouth shut, Clay stumbled on, "Well, you know, one step forward and two steps back, that sort of thing. Bold as brass one minute, butter-soft and sweet the next. Drive a man right up the wall! Well, it would *this* man, anyway,'' he finished with a lame attempt at humor.

"So you think she's leading him on," Sam mused. "I can see how she might be considered a flirt, even, Heaven forbid, a bit of a tease. Such a pretty woman, so warm and friendly and loving—has to be an act, right? Couldn't possibly just be her nature, right?'' Her voice, scathingly sweet and reasonable, made him wince. "Bold and brassy, shy and sweet, all in two minutes time? Why, that little trollop!''

"Sam, come on,'' Clay protested. "I wasn't putting her down. I like Valentine, you know that.''

"Lucky for you, I do know that. But I always thought liking went hand in hand with respect. In fact, I cannot for the life of me see how the hell you can have one without the other!''

With effort, Sam subdued her temper. The man looked purely miserable, she thought, quite liking the effect her disdain had on him. "Clay, Valentine is an innocent, with principles and morals strong enough and high enough to build a ladder to Heaven. To put it bluntly, she's a virgin. She is also the purest person I've ever known and it's quite possible I would kill for her. In fact, if you let slip that I told you this, I'll kill you. Keep that in mind at all times.''

Gently she reached up and closed Clay's mouth.

"I'll be damned,'' he finally decided.

"Possibly.''

"I mean, she's so . . . she gives off such an air of . . .''

"Sensuality? Yes, she does,'' Sam agreed coolly. "But that's natural, too, not something she puts on and off when the situation calls for it. I do have to admit, though, that it's become more intense since she's known Jordan. So maybe she's a little wound up herself.''

"Yes, I can see how that could happen.'' Clay sighed. "Look, I'm sorry I've been so dense and I apologize.''

"Apologize to her.''

"I will. So, I'm not to mention this to Jordan?''

"One word and I tear off your lips. Is that clear enough?''

Clay laughed. "Yes, ma'am! Tell you what, you go on home and convince her to come party with us, and I'll pick you both up in—" he checked his watch—"forty-five minutes."

"Oh!" Absurdly unprepared, Sam flushed all over. "No, I'm sorry, I can't, Clay, I still have a problem with this, a personal problem this time. Dating the boss creates a situation that . . . well, it's just not something I want to get into. There's already some talk about us, you must know that. In fact, you'd have to be awfully dumb not to know," she snapped, annoyed at feeling so rattled.

He smiled. "Yes, I know."

She frowned. "Doesn't it bother you?"

"Only if it bothers you. To tell the truth, I'd be proud as hell to even be rumored as your paramour."

Sam's mouth opened, but nothing came out. For the first time in her life she was rendered speechless.

Clay sandwiched her hand between his warm, hard palms. "But since it's just the employer-employee relationship that's bothering you," he continued, his gray eyes alert to even a hint of denial, "that's easily taken care of."

"Oh? How?" she asked warily.

"I think that because I was your first contact in this job market, you've confused our roles. You're the head of your own firm, aren't you?"

"Yes, but I don't see—"

"Then you don't work for me, you work for yourself. I'm your client, Sam, not your boss."

She laughed tightly. "I think you're splitting hairs."

"No. I'm stating facts."

When Sam found her voice again it was far too throaty. "Maybe you're right, I have been thinking of you as my boss rather than as a client. Because of the unusual circumstances surrounding our first meeting, I felt . . . obligated, I guess. But of course I'm not. Not any more than usual, I mean."

Uncommonly flustered, she drew herself up to statuesque dignity. "Okay, I'll see how Val feels about it. I must warn you, though, she's not too keen on boating."

*   *   *

Across town, Valentine was showing Vera Loving her library,
a dark-paneled room with many empty shelves and few books.

"Oh my, ain't this nice," Vera said, gazing around the
handsome room. She wore yellow shorts and shirt and looked
like a stray sunbeam. "You a reader, too? So am I! Self-help
books, positive thinkin', stuff like that. The kinda books that
get you through the tough times," she confided. "Ozell makes
fun of them, the sorry bastard. So I won't let him touch my
books. But I'd be glad to lend you some."

"And I'd be glad to accept," Valentine said. She wasn't
fooled by the woman's derogatory names for her husband. The
warmth they radiated could melt snow. "Is that how you got
through all that terrible trauma, with books?" she asked softly.

"Yeah, they kept me goin', helped me see the light. Oh, I
ain't saying I was a saint. I had my times of cussin' and wee-
pin' and wailin', 'Why me, God, why me! It ain't fair,
goddammit!' " Her smile askew, Vera shook her head. "Ain't
it strange how it always feels better if you can put the blame
on someone else, instead of just tellin' yourself, Okay, this
happened. Now deal with it."

Valentine averted her gaze. When Sam had referred to Vera
as "that squirrely blonde next door," Valentine hadn't bothered to refute the lighthearted slur. It didn't seem that important at the time. It did now. "And you dealt with it. You
humble me, Vera, you know that? I think you're a very spiritual person, very enlightened. Unlike me," she added ruefully.

"Oh, I don't know 'bout that." Vera's diffident smile
turned beautifully wry. "But if so, well, you know the saying;
'Before enlightenment, chop wood, carry water. After enlightenment, chop wood, carry water.' "

Valentine smiled even though she failed to see the humor.
Or even the meaning of that saying, she thought, discomfited.

"Life goes on, in other words," Vera supplied.

"Yes, I . . . I guess it does." Feeling incredibly obtuse, Valentine glanced at the folder Vera held. "What do you have
there?"

"Historical stuff on your house. It's called Rosehill Manor, named that because its mistress was crazy about roses. Had four hundred of 'em at one time. That's all I've read so far." Vera opened the folder. "Says here it used to be a fifty-acre estate. Hard times forced 'em to sell off the land, I suppose." She turned a page. "Let's see. . . . Oh, the house was built as a wedding present for Elisse Manning nee Du Veaul from her parents. And so on and so on . . ." She flipped another page. "Ohmigod, she died in childbirth just four years later! That poor little thing," Vera mourned.

"Here, let me see," Valentine said. Taking the document, she read swiftly. "The house was sold immediately afterward to a lumber baron . . . oh, Vera, isn't that sad! To be in your lovely new home, happily married and carrying your first child—and then to die?"

"That stinks," Vera agreed. "But sometimes life does." Her shrug was calm acceptance of something that just was. "Well, that's Ozell hollerin', so I better run. He's got the tiller out, so if you know where you want your garden?"

"Ozell does manual labor on Sunday?"

Vera shrugged. "Sure, why not? You think if God had a garden needin' plowin', She'd just sit around waitin' for Monday?"

"No, I guess not. Sam's working this afternoon, too." Reluctantly Valentine put Elisse's story aside for now. "Come on, I'll show you where God wants the garden," she said puckishly. Vera cackled. Valentine's response was an affectionate hug, and on a deeper level, an apology.

Basking in their warm rapport, she pointed out her chosen site for a future garden, then returned to the sunny kitchen.

A short time later Sam blew in like a gorgeous whirlwind. "Val? Oh, there you are!" She grabbed Valentine in a bone-crushing hug. "Listen, babe, it's wholly your decision whether or not you have sex, and when. Always remember that."

Leaving her openmouthed cousin to ponder that, Sam sped down the hall to her bedroom, shedding clothes as she went. "Can you come here for a sec?" she called. "I've something to tell you."

"Okay." Valentine followed her trail, picking up clothes like a chicken pecking grain, she thought, enjoying her whimsy. She stopped inside the bedroom door and eyed her cousin, who was down to a bra and skirt. "What's up?"

Sam hesitated, wondering if she should bring up Clay's boating invitation. Not yet, she decided. "Val, for goodness sakes, stop looking so wary!" she said, laughing.

"Well, you look different, Sam, sort of radiant," Valentine accused. She dumped the discarded clothing on a chair. "Why? And why that Dear Abby advice about my sexual choice?"

"Because I know you've been wrestling with it lately. *'Is it time to surrender my precious jewel? Is Jordan the Select One?'* " Sam mimicked affectionately. "That kind of stuff. Just remember, kiddo, I can read you, too!"

Valentine flushed all the way to her toes. Denial would be a lie; Jordan was always on her mind lately, as if something were giving her a gentle push toward him. Probably her body, she thought, mouth quirking in acknowledgment of the sensual longing that built little fires here and there without regard to what her brain was up to. Steadily she met Sam's sparkling green gaze.

"And your advice on that kind of stuff?"

"Oh, well, that's a choice that every girl has to make for herself," Sam said, losing some of her cocky assurance. "Just go with your feelings, I guess. Your deeper feelings. That's the best," she conceded. "But the rest of the time wasn't all that bad, either!"

Valentine chewed her lip. "Even though love was absent?"

Sam shrugged. "What's love got to do with anything?"

"Well, jeez, Sam, silly little me thought love had plenty to do with anything!"

"A pretty thought," Sam conceded. "Romantic, too. But in real life? Impractical at best, self-deception at worst."

"I see. So what you're saying is that mutual commitment and caring are antiquated concepts," Valentine concluded with a hollow sense of loss, for she had always honored Sam's word.

Feeling defensive, Sam shrugged. "Positively Victorian. At least as far as I'm concerned."

"I hadn't looked at it like that. Maybe that's why I'm still burdened with virginity at my advanced age," Valentine quipped.

"A woman's choice, honey," Sam reminded, wishing she hadn't shot off her mouth to Clay. "Oh, what I started to tell you is that Jordan has invited us out on his boat." Quickly she outlined the entertainment plans for the evening. "Sounds great, huh! I accepted for us, so get cracking, Mouse. Clay will pick us up in about thirty minutes."

Valentine's first reaction was exhilaration. Thoughts swarmed her mind, but strangely enough, something else snagged and held her attention, the word *Mouse*. Her nickname, formerly warm and fuzzy, now felt uncomfortable, like a too-tight shoe. Because I've outgrown it, she realized with a tiny shock.

"It just doesn't fit anymore, Sam," she marveled aloud.

As usual, Sam looked puzzled at the seemingly random remark.

But this time Valentine didn't explain; she wanted Sam to realize for herself that the nickname was no longer applicable.

Needing a diversion, she murmured slyly, "So it's you and Clay now, huh?"

"We've become friends, yes. He's an easy man to like," Sam admitted. "So is Jordan, so go get dressed. Slacks, I think. Oh, and a sweater; Clay says it gets cool on the lake at night. You are going, aren't you? If you don't, then neither am I."

"For you, I'll go," Valentine said blandly. "I'll drive my own car. That way we can all leave when we want. No arguments," she warned. "Just hush up and tell me how to get there."

Frowning, Sam told her.

Valentine went to her own bedroom with a little skip in her step. Sam was right on the nose, she thought; to have or not to have sex was her own personal, private decision. So was where and when. And why. Just simply wanting to make love with Jordan—and she did, badly, hotly, achingly want to make love with Jordan—was reason enough, wasn't it? It didn't have to mean anything. Besides, she was tired of being out of step with the rest of the world.

"So okay, take charge, September Valentine," she instructed, peeling off her clothes. "Yank this relationship out of his hands and into your own. Start something, for God's sake," she growled, jerking open the shower door. After weeks of biding her time she was suddenly suffused with the urge to act.

Even after an icy rinse, her body felt hot, taut with tension. Excitement, wonderfully wild and heady, created an extra beat in her pulses. "Good grief, girl, get a grip!" she grumbled, stepping into new red satin bikini panties. Her reaction to his lovemaking would probably be that of a snowball rolled atop a warm stove. "You'll dissolve, you naif," she accused her merry-faced image.

Remarkably unperturbed by the threat of dissolution, she picked up Elisse's picture and waltzed it around the room. Stroking a finger down one glass-protected cheek, she whispered, "Elisse Du Veaul Manning. I'm so sorry your life was cut short. It looked to be such a good life. A husband, a lovely home, a baby on the way. And then in the blink of an eye, you're gone and it's all over."

Nonsense, it isn't over. Love never dies, Valentine, you know that, the familiar inner voice chided.

"Well, it still seems sad to me, to have everything and then have to leave it," Valentine countered. Having spoken aloud, she glanced over her shoulder to make sure no one had heard. "They'd think I'm nuts. Which is a definite possibility, seeing as how I'm talking to the dead." She sighed.

But her words and her frame of mind were pleasingly opposed. She liked being on such good terms with her intuition or conscience or whatever it was that spoke from deep within her heart. Elisse had somehow become a symbol of that small voice.

Replacing the picture, Valentine went to her closet. She ignored Sam's decree of slacks and sweater, choosing instead a simple rayon dress in a dark, tiny print. White buttons ran from low, round neckline to hem. She added white sandals and gold earrings, then tied back her hair with a white silk scarf.

Her pace hastened as she heard Sam and Clay drive away. Before following them, she stopped in front of Elisse's picture again. "Well, here goes. I don't know exactly what, but whatever it is, I'm ready for it," she assured the lovely lady, and felt a powerful burst of reassurance.

Savoring this eerie sense of communication, Valentine went downstairs to her car.

Covertly Jordan checked his watch again. Clay and Sam were comfortably ensconced on the cushioned banquette that ran along the back of his boat. Valentine, however, was nowhere in sight.

When, finally, she drove over the grassy meadow and parked beside his truck, he stepped onto the dock to meet her, his mouth arranging itself in a wide smile. The wind blew that scrap of a skirt around her legs and she looked downright edible.

"Hi, Jordan," she called with a languid wave.

He grinned, and lifted his bottle in teasing salute. "Hello, Valentine. You look gorgeous."

"So do you," she said, ogling him, a saucy smile crinkling her eyes and making him laugh from the heart for no reason at all. But he was glad he'd taken time to shower and change his clothes after his outing with the kids, and that he smelled woodsy instead of fishy.

He took her arm. "Sam said you were scared of boats. Are you okay with this?"

"Of course I'm okay, I outgrew that years ago." Her gaze shifted to the boat. "This is a big, stable vessel and I'm sure I'll love it. Hi, Clay!"

Clay, superbly at ease in jeans and a striped sports shirt, waved at her. Sam, classy elegance in green tailored slacks and a paler sweater set, frowned at her. "You wore a dress."

"I did indeed," Valentine said. She brushed by Jordan and left him standing in a mist of exotic perfume. With Clay's assistance, she stepped aboard. Jordan followed. She sat down, crossed her legs, and wrapped her fingers around the railing. "Thank you, Clay. You look gorgeous, too, if you don't mind my saying so."

"Don't mind at all," Clay replied with an ornery grin.

She laughed and winked at Sam, who immediately asked, "Did you have any problems finding this place?"

"Piece of cake, Sam." Valentine tossed back her hair. "Jordan, are you going to attend me or just let me die of thirst?"

Jordan came out of his negligent lean against the rail and opened the cooler. "What's your pleasure?"

You, her eyes said. "Bottled water, if you have it."

He opened it for her. Valentine took the bottle and pressed it against her forehead for a moment. She still felt hot and flushed, and watching Jordan's graceful movements didn't help. His lithe body was beautifully defined by trim black jeans and a black T-shirt. He caught her staring at him, which added a blush to her flush.

She diverted her gaze to Clay and Sam. The two sat apart, but their auras easily spanned the gap between bodies. Smiling to herself, Valentine wondered if her cousin had any idea of the revealing radiance enwrapping her like a gossamer garment. Clay had a glow, too, she noted. They were both dancing around an emotional maypole, oblivious to its entangling ribbons.

Soon Jordan sat down in his leather captain's chair and navigated the big craft away from the dock and down the channel. There was a tinge of lavender to the evening sky, and in the sunlight's last glow, the expensive homes dotting the shoreline took on a fairy-tale look. Valentine's gaze was torn between the scenery, and his strong hands on the wheel.

His strength and competence were reassuring, and the water blessedly calm. Eventually her tight grip on the railing loosened as they motored along. Emboldened by her small victory, she stood up and made her way to the captain's chair. She slipped her hands over Jordan's shoulders, a casual clasp that helped maintain her balance.

He smiled at her. "That's where I live," he said, pointing to a white stone tower set well back from the shoreline. "Tenth floor: water view."

Thrilled, and too easily impressed for her liking, Valentine responded with a low, "Wow. Very nice, Jordan. Condominiums?"

"Um-hmm. Covered parking, maid service, restaurant on the grounds, all very convenient."

"Sounds wonderful," she enthused. "I can't wait to see it."

A noncommittal smile creased Jordan's cheek, an oblique response she could not decipher with any surety. After a moment's thought, she decided to put a positive spin on it.

The pleasant cruise terminated at another pier in front of a ramshackle restaurant. As they walked up the rough boardwalk, delicious aromas beckoned. Loud music hammered the air, and some wild dancing was taking place on a huge, covered terrace overlooking the water.

"Country line-dancing," Jordan said. "We'll give it a whirl before we leave."

Valentine laughed and caught his hand. She felt vibrantly alive, fizzy with the evening's promise of fun and excitement.

And when it's over, you'll be alone with Jordan.

The sweet, sly whisper caused her heart to skip a beat.

Nightfall. Still aboard the boat, Valentine waved as Clay and Sam drove away. Checking first one thing and then another, Jordan prowled the dock, as lithe and lean and powerful as a panther in the elongating light cast by a tall pole-lamp. She drew a deep breath and slowly released it in an effort to shed some tension.

"Umm, this is nice," she murmured. "I've so enjoyed the evening, Jordan. Line-dancing is such fun—different, but fun, once I got the hang of it. You're a good teacher. So's Clay."

"Thanks. I'm glad you enjoyed it. That's one of our favorite hangouts." Jordan tested the tie-ropes before reboarding.

"Sam wasn't too pleased about you driving home alone, down narrow, winding roads in the dark," he remarked. "Neither am I, for that matter."

With a sultry laugh, Valentine curled her hands above her head and stretched. "Sam worries too much. So do you."

Jordan grunted. "Maybe. But if you'll wait until I unload the boat, I'll follow you home."

"If you wish," she gave languid approval. "But I'm not ready to go home just yet. It's so beautiful out here, Jordan, the water, the moonlight, all those stars."

"Yeah, must be five or six of 'em," Jordan said, glancing at the sky. "Be careful!" he snapped as she grabbed a stanchion and swung up on the second rung of the safety rail.

"I am being careful." She frowned. Why was he so uptight? For that matter, why was he just standing there on the dock? Couldn't he read her signals? "I'm chilly," she added, shivering. "Guess I should have brought that sweater."

"My windbreaker's there on the seat." He stepped aboard and reached for the jacket since she made no move to get it.

"Your arms would be warmer, Jordan. And safer," she added, swaying as the boat rocked in the wake of a passing craft.

"Dammit, Valentine," Jordan growled. All evening he'd strained to keep a safe distance between them. But what man could resist such a sweet request? He stepped up behind her and framed her shoulders with the jacket, then with his arms.

Relaxing, she leaned back into the bulwark of his hard body.

Jordan went rigid. Her firm little bottom was just a breath away from his vulnerable manhood. If she moved . . .

She moved.

He sucked in a breath. When he inhaled, he breathed in *her*, but damn it all, he did have to breathe! "Tell me . . ." He cleared his throat. "What made you afraid of boats?"

"When I was eight I was trapped under an overturned dingy and nearly drowned. Since a half-dozen relatives jumped into the lake to rescue me, the danger was minimal. But basically I'm a coward, so I panicked."

"You? A coward? I don't believe that for a minute. Sam

said it was your idea to pull up stakes and move west. To leave everything that's familiar, no promise of jobs, very little money; that, my friend, takes courage.''

The pleasure she derived from his compliment left Valentine momentarily speechless. That it could mean so much! She felt aglow from inside out. With an airiness she was far from feeling, she replied drolly, '' 'Tis said that praise, like perfume, should be inhaled, not swallowed. So pardon me while I take a deep breath.''

Jordan's laugh came from deep in his chest. "You are the most unpredictable woman! I never know what you're going to say. Have you always been so capricious?''

"No," she replied with rueful candor. "Until I came here, both I and my life were as predictable as a sunset. I didn't have to make decisions—others were delighted to do that for me. And I was happy to let them. It's a funny thing about decisions, Jordan. If you don't make them, well, no decisions, no responsibility; no responsibility, no blame. You're home free.''

"That sounds . . . parasitic," he said, his voice flattening.

"Oh, no, nothing like that. I helped out and cared for other people, truly I did. When Grandma Fiona was so terribly ill, she didn't want anyone but me around. I stayed with her day and night during those last few weeks, feeding her, bathing her. Loving her.'' Valentine sighed. "But out in the world, a passive role is just so much easier than the active. I was like a clam in its snug little shell.''

Unable to refrain, Jordan kissed her hair. "So what triggered you into leaving your shell, little clam?''

Valentine hesitated, longing to confide in him. But if she didn't understand the irrational feelings that had driven her out into the world, or the soft, gentle voice that sometimes pushed her into decisions, then neither would he.

She shrugged. "Maybe I started growing up.''

The tiny movement tested Jordan's control. With effort, he spoke calmly, albeit huskily. "When will you know for sure?''

She laughed. "Beats me! Why do you ask?''

"Oh, my sister Glory; sometimes I wonder if she'll ever

grow up. I thought when she married that I was finally free. She was the last one, the rest had flown the nest by then—but her husband turned out to be a Class A heel. I know it was traumatic for her, but . . . She just seems to hang on to it!'' he blurted.

'' 'Poor little me' syndrome?'' Valentine murmured, rubbing her smooth cheek against his somewhat bristly one.

''No, not at all,'' Jordan said loyally. ''She got hurt pretty bad and it takes time, I guess. I don't even know why I brought it up.''

''Maybe because you've been making her decisions for her?''

''I've helped, yes.'' Disliking his defensive tone, Jordan tacked on a careless, ''Force of habit, I suppose. I've always done . . . God, Valentine!'' he rasped as she turned in his arms.

''Umm?'' Facing him, her warm breath whisking his mouth, her hands loosely clasped behind his neck, she drew down his head and kissed him.

It was a tenuous kiss, given with the same unsureness etching her other movements. Her hesitancy licked at the tinder of his desire, tiny flames, crouched to leap. Thin fabric was all that separated their bodies and he could feel the heat rise between them. Her firm breasts ached his chest with the tantalizing knowledge that she wore nothing beneath the dress. The muscles in his arms and shoulders drew wire-tight with the urge to crush her into the rest of him.

He resisted. But his mouth, independent of his will, took over the kiss and ravished the sweetness between her lips.

The boat rocked, nearly throwing him off balance. He diverted his mouth to her hair until the world stopped spinning. He wanted her with an intensity that would have shocked him had he been capable of thinking.

And she wanted him. That sweet knowledge burned hot and bright in the deep, dark forests of his mind.

He burrowed deeper into her hair. Think, Wyatt, think, he exhorted his fuzzy brain. All right, he didn't want just sex, although Lord knew he needed some. He wanted . . . things that he had never wanted before. But if he put names to his deeper desires, then he'd have to ponder them, too, and he had enough on his mind.

"Jordan?" Soft, silky, seductive.

Steeling himself, he pulled back from her and set his hands on her shoulders. "Valentine . . ." When he tried again, his voice, though too husky, was just light enough, with exactly the right amount of fond, teasing humor; an incredible feat. "Valentine, I like you. I like you a lot. Really, I do."

She stirred, and Jordan spoke faster. "You're sweet, smart, sexy. I find your naivete and innocence very appealing—"

"Could you be a little more patronizing?" she asked dryly.

"I'm not patronizing you, I'm simply trying to say something that needs saying. At least *I* think so," he said, disliking his testy tone.

"What?"

"What?" he repeated, momentarily confused. "Oh. Well, for starters, what I want from you and what you want from me may be two very different things."

"Could be," Valentine agreed coolly. "If you're the kind of man they say you are."

"Yes, it very well could be and I think we ought to . . ." He stiffened. "What do you mean? What kind of man?"

"A ladies' man. The love 'em and leave 'em kind."

"I've never claimed to be a monk, but on the other hand, I'm certainly not a Don Juan, either. Who's this *they* you refer to?"

"Deke. But he wasn't being mean, Jordan," she added quickly. "He just didn't want me to get hurt."

"I don't want you to get hurt, either. So maybe you'd better listen to ole Deke," Jordan drawled. His opinion of Deke had gone up a notch even if it did make him burn. "Maybe he sees the same thing I do—that you and I have different agendas."

"Meaning?" Her breath brushed his mouth.

"Meaning that you're marriage and kids and white picket fences," Jordan said just short of a rasp, "and I'm just the opposite. I don't want commitment, I don't want kids, and the only urge I get from a white picket fence is to burn it down."

"You don't like kids?"

"No." That wasn't true. He sighed. "Yes, other people's kids. My sister's boys more than satisfy any paternal urges I might have."

He shifted under the burden of her silence. Easy and humorous, he warned himself. "So, sweet Valentine, while I enjoy our friendship and being part of your life, I think our relationship should stay just as it is. Warm and friendly, but nothing else."

Silence again. Heavy, *heavy* silence.

"Regardless of how right it feels," he stated, "I think we both know that sexual involvement would be a mistake."

"We? *We!*" she cut in, voice hot with outrage. "May I remind you that it was you who grabbed and kissed me—and who keeps right on kissing me every chance you get?"

"Because I had to kiss you, I was dying to kiss you—you're a very kissable woman!" Jordan ran a hand over his face, his tone changing to irony. "Okay, guilty as charged. But you bear a little of that guilt, you know. You're very appealing, Valentine, damn near irresistible, in fact." He forced a chuckle. "Even so, although I want to—indeed it may kill me not to—I'm not going to make love to you."

The supple body he held suddenly transformed into a slender stone column that slowly drew away from him.

The light was too dim to see her face. But her voice was clear enough, cool, strong, faintly amused as she replied, "Well, Jordan, I don't remember asking you to make love to me."

Stepping down from the rail, she picked up her purse and walked off the boat.

Chapter 10

"Valentine, wait!" Jordan called. "Give me a minute to secure the boat and I'll see you home."

"Thank you, but I'm perfectly capable of seeing my own self home," Valentine said crisply.

Ignoring his response, she walked to her car with fierce composure and a crushing sense of her own foolishness. "I practically offered myself to him on a platter!" she muttered. An offering that had been gently, tactfully, kindly rebuffed, she acknowledged, burning with something that alternated between anger, outrage, and a formless smear of shame.

And hurt. God, it was infuriating how much it hurt! It stripped away her defenses, left her feeling nakedly exposed.

But she'd reacted well, she assured herself. She'd carried it off. Hadn't she carried it off? Yes. He hadn't a clue.

That mattered too much for her liking. A little less anguish and a little more sangfroid would be nice, she thought with acrid humor. Unlocking her car door, she got in, slammed it shut, started the engine.

Lights, Valentine!

"Lights, yes." Grateful for the reminder, she turned on the headlights, her gaze riveted to the man striding toward her car.

In the moonlight Jordan looked enormously tall and powerful. To think that she had actually thought she could tame all that power and passion and raw male energy! "Dumb, Valentine, dumb," she lashed herself. "Classic dimwitted behavior."

Tires screeching, she tore out of the grassy lot, her eyes hot with unshed tears, her mind a hornets' nest of discordant thoughts. The treelined road was pitch-dark except for her headlights. She floored the gas pedal, her ears stubbornly deaf to the sound of flying gravel as she took another curve much too fast. She was focused on one thing and one thing only, holding it together.

She had a tight grip on this undefined but frightening "it." In control, Valentine reassured herself. She refused to give into seething emotions. She would not acknowledge the fears milling at the back of her mind no matter how sharp their claws.

Men, she reminded herself, dealt with rejection all the time. So could she. No whining, no crying, no bitching. She was angry, yes, but that was normal. The lovely, golden magic she had created tonight had been turned to lead.

And he'd done it. Deliberately. And made her feel foolish. So of course she was goddamn angry! But nothing else. No deeper feelings, she asserted, fiercely resistant to caring any more than this.

Even so, she had to replay the scene with Jordan. To her annoyance, she examined it with adolescent intensity, probing for missed cues. There really wasn't much to work with, she admitted with searing honesty. He had made himself quite clear. He simply didn't want to get involved with her beyond the point of friendship.

Would he have resisted Gaby? The question wormed its way into her mind and stuck there, insisting she answer it. She refused. "What the hell does it matter?" she hissed.

It mattered. Her hands clenched around the steering wheel. She hadn't given much thought to the tall blonde who'd accosted him in the piano bar on their first date. After all, Jordan wasn't a monk, he liked women.

He even likes me, she thought bitingly. Just not *that* way.

But that wasn't true; she knew he desired her. "I don't care what he thinks about me or anything else!" she gritted. But that wasn't true, either. . . .

Rejection is painful, a soft voice commiserated with her disavowed turmoil.

"It stings," Valentine conceded tightly.

It hurts.

"A little," came another grudging concession.

More than a little. Rejection can be devastating if taken personally.

"How the hell else *would* you take it!" Valentine exploded. "The man as good as told me to take a hike! Well, he can just—oh God!" she gasped as her headlights suddenly illumined trees instead of pavement. She slammed on the brakes. Tires squealed and skidded into a spin. For a terrifying instant the car was very nearly airborne. Then, miraculously, it regained traction and righted itself. She was back on the road, the speedometer registering a steady thirty-five miles per hour.

She was shaking—it had all happened so quickly!

Calm down, Valentine.

"Good advice, Valentine," she agreed, slowing even more. She'd die if Jordan found her sitting in a ditch less than a mile from where she'd left him!

In a few minutes she was on the wide, well-lighted freeway. Relieved that her near-mishap had gone undetected, Valentine tucked right back into her disturbing thoughts again.

It really wasn't personal, Valentine, the inner voice confided. *Jordan has his own problems. He's just as vulnerable as you, just as subject to his feelings. And like you, he has difficulty with deeper emotions, particularly the ones that require something from him. He thinks he's given all he can, that he cannot take on any more without endangering his basic self. He's unaware of the reservoirs of courage and compassion that exist just beneath his primal fear. His wounds are deep, Valentine. The darkness of past experiences overshadows his hopes for the future.*

Valentine reacted with stunned surprise to this outpouring of intimate knowledge. Jordan was still an enigma to her. She hadn't a clue as to what motivated the man, so where was all this coming from? Was she hallucinating? Crazy?

Was there someone else in the car with her?

Goose bumps raced up her arms, and she actually checked the rearview mirror to confirm that she was alone before coming to her senses. Chagrined, she gave herself a hard shake. Obviously she was involved in another of her self-arguments.

It seemed a safe assumption and she ought to stop right there. But something—curiosity, perhaps—impelled her on.

"I . . . I don't understand," she whispered, licking her lips. "What wounds? What happened, what's his problem?"

She held her breath until the soft, eerie response resonated through her mind. *An overload of responsibility, forced upon him by circumstances beyond his control.*

"Well, what?" Valentine hissed, tantalized beyond endurance by this oblique response.

To say more is a violation of his privacy. He alone must decide whether or not to confide in you. But he gave you a clue when he spoke of his sister.

"What, that he feels responsible for her well-being? Big deal. I've felt responsible for other people's well-being: Mom's, Sam's, Grandma Fiona before she died, and I'm okay. That's just the way it is, just part of life."

Valentine waited. She wanted to continue this intriguing disputation despite her jittery nerves. But nothing beyond a kind of white noise filled the suddenly enormous silence.

"Okay," she whispered, shivering as her safe assumption lost credibility in another icy chill of wonder. "Okay, what just happened here?"

No answer. But she had to have an answer, a logical answer to a mysterious happening. . . .

A shake of head rejected that. Nothing mysterious about it, she asserted, expelling a breath of relief as another possibility blessedly came to mind. She had "read" him just as she did the other people who made up her inner circle. Somehow or other she had breeched the wall Jordan kept around his private self. "And was able to tell what he was thinking and feeling!" she exclaimed softly.

Would this breakthrough last? "Oh God, I hope so!" she whispered, tantalized by its possibilities. If she knew him better, understood the reasons behind his fear of commitment, then maybe there was a chance. . . .

Valentine was shocked to realize she'd made it home, driving on automatic apparently; for she had no recollection of actually entering town. She parked beside Clay's car and walked around to the front of the house.

Headlights outlined her path; Jordan was right behind her. She paused, waiting for him to draw abreast.

He rolled down the window and leaned across the seat to say, "Just wanted to make sure you got home okay."

The clarity of his statement spotlighted its lack of undertones or hidden meanings. He was still a blank to her, Valentine realized. Her intimate glimpse of this perplexing man had been a momentary aberration.

Aching with disappointment, she stared at his shadowed face, seeking to discern his expression. Impossible.

"Jordan, I told you that wasn't necessary." Her voice softened. "But thank you for caring."

"Dammit, I do care, Valentine," he said gruffly. "Why is that so hard to understand? You're a friend and I take care of my friends."

Valentine's puckish smile filtered into her voice. "Well, at least we have that in common. Good night, friend Jordan. See you!" Turning, she ran up the steps and hurried inside.

"Hey, honey!" Sam called. She and Clay were having coffee in the den.

"Hi, guys," Valentine said, smiling.

Eagle-eyed, Sam scrutinized her cousin. "Have any trouble getting home?"

"Nary a bit, Sam."

Clay stood up and walked to the arched doorway she leaned against. "Valentine, I think I owe you an apology—several apologies, in fact. I'm sorry I misjudged you," he said simply.

Valentine nodded, sensitive to the gist of his apology if not the actual details. "Accepted. Thank you, Clay." Responsive to a sudden rush of affection, she cradled his face and brushed a kiss on his firm mouth. Drawing back, she exclaimed, "Delicious! Sam, have you sampled this yet? Going to waste, Sam!''

Forced laughter, like a stream of bubbles, floated out behind her as she ran upstairs.

Sam just stood there, rooted to the floor by the fiery blush engulfing her entire body. Her cheeks burned with the blood-rush of embarrassment. The asinine embarrassment of a teen-ager, she acknowledged, her eyes flashing as she met Clay's gaze.

Lacking her usual grace, she moved toward him . . . placed her hands on his shoulders . . . pressed her lips to his, all in exquisite slow motion.

Clay didn't move a muscle. Despite his fevered urges, he had made no demands on her, respecting the invisible barrier she had thrown up between them as something she needed. As her soft mouth brushed his with immeasurable sweetness, he was blazingly aware of his growing need for this lovely woman. Simultaneously, he felt proud of himself for resisting this extreme and provocative temptation to take what he wanted.

Doubtless the old Clay would have made a grab. But he was different now, a changed man. Somehow, just knowing her had done what all his years of experience couldn't.

She slowly drew back and released a long breath. ''Valentine's right,'' she murmured as if to herself. Her mouth curved. ''Thank you, Clay.''

He inclined his dark head. ''Thank *you*.''

She laughed. ''You're welcome. Good night, Clay. Thanks again for a lovely evening.''

''The pleasure was all mine,'' Clay said, smiling. Desire still flickered like fireflies under the surface of his tight skin, an altogether lovely feeling, he decided.

''See you tomorrow,'' she said.

''Tomorrow,'' he echoed like a bright promise.

The storm that came with dawn finally lulled Valentine to sleep. She awoke at ten to a freshly washed world of shining green foliage and white clouds drifting across a forget-me-not blue sky.

Her interior landscape was far less tranquil. The instant she became alert her mind shot back to the prior evening and the information about Jordan she'd accessed on that strange drive home. In retrospect, it didn't seem all that insightful. All she'd really learned was that he had a strong aversion to taking responsibility for other people's lives.

He refused to make love to her. Did that display integrity or disinterest? She'd like to think the former, but her ego was a pathetic little thing at the moment. She closed her eyes, wishing she didn't have to face the world today. She was tense, cold, tired and aching. What else? Confused. Hellishly confused.

Impulsively she got up and dialed her mother's number. Ed's slurred voice stung like a wasp in her ear. Julia was at work, he said. Then he went into a furious tirade that included foul language and hurtful accusations.

Unable to talk sensibly with him, she hung up. Tears stung her eyes. He'd accused her of bailing out on them. Well, maybe she had, who knew?

Sighing, she skimmed off her T-shirt and headed for the bathroom. That sense of urgency was back again, like an itch she couldn't scratch because she couldn't reach it. Or even find it, she reflected, dragging a towel punishingly across her wet skin.

Somber-faced, she dressed in jeans and a sleeveless cotton sweater and went downstairs to find her cousin.

Sam had already left for Clay's office. Distracted and moody, Valentine went into town to run some errands. When she'd finished, she stopped at a fast-food restaurant for chicken pita fajitas slathered with guacamole sauce. A high-calorie lunch, she acknowledged, but incredibly soothing.

Afterward she strolled the mall, another mood-settling experience. She felt almost decent by the time she returned home.

Sam, green eyes flashing and red hair bristling, at her most imperious in a navy pin-striped suit and silk blouse, met her at the door. "Where the devil have you been?" she exploded. "I called you here, on the cell phone—dammit, I must've paged you a dozen times! Weren't you wearing your beeper?"

Taken aback, Valentine blurted, "No, I . . . I needed time out, so I left it at home."

"Time out is a luxury we can't afford, not when it keeps a client waiting," Sam snapped. "You were supposed to pick up those fabric and wallpaper samples and meet me at the Clayton house at a quarter of eleven!"

"Oh, no!" Valentine groaned. "Sam, I completely forgot about it! I'm sorry, truly I am!"

"Well, sorry doesn't cut it, Valentine! I ask you to do one little thing for me, one lousy little job, and you blow it! If I can't rely on you—"

"Sam, that's not fair, you know you can rely on me," Valentine said, low and intense. "I made a mistake, that's all."

"I'm not concerned with being fair, that's the least of my worries," Sam retorted. "Not only did we look unreliable, we looked incompetent. I felt like a fool standing around wasting a client's time while I tried to contact an associate who had evidently disappeared off the face of the earth!"

"I'm sorry, Sam," Valentine repeated, the only thing she could say, given the circumstances. "It won't happen again."

The quiet apology irritated rather than pacified Sam. Fired up and needing to vent her wrath, she cast her young cousin an acidulous look. "Let's hope not. I run a tight ship. Or at least I try to. I can't afford screwups like this one." Wheeling, she headed for her office.

"Sam, for godsakes, I took some time out to think! Maybe you ought to try that. Then you wouldn't be so uptight over something you want so badly and could have in an instant if you weren't scared to death of your feelings!" Valentine shouted.

Sam stopped dead. "What the hell are you talking about?" she asked, slowly turning to face her.

"I'm talking about Clay. You love him, Sam."

"And you are out of your mind."

"You deny having special feelings for Clay?"

Looking amused, Sam replied, "Of course not. I've just never considered lust to be all that special, that's all. Natural, but hardly special. Now if you'll excuse me, I've got work to do. Like reschedule my entire afternoon, beginning with my appointment with Mrs. Clayton. After I pick up those samples, of course."

"I'll pick them up."

"Never mind, I'm going downtown anyway." Sam grabbed her purse, slung it over her shoulder and stomped back to the foyer. "What the hell's this, a lottery ticket?" she asked, spying a scrap of paper on the hall table. "I thought I'd made it clear how I felt about gambling!"

"Sam, I spend two bucks a month on the lottery. Is that going to put us in the poorhouse?" Valentine retorted.

Sam's color rose. "I just wish you'd respect my opinion, that's all. But I guess that's too much to ask." The ticket fell to the floor. "I have a late meeting so I won't be here for supper." Her slender back stiff with anger, she walked out the door.

Valentine sagged against the bannister. She hated fighting, especially with her cousin. Sam's scorn and disapproval scourged her tender heart like twin whips.

The telephone rang. It was Deke.

Valentine made a ferocious effort to pull herself together. "Deke! Are you in town? If not, why not?" she demanded, wiping away tears. She listened, laughed in the right places, declined his invitation to fly to Jamaica for the weekend, thinking to herself that he felt quite safe in issuing these outrageous enticements because he knew she'd say no.

"One of these days I may surprise you, Deke," she said, only half joking. "Are you free for dinner tonight? Mexican, my treat. ... Okay, seven o'clock."

After she rang off, Valentine felt a little better. Deke was always fun to be with, sometimes wickedly so, she mused, remembering the shadows in his aura. But at least she knew how he felt, what he thought about things. And those shadows could be erased if she put her mind to it.

Her attention fractured as Vera popped in the door. Caught

tear-streaked and still sniffling, Valentine discarded any
thoughts of concealing her distress from her friend.

"Hey, you've been crying! What's wrong? Who made you
cry?" Vera demanded, absurdly pugnacious.

"Oh, I had a fight with Sam. Besides that, I've been ro-
mantically bruised," Valentine said. Pleased with her flippant
response, she impulsively added, "I wanted to get closer to a
guy and he turned me down."

"You're kidding!" Vera was astonished. "What, is he
nuts?"

Valentine gave a weak laugh. "As good a reason as any, I
guess. Thank you, I feel much better! Did you need something?" she asked, sobering as she took a closer look at her
friend.

"I wanted to show you this picture," Vera responded, suddenly diffident. "You know, you've never been in my living
room, but I've been in yours dozens of times. Funny, huh?"

"Yes, it is, I guess," Valentine replied, feeling negligent.
"But I always come to your kitchen door, you know? And
your kitchen is so warm and inviting, Vera, a person just sort
of naturally stops there."

Vera's smile accepted her explanation. "Well, my point was
that since you'd never seen my living room, you've never seen
a picture of my daughter. We just got this one today and it's
a beaut!" she said, holding out an unframed photograph.

Her stomach tightening, Valentine took the picture. In truth,
she hadn't wanted to see Vera's daughter. As she had feared,
her immediate reaction to the distinctive face of a Down's
child was a disconcerting mixture of love and appalled pity.
For a terrible instant she didn't know what to say. The normal
responses were dismayingly unsuitable. *I can't very well say
Shanna has her mother's eyes or her daddy's grin*, she
thought, suddenly flooded with sorrow.

But Vera, she noted, was smiling.

"Oh, my, Vera, I didn't realize—why, she's a young lady,
not a child!" she exclaimed, truly surprised. Despite her squat
little figure, Shanna possessed a remarkable air of dignity.

"And all these lovely plants around her—what's she doing here?"

"Her job," Vera replied proudly. "The place where she lives is a working community. The tenants make stuff and sell it, not just plants, but pottery, sculptures and such. Shanna's so happy there she didn't even want to come home for Easter! They work and get paid just like normal people," Vera went on in a joyous spate of words. "Shanna's a greenhouse attendant. She loves plants. And they love her, too, Valentine."

"That's great!" Valentine said, inwardly wincing at the inadequacy of her response. "I didn't even realize there were places like this."

"Well, there's not many. And this one's struggling like mad to make it. I . . . I thought you might like to keep the picture for a day or two, so Sam could see it, I mean."

"Yes, of course." Valentine looked at Vera and immediately heard her unspoken words. "Oh, Vera, this is your way—a kind, sensitive, wonderfully perceptive way—of introducing Sam and me to your daughter, isn't it," she queried gently.

Coloring, Vera glanced at her, then glanced away. "Well, sometimes it's hard for people to meet her without any idea of . . . of how she looks. 'Course, I don't see her the way most people do, like something too pitiful to look at directly. I see her as a shinin' being—I mean, just look at those eyes," she said with fierce intensity. "Not a speck of meanness, just pure goodness and sweetness."

"Like an angel in disguise," Valentine supplied softly.

"Yes! Oh, Jesus, you do understand, don't you! I knew you would, I just knew it!" Vera exclaimed. "That's no exaggeration, either; havin' her in my life has really changed me, changed the way I look at—at everything, good or bad." She sighed. "I ain't tryin' to snow you, Valentine, it's been hard raisin' her. My heart's broke a thousand times watchin' her try to make herself a place in the world. A world that's not very kind to them that's different. But when it gets tough, I just remind myself that she's not a human being havin' a spiritual experience, she's a *spiritual* being having a human experience." She smiled wryly. "Not your usual experience, that's for sure. But it's the one she chose."

"She chose?" Valentine echoed. "Good God, Vera, you think she *chose* to . . . to be like this?"

"Yeah, I do," Vera answered a bit defiantly. "It's either that we think we choose the trials and traumas of our lives ourselves, or that we've got a mean, uncaring, even downright sadistic God in charge of the Universe."

Eyeing her friend, Valentine leaned against the kitchen counter. "Jeez, that's pretty deep, Vera. Over my head, to be truthful. But it's certainly food for thought. And I will keep the picture. Sam will be as pleased as I to meet Shanna the next time she comes home." Another brief, intense glance at Vera compelled her to add, "Hey, I'm not busy—anything else you want to talk about?"

"Naw, I just . . . Do you believe in miracles?" Vera asked abruptly.

Valentine blinked. "Well, I . . . I've never got right down to asking myself that question, but right offhand, I'd say yes."

"You honestly believe they're for real?"

Puzzled, Valentine studied Vera's angular face. "Yes, sure. Why not? Lots of people do. Why do you ask? Vera, is everything okay with you? I mean, you seem kind of uptight."

"Oh, I'm fine. I was just wondering, that's all. You know us geniuses, our bright minds always overflowin' with questions!"

"That's us," Valentine agreed and joined her friend in a hearty laugh. Vera Loving was a bit of a mystery herself.

Jordan Wyatt came in from work with a bitch of a headache. The telephone's loud peal made him wince. Tucking the receiver into his shoulder, he uncapped an aspirin bottle. Gaby's voice was a surprise; he hadn't seen her since the Houston Rodeo.

"Jordan, hello!" she said warmly. "I'm en route from the Valley on my way to Dallas. Can I overnight with you?"

Jordan hesitated, startled by his conflicted reaction. He'd

always enjoyed having Gaby as a houseguest. What had changed?

"What's the matter, bad timing?" she asked.

"No." He sighed and rubbed his aching brow. To find himself in the position of rejecting sexual pleasure with two women in the short space of two days struck him as ludicrous, considering that he was wound up like a coiled spring.

Hurting females was alien to his character, yet here he was, walking on eggshells again. "I'm just not up to fun and games right now."

"Ah, poor baby! Your allergies acting up again?"

Her cooing sympathy unsettled him further. "Gaby, I'm sorry—"

"Oh, that's all right, Jordan. I'll sleep in the guest room. No problem. See you in twenty minutes," she said, and hung up.

Jordan put down the receiver and hurriedly swallowed several aspirins. Why this reluctance to see Gaby again? More to the point, why was he so ambivalent about having her here tonight? Dammit, they were two mature, consenting adults, capable of picking up again from where they'd left off.

Not like Valentine, he thought, ranging around the living room like a caged tiger. He did not want to think about Valentine.

He made another lap around the room. It would help considerably if she'd just blend in with the other women he knew. But no, she was different, beguilingly so. Even now, with his head pounding and muscles aching, he had to smile, remembering. The way her hands flew about as she chattered in that breathy voice. The way she nibbled her lip in uncertainty. Her heart-clutching habit of tipping her head to one side and regarding him as if measuring his worth, making him hope rather desperately that he wasn't found wanting.

The wind chimes of her laughter, he thought, smiling softly. The sheer magic of her touch, her kisses. Sweeter than honeycomb. "Damn, Wyatt," he said, shaken by his vivid imagination. He could have had it all. But the cost was just too damn high. You didn't fool around with a woman like Valentine—

The doorbell rang. It was Gaby, undemanding, carefree Gaby.

He answered it, his mouth forming a warm, welcoming smile.

It died aborning. Gaby, in a miniskirt and cropped sweater that displayed hillocks of breasts and miles of long, lithe legs, was seduction personified. And he—a virile, red-blooded, Texan male—was dead from the waist down.

Chapter 11

That evening, Valentine dined in a restaurant high above downtown Houston. The music was "Mood Indigo" and the atmosphere quietly luxurious. Even the air smells sumptuous, she thought, flashing her companion a conspiratorial smile.

Sitting beside her, Deke Salander managed to keep his grin under his mustache. Deke knew he looked at home in these plush surroundings. The knowledge was richly satisfying; it had taken a long time to create his patina of unshakeable confidence.

The trick was to appear supremely at ease wherever he found himself, he thought expansively. He had developed personas for every situation: the good-old-boy with backcountry drawl; the impeccable gentleman; the polished, soft-spoken Texan of folklore; the cold, hard-eyed businessman. All stupid prejudices that could be used to advantage, even with Valentine.

"Which is the real man, Deke?" she'd once asked him, amazed at discovering yet another facet of his self-made personality.

"Damned if I know. Maybe all of 'em—maybe none," he'd replied. She had looked at him with affection—and what he took to be admiration—shining in those incredible eyes.

The memory graveled his voice as he asked, "This place meet with your approval, Valentine?"

Tilting her head, Valentine scowled at him. But her mouth twitched madly, ruining the effect.

"I'll reserve judgment until I've sampled the cuisine. But I am glad you honored my request not to go anywhere fancy," she harrumphed, eyeing him with feminine pleasure. Deke looked positively elegant in a dinner jacket. His snowy shirt was a superb foil for his tanned skin and glossy black hair, and the arrogance of power and wealth set well on his strong shoulders.

Even his mustache was in fine form! "Tonight was supposed to be my treat, you know," she ended with a rosy pout.

"Oh, it still is," Deke assured her.

Shifting on the velvet seat, he crossed one high-gloss leather boot, with gleaming alligator uppers etched with intricate designs, over the other. "And the food here is great, much better than that Tex-Mex place you mentioned, trust me."

"Huh. At least I could afford the food at that Tex-Mex place. And I could've worn my jeans, too."

Deke grinned. When he'd appeared on her doorstep earlier, one look at his beau monde attire had sent her flying upstairs to change clothes. "How's the wine, honey?" he asked, savoring the expensive stuff with a satisfaction that had little to do with taste. "You don't mind if I call you honey, do you?"

"Not in the least. And the wine's good," Valentine said innocently. She stretched out her legs and admired her own honey-colored, calf-skin boots with cocoa stitchery and embossed leather uppers. Deke had presented them to her when he'd picked her up for their date, and she promptly put them on. When asked how he knew her size—they fit perfectly!— he smirked and told her he knew everything.

Had he not dissuaded her, she would have worn her cowboy hat, too. Even with this soft-skirted dress, the boots looked snazzy. Rakish, she thought, turning her foot this way and that. She glanced around the room, noting the stylish women with their big hair and even bigger diamonds. None of them wore boots, but who cared? Not Deke, and therefore, not Valentine.

Watching her, he asked, "If I had given you fancy jewelry

instead of fancy boots, you'd have declined my present, right?"

"Are you crazy?" she retorted, widening her eyes comically. "I adore presents, of *any* kind."

"Even the kind that, ah, endanger your reputation as a lady?"

Her mouth drooped. "Especially that kind."

"Unseemly," he said knowingly.

"Yeah." She heaved a doleful sigh.

Deke laughed aloud.

Pleased by his enjoyment, Valentine patted his hand. He was so good for a woman's ego, especially one that had been seriously deflated. In his company she felt pretty and vivacious. She didn't have to wonder if he approved of her—he obviously adored her. And that felt damn good, she thought defiantly. It was a powerful antidote to the ache Jordan had created in her chest.

While Deke ordered their meal she got up and strolled to the window. The restaurant topped one of Houston's skyscrapers and the panoramic view was breathtaking. She wondered if Jordan would ever take her to a place like this. Probably not. This was not his milieu.

Would you feel the lack so terribly?

Valentine smiled as the soft, sly question flowed like an oil slick through her mind. Her blunt answer evoked another inner smile; lunch in a hamburger joint with Jordan beat pie in the sky anytime.

Deke came up beside her and draped an arm around her shoulders. "Nice view, hmm?" he asked with a proprietorial air.

He probably owns the darn place, she thought, smiling at him. "It's fabulous, Deke. What did you order us for dinner?"

"Kobe beef: A porterhouse for me, a filet mignon for you. It'll be delicious, I promise."

It was. Valentine thought she had never eaten such lusciously tender steak. "A person could get used to this sort of thing," she murmured, lifting her glass in salute.

Her gaze lingered on Deke's rugged face. A person could

get used to that, too. "I bet that's a real obstacle for you. I mean, how do you know what a woman wants from you when you have so many desirable attributes?"

Deke studied her over the rim of his glass. "You tell me."

"You mean what do I want from you? A fair question." She considered it. "Just to be your friend, I guess." Her mouth curved in an impish smile. "I know I'd sure as heck hate to have you for an enemy!"

His black eyes glinted. "You think I'd be a formidable foe?"

"I know you would," she said lightly. Her gaze leveled to his. "Speaking of friends, why do you count men like Reed Ballinster as one?"

His eyebrows shot up. "You don't like Reed? That's mighty quick judgment; you only met him that one time, the same night you met me, if memory serves me right."

"It's not judgment, it's discernment. I suppose he's very powerful and thus useful, but no, I don't like him. He has no principles, no personal integrity. You do. But tar will rub off regardless of how lightly you brush against it."

Deke regarded her with a puzzled frown.

Small wonder, Valentine thought, wishing she hadn't started this. "You're an honest businessman, Deke . . . for the most part, anyway," she plowed on. "Maybe a few deals that were, uh . . ." Her hands flew about like startled birds as she tried to skirt the hole each word deepened. "I mean, I know you've done things that probably won't bear close scrutiny. Like Sam said, you don't get rich by being nice. But there's a lot of good in you. I can see it and I can feel it. Furthermore, you've been blessed with the opportunity to make amends for . . . for whatever might be darkening your conscience."

Caught between amusement and affront, Deke sat back and stared at her. He wasn't accustomed to such candor. He didn't even know how to react to it.

"This is a damned peculiar conversation, but I've gone along with it this far, so . . ." Sarcasm etched his tone. "How can I make amends for my dastardly whatevers?"

"By using some of that money you've piled up to help others less fortunate than you."

"Ah, yes, of course. Now why didn't I think of that?" he asked himself.

Color swept her cheeks. "I'm sorry, that was presumptuous of me. I know nothing of your philanthropic activities."

"No, you don't," he agreed mildly. "So why am I being vilified?"

"I'm not vilifying you!"

"You're not, huh?" A sardonic smile crinkled his eyes. "Someone once said that every American aspires to be what every American despises, *rich*. Admittedly a sweeping indictment, but still, it fits a helluva lot of people. I didn't think it fit you, though."

"It doesn't, honest! I don't despise wealth or think any the less of you because you've got money. In fact, I envy you. It must feel great to make it to the top! And I've always thought how wonderful it would be if you were financially able to do things like . . ." She sighed, seeking the right words. "Sometimes I just ache to, well, to help people. You know, like when you hear or read about some woman who's taking care of several throwaway children without any help and she's months behind in rent, or some mission is trying desperately just to stay open . . . or a brilliant concept for helping retarded people help themselves is barely making ends meet because their funding depends on charitable donations. If you could step in and solve the problem just by writing a check, wow!" she said softly. "That must be a terrific feeling."

Deke's faint smile deepened the color in her cheeks.

Her chin came up. "Okay, so you're thinking I'm a sucker for a sad story. You may be right, I don't know. But I do know that you're worthy of love, honor and respect. And quite frankly, I don't think you're getting it from . . . from your inner circle. I think some of them are unfit to lick those handsome boots of yours and you ought to just cut 'em loose."

"You don't even know my inner circle." He signaled for the waiter.

"No, not personally. But feminine intuition tells me I'm

right. They need you lots more than you need them." She
wrinkled her nose. "End of sermon, cross my heart."

"Good," Deke grunted, more disturbed than he let on. She
was unnervingly direct. In the world he inhabited, saying exactly what you thought was both foolish and dangerous. He
turned his enigmatic gaze on her again. "It's been a while
since anyone worried about me. Feels kind of strange. But I
can take care of myself. Been doing it for a long, long time."

Looking up in time to catch her tender smile, Deke felt a
rocket slam into his excellent defenses. "You know, when I
first met you, I thought, 'With those eyes, she has to be an
angel.' Then you grinned at me, and while I didn't exactly
know what you were—beyond the cutest thing I'd ever seen—
well, an angel you definitely were not."

He ordered two brandies before continuing. "We've known
each other for five months now, and I'm still not a damn bit
closer to figuring you out," he confessed. "So what are you,
Valentine?"

Startled, she replied, "Just a woman, Deke." Her impish
grin got loose again. "Twenty-three and pure as the driven
snow, but otherwise, nothing special."

"Can't say I agree with that 'nothing special' stuff," Deke
drawled. An eyebrow winged up. "Pure, huh? Jesus!" He
began laughing. "You're still dating Jordan?"

Valentine blushed; she could practically see the thought
tickling his mind. "Now and then." She met his gaze although
she would rather not. "You were right, Deke, he is allergic to
commitment. Petrified, actually. I don't think the man knows
quite what to do with me," she ended with whimsical irony.

"I don't doubt that." Deke's chuckle grew into a satisfied
laugh. "Poor bastard's probably half-crazy by now!"

"Naw, to him I'm water off a duck's back!" Seeking a less
personal topic, she said, "Tell me about your ranch."

Deke hesitated, loathe to abandon the intriguing subject.
Shrugging, he replied lazily, "It's not big, as ranches go, only
a few thousand acres in the Hill country."

"A few thousand acres isn't big?"

"Naw, just an oversized backyard, that's all."

"Huh." Valentine watched as he lifted one of the gorgeous crystal snifters from the waiter's tray and swirled its tawny liquid. She accepted hers and took a fiery sip. "Whoa!" she gasped, eyes watering. "So . . ." She stopped and coughed. "What is the Hill country, anyway?"

"Just plumb pretty, honey," Deke said quietly. "It cleanses a man, you know? No matter how dirty you get, no matter how soiled your hands, when you return to the hill country, you're cleansed. It's like a diamond; hard, but beautiful, too. The water's clean enough to drink and the air's clean enough to breathe. Don't find that in too many places. It's rocky land, not too fertile, but it grows cattle. Grows some fine men, too."

"I know. I see one fine man it's grown."

Deke reddened at her soft declaration. "Well, it's got a little bit of a bad side to it. Sometimes the rains don't come for so long, you think the land's gonna dry up and blow away . . . dust so thick and white the foliage on the trees turns a dingy gray. But the trees survive and so do the people."

He paused for a sip of brandy. How much he loves his land, Valentine thought. The black eyes gleamed as he grinned at her, and she felt again the magnetic pull of an exceedingly virile male. She dared another sip of brandy. "So the ranch is your refuge, then."

"Yeah, I guess you could say that. I only bought it because that was one of those promises a raggedy, snot-nosed kid makes himself when his belly's hitting against his backbone."

Valentine, aware of the drama behind his casual tone, asked softly, "You had a tough childhood? Where were you born?"

"Near Harlingen, in the Valley. Grew up in the picking fields."

"Your parents were transients?"

"Never saw my father, so I don't know about him. My mother died when I was six." His musing gaze traveled beyond her to the unimaginable distance encapsulating his past. "Finally a family by the name of Cordoba noticed me hanging around the weighing shed and took me in. Made me a pallet alongside their own six kids."

"Where are the Cordobas now? Do you ever see them?"

He pulled his gaze back through time, to her tender face. "Twenty-one years ago they went back to Mexico and bought a fine house on a mountaintop high above the stink of Mexico City. No more hard labor for them, no financial worries."

"*You* did that for them," she put in.

The flush under his tanned skin was perceptible. "Yeah, another promise that hungry kid made to himself." He shifted, still not comfortable with unguarded conversation. "What about you? What kind of childhood did you have?"

"Mostly trauma free. I was always a little scared of my stepfather. He's one of those people who seem to have to keep a tight rein on themselves, you know? Keeps you on edge wondering what would happen if that rein snapped. But that's about it for trauma," she said, glossing over the last few years. "Looking back brings sweet memories: lilacs and fresh berries, waffles and hot syrup on a cold winter night, freshly washed sheets whipping in a spring wind, deep summer evenings redolent of suppertime and fireflies and kids laughing in the dusk . . ."

She glanced at him and shook her head. "Lord, I do get carried away, don't I! Okay, enough said. That's lovely music—would you care to dance with me, Sir Salander?"

On the tiny dance floor, Valentine came into his embrace testingly. The elixir of fine wine and brandy heated her blood and created a glowing pool of warmth in the pit of her stomach. She felt blazingly reckless. She ached to be held, wanted desperately to be kissed.

She wanted Jordan.

"Damn," she muttered and wound her arms around Deke's neck.

He had a good body, a hint of spreading waistline, but still strong and hard against her softness. She wondered about kissing him. What would his mustache feel like? Intensely curious, she cupped his head and placed her lips to his. Warm, firm, quite nice; she acknowledged. But no sparks, no head-spinning warmth radiating from every point of contact, no breathless loss of reality. Wishing she hadn't discovered the latter fact, she carefully withdrew from the kiss. It felt sinful playing fast and loose with his emotions.

"Sorry," she said. "Ordinarily I'm not so bold. It's that brandy you made me drink."

"I made you drink?"

He was laughing. Immensely relieved, she made some flippant retort and decided to put their relationship back on a safer level.

Good, an inner voice applauded her decision. *He isn't the man for you.*

Valentine marveled at her absurdly conflicted self, for even as she agreed with this assessment, another part of her mind was busily listing the many points in his favor: nice manners, manicured nails, good taste, a quick, humorous mind and he thought she was wonderful. All scoring points. He was well-to-do. *Rich*, she thought, making a moue at her primness. But hey, that counted. That counted a lot when one was looking at a man as the father of her children.

Not that she was looking. Just making an observation, she told herself. But still, a woman would be a fool to dismiss this attractive prospect out of hand.

Deke's arm tightened around her back, bringing them close again. Leaning his mouth to her ear, he said roughly, "Listen, little girl, don't you give your dreams to Jordan Wyatt. He'll break your heart, sure as hell."

Startled, Valentine stumbled over his feet. "Deke, that's an awful thing to say about Jordan!"

"Awful, but true."

Since she had lost any semblance of grace, Valentine stopped dancing. She stared at Deke, wondering if he was sincere, then realized with a hot rush of resentment that he was.

She knew he meant well. But she felt hostile. "It might be true right now, but people can change, Deke."

"A leopard can't change its spots no matter how much it might want to."

She let her hands drop to his shoulders. "People aren't leopards and that's a very cynical observation. People do change, given enough reason. It's called growing, Deke, not just intellectual growth, but spiritual and emotional growth as well. Otherwise, we just stay the same, making the same stupid mistakes and the same dumb choices because we draw the same half-baked conclusions. It's the living soul that makes the difference."

"My soul stopped living a long time ago," Deke said indifferently.

In a flash she rounded on him. "Don't you dare even think such a thing, Deke Salander! You're more than just this body—this body isn't you! It's just the house you live in; a wonderfully intelligent, dynamic, living house; but still just a useful vehicle. You, my dear friend, are immortal, and like it or not, you'd better start realizing you'll have to deal with that when you exit this world. *Judge not, lest you be judged.* And by the same narrow standards, you can bet," she wound up with ringing conviction.

Deke arched an eyebrow. "Hellfire and brimstone, Valentine?"

"Goodness no! I just meant . . ." She looked up at him, her lips twisting in wry admission. "Okay, okay, I was preaching. Again. Jeez, wouldn't Uncle George be proud of me!"

At that point, the music obligingly ended. Scarcely breathing, Valentine led the way back to the table. Anxiously she watched Deke for signs of anger. She'd said a lot more than she intended. Why the devil had she said anything at all? Why this compulsion to change him, free him from his self-made prison? She had never talked this freely with Jordan. She wouldn't dare. His opinion meant too much to her.

But Deke's meant a lot, too. Ill at ease, she sat down and clasped her hands, waiting for Deke to speak. He was probably horribly embarrassed.

Looking unperturbed, Deke settled himself beside her and signaled for another brandy. He grinned. "So who's Uncle George? And why would he be proud of you?"

The next day, eager to make up with Sam, Valentine told her all about her fabulous date with Deke. "And he kisses good, too," she confided.

Sam's green-eyed glance wasn't exactly hostile, but it wasn't friendly, either. "You planning to test out every man you meet, Valentine?"

"Well, no . . . Well, I just might!" Valentine's eyes narrowed as she caught the undertone in Sam's question. "Are you jealous because I kissed *your* man, Sam?"

"Oh, don't be ridiculous," Sam replied, straightening the lapels of her tailored white pantsuit. "I just don't think Deke Salander is someone to fool around with, that's all."

Valentine put another glass in the dishwasher. "You still have something against Deke?"

"Oh, he's okay, I guess. I just don't consider him a suitable match for you."

"Why not?" Valentine demanded, ready to defend him even though she herself was still smoldering over his negative remarks about Jordan.

"For one thing, he's old enough to be your father."

"That's a low blow, Sam! You make him sound like an old man. And he assuredly is not! He's attractive, vigorous—"

"No argument there." Sam closed her appointment book. "I simply meant that he's much older than you. And far more experienced. In everything."

"So maybe I'll learn something. Then I won't be such a simpleton."

"I didn't say you were a simpleton," Sam replied with vast patience. "Just green as grass."

"No argument there." Valentine glanced at her with a tiny smile. Sam stood with a hand on each hip, her mouth pursed in exasperation. "You know who you remind me of standing there like that, Sam? Aunt May, red-faced and proclaiming, 'Your whole future, just pissed away!' "

Sam gave a choked laugh. "Jesus, Val, talk about low blows! But okay, I give up. Trying to reason with you is like talking to a mule." She started toward the door. "Don't forget to call UPS and ask where the hell my packages are. They were due yesterday." On that grim note, she left.

Valentine watched her go with a troubled gaze. Maybe her cousin's mood was due to PMS, she mused. Whatever the cause, she hoped Sam got over it by the time she came back home tonight.

No such luck. The next two days passed without much change. Except for business-related matters, Sam spoke in monosyllables if at all.

Her mood was infectious. Valentine even caught herself snapping at Vera when she called to ask if they could get together. Instantly apologetic, she said, "I'd love to, Vera."

"Thanks, Val. I know I'm imposin', but I really do need to talk to someone and you're my best friend."

Valentine inwardly sighed as she sensed how troubled Vera was. She's practically emanating distress and I've been too self-absorbed to see it, she thought. And I still don't want to see it. I just want to roll back up into my fetal knot of self-ishness and shut out the world!

"And I want to listen, Vera. Give me ten minutes to clean up, then come on over. I'm making some fresh iced tea." Hanging up, she hurried upstairs to shower and dress.

Before returning to the kitchen, she paused by her photo table. Her mother's gentle nature radiated through the matte finish of her picture. Touching the frame, Valentine felt the familiar prick of guilt and sorrow. Although she'd talked with Julia just last night, she hadn't been at all convinced by her claim of being "fine, darling, just fine."

"It's my pain, too, Mom," she whispered. She tucked a fingertip kiss on her mother's picture, then ran downstairs.

Vera came in a moment later.

"Good timing, honey, the tea's ready," Valentine greeted her. She poured two iced teas and joined her friend at the table.

"What's wrong, Vera?" she asked without preamble.

Vera's cornflower blue eyes suddenly swam with tears. Quickly she lowered her head. "I don't know that it's wrong, exactly. But it's very hard to get a handle on, that's for sure." Her head lifted. "I'm pregnant."

The bald statement jarred Valentine into a sharp gasp. "My God, Vera!" she whispered as its many negative implications struck her sensitive heart. "Honey, are you sure?" she asked, for Vera's loose smock concealed any hint of impending motherhood.

Vera nodded. "I went out and bought one of those pregnancy tests. It was positive, so I bought another one, different test, same results. Since my periods are irregular, the best I can calculate is between four and five months. I know I don't look it, but I never get big with my babies."

"*Five months*! God, I'm just . . . this blows my mind, Vera!" Hastily Valentine lowered her voice and sought words that would neither wound nor deepen Vera's anxiety. "How do you feel about it? And Ozell? How's he taking it?"

"Dammit, I don't know how *to* feel about it!" Vera cried, wiping tears. "And I haven't told Ozell yet."

"I see. How does your heart feel about it?" Valentine reworded her question.

"Singin'. It's singin'," Vera said, looking embarrassed. "Stupid, given my history, I know that. But all those years I prayed so long and hard for another baby, a perfect, healthy baby boy, a son for Ozell." Her words became a rushing stream. "And now here I am, forty-two and pregnant and—oh, Val, is this some kind of cosmic joke? Christ, I'm so scared! And how am I gonna tell Ozell? He'll be so . . . Oh, hell, I don't know what he'll be," she ended with a weary sigh.

"He'll be supportive and loving, as usual." Valentine touched her hand. "Aren't there tests that will tell you if . . . that will tell you?"

"Yes, there's a test. Amniocentesis." Vera got up and walked to the sink to wash her face. She dried it, then turned with a wobbly smile as Valentine joined her. "But I'm afraid to take the test. I don't know if I could stand what it might tell me. I love my Shanna to death, but I—oh, Val, I just don't think I could bear having another Down's baby!"

Acting on an urge so deep and intense that it electrified her senses, Valentine suddenly spread both her hands over Vera's belly. Something ran through her fingers, something vital, something that connected with her own life force.

When she spoke, the words welled up from some ancient

source, firm, sure, absolute: "Do not fear, Vera. Your babies are perfect in every way."

Vera paled. "What . . . are you saying?"

Suddenly appalled by what she'd done, Valentine snatched back her hands. Ashen-faced, she stared at Vera. "Oh God, Vera, I don't know!"

"Yes, you do—you do, Valentine!" Vera whispered. "You *know*. I can see it in your eyes. You're psychic, aren't you? And you say my baby is perfect! Oh Jesus, thank you, thank you!"

Feeling stunned, Valentine shook her head. "Vera, I don't . . . I'm not . . . Maybe I am a little psychic, but I've never done anything like this before! Please, don't hold me to this," she pleaded. "I don't know what came over me—my God, to tell you such a thing! It's so—so presumptuous! I had no right to make such a statement, no right at all!"

"Yes, you did. You *did*, Val." Vera caught her shoulders. "Don't be afraid of your gift, just accept it and consider yourself blessed. I do!" Abruptly, she released Valentine and backed against the counter, her eyes enormous. "You said . . . oh God, you said my babies are perfect. My babies, Valentine!"

"Yes, I . . . yes, two—there are two," Valentine stammered. She was shaking like a leaf.

"Twins!" Vera choked. "And they're fine?"

"Yes, twins. And they're fine," Valentine echoed tonelessly. Tears spilled down her face as she heard her reassurance. It felt so right to give her despairing friend new hope. But it was such an enormous hope! And yet it felt so right.

"Valentine, do you believe this?" Vera pressed, unable to stop herself.

"Yes, I believe it," Valentine said, stronger now although she had no idea why. "So much so that I'll go with you to have that test."

"Oh, Valentine, don't cry. I know you're scared of giving me false hope, but I also know you wouldn't hurt me for the world. I've always felt you were different," Vera declared softly. "Special, you know? I trust what you said, enough so that I can go have that test now."

"Because of what I said." Valentine sighed.

"Because of what you said," Vera echoed with a piercingly sweet smile. "And you don't have to go with me, honey. I thank you for your kind offer, but Ozell and I can do it." She grabbed Valentine in a bone-crushing hug. "And I'll call you first thing we get the results."

"You'd better!" Valentine said, releasing a trembling breath. She was still confused about what she'd done. But the die was cast now. All she could do was wait.

And agonize.

And pray.

She did a lot of both during the rest of the day. Especially after Vera called to tell her the doctor's appointment was all set. "I'll tell Ozell tonight," she said.

"God Almighty," Valentine beseeched as she rang off. Vera's voice had been so joyous.

"And what if I'm wrong, Sam?" Valentine asked, after relating the incident to her cousin. "I've never done anything like that before. What if I'm wrong?"

Sam, visibly upset, flung her hands out in appeal. "Val, I swear, you're making me a basket case, you know that? First you read people's minds and now you read stomachs and predict twins, for God's sake! What next, séances? Right here in our living room? I mean, my God, do you believe what you said?"

"I believe that anything is possible," Valentine offered.

"Which means pigs will be flying soon? Oh, stop that, it isn't fair to cry," Sam snapped, sighing. "All right, all right, let's try to put a positive spin on this. At least you gave her the courage to go to the doctor and take that test. Which is what she should have done in the first place, but that's beside the point. Because of you, she'll have intelligent feedback from medical people—"

"Instead of spooky feedback from a weirdo," Valentine finished for her. "Okay, you're right, she did need to get herself to a doctor. So if I motivated her, well . . ."

"The ends do not justify the means, Valentine," Sam said. "Now stop wallowing in whatever it is you're wallowing in and leave me to shower in peace."

"You could be a little more supportive," Valentine said, but kept it beneath her breath. She knew that Sam had her own problems. Part of the redhead's angst centered around Clay. He made her feel vulnerable and no longer in charge of a relationship, which was a serious affront to Sam's carefully constructed self-image.

Valentine had no trouble understanding that particular feeling. Even so, Sam's crankiness wasn't easy to live with. By the weekend her own frustration was screaming for an outlet. Happily, she found one.

"I'll be damned," Clay declared as he hung up the telephone.

"What's the matter?" Jordan asked.

"That audacious little spitfire!" Clay jumped up from his desk. "She took out the wall! Can you believe it? She got herself a sledgehammer and took out the frigging wall."

Jordan made the connection in seconds. "Valentine?"

"Valentine. Just knocked it down, Sam says. Rubble all over the place. And somehow it's all my fault," he marveled.

Jordan hid a grin. "The wall between the dining room and whatever?"

"Yeah. She'd just finished her demolition derby when Sam walked in. They had a screaming contest, Sam says, but is she repentant? Hell, no! Valentine, I mean, not Sam. Sam's apologizing all over the place."

"The wall you promised to remove when they took the house?"

Clay scowled at him. "I don't recall making any such promise. And now I'm to send someone out there to fix it. Well, I will, but Valentine's getting the bill, by God she is."

"Oh, sure she is," Jordan said, letting loose his bedeviling grin. "Face it, Clay, you're a mooncalf when it comes to those two women. You'll growl and rant a little, then you'll fix it."

"You're right." Clay sighed. "I am soft in the head on that

point, but so are you, my friend. They've got both of us wrapped around their little fingers."

"The hell you say," Jordan snorted, grabbing his jacket. "Speak for yourself, friend. I passed that stage a long time ago. Immune to 'em now."

"Uh-huh." Clay got his jacket, too. "Well, let's go and check the damage. I assume you are coming along?"

"Yeah, I'll follow you there." Despite his poker face, a laugh rumbled in his belly as Jordan strode to his truck. "Dammed sledgehammer's probably bigger than she is," he told Clay. The humor of the situation overwhelmed him and he threw back his dark head in riotous laughter.

His amusement lessened the closer he drew to Valentine Townsend. Why the hell had he tagged along? This was Clay's problem, not his.

The hunger in his gut had a ready answer; he hadn't seen her in over a week, and he just flat-out missed her. Which brought up another plaintive *why?* She had already proved she could tie his brain up in knots and turn him into a babbling idiot. His memory didn't need refreshing.

He parked in the circular drive and slowly got out. He ought to keep a prudent distance between them. Like a mile or two, he thought half-humorously. But to do so would mean sacrificing something he very much enjoyed, the elusive element of something rare and wonderful that seemed to reside only in this house.

The simple act of stepping through her door had all the tantalizing qualities of a long-ago Christmas morning. "Val?" he called.

"She's outside somewhere; would you get her?" a harassed Sam asked him. "Tell her to get in here and face the music."

"Yes, ma'am," Jordan said. He glanced at Clay with a straight face, then strolled back outside, whistling. "Yo! Valentine?"

"Around here."

The sound of her soft voice pulled him on leash to the side of the house. Valentine sat in a secluded bower formed by rampant wisteria vines. White clematis flowers flickered among its deep green foliage. Jordan picked one and gave it to her with the courtly grace that came so easily around her—if he didn't think about it.

"Thanks, Jordan." She lowered her nose to the flower, then looked up at him and said wryly, "Guess you've heard I went insane and destroyed a piece of Clay's house?"

"Um-hum." He leaned against a tree. "Sam says you've got to come in and face the music. Big music, too; Clay's declared himself rendered fine as lard by your audacity."

Her lashes fanned down. "It's not funny. Sam's mad at me again. So's Clay. I don't know what all the fuss is about. It wasn't a load-bearing wall, it wasn't even original to the house. Someone just slapped it up and carved a door in the ugly thing. Just ruined the dining room. But you'd have thought I took a wrecking ball to the whole house, the way Sam carried on. Seems like I can't do anything right lately, not where she's concerned."

The quiver in her voice caught Jordan's breath in a long sigh of conflict. Her shoulders were hunched, and that annoyed him. Gently he drew her to her feet. The glint of tears on her lashes was another sharp stab. "Oh, honey, it'll be all right," he said helplessly, and gathered her to him.

She put her arms around his neck and lifted her face in a gesture so natural he was powerless to resist the need it expressed. He kissed her. And kept on kissing her. Because she was kissing him back. Also because he simply forgot to stop.

It went on and on. Time stood still in their leafy bower; reality slipped away. Her lips opened and his tongue plunged in and drowned itself in honeyed wetness. Hands with a will of their own slid down her slender back and into achingly soft curves. She made a little moaning sound and that was lovely, too. He pressed her closer when it was impossible to press her any closer and still remain erect; he kissed her until his senses reeled and anything was possible.

"Valentine," he whispered with burning intensity, feeling her seductive little wriggle as a shuddering thrill. She moved against him again and it felt so good that his mind spun a kaleidoscope of utterly glorious images.

The tantalizing pressure of her belly expanded his fantasies until, for a wild, crazy instant, she was naked in his bed and he was lost somewhere between insensible rapture and flaming delirium.

She wriggled again. Jordan groaned as he realized just why she was moving so much. Not to excite him. To *escape* him. This was so incredible that he wrapped both arms around her.

There was no doubt as to her desire, or to his. Yet her palms were pushing, not angrily, but slowly, and curve after curve was withdrawing from the aroused flesh and muscle that blindly followed. With huge and gallant effort, Jordan loosened his clasp.

Thick, dark lashes veiled her eyes. Her mouth had a soft, swollen look from his kisses, and he hungered mightily to take it again. Her throaty plea stayed his intent.

"Jordan, please." Her cool fingers laced around his face. "Please, I'm just too tired for this tonight."

The words bounced across his mind and made no sense whatsoever. Jordan stared at her with baffled wonder. My God, he thought, and for an instant he didn't know which was more astonishing, that he could still think, or that she could wreak such havoc in the space of a moment. His heart was pounding; his breath coming in short, hard bursts; and a fire blazed merrily in his groin.

This obdurate passion, he thought, deeply shaken. This magnificent woman. And this poor, wickedly tormented man. Why was he drawing her closer and dropping tiny kisses on her hair? And why, he wondered furiously, did she make him feel he was standing on the edge of an abyss between warm, familiar ignorance and the alarming threat of brilliant insight and discovery?

There were no answers and he was accustomed to being answered. Jordan was just getting up a good head of steam when her eyes opened. On the instant his indignation drizzled away, replaced by throat-strangling tenderness. Of course she was tired, he chastised his impatience. Hadn't she just knocked down an entire wall?

The peach-glow of sundown revealed faint lavender shadows under her eyes. He brushed a kiss there, then went on to solace the soft droop of lips, her smooth cheeks, that pointed little chin, before he got his mouth under control. She sighed and leaned her head to his chest. He held her as if he held the rarest, most fragile of porcelains. When a man's a fool, Jordan thought wearily, he might as well be a fool all the way.

He blew out a long breath. "You're the only woman I've ever met who can do this to me. What happens when we get together is wholly incredible. Instantaneous combustion. Absolutely mind-blowing."

"I'm the only one?" she asked with a swift upward glance.

He laughed. "The only one. Which is a good thing, because otherwise I doubt I'd have survived this long," he ended dryly.

Her pleased smile was ample reward for his not-entirely-a-joke response. Rummaging through the rags of his self-discipline, Jordan stitched together enough to help him step away from her. "You okay now?" he asked, giving her pert nose a little tweak. "I need to get on home and clean up, get something to eat. And you, Ms. Townsend, need to go in and face the music, let ole Clay stomp and roar a little more. He needs to get it out of his system before he chokes on it," he confided.

She giggled. "Okay, I'll take my medicine like a good little girl." They parted at the steps. "Jordan?" she called as he headed for his truck. "Call me?"

He stopped, feeling in danger of taking root here. An unruly part of him turned around and replied, "I'm having a small party Sunday night. Want to play hostess?"

"Okay!"

"Okay. I'll call you with the rest of the details." *As soon as I know what they are myself,* he thought but did not say.

"Jordan? What about Gaby?"

He blinked. "What about Gaby?"

"Maybe she's accustomed to being your hostess. I mean, you two have been friends for a long time."

He frowned. "Yeah, we have, but I asked you, didn't I?" That radiant smile lit her face again. "Seven o'clock," he said, stern as hell. He turned on his heel and strode to the car, his mind on Sunday night. Now he had to find some people to come to a party he hadn't even planned on having.

"Jordan's leaving," Clay said, glancing out the dining room window. "You think he got our wildcat tamed down?"

"I hope so." Sam sighed. "Clay, thanks for not blowing a gasket. You had every right to; seems like you've had nothing but trouble since we rented this house from you," she said, twisting her hands. "All the renovations you okayed, the new appliances, new flooring; just one thing after another." She glanced at the raw scars of Valentine's remodeling efforts. "And now this. I just don't know what to say, or even what to think about Valentine's behavior. She's changed so much in the past few months!"

"Oh, come on, Sam," Clay said, shifting with discomfort. "She gave me fair warning, didn't she? Told me the wall had to come down! I just didn't take her seriously. A mistake I won't make again, I assure you."

Sam averted her gaze. "That doesn't absolve her. Or explain her. Sometimes I feel like I don't know her anymore, that I'm living with a stranger!" she burst out angrily. "Like someone has taken away my sweet, malleable little Mouse and replaced her with this . . . this alien!"

Clay smiled and took her hand. "While I doubt she's actually been replaced by an alien, I do agree that she's changed since I've known her. Maybe she's just growing up, Sam."

"I don't want her growing up!" Sam blurted. She flushed as her words rang through the room. "I mean . . . oh, hell, I don't know what I mean."

"I think you meant exactly what you said, Sam," Valentine declared quietly from the doorway. "And I love you so much that I wish with all my heart that I could oblige you. But I can't. Apparently it's an autonomous condition; happens whether you want it to or not." Her gaze went to Clay. "Clay, dear Clay, what can I say . . . Jeez, listen to me, I'm a poet and didn't know it," she murmured with a quick, mischievous grin. "Anyway, I'm sorry for breaking your wall and I apologize. I will pay whatever it costs to clean up what I have wrought.''

"Damn right you will," Clay growled. "And I accept your apology." He smiled at Sam. "Now that we've got that all cleared up, what say we get a bite to eat?" His expression underwent a severe change as he looked at Valentine again. "If you promise to behave yourself, you can come, too."

"Thank you, Clay, but I think I'll stick around here. I may go out for a while myself later."

"Go out where?" came Sam's prompt inquiry.

Valentine shrugged. "Oh, I don't know. Just out." Sidling closer, she kissed Sam's cheek. "I love you, Sam."

"Valentine . . ." Sam sighed and looked at Clay. "Okay, okay, I'll shut up. Just be careful, will you? It's a jungle out there. God, I can't believe I said that. Good night, Mouse. Let's go, Clay, while I'm still coherent."

Mouse. Shaking her head, Valentine curved an arm around Sam's waist and walked with her to the porch. "G'night, you guys, have fun. And don't hurry back on my account!" she called as they started down the drive.

With the old house quiet again, Valentine felt too lonely to go back inside. She sat down in the porch swing. The creaking of its chains filled the silence. Night crept down, bringing its own kind of loneliness, poignant and sensual. The desire Jordan's kisses had aroused eddied and flowed like a living current. It ached. She couldn't believe how much it ached, a hot, throbbing demand deep within her body. Pressing her thighs together only intensified it. At length she got up and strolled through the dewy yard, heedless of wet slippers.

"So now what, Valentine?" she mumbled, growing impatient with her aimless ramble. She didn't know *now what*. All she really knew was that she wanted to make love with Jordan Wyatt; wanted it with a clean, fiery passion that simply would not be denied.

He'd felt it, too, she assured herself. He had kissed her with such profound passion . . . wasn't there something profound about it?

"The only one," he had said. Didn't that mean something

more than the sum of its words? And the way he'd held her, so sweetly, with such exquisite tenderness. Of course, he was by nature a tender man. But still . . .

Why not just go to him?

"What, and swallow what pride I've got left? Not on your life!" The words erupted in a geyser of ego-alarm.

Valentine sighed. "Besides, my pride's such a tiny thing, I doubt I could even find it," she muttered. Absently she placed a hand on the rough trunk of her tree—and recoiled with a startled gasp. She could actually feel life surging through the gnarled old oak.

Imagination, she told herself. But even about that she wasn't sure.

Suddenly fed up with her indecisiveness, she whirled around and raced back to the house, up the stairs, into the bathroom. A quick shower with gardenia-scented soap, a swift rubdown, an even swifter slide into red bikini panties and matching bra. She was acting on pure, primal impulse and she knew it, so it was better not to question. She slithered into a red sundress, found some slippers and flew downstairs again. If she stopped to think, she'd grow fainthearted and start worrying about where her romantic nature was leading.

Her hair had come loose; she brushed it as she drove. Doubts about the wisdom of what she meant to do laid siege to her mind. Simultaneously she felt an almost primordial need for haste. Her foot pressed down, lead-weighted, on the gas pedal. *Hurry, hurry, hurry!* The urgent words sang through her head.

It was only when she stood in the hallway outside Jordan's door that the fullness of her intentions struck home. Suddenly weak-kneed with fear, she leaned against the wall. What on earth was she doing here! He'd rejected her once; what made her think he wouldn't do it again? That brief, unsatisfying bit of lovemaking under the wisteria bower?

"He just kissed you, that's all," she reminded herself. A few kisses did not constitute an invitation to a man's bedroom.

She couldn't chance it. She wouldn't chance it. Not again. "If I had an ounce of sense I'd go home. And I do have an ounce of sense, so . . .'' She took a few steps, stopped again. "Oh, *blast*," she hissed, and suddenly laughed. She had to laugh—this was getting too damn weird! She turned back to the door.

Valentine, Valentine, a soft inner voice chided. Why are you so hesitant? Love is worth any risk, don't you know that? With all its fire and passion, its glorious anticipation, its challenging doubt and anxiety, love is one of Earth's richest experiences. It's a celebration of the emotions, a bacchanal of feelings! Don't be afraid, dear one—embrace the risk, delight in the challenge. Live, Valentine!

Shaken by the vibrant joy in that admonition, Valentine stiffened. Who had spoken? Where was the source of this mysterious voice? In her mind, yes, but where in her mind?

The scent of hyacinths wafted around her, then vanished like the illusion it must be. She tried to use the same old argument, but it didn't work this time; she couldn't recall ever talking to herself like that. The flowery words, even the cadences, were not symptomatic to her manner of speech. But if they weren't her thoughts . . .

Oh, for goodness sakes, of course they were her thoughts! They had poured through her mind like a glorious golden shower.

And yet, and yet . . .

A sudden rush of love filled her to overflowing. "Celestial love," Valentine whispered, her mouth curving sweetly, tenderly. "Whatever part of me spoke just then, I thank you." She listened as if for an answer. "Is this what's meant by the Biblical injunction to love thyself?" she murmured, eyeing the ceiling.

Another possibility struck her, making her shiver. "Is this you, Elisse?"

Don't be afraid, Valentine. Cast out your fear, my darling girl.

The voice whispered away like wind passing through the trees, heard but not seen, but most surely there. And most surely coming from a source other than herself, Valentine decided.

Grandmother Fiona? No. Ahead of her generation Fiona might be, but she would not be urging her granddaughter into a man's bed!

Valentine laughed and placed a coral-nailed fingertip on the doorbell. Whatever the explanation, she felt more confident, a little braver. She gave the bell another push.

Remember what you've learned about Jordan.

The reminder flowed through her mind like the whisper of silk. Before she could decide how to react to it, Jordan opened the door.

Chapter 12

Jordan wore a stunned expression and the bottom half of navy silk pajamas. He was so beautiful he took her breath away.

Valentine cleared her throat. "Hi, Jordan."

"Valentine! What are ... I mean ... well, this is a surprise."

"A nice surprise, I hope," Valentine replied, wishing that she could see what lay beneath his exterior reaction. His hair was rumpled. She glanced beyond him, past the foyer into the living room. A single lamp shed its pale radiance, and music whispered in the background.

What if he had company? The appalling question rolled across her mind like a thunder clap!

"Oh God, I didn't think—it just never occurred to me, I swear!" she said in a hoarse whisper. "But if you do, I'll leave."

"If I do what?" Jordan asked, utterly baffled.

"If you're with someone ..."

"No, I'm not with anyone, I'm alone."

"Oh. Well, then!" she said, breathing again. A slow, secret smile played around the corners of her mouth as her gaze roamed the contours of his naked chest. Lazily she met his turbulent blue eyes. "Well, may I come in, Jordan?"

"Oh! Yes, of course." He plowed both hands through his hair. "Please, come in, Valentine."

"Thank you." Valentine's dignified response masked the feathery laughter tickling her throat. She loved seeing him so flustered! It empowered her.

Only the tiniest twitch of mouth betrayed her amusement, but Jordan noticed it. He reddened. "You'll have to forgive me, I'm a little rattled. It is after ten and I . . . I guess you're about the last person in the world I expected to see."

"Would you rather I go?" she asked, making no move to enter.

"Christ, no! I just want to be sure you know why you're here. Me, too, for that matter." He drew her inside and shut the door. "Why this unexpected visit? Spur of the moment?"

"No, I gave it some thought." Valentine walked into the living room and stopped in front of a window. Down below, stretching out into the distance, lights glittered like a handful of jewels strewn by a careless hand. "Beautiful view, Jordan," she said with a catch of breath. He had come up behind her and his clean, spicy scent wove a cloak of warmth around her senses.

"Thanks. I like to sit here at night, have some wine, think, plan—"

"Brood."

He laughed. "That, too. Well. Please, sit down, make yourself at home. That's an attractive dress. Would you like some wine? This is an excellent red." He gestured at the wine he'd been enjoying.

"No, thank you."

"A soft drink then. Or a wine cooler?"

"No. Nothing, thank you." She shook back her hair.

Jordan inhaled sharply. "Are you going to tell me why you're here? Or just leave me twisting slowly in the wind?"

His strained attempt at humor pleased her. "I'm here because we've left too many things hanging, Jordan. I want to finish what we started on the boat."

Jordan savaged his hair some more. "Are you sure, Valentine?" he asked. When she nodded, his smile grew absurdly tender. She stood with a hand on her hip, as delicate as a flower and resolute as an oak.

He brushed her cheek with the back of his hand. "Honey, maybe we should talk."

"Maybe we shouldn't." Rising up on her toes, she wound her arms around his neck and reached for his mouth with hers. When their lips touched, she sought to deepen the sweetness of contact by swaying into him. If he didn't touch her now, if he didn't respond to her ardent invitation, she would die, Valentine thought giddily.

Her breath of relief whispered out on his lips as he locked her in his arms and pulled her closer. For a moment he kissed her with unconcealed hunger. Then he broke off and leaned his forehead against hers.

"Listen, Val, if this goes much further, I won't be able to stop," he said hoarsely. "It's been too damned long, baby, and I—dammit, I'm not made of steel!"

"Feels like you are," she murmured.

He swore, mixed it into a strangled laugh and pulled her tighter against him. His kiss was almost punishing. A delicious warning, she thought. She closed her eyes and simply clung like a limpet, soft, boneless, infinitely yielding.

"Valentine," he tried again, his voice ragged. "I don't know if this is right."

"It's right—you know it is," she replied breathlessly.

"I mean for you. It's you I'm—"

"Hush, darlin'," she chided. She kissed him again, her tongue flickering through his lips like touches of fire.

He groaned and ran his hands down her supple curves.

Sensation flamed through her entire body. She expanded the kiss, her whole being riding on it, imploring him with her mouth, her fingers, her low, sultry murmurs.

"I can't take any more of this," Jordan muttered. To her delight, he swept her up and carried her to his bedroom.

"A fine way to get around," Valentine said, laughing as he kicked the door open. A lamp on the night table illuminated the ivory-walled room and she had a blurred impression of a huge, rumpled bed with a brass headboard.

"Who rumpled the bed?" she asked as he set her down.

"Me. I turned in early but couldn't sleep."

Satisfied, she stepped away from him to turn off the lamp.

"No, baby, leave it on," Jordan said, "I want to see you."

Valentine dropped her hand and formed a careless smile. Drawing aside her hair, she turned her back to him. He unzipped her dress, then slipped it off her shoulders. The soft material flowed over her hips and fell in a scarlet pool around her feet.

His sharp intake of breath filled her with fierce exultance. She shivered as he stepped in close behind her and cupped her breasts. The firm little globes fit snugly into his hands. The sensation was lovely; rough skin against soft, tender flesh. When his lower torso brushed against her buttocks, she could feel his excitement made manifest in hard, needful flesh.

In a surge of hot impatience, Jordan turned her to face him. "You are very beautiful," he said.

It sounded mechanical, something said by rote. Valentine looked up at him and felt a bone-weakening thrill. It wasn't mechanical. His lips were parted and he was looking at her as if she were food and he was a very hungry man.

"So very beautiful," Jordan whispered. Her hair gleaned like ebony silk against her ivory skin. Her tiny waist made the richly rounded curves of her hips a visual feast for masculine eyes. Black and curly, her pubic hair had been shaped, bikini-style, into a loin-heating vee. His mouth was dry and his heart pounded. She was an exquisite ivory figurine, and he was going to kiss every inch of her.

Slipping off his pajamas, he stepped toward her, gathered a handful of hair and let it pour through his fingers like liquid silk. Her gaze stayed on his face and he was drowning in those violet eyes! "Oh, Valentine, do you know how lovely you are?" he asked, deeply, reverently.

She shook her head.

Jordan stared at her. "But you must have been told—"

"I've never undressed in front of a man before," she confessed with a winsome smile.

He licked his lips. "I—don't understand."

"Oh, Jordan." She sighed. "Will you freak out if I tell you this is my first time?"

"Your first time," he repeated dumbly. "You mean you're
. . . Jesus, Val, you're a virgin?"

"Why so stunned?" she asked, finally succeeding in arching an eyebrow.

"Because I *am* stunned, dammit! You're so—I just don't
see how you could still be a virgin when . . ." Jordan shook
his head. "But you are? Ah God," he groaned, realizing what
this meant. They couldn't make love. He couldn't take his
pleasure with a virgin. Not *this* one. He cared too much to
screw around with Valentine Townsend. That didn't make
much sense at the moment, but it was how he felt.

Breathing hard, he stared at her. Her lashes promptly fanned
down and she nibbled her bottom lip. He mauled his hair and
groaned again. She was standing there temptingly naked and
he was standing here buck-naked and so hard he ached—and
now she tells him? Jordan staggered, nearly overcome with
the irony of it. For so long he'd battled his natural instincts
and now . . . His laugh snarled in his throat like a tangle of
blackberry vines.

"Jordan? What's wrong?" she asked softly.

"What's wrong?" he echoed, incredulous. "You wait until
we're practically in bed to tell me you're a virgin, and you
ask what's wrong?"

"I should have told you sooner," she conceded. "But I was
anxious about how you'd react." Her lips quirked in that endearing way. "Which I had every right to be, I'm thinking!"
Lowering her voice, she smiled up at him. "Don't stop now,
Jordan. I fear I'll ignite if you do."

A strangled laugh burst through Jordan's throat. "Valentine,
Valentine, what am I going to do with you?" The question
was posed more to himself than her. Sighing, Jordan cradled
her face. "Sweetheart, you must know how much I want you,
I haven't been too good at concealing it."

"So what's the big deal, then?"

"The big deal is that you're not just any woman," he said
irritably. "You're someone I've grown fond of and that makes
a difference. Honey, what I said on the boat—"

"Still goes," she finished for him. "I know. But that

doesn't apply here, because that's not what I expect from this
. . . this affair.''

"All right, I accept that," he said. "But what do you expect, then?"

"Exactly what I bring into it: respect, admiration, caring,"
she said succinctly. "I respect you as a man, I like and admire
you as a person, and I care for you as a friend. Obviously I
think these feelings are mutual or I wouldn't be here. Because
it would trivialize our lovemaking if they weren't, and I
couldn't . . ." She shrugged. "Well, I just couldn't. Is it mutual, Jordan?"

Jordan growled her name deep in his throat. "Dammit, if it
wasn't mutual, I wouldn't be standing here arguing with you!"

"Wonderful!" came her throaty murmur. Her fingertips
played a riff down his bare back, causing him to shiver. "If
you want to hear me say it, then I will, Jordan. I want to make
love with you. *Now*. Right now." Her nails traced erotic patterns across the naked flare of his hips. "Right . . . this . . .
minute."

"God, what you do to me!" he muttered thickly. She gave
another sultry laugh. Jordan caught his breath as her fingers
reached his belly. *The hell with it. I've got to have her*! He
cupped her luscious little rump, pulled her in close, ravished
kisses on her taunting mouth. When he drew back, she broke
the embrace and gestured to the bed. He grinned, pleased by
her impatience. It was then that he became aware that she
hadn't really looked at him. Catching her arms, he turned her
to face him. She fingered the hair on his chest, but her gaze
stayed above his waist.

Perplexed, he asked, "Valentine, haven't you ever seen a
naked man before?"

The soft wave of color traveled visibly up her breasts to her
cheeks. "Well, of course," she said with a charming touch of
indignation. "I've lots of boy cousins, you know."

"I said a man, not a boy. There's a difference, honey."

Her blush deepened.

"Valentine, look at me," he commanded.

Obeying, Valentine felt a vivid shock at the sight of his

smooth, muscular body. Her cheeks burned. She was behaving like a teenager rather than the mature woman she was! But naked men are so disturbing, she thought in hot confusion.

"You're right," she said, dry as alum. "There's a helluva lot of difference between a boy cousin and a full-grown man."

Jordan drew her back into his arms. "Oh, baby, don't be afraid of me, I won't hurt you. Valentine . . ." Desire coursed through him like living fire. He sought to restrain it. He had to be gentle, but his thickening voice attested to the strain on his embattled self. All the nights, weeks, months of pent-up passion were explosively evident.

"Ah God," he groaned as his hands escaped to fill hungry fingers with deliciously soft, naked woman, bringing her into him until they touched with an intimacy too electrifying to resist.

Her nipples were hot little points on his chest.

"Oh, baby, I can't—God, you get me so hot, I want to—how on earth did you stay a virgin this long?" he rasped.

"I'm just picky, Jordan," she responded, her breathing quick and shallow. "And you're the man I've picked to be my teacher. No one else ever got past first base." She smiled. "That makes you kind of special, don't you think?"

Jordan's reaction rendered him temporarily speechless. Mind-numbing warmth spread through him in caressing waves even as the pressure of the situation hit home. Groaning, he buried his face in her hair. Her heady scent engulfed his senses until he reeled with it. Gently, gently! he reminded himself. But the blaze in his loins raged out of control as he gripped her hips and lifted her up until he was hard against that be-witching valley.

She melted into him in a sweet, sweet fusion of bodies and mouths. Jordan tumbled backward onto the bed without re-leasing his hold on his woman.

Valentine gasped aloud. The feeling of naked skin on naked skin took her breath. Mindlessly she clung, her body hot and eager for possession. The urge to get closer was a strident command. She didn't know what to do, where to touch. So she lay still and just reveled in the sensations sweeping through her in vast, sensuous waves.

For a long time Jordan simply kissed her, deep, hungry, exploring kisses, on her face, her neck, her arms, the soft, inner skin at her wrists. Her uptilted breasts were delicious, the soft little buds rousing as he sucked and nibbled. He kissed her tiny waist and each rounded hip. Her flat little belly was like silk under his lips . . . her navel a hollow which he probed before moving down to her knees. He traced sensuous patterns down her slender calves to the top of each small foot and back up to the moist warmth of her inner thighs. He buried his mouth deep in her pubis, his tongue searching, finding, tasting. The sensitive bud of womanly pleasure was dusky-sweet to his tongue.

"Oh, Valentine, you taste so good, so good . . . God, you are sweet!" he muttered thickly without raising his mouth from her fragrant skin.

Valentine trembled at the sensation of his voice vibrating against intimate flesh. He nuzzled deeper, parting her tumid lips, and he was kissing her where she had never been kissed . . . and it felt . . . odd . . . it felt . . . she didn't know how it felt. The pressure building up in her loins was such exquisite pain. She caught his head and pressed it down to bring his mouth against the source of that fire, but this wasn't quenching it. She writhed under his caresses with a low, guttural moan.

His fingers entered her, found resistance, and she tensed. Jordan immediately withdrew them, but he'd felt the lubricant of her excitement, and he could take no more of this delectable torment. He lowered himself upon her and parted her thighs.

"Valentine, relax, don't . . . tighten up, honey," he panted. He felt monstrous, so huge and swollen he couldn't possibly . . .

And then he was.

Groaning her name, he plunged into her with wild, incendiary pleasure. He heard her sharp hiss of breath. One part of his mind yet cautioned him to go easy. *Slow down, Wyatt!* that thinking part of him warned. But he had never been so high, never experienced such volcanic excitement or felt so helpless to control it. Within seconds he lost command of these powerful forces. They splintered in a convulsive burst of release.

Valentine shut her eyes. So this was it, she thought dully. She also thought she had never been so disappointed in her life. After that first stinging bite of pain, his deep thrusts were intensely pleasurable and she was just beginning to feel so good—and now this. She hadn't really expected the clash of cymbals and bells ringing and all that crap. She furiously defended her urge to cry. But certainly she'd expected more than this. Where the hell was ecstasy? She felt totally cheated.

It was laughable in a way. In a very small way. All the hours spent wondering, fantasizing, dreaming. And now this. She laid her fingers on his shoulders with exact placement, and waited.

"Valentine." His voice was a harsh gasp of insufficient air.

She felt his heart thudding against her breasts. Was it supposed to pound like that? She tried desperately to recall something from her novels, but her mind wasn't working. She really would like to cry.

In slow motion, Jordan raised his head to meet violet eyes watching him with half a dozen different emotions, none of them good. Confusion tinged them, deepening their vibrant hue until he thought he could fall into them and vanish if he ever let himself go.

"Ah, Valentine," he whispered, kissing her twist of lips. "Honey, I'm sorry, I lost control."

Her gaze met his, dead-level. "You mean you screwed up."

"Uh, yes, in a manner of speaking. Val, I am sorry," he said urgently.

Looking deep into his eyes helped Valentine choose her reaction. "Why did you screw up?" she asked curiously.

"Because I . . . you . . ." Jordan expelled a breath as he felt the bitterness of his confession fade to irony. "Because it was too long needed, that's why!" he half roared.

Her tiny, wicked smile eased his mind considerably.

"But now we can concentrate on showing you what making love is all about, honey," he asserted, his confidence reviving.

One screwup was surely his limit for the night. Withdrawing, he rolled off her fragile body.

She slid to the edge of the bed and stood up. When he caught her gaze, color swept her cheeks again. Her awkwardness clenched his heart. God, she was such an innocent! She really was, he thought with renewed shock. In this age of liberated women who grabbed his cock before he had a chance to grab at anything, it seemed incredible that she could be so sexually inexperienced.

He parried a stab of guilt. There was no reason to feel like a knave. He'd had to have her, had to taste the intimate sweetness concealed/revealed by those bewitching eyes. She wouldn't regret her choice of teacher, he vowed.

When she emerged from the bathroom he lay waiting, his hands folded behind his head. She glided across the carpet, set a hand to each hip and looked down at him with a provocative smile.

"Are you too tired to continue, Jordan? I could perhaps take up this lesson at another time ... or with a less exhausted teacher," she purred.

"Oh God! Come here, woman!" With an exultant laugh he reached out and pulled her supple body down atop him. Happily he let his hands loose in the glory of her hair.

She wriggled. "My goodness, you feel good," she said in pleased surprise.

Jordan grinned. "You don't feel so bad yourself, honey." Gently he turned her on her side, then guided her hand down between his legs. "Touch it, Valentine. It's not so frightening, is it?" he teased.

She snatched her hand back. "Jordan, I'm not a child; if I want to hold it, I'll do it," she rebuked. Then her fingers curled around his penis as though she held a broomstick.

He bit his lip. "Um, well, but not like that, like this." His voice deepened as silken fingers caressed him, altering his flesh to a hard shaft that throbbed in the palm of her hand. "Oh, yes, like that, baby. Like that."

At first Valentine was too overwhelmed to let herself go completely. It seemed imperative that she hold her innermost self in reserve, taking all the pleasure he had to give her while still protecting her emotions. But she kept forgetting why, and even how. He was kissing all around her neck and it felt so good! What his hands were doing couldn't even be described. She wanted so much to give him pleasure in return.

"Jordan, what do you want me to do? Where do you like to be touched?" she whispered.

"Do whatever you want, my baby. Touch me anywhere—just love me, kiss me . . . I do love to kiss you," he muttered against her mouth, her soft, delicious mouth. "Valentine."

She thrilled to hear her name mingling with the intoxicating heat of their kisses. She held him, caressed him with a wantonness that exhilarated her, and electrified him. "Jordan." Her voice was throaty, fevered with need. She ached with it. Passion pulsed its rhythmic contractions deep within her. "Now," she whispered, pulling him to her. "Now."

When his long body covered hers, Valentine parted her legs for him in a gesture so natural it resembled some primal dance movement. Instinctively she arched to meet that first breathtaking thrust. He caught her mouth, opening it with insistent pressure as he pushed deep within her on a gusty groan.

His hoarse voice shivered her. His broken words added immeasurably to her pleasure. He had said nothing the first time, but now he murmured and whispered on her mouth, and she loved it. She loved *this*. Something rippled through her body. She gasped as it intensified, wave upon wave unfolding in a splintering of self, building and building until she dissolved, liquefied into a shower of radiance—oh, yes, she thought wildly, oh God, yes, this is it!

Jordan gloried in the pleasure he was giving her. Her writhing body tormented his, but sweetly, so blessedly sweet—and then he felt the convulsions inside her, gripping his manhood, expanding, tightening, driving him magnificently mad.

"Do you like this?" he asked urgently. "Tell me what you like . . . say things to me."

"Oh, Jordan. Love me—yes—yes, yes—" Valentine trembled with it, shuddered and cried aloud on the cresting wave.

It was, she thought with some tiny corner of a still thinking mind, a mighty clash of cymbals!

An eternity later his sky blue eyes met hers, his low, rich laugh a paean of masculine satisfaction. Jordan did not have to question, for he was well acquainted with a woman's after-sex aura. But this time was different. She was different. And he wanted—needed to hear it spoken.

"Well, my sweet Valentine, what say you now?" he asked, probing her kittenish smile with a fingertip.

"Oh, Jordan!"

Her joyous exclamation was rich emollient to his ego. He had just introduced a woman to lovemaking and done a damn fine job of it. Lord, but he felt good! Arching his head, he laughed again, for it had to be expressed and a man did not burst out singing just because he'd had some fantastic sex.

She frowned. "Why are you laughing?"

"Ah, Valentine," he whispered, kissing her. "Because I feel so good, so marvelously good." Another laugh erupted through his that. "And because I remembered that old movie *Fiddler on the Roof*! Every time that old guy got to feeling real good, he burst out singing and I feel like ... singing!" On the last word, he rolled over and pulled her into his arms.

She made a little cuddling movement, her softly given "umm" ending on a contented sigh. He was surprised at the curious emotion this small gesture evoked.

For a time they drifted on this euphoric fulfillment. Jordan's blissful cloud hit a bump now and then when he tried to sort out his feelings. This was her first time to make love. Funny how it felt like his first time, too.

"Tell me," he murmured, "what do you think of lovemaking?"

Fleetingly Valentine wondered how another woman would respond, then reversed herself. She didn't want him remotely reminded of other women.

"Well, the moon didn't stand still."

Jordan made a strangled sound. "You were ... watching the moon?"

She stared at him. "When on earth did I have time to watch the moon?"

He groaned and wrapped her in his arms.

Valentine appreciated the respite. She didn't know how much longer she could keep up this lighthearted pretense. Casual acceptance of something so profoundly moving was almost beyond her. How could she not express it when her entire body ached, throbbed, sang with soulful joy! No wonder people cried out to God during intimacy! Jordan still held her, his long frame positioned so that her breasts cushioned his face. She stroked his hair, marveling at the intense pleasure such a small act gave her. But then, she was engulfed in a veritable flood of the most extraordinary feelings! She closed her eyes, reluctant to speak for fear of saying the wrong thing, and hoping he wouldn't speak for the same reason.

"Umm, that was so good, baby," he mumbled, sighing.

Don't spoil it, she thought imploringly. *Don't downgrade this beautiful intimacy we've just shared!*

He turned onto his back and drew her close again. She pillowed her head on his shoulder and curled her fingers through the hair on his chest. A quick peek at his face caught him smiling. She smiled back and he hugged her. What happens now? she wondered. He reached out with his free arm and switched off the light.

Silence settled around them. Valentine was intensely aware of time passing. The cashmere-soft darkness seemed intent upon revealing what she was trying desperately to conceal. Or at least deny, she thought, biting her lip as the words surged against her throat. She sank her teeth deeper into her bottom lip. The things she might say raced through her mind and she edited them, then rejected them one after the other. For what she wanted to say was simple enough.

She wanted to tell him she loved him.

She burned with the need to tell him!

I love you, she rehearsed. *You don't need to get all uptight over this and you don't have to respond. I just want to say I love you. It's a gift I give you with no strings attached. . . .*

Yes, that would be all right, she decided; that would eliminate any pressure he might feel to say he loved her, too. Certainly she didn't want him thinking he had to say it.

But if he didn't, it would break her heart. *Which seems to cast doubt on the claim of no strings attached, doesn't it, Valentine!* She sighed, disliking the mocking thought, but forced by self-honesty to examine its merit.

It has a lot of merit, she admitted. They'd had sex. Great sex. So naturally she was now madly in love with him. Like an icy splash of deja vu, she felt again the crushing sense of her own foolishness. Idiot! Thank heaven she'd kept her mouth shut!

Hearing her hard sigh, Jordan asked, "What's the matter? Can't sleep?" He chuckled. "Me, either."

He turned onto his side and kissed her. A quivery thrill raced down her stomach, snatching her breath as his hand followed its path. "Oh, Jordan, I want . . ."

"What, baby? What do you want?" he asked, his husky voice so exciting she shivered.

"You. This," Valentine whispered. She pulled him down atop her and gave herself up to his sweet, sweet magic.

It was a slow, unhurried time of loving, and it was marvelously good.

Jordan drowsed.

Although weary, Valentine couldn't relax. It must be very late. Sam would be home. Worrying about her? Had she noticed the car's absence? Surely she would guess where it was. But still . . .

"I have to go," Valentine decided. Sitting up, she rolled to the edge of the bed.

"Not yet, honey," he protested, reaching for her.

"Jordan, it's nearly dawn. I have to go," she said firmly. "Turn on the light, please?"

Grumbling, Jordan snapped on the light, then swung his legs to the floor.

"Why are you getting up?" she asked.

"To see you home, of course. If you really must go, then I'll follow you."

"Oh, don't be silly," she said shortly. "I got myself here and I'll get myself back."

He grabbed his jeans off the valet chair. "I'm not being silly, I'm being a gentleman."

"You may think you are, but it doesn't seem that way to me. In fact, it's kind of insulting. I'm a woman, not a child."

"I'm fully aware of that," he answered with a slow, sexy smile. "But if that's what you really want—"

"It's what I want."

Tossing aside the jeans, Jordan pulled on his pajama pants. Her firm statement had to be respected, whether or not he agreed with it.

After dressing, Valentine stood in front of the mirror and brushed her hair into some semblance of order. Her mind was now preoccupied with making a graceful exit. Just what did one say, anyway?

Jordan came up behind her, stepping in close, cupping her breasts as their eyes met in the mirror. "Thank you, Valentine," he said deeply.

Thank you? her heart cried out. Just *thank you* for a night that had left her shaken and disbelieving? A night filled with emotions that were, to her, so complex and mysterious that she couldn't even name them all? Keep it light, Valentine, she pleaded. This is all so commonplace to him. Don't let him see how much it meant to you!

"And thank *you,* Jordan," she said.

"For what?" Her mouth curved into a deliciously wry smile that ignited his own.

"Why, for taking the time to break in a little greenhorn! Deflowering maidens must exact a wearisome toll!" Valentine's teasing tone concealed the pain of leaving him. She ached to see a similar response in him, but apparently she was just another conquest.

He kissed her neck. "It was my pleasure, ma'am."

Mine, too, she thought, nuzzling his cheek. So why did I automatically assume it was solely *his* conquest? *I* came to him, *I* made the choice. Grateful for this small empowerment, she eased from his embrace and walked into the living room.

She was still dead set against betraying her true feelings and her nerves were dangerously frayed.

Battling her urge for haste, she picked up her purse. "Bye, Jordan. See you," she said, and turned toward the door.

"Will you? When?"

The urgency in his questions flowed through her like a honeyed balm. "Tomorrow. I'm hostessing your party, remember?" She stretched up and kissed him. "Good night," she said, and walked sedately out the door.

After she left, Jordan lay sleepless, missing, with a peculiar ache, the warmth from Valentine in his bed. It still felt wrong not to see her safely home. Sure, he'd had women leave his bed with a sweet "good night" and gratifying unconcern about the logistics of it. No big deal. But this was Valentine, which always made anything a helluva big deal. Factor in her virginity and the difference became downright unwieldy.

A hard sigh rent the silence of his lonely bedroom. True, he had lost himself in her. But what got to him was that for the first time in his life, it wasn't just a woman's essence— this was Valentine. Not once had he been oblivious of that lovely fact. Not once, he marveled. Even in the deepest throes of ecstasy, he was aware that he was making love with September Valentine Townsend.

It made him uneasy. Deeply uneasy.

Chapter 13

Sam poured another cup of coffee and took it out to the veranda. She was tired, edgy, and very annoyed. How could she sleep with her young cousin out running around till the wee hours of the morning? She had a perfect right to be cranky.

"Hi, Sam," a soft voice interrupted her fit of pique.

Sam took one look at that radiant little face and made a momentous leap to the correct conclusion within seconds of eye contact. But she said nothing beyond a bland, "You feeling okay this morning, Val?"

"I'm feeling fine, thank you." Valentine gave her a sidelong glance. Then, looking her full in the face, she whispered, "Oh God, Sam!"

"Oh God, Valentine," Sam mimicked, ruffling the satiny hair framing her cousin's soft, glowing face. "I love you, Val," she said with a tenderness that surprised them both.

"I love you, too, Sam." Blushing under the scrutiny of intense green eyes, Valentine smoothed her messy hair. "I'm sorry if you worried about me last night. I should have called."

Sam chuckled. "I'd imagine calling was the furthest thing from your mind last night! But I'm sorry, too, babe. I've been a tad cantankerous lately and I don't know why."

"Maybe because you're a control freak?" Valentine suggested sweetly.

"I am not a control freak. I am, however, accustomed to being in charge and you keep throwing me for a loop, Cousin. I may have gotten a little overwrought—"

"A lot overwrought. But I understand. I guess it's hard to cut those apron strings, huh?" Valentine quipped. She grinned. "So, Sam, darlin', who's the bold one now? And who's the one holding back, shaking in her size nines because she's never, ever, felt such overpowering need for one very special man?"

Sam made a face at her. "Okay, gloat. Go ahead, get it out of your system. Maybe I'll just do a little gloating myself. After all, I'm the one who kept telling you what you were missing. Surely I'm due an 'I told you so'!"

"Are you ever," Valentine said fervently. "It was so wonderful I—oh, Sam, for the first time in my life I wanted to say those words!"

"Those words?"

"Yeah, you know, *those* words. I wanted to say 'I love you, Jordan.' Actually that's four words, but—"

Sam wheeled around. "You didn't, did you? My God, Val, that's the worst blunder a woman can make!"

Valentine eyed her. "What, saying it first?"

"Saying it at all. And to say anything after great sex—Val, a woman isn't quite sane right then. Not even rational, for that matter."

Valentine turned away. "Yeah, I kind of figured that. All those wild, crazy feelings . . . wouldn't be too smart to say anything while under the influence," she conceded drolly. "You'll be much relieved to know I said nothing."

"Well, thank heavens for that!" Sam glanced at her downcast face. "Oh, Val, I'm sorry. I didn't mean to, well, to rain on your parade," she said softly. "Have fun, love, enjoy those wild, crazy feelings. There's nothing to compare with them. Except maybe killing a whole bottle of bubbly all by yourself. I seem to recall that experience as being a little wild and crazy!"

She sobered. "Just keep in mind that you're playing in the big leagues now, so be careful. As much as I need to swat your bottom at times, I really don't want you getting hurt."

"Don't worry, I can take care of myself. Any coffee left? I need some caffeine—I'm limp as a rag," Valentine said, collapsing on a lounge.

Sam muttered something better left unsaid and fetched her some coffee. "Don't forget the party tonight. Clay says it'll just be a dozen or so people. Unless of course, more show up, which tends to happen with Jordan's parties." She perched on the railing. "Clay suggested an afternoon swim if you're interested. At least lie around the pool and get a little sun. I'm taking him up on it."

Valentine nodded, a half smile on her mouth. "Sam, why are you still denying yourself? With Clay, I mean."

Sam sprang to her feet. "Because it's too damned important, that's why! I already told you that. Jeez, Val!" Still grumbling, she went back inside.

Laughing to herself, Valentine got up and walked out into the warm, steamy day. She felt so different this morning, so altered. An irrevocable difference, she conceded. But she refused to sanction her niggling doubts; last night's decision had not been a mistake. Even in the glare of sunlight, giving Jordan her virginity felt beautifully right.

"Elisse wouldn't have told me to take a chance if it was wrong," Valentine whispered with firming certainty.

Leaning against her oak tree, Valentine replayed what Jordan had told her about his childhood. No wonder he avoided commitment, she thought sadly. But she could break down those self-protecting barriers and free him from the past. She knew she could! "And maybe I can't confess my love, but I can show it," she muttered, then laughed aloud as a sudden wild, sweet happiness seized her. How could he help but reciprocate!

Filled with confidence, her spirits soared to incredible heights. Last night, she thought deliciously, had been an awakening in more ways than one! She was tempted to turn a handspring, but refrained. Instead she wandered around the yard in her pink wrapper, barefooted, hair uncombed; a mess, she admitted, but who cared?

Next door, Mrs. Belmont's prized dahlias had begun to droop, but Valentine's garden flaunted its rich, green sheet of weeds in splendid defiance of the gathering heat. A disgrace, that darned garden, she thought with righteous penitence. But Ozell said it was too late to plant veggies now, had to wait until fall. Someone should mow the lawn pretty soon, though.

"I know what. I'll get a goat! Maybe two or three. Goats love nutgrass," she shouted to the blue, blue sky.

Jordan's eyes were blue. "Heavenly blue, divinely blue," she sang, then flung her arms skyward and performed a series of graceful pirouettes. These sleek, oily movements came from a specific source, she acknowledged; a little loving did indeed smooth the kinks and oil the muscles!

"Oh God, I feel wonderful!" she crowed. "I absolutely adore Texas, I absolutely adore Ozell and Vera, I absolutely adore green, green nutgrass!"

Dancing along the edge of the yard, where her nutgrass bumped up against the border that protected Mrs. Belmont's impeccable lawn, Valentine continued her zany outburst. "It was so good between us," she explained to a butterfly. "Jordan is a fantastic lover." She stopped dead. "Oh my God, I've got a *lover!*"

A loud gasp commanded her attention; Valentine looked up just in time to meet her neighbor's horrified eyes. "Uh, hi, Mrs. Belmont!" she said, flushing all over.

Daunted by the elderly matron's curt nod, Valentine turned and raced back to the veranda. She stretched out on a lounge as soporifically as a contented cat. She yawned, eyes closing . . .

Across the way, Mrs. Belmont watered her dahlias while glaring so ferociously at the nutgrass, it should have wilted from the blast. "Goats, nutgrass, and loose women," she muttered incredulously, *"right next door!"*

Valentine awoke with a plaintive cry. She was totally disoriented as to time and place, and even Sam's familiar face failed to help find her balance.

"Oh, honey, I'm sorry, I didn't mean to startle you!" Sam

exclaimed, removing her hand from Valentine's shoulder, which she had shaken to rouse her.

"It's all right," Valentine said fuzzily. Recall returned in a rush. She'd stretched out on this lounge to finish her coffee and had fallen asleep. Her mouth was cottony and her body damp with perspiration under her pink wrapper.

"Good grief, how long did I sleep?" she blurted.

"You were still awake when I left at eleven, but I was gone nearly five hours, so you must've had a pretty good nap." Sam grinned. "Miss some sleep last night?"

"A little." Valentine licked her lips. "Oh, Sam, I just had the weirdest dream! Grandma Fiona was there, standing in front of a shiny metal gate, and she wouldn't let me in no matter how much I begged!"

"That is weird," Sam said with a quick glance at her watch.

"It gets weirder." Valentine rubbed her eyes. "After I left her I went on to . . . to somewhere, I don't know where. Just up there above the clouds, sort of drifting along. But with a definite direction. I mean, I knew where I was going and how to get there. And the people were familiar, even though I don't know them here on Earth. Elisse was there, too—"

"Elisse? You mean the woman whose picture you found in the attic? The dead woman?"

"She didn't feel dead to me. She was so beautiful, Sam, so radiant! And so filled with love. Everyone was! I felt"—Valentine shook her head—"I felt completely and unconditionally cherished, like I was very, very precious."

Sam smiled. "Well, you are precious, Mouse."

"You don't understand," Valentine said sharply. "By precious I mean something really different, something extraordinary. I didn't want to come back. I was arguing my case when something snatched me back. You, I guess, when you shook me."

"Well then, thank goodness I shook you," Sam said, but her quip fell flat. "Val, for chrissakes, you're scaring me with all this talk of . . . whatever it is you're talking about."

"Well, here's something even scarier." Valentine sighed. "Sam, I haven't told you everything that's happened to me since the plane crash. I've been . . . God, this sounds really nutso even just thinking it," she said, sighing again. "I hear voices. At first I thought I was just arguing with myself—"

"Which is just what it is, honey," Sam quickly agreed: "You've always carried on debates with yourself."

"Yes, I know, and for a long time I tried to rationalize it that way. But last night when I went to Jordan, I was nervous, not sure I was doing the right thing, and when I reached his door I got cold feet. I was trying to boost my courage when this inner voice took over the job. It really helped me, Sam. My fear just evaporated."

"Valentine, that can be explained."

Valentine's mouth tightened. "Maybe it can. But what happened the night I was driving home from Jordan's boat isn't so easily explained. I was upset, angry and hurt and blaming Jordan, and I . . ." She paused, then decided to omit the ditching incident. "Well, suddenly here's that voice again. Sam, it told me many personal things about Jordan, about why he's so freaked by commitment and stuff like that. And when I wanted more information, she said—"

"She?"

"Yes, she; it's a woman's voice, very soft and sweet. She refused to answer my questions, saying that she didn't have the right to reveal details of his life, or something to that effect. According to her, it was wholly his decision whether or not to confide in me. She couldn't interfere."

"I see," Sam said neutrally. "And who do you think this voice is?"

"I . . . I don't know," Valentine hedged.

"Which makes me think that we'd better just let the matter lie and keep it between ourselves," Sam said, crisply dismissive. Noting her cousin's rebellious look, she added with a throaty chuckle, "You know what Aunt Virginia always says—certain things are best not discussed outside the family."

"Dear Aunt Virginia," Valentine murmured. "I miss her sage counsel. Which makes it so nice to have you standing in for her."

"Touché." Grimacing, Sam checked her watch again. "Listen, you've got less than an hour to get ready for Jordan's party, so I suggest you hit the shower."

"Oh, jeez, is it that late?" Valentine shot to her feet. "You and Clay'll come with me, won't you? Jordan will need help getting set up, greeting guests and such, and I'm not very good at that sort of thing. Besides, I'm a little nervous, Sam," she admitted. "Meeting Jordan's friends after . . . well, you know, after last night, makes me feel kind of squirmy inside."

"Val, you don't have a scarlet letter branded on your forehead, trust me," Sam replied, vastly amused.

Valentine grinned. "Okay, okay." She stood up and stretched luxuriously. "Time for a shower. I feel downright dehydrated!" she said, heading for the door. "Sam, do me a favor? Call Mrs. Belmont and tell her we're not really getting a goat?"

She ran into the house before Sam could form the question.

In her bedroom, Valentine shed her clammy robe, flipped on the overhead fan, then picked up Elisse's picture. "Elisse. What were you doing in my dream?"

Although the question raised goose bumps on her arms, only the gentle whirr of the fan broke the silence. Valentine replaced the picture and went into the bathroom.

Standing under the invigorating shower, she closed her eyes in voluptuous enjoyment, which left her mind free to romp. She hadn't argued with Sam, because it seemed like pretty sound advice not to announce to the world that Valentine Townsend heard voices. Her personal response to the situation was contradictory enough; even while feeling wonderfully comfortable with it, she was uneasy about the voice.

"I welcome you, Elisse," she whispered testingly.

The answer came with downy warmth. *Thank you.*

Valentine stilled. A delicious chill and her spontaneous laugh flowed together in perfect, if absurd, harmony.

She exited the shower and hurriedly toweled off, her mind racing. Was it really Elisse's voice she heard? Did Elisse speak to her? If so—and it was a very big *if,* Valentine assured herself—why would a woman who had died long before she was born want to communicate with her?

And how did she do it? Assuming, of course, that she did, Valentine added quickly. Mental telepathy? Or was she a ghost, her sheet-wrapped form floating through the air?

"Oh, nonsense!" Valentine said briskly. She didn't believe in ghosts. "I also don't believe in phantoms, disembodied spirits, or Fairy Queen Mab, for that matter," she informed her rosy image. "So why do I believe that a mysterious inner voice is speaking to me?"

A guardian angel, Vera had said. Was it possible? Valentine wondered. Sure, she'd heard of them. "But darned if I've ever heard of chatting with one," she muttered.

Giving up on making sense of something that made none, she filled her mind with thoughts of another night in Jordan's big, tumbled bed. The ensuing excitement created a tremor in her hands and an extra pulse in her blood. She put on a fluid jersey dress the color of evening and knew with giddy pleasure that she looked terrific. At once sweetly decorous and outrageously sexy, the frock's halter top concealed in front what it bared in back, lots of skin.

Sam gave a long, low whistle when she came in to announce Clay's arrival. "Fantastic dress, Val!" she crowed. "Now let's give you a hairdo to match." She coiled Valentine's hair atop her head and fastened it with a white silk magnolia, leaving only a long, curling tress to cascade over one bare shoulder.

"Gorgeous! You'll have a certain man begging for mercy before this night is over!" Sam predicted before heading back downstairs where Clay waited with saintly patience.

Valentine trailed along behind her. Sam was sheer elegance in dark green silk shantung. "You look gorgeous, too, Sam. And you've already got a man begging for mercy. Hi, Clay," she caroled, giving him a saucy grin.

The poor man was a powder keg of pent-up passion, she thought impishly. "The question is, when are you going to take pity on the poor thing, Sam? End his calamitous misery?"

"Valentine, will you shut up?" Sam groaned.

"Well, Sam, that's a nice thing to say. Did I not knock down an entire wall for you?" Valentine asked, much aggrieved.

"Yes," Clay remembered, "and you're going to pay for that wall!"

"The devil I am. It was in our contract that you knock down that wall. You breached our contract, Clay Tremayne!"

"We don't have a contract!"

"Did anyone ever tell you you're sexy as hell when you're mad?" she cooed. Before he could answer, she flung her arms around his neck and kissed his cheek. "That's because I love you. I have no hidden agenda, believe me."

"You seem to love everyone these days." Sam sighed.

"Ha! Sneer if you must, Sam, but remember: *'There's nothing worth the wear of winning but laughter and the love of friends,'* " Valentine quoted. "Belloc, I believe. And did not Barrie exhort us to *'Let no one who loves be called altogether unhappy. Even love unreturned has its rainbow'*? And Emily Dickinson said—"

"Valentine!" Sam shouted.

"What?"

"Shut up."

"Oh." Laughing, feeling explosive with love for these two dear people, Valentine tossed her head. "Okay, fine. Go ahead; seal tight your closed little minds lest a feather of knowledge tickle your intellect and reveal its cultural ignorance."

"What wise old bard said that?" Sam asked skeptically.

"I did; S. V. Townsend. Well, shall we go?"

"God, yes. Let Jordan deal with her," Clay muttered, his mouth twitching as he met Sam's sparkling gaze. He felt embarrassingly happy, and helpless to resist Valentine's high spirits. So he stopped trying. Wearing a woman on each arm like a fine pair of bracelets, he escorted them to his car.

Valentine's heartbeat accelerated before they ever reached Jordan's door. It gave a convulsive little jump when, in response to Clay's knock, his voice came over the intercom.

"Valentine? Come on in, the door's open. Be with you in a minute."

Clay opened the door and ushered them inside. "Wow, nice!" Sam said, looking around. "This is a great concept, Val!"

"Isn't it?" Valentine agreed, covertly assessing her surroundings. The only thing she remembered from last night's visit was the huge expanse of windows. His public rooms were really just one enormous space—designed by Jordan during the building stage, Clay told Sam—each area defined by tall, white ionic columns. By clever positioning of furniture, he could redesign the room as flowing space that easily accommodated thirty or more guests.

"That's probably about what he'll have tonight," Clay predicted.

"How many did he invite?" Sam asked.

"Twenty, but word gets around," Clay said. "Spur-of-the-moment parties are casual things."

Valentine startled. "Spur-of-the-moment? Jordan didn't plan this party before . . . well, before?"

"Well, Jordan likes to party," came Clay's vague reply.

"So does Clay," Jordan said, clamping a hand on Clay's shoulder as he joined them. "I've seem him round up a bunch of people in the afternoon for a barbecue that evening."

Clay shrugged. "I just do what you did, call Sugar Lee, pay her an enormous sum of money and *viola!* a party happens. I'll give you her number in case you need her services sometime," he told Sam.

"Thanks, but I doubt I'll be paying anyone an enormous sum of money to make a party for me," Sam sniffed. "Besides, I can fix a mean spaghetti dinner for ten in half an hour."

"Well, remember, *duh*, we're bachelors, just pitiful, helpless single guys without a clue," Jordan reminded her.

His gaze lit on Valentine with the impact of liquid blue heat. "Hey, beautiful, how you doing? Hello, Sam. Damn, but you look good!"

"Thank you, Jordan. I feel good. So do you, it seems,"

Sam replied dryly. She kicked off her three-inch heels. "Well, we're here to work, so tell us what you want done."

"Just having you here is all a man could ask for," Jordan waxed romantic. He grinned at Valentine, the sweet, crooked grin that had the power to captivate and seduce. Fearful that she wore her heart on her face, she looked away. He was having this party just for her! *All this trouble just to cheer me up,* she thought softly. And she'd learned something else about Jordan Wyatt. He loved parties.

Of course, she found everything about Jordan fascinating, Valentine conceded, helplessly smiling as she met his electric blue gaze. His white silk shirt, open at the throat, revealed tanned skin and dark wisps of hair that ignited stimulating memories of last night. Warmth flushed her. Quickly she averted her gaze to the vivid pink silk flowers spilling from the fluted mouth of a waist-high, white ceramic vase. Elsewhere, plants, books, and a basket of shiny green apples lent their grace notes to the scene. Wondering who had decorated his home, she made a mental note to ask him later.

He brought a tray of drinks and they gathered in front of the wraparound windows to watch the sunset on the lake. From the secluded kitchen came sounds of food preparation. The vaunted Sugar Lee, she supposed. This room, too, could be opened to circulating guests by folding back the louvered wooden doors.

"This is really an excellent design, Jordan," she offered during a break in conversation.

He looked pleased. "Thank you. I don't much care for small, enclosed spaces. A little claustrophobic, I guess."

Ah, she thought, another bit of knowledge. She glanced at a bookcase, noting many Western novels, including what appeared to be the entire works of Louis L'Amour. "You're a reader, I see," she commented.

Sam smiled. "You've passed a test of sorts, Jordan. Val's heavy into reading. If she was missing at a family gathering, we knew we'd find her in some quiet corner with her nose buried in a book. Romances, of course; Estrada, Roberts, Krentz, Somerfield, Daily," she reeled off authors' names.

"She's read *Gone With the Wind* twice and saw the movie three times!"

Jordan grinned at Valentine. "You like romances, hmm?"

Her chin snapped up. "Yes, I do."

"Hey, that wasn't a judgment! I've got four sisters, remember?"

"Bet you've never read one, though," Valentine countered. "If you did, you might learn something about women." She slanted him a glance. "Personally, my favorite movie scene is when Rhett Butler scoops up Scarlett and carries her up those elegant stairs. My second is when he busts down her door." Her tongue made a lap around her upper lip. "Fantastic fantasy fuel."

"Valentine!" Sam exclaimed, honestly shocked by her cousin's provocative remark.

"Well, it's better than kissing your horse, Sam," Valentine said. Arching a brow at Jordan's grin, she added, "What's exciting about riding off into the sunset with just a horse for company?"

"She has a point, Sam," Jordan said, chuckling. The telephone rang. He answered it, then handed the receiver to Valentine. "For you."

"For me?"

"Oh, yeah," Sam remembered, "I put on that call-forwarding doodad before we left the house."

"I didn't even know we had a call-forwarding doodad," Valentine muttered. Perching on a big, puffy ottoman, she murmured a wary, "Hello?" She jumped up again. "It's Deke," she said in a happy aside. "Hi, Deke, what's up?" She listened, laughed, shook her head. "I'm at a party . . . at Jordan's." She glanced at Jordan. "I don't know why he didn't invite you . . . okay, I'll tell him." Putting a hand over the receiver, she addressed Jordan again. "Deke says you forgot to invite him, but that's okay, he forgives you, and what do you want him to bring?"

The outburst of laughter nearly obliterated Jordan's response. Relaxing, Valentine laughed, too. "Deke, you're a scoundrel, you know that? But Jordan says bring a couple

cases of iced-down beer and come on down. . . . Well, buy a
cooler and ice 'em down, Deke. See you soon," she said, and
hung up. Her mouth quirked. "Was that nervy or what?"

"For Deke? Or what," Clay replied, still amused.

"Amen," Jordan said.

Valentine wondered if his unconcerned smile was genuine,
or a masking device. She'd give anything to know what he
was thinking!

The doorbell rang, and he opened the door to his first guests,
a handsome young Asian couple. After that, people arrived in
a steady stream. An eclectic group, his guests so differed in
age, class, race and culture that Valentine marveled aloud.
"My goodness, Jordan, your friends are so . . . so diverse!"

His eyes narrowed. "Do you consider that good or bad?"

"Why, good, of course." She drew back. "It hurt that you
had to ask me that. I'm not a bigot, Jordan."

His voice gentled. "I'm sorry." He tipped her chin up with
a fingertip. "Show me where it hurts and I'll make it better."

"Here." She touched her bottom lip.

His dark head leaned to hers, a chuckle brushing her mouth
as he kissed the pinpointed spot. "Better?"

"Better," she said, glorying in his tender smile.

The apartment grew crowded, yet traffic flowed freely. Bemused, she watched as Jordan moved among his guests, stopping now and then for a shared laugh, a joke, a genuinely glad
greeting. She was captivated by this engaging, heretofore un-
suspected side of his personality. He had the looks, the wit,
the charm to which people naturally gravitate, but what she
found most endearing was the affectionate, outgoing nature he
openly displayed. Was it real, or just a social veneer? Whatever, it worked magic, she reflected, breaking out in a smile
as he glanced at her. The atmosphere was as sparkling as fine
wine and just as intoxicating.

For Valentine, already distracted by Jordan's charisma, the
spate of introductions ran in one ear and out the other, snag-
ging only when an attractive woman spent a few minutes more
than necessary with him. Knowing what another person
thought or felt wasn't always a bonus; she hated the little

worms of jealousy created by overly warm, feminine greetings.

This included the gorgeous blonde named Gaby, who pounced upon Jordan with a gusty kiss. To Valentine's relief, his greeting was casual, his smile seemingly indifferent to her abundant charms. Her slender hands flying, Gaby engaged him in animated conversation. A mutual friend had told her about the party, so she'd decided to drop in for a few minutes. "I hate dashing in and out, but I'm flying to Nashville tonight to check out a fine Tennessee walker!" she confided with breathless excitement.

Jordan seemed genuinely interested in her new horse, and that struck a nerve. Feigning a similar interest, Valentine moved closer until his chest warmed her back. He slipped a hand around her shoulder with a naturalness that thrilled her soul. Feeling more secure, she glanced at Gaby and wished she hadn't. Resentment smoldered beneath the woman's gaiety. Obviously she and Jordan were better acquainted than he let on. How much better? Looking at Jordan was similar to trying to penetrate wood.

Firmly she squashed her fevered speculations. Jordan's past was just that, past. He belonged to Valentine Townsend now. She tilted her head and gave Gaby a supremely unbothered smile. But she didn't mind at all when the voluptuous blonde left.

At ten o'clock the party was still going strong. Liquid refreshments flowed like spring water; food covered the kitchen counters, the dining room table, and very soon, every flat surface that would hold a plate or glass. Nibbling on something called a buffalo wing, which on closer inspection proved to be the meaty part of a chicken's wing, Valentine was struck by how good it was. She was surprised to find herself heading for the kitchen, impelled there by her sudden strong desire to meet the caterer, Sugar Lee.

A sturdy, ginger-haired woman with tawny eyes and pale, freckled skin, Sugar Lee was taking a break in the walk-in pantry. Stopping just inside the door, Valentine said nervously,

"I wanted to tell you how wonderful the food is."

As was so often the case, five minutes later she knew the woman's entire history, the pertinent parts, anyway. Sugar Lee, twenty-seven, was a waitress. She had nursed her father and then her mother; and after their deaths was given custody of her younger brothers. She loved catering parties and hoped someday to be able to do it full-time. "Make a hard-scrabble living at it, at least," she said from her weary lean against a shelf.

"You will. And it won't be hardscrabble, either." Valentine didn't know why she spoke with such conviction, but it felt like the truth.

A mixture of hope and doubt darkened the golden eyes she gazed into.

"It will happen," Valentine repeated, clasping the woman's hands. Then, feeling a little confused herself—for she had as good as promised the woman success—she pasted on a vague smile and returned to the party.

A few minutes later, Dan Marshall, the policeman they had met their first day in Destiny, came bounding in. "Finally, someone we know!" she whispered to Sam before hurrying over to greet him. "Great cowboy boots, Dan! Wish I'd worn mine!" she lamented.

He grinned. The rugged, good-natured face that had immediately inspired her trust now aroused a powerful urge to hug him. So she did, exuberantly. He in turn gifted her with a choice bumper sticker. "Armadillo: the Texas turkey," she read aloud. "Well, thank you, Dan. I'll treasure this."

Beaming, he gave her the rundown on this exotic critter, which fully deserved to be the official state emblem, he declared. Her gleeful laugh warmed his heart to such an extent that Dan invited her to go with him to a cow-chip toss in El Campo.

"Cow chips?" Sam said, joining them. "You mean those . . ."

"Yep, pats of cow manure," Clay supplied, slipping an arm around her slim waist.

"I'll be a sonofagun," Valentine declared.

"Me, too, among other things," Sam decided, giving Dan Marshall a jaundiced look.

"Well, *I* believe you," Valentine soothed him. "Come on, drinks are on the house and I'm your hostess. So what'll it be, cowboy?" Linking arms with him, she steered him toward the bar.

To her surprise, Ozell and Vera Loving came in shortly afterward. "I didn't know you'd invited them!" she told Jordan.

"Well, I knew you liked them, so . . ." He shrugged.

"Thank you, you sweet man," she murmured for his ears only.

Vera looked smashing in a loose turquoise shift and barefoot sandals, her hair more or less chignoned. Ozell wore a sports jacket with nervous aplomb. He bobbed his head in Valentine's direction and headed for the bar.

"Val, can we talk a minute?" Vera whispered.

Still puzzled by Ozell's evasive greeting, Valentine froze, her heart thudding with trepidation. Obviously Vera had news. Good or bad? Valentine couldn't tell because her own self-doubt blocked her psychic senses. Swallowing over the egg-sized lump in her throat, she led her friend to the guest bathroom.

Chapter 14

*V*alentine closed the bathroom door and wheeled to face Vera. "What's up?" she asked, her voice fluted with fear.

"God's in his Heaven and all's right with the world," Vera said simply.

Valentine's knees went weak with relief. "Oh, Vera! Everything's all right, then? You're all right and the baby? I mean babies—dammit, tell me!" she half shouted, grabbing Vera's thin shoulders in a death grip.

"Yes! Yes! Yes!" Vera yelled back.

"Oh, thank God, thank God!" Valentine flung her hands heavenward, then seized Vera in a convulsive hug. For a moment they just held each other, two women caught up in a miracle.

"Ozell?" Valentine managed to ask.

"So petrified he can't talk, so happy he can't move, so thrilled—well, you get the idea. He's a fence post right now. Also he's kinda scared of you."

"What? Vera, I don't want Ozell to be scared of me!" Valentine cried. "I love you guys. I don't want this to affect our friendship! Make him see that I'm just me, just Valentine, not some freak!"

"Oh, honey, no, he's not seein' you as a freak," Vera assured her. "Just the opposite, in fact. He thinks you're Mother Teresa or somethin' like that!"

Valentine burst out laughing as a memory zinged through

her mind. *Mother Teresa you are not, Valentine....* She couldn't recall who said it, yet she could almost taste the deliciously dry humor of that little barb.

She gave Vera an affectionate squeeze. "Tell Ozell I haven't qualified for sainthood yet," she said with her own puckish humor.

"Shoot, I already told him that!" Vera hooted. Her tone softened. "The doctor said the babies were perfect, Val. And he's gonna watch me like a hawk. The slightest sign of trouble and he'll put me to bed for the duration. But heck, whatever he thinks best!" Drawing back, she smiled down at Valentine. "Provided you think it's best, of course."

"Me? Good God, I don't know anything about childbirthing! No, you listen to your doctor, Vera," Valentine adjured. She spread her hands just a breath away from Vera's stomach. "Could I . . . do I dare?"

"Trust yourself, Val," Vera said tearfully. "I do."

Delicately, with a mysterious accuracy that needed no learning, Valentine placed her hands over the babies' minute forms and closed her eyes. A laugh bubbled through her lips. "What a time you're going to have with these two. They'll run you ragged, Vera!" She sobered. "*Chaim* . . . I hear the word *Chaim*. Pealing, over and over again, like joyous church bells. I don't know what it means, Vera."

"It means life," Vera said softly.

Valentine's eyes opened. "Life? Really? Oh, jeez, that's just beautiful. A beautiful message from . . . I don't know who it's from. I don't hear anything else." She removed her hands.

"It is a beautiful message, no matter who it's from," Vera said. "Val, would you be my children's godmother?"

"I'd be honored," Valentine said. "Will you make an announcement tonight?"

"No. It's too private to bring up at a party."

Valentine quickly agreed. Composing themselves, they returned to the merriment in Jordan's living room.

Drawing Sam aside, Valentine told her the news.

"Thank God, Val! You're off the hook, with no damage

done. Just don't do anything like that again, okay? Makes me a nervous wreck!''

"Me, too," Valentine admitted. "I'd love to tell Jordan. But I doubt he'd understand," she added when Sam frowned.

"I know he wouldn't. I don't understand and I'm right in the big, fat middle of it," Sam said. "Unless you want to scare the man off, I'd advise you to keep this to yourself, sweetie."

"Well, I sure don't want to scare him off," Valentine agreed. Spying Jordan's flushed face, she laughed softly. "I've never seen him really having fun. He's always sort of guarded."

"Uh-huh. And here he is letting it all hang out in front of God and everybody," Sam drawled. "I wonder if you had anything to do with that?"

"Me? Of course not. It's because they're his good friends. And also because he's had a few drinks," Valentine concluded, grinning as he gave her a naughty wink. He was so lovable she fairly ached to hug him.

Deke arrived, his driver trailing behind him with a beer cooler. Deke had already sampled its contents, Valentine realized as he scooped her up in a bear hug and his breath swept her face. Thank God he wasn't driving tonight!

"Deke, you rascal, put me down!" she commanded, but he just held her clasped against his broad chest while he grinned at Sam and inquired as to her good health.

Jordan was in the kitchen freshening his drink. Before he'd added so much as an ice cube to his glass, Valentine's laughter erupted, mingling with the roar of a very smug, very satisfied male. An instant later Jordan strode into the room. He stopped short, blue eyes slitting as he spotted his woman locked in the arms of his good friend, Deke Salander.

It wasn't that the mustachioed pirate was hugging her—which he had no goddamned business doing. It wasn't the laughter lighting her pretty face, or the feminine delight evident in her sparkling eyes. It wasn't Deke's wicked grin, although that alone was infuriating. What the hell was it then? Jordan couldn't say, but he knew one thing with rock-bottom certainty. He had never felt so enraged, so just plain savage, in his entire life. It shot up from the core of him, a caveman ferocity he didn't even know he possessed. Some part of his brain was aware of and astounded by it, but the rest of him crouched in the long grass, tail switching, ready to spring.

With feline speed and no coherent thought, he was across the room before even deciding upon a course of action.

Clay knew trouble when he saw it coming. Swiftly, casually, he placed himself between his two friends.

Deke looked startled.

Dan said, "What the hell?"

Jordan, facing Deke, made a dangerously quiet suggestion. "Why don't you put her down, friend?"

"Well now, friend," Deke replied in a slow, liquid drawl that increased Clay's concern. "Maybe she doesn't want down. What do you say, honey?" he asked Valentine with a devilish grin. "You want me to put you down?"

"Yes, I want you to put me down, you idiot!" Valentine hissed, then spoiled it by giggling. She could feel Jordan's animosity. And while she was properly concerned, the feminine nucleus of Valentine positively delighted in his masculine resentment of another man's attentions to her. At the same time, she didn't want either man embarrassed, and was very glad that only three or four people had heard the exchange.

When Deke released her, she turned and smiled at her affronted lover. "Thank you for rescuing me from this brigand, Jordan. You're a true prince," she said puckishly. "Deke, come with me, I have someone I want you to meet." Taking Deke's hand, she towed him to the kitchen.

"Seems my hugging you got Jordan a little hot under the collar," Deke observed with a sideways glance. Noting her smile, he added dryly, "I can tell you hated it."

"Well, any woman would," she said. "I hope you didn't mind being called a brigand? I meant it in the very best way."

He laughed, black eyes gleaming. "Oh, I knew that. Now what did you drag me in here for?"

"For this." Relaxing, she handed him a plate of canapés, including the spicy buffalo wings. "Taste these and tell me if they aren't the best finger food you've ever eaten.''

Slanting her an amused look, he complied.

"Well?" she demanded.

"Delicious," he agreed.

"Oh, good. Deke, you magnificent man, I have a sporting proposition for you," she enthused. "The young lady who made all this good stuff needs a hand in getting started in her own catering business, full-time instead of just moonlighting from her waitress job. She's a good, decent, hardworking woman who deserves a break; and you won't lose a penny, I promise. Now before you leave here tonight you get her name and number and call her, you hear?"

Deke frowned. "That sounds like an order."

"It is. But it's also a request. A favor, if you will." Valentine gazed up at him, her expression terribly earnest. "You know, you don't meet that many really good people, Deke. So when you do, you honor them with your respect and help." Her grin broke out, infectious as measles. "If I could do it I would, but I'm poor as a church mouse at the moment. Okay. Now there's another lady I want you to meet. You'll love her. I know I do," she said, ushering him back to the party. She looked for Jordan but didn't see him. "Vera? Come here a minute, I want you to meet someone very special."

Vera obligingly trotted over.

"Vera Loving: Deke Salander," Valentine said.

"I've heard of Mr. Salander," Vera replied deferentially.

"Good, then you already know what a sweetheart he is," Valentine said. "Tell him about your daughter, and the school she attends. He's so interested in things like that, aren't you, Deke?" she inquired, patting his cheek.

"Good God, I'm being set up!" he exclaimed. "Manipulated, even." He burst out laughing as Valentine tried to appear innocent and succeeded only in looking sheepish.

"The things I do for the sake of your soul, Deke Salander." She sighed. "What goes around comes around, remember that. Now if you'll excuse me, I need to find Jordan, see how he's faring."

Jordan stood in an alcove chatting with Dan Marshall.

"Will you excuse us, Dan?" he asked as Valentine stopped beside him.

She waited until they had a small pocket of privacy. "What was that all about, Jordan?"

Jordan sipped his drink. "What was what all about?"

"You know perfectly well what I mean."

"Deke?" He shrugged. " 'Much ado about nothing,' I guess."

"If you find that rationale helpful, then by all means go on thinking it." Valentine lowered her gaze as something cold, like threads of steel, stiffened her spine. "Because you see, I'm naturally a warmhearted, affectionate person. I touch, I hug, I love people and I show it. That's my nature, Jordan. Deal with it." She turned on her heel and walked back to Deke and Vera.

Their conversation made little impact on Valentine's agitated mind. She was too busy wondering how the evening would end.

Nibbling a fingernail, Valentine kicked off her shoes and curled her legs on the couch, noting with narcisstic pleasure their flowing contours. Her pensive gaze followed Jordan as he closed and locked the door behind their last guest. She'd wanted to be alone with him all evening, but now she felt nervous and awkward. When he glanced at her and flashed his sexy grin, her thighs tightened around the coiling heat of desire. She sighed. Being a woman was hellishly confusing at times.

Jordan moved about the room with easy assurance. She tossed out a perfunctory, "It was a lovely party, Jordan."

"That's because you were the hostess. How could it be anything else?" he asked. "Thank you, Valentine."

"You're welcome," she replied, flushed with pleasure. "Jordan, I hope you aren't mad about what I said earlier? I didn't mean to be harsh with you. I just wanted you to understand that when I like someone I show it."

"I know." He snapped off a lamp. "And I deserved the chewing-out. I was way out of line."

"I hope you told Deke that."

"I did. Hated every second of it, of course, but . . ." He shrugged. "He'd already figured out why I came on so strong."

"Why did you?" she asked, watching him alertly.

"I was jealous."

Valentine's heart jumped. "You were?"

"Yeah, I was. And it blew my mind, honey. I'm not a jealous man by nature, but tonight . . . I was damned jealous. Deke's a formidable rival."

"He's not a rival, Jordan. There's only you," she said so softly he had to strain to hear it.

"Thank you. I needed that." Jordan pulled her up, tipped her chin and kissed her, then drew back with a gentle smile. What an odd mixture this woman is, he thought: bold and saucy, shy and innocent, sexually inexperienced, yet radiating a sexuality that knotted his belly. Her eyes met his again. Didn't she know what she could do to a man with those eyes? Or maybe she did. He was so hard he ached.

"You should never be allowed to wear blue, not with those eyes," he said. "Pretty blue eyes . . . a little bluebird." He smiled. "Bluebird," he repeated.

"Well, it beats Mouse," she said.

He threw back his head and laughed. "How'd you get that nickname, anyway?"

"Oh, I was small as a child, so . . ."

He nibbled her lip, and she raised her face just enough to catch his mouth full-on. The kiss kindled the passion smoldering within him. It swelled and burst into flames, a wildfire, he suspected, that would never completely burn itself out.

"Was I too rough?" he asked when the world stabilized again. "I wanted to love you tenderly, I meant to be so gentle. But you just—God, you just turn me inside out, honey! I've never felt such an intensity of passion."

"Jordan, is that true?" she asked curiously. "Or just some of the sweet lies that spring to male minds at times like this?"

"I don't lie to women," he said, indignant. "Why would you ask that? Someone lie to you?"

"Everybody's been lied to at one time or another, I imagine. At the time I thought it was important, but now . . ."

"But now?"

"Now I realize it didn't matter worth a hoot. Water over the dam," she said dismissively. "You said your parents are dead. When did that happen?"

Ever so subtly, he stiffened. "Mother died just a couple years ago. The old man . . . well, actually, he isn't dead, not physically, anyway. In fact, I've had several messages from him this past year. They were on my machine, so I never really talked with him."

"You didn't return his calls?"

"No."

"Why not?"

"I have nothing to say to my father."

She ran a fingertip down his belly. "How do you know unless you talk to him? You might find you do have something to say."

"No." Jordan struggled for his habitual control, but the words just boiled up from inside him, hot as lava and just as irrepressible. "He ran out on us, Val. He left us with no money, a pile of debts, a mortgaged house which we lost to the bank. Mother's drinking kept getting worse and finally, at twelve years old, I had five kids and an alcoholic on my hands without the slightest idea how to cope. I was wholly inadequate for the job. I didn't know what the hell to do!"

He flung an arm across his brow. "Except apply for welfare. Yeah, a trailer camp and food stamps, that's the legacy my father left his family. And now, after nearly twenty years of silence, he has the gall to contact me! Hell, I'd assumed he was dead."

"I'm so sorry, Jordan." She caressed his cheek. "Maybe talking with him would relieve some of your resentment, at least get it out in the open rather than let it eat at you."

He stiffened. "Nothing's eating at me. That's the past. My focus is on the present."

"Sometimes the past can taint the present." Getting no response, she snuggled closer. "I have several relatives who live in trailer camps."

"Not like that one, you don't," he said grimly. "That was where you lived when you hit bottom."

The tug at Valentine's heartstrings evoked a hard sigh. "Your mother was an alcoholic?"

His jaw tensed. "My mother was a lovely woman, not very strong. I always thought of her as a fragile flower, in fact," he said angrily, defensively. "She had these spells of depression—sometimes she couldn't even get out of bed. So when he left . . ." He paused. "It wasn't her fault. She had to drink to make it through those terrible downtimes."

"She could have gotten treatment," Valentine ventured.

"It's easy to come up with facile solutions when you're not actually involved," he replied tightly. "Treatment for clinical depression wasn't so easily had back then. Not without being committed."

"You're right. I'm sorry," Valentine said. "Apparently you did cope, though, and quite well, too. Your sisters grew up to be fine young women, your mother survived most of that twenty-year absence—"

"But not my brother."

The bitterness in his voice shook her like a violent wind.

"Oh, darling, what happened?" she cried.

"He was run down by a truck."

"And you blame yourself for that?"

"I was responsible for his safety," he said flatly. "I was supposed to be watching him."

"Even the most seasoned caretakers can't be ever vigilant," she said, her voice soft with sympathy. "What happened?"

He hated sympathy; he craved hers. "The trailer park bordered on a busy highway. He threw his ball over the fence and went to get it. I was chatting up the resident sexpot at the time." His teeth flashed. "At sixteen, boys find sexpots compellingly interesting. I never even saw him leave the yard—just heard that God-awful squeal of tires." He shook his head. "Well, that's my sad tale. What's yours?"

"I don't really have one."

"Good. I'm glad you don't, baby. I'm sorry I got into all this garbage, I don't want anything to spoil this lovely evening." On impulse, he moved off the bed, and returned with a handsomely bound magazine. "Here," he said gruffly, placing it in her hands. "Page forty-seven."

Valentine sat up and placed the magazine over her lap. "Lucky magazine," he said. Sitting down beside her, he drew up his knees, his gaze pinned on her face. He grinned as her eyes rounded.

"Why, Jordan! This is your house! It says Jordan Wyatt, architect. Oh, Jordan, it's beautiful! It's so different . . . exciting, yes, an exciting house. 'A unique visual concept of space,' " she read. " 'Youngest architect ever to receive this award!' "

She looked from the house to the man, and her expressive smile filled some raw emptiness way down inside him. She lifted her hand to his cheek and kissed him. "It's wonderful, Jordan. And the odd thing is, I'm not the least surprised. When—"

"Last year," he said negligently. "I wasn't even going to submit it. It seemed sort of arrogant, given the caliber of the competition. But others, including Clay and Deke, insisted. So I did. I went around in a state of shock for months afterward," he said with a self-deprecating laugh.

Laying the magazine on the bedside table, he scooted back into position, then drew her into his arms again.

"This working with Clay on spec houses," she mused. "Does that utilize your talents to the fullest?"

"Clay builds quality homes and he has a fine reputation, so it's a pleasure working with him." Jordan paused, but the spate of words would not be stopped. "But I don't just do his houses. You know that office complex in Sheridyn Park? That's mine . . . admittedly a direct result of that award, but I greatly enjoyed designing it." He nuzzled into her shoulder, wondering why he went into such detail, and why her skin was so soft. But it was, and he was, and he enjoyed both.

"And when it's finished, it'll be a very fine building, I

think," he continued. "It's leased nearly to capacity already. Am I boring you?"

"I do hope you know better than that," Valentine said. She kissed him, sweet, velvety brushes of lips against lips, slow seduction. She trailed her fingertips down his belly to his pliant manhood. It hardened under her touch. Thrilled, she twisted in his arms and brought her body full against him.

His blue eyes grew intense and heated. "Valentine." It was a passionate sighing of her name before his mouth covered hers.

Jordan was very tired and very sleepy, but liquid fire flowed through his veins again, its tantalizing promise of ecstasy impossible to resist. Holding her mouth captive, he turned onto his back and lifted her atop him, a slow, deep impalement that made her gasp with delight. Then, without withdrawing, he turned until she lay beneath him.

She moved with him, a soft, silken, immensely satisfying rhythm. And this time he managed to love her tenderly, savoring to the fullest her joyful pleasure before he took his own.

Eventually they turned off the light, and darkness enwrapped them like a cashmere blanket. Profoundly fulfilled, Valentine drowsed, half-awake, half-dreaming, unable to separate reality from fantasy. Yet when she awoke to morning's gray light, she knew immediately where she was and who lay beside her.

Jordan still slept. She snuggled closer and smiled when his arms swept her into the hard warmth of his body. *I'm the luckiest woman in the world*, she thought fiercely.

Despite her bliss, she couldn't help wondering; how far did that luck extend? And how long would it last?

Her luck extended as far as she could dream, Valentine discovered three weeks later. On a Friday afternoon she tore into the house in a state of great excitement.

"Sam?" she yelled. "Sam!" No answer. Damn! The Blazer sat in the driveway—she had to be home. Valentine set down her bag of groceries and searched the house with spiraling impatience. A few days ago Sam had blown her stack because

Valentine, motivated by a dream, had spent fifty dollars on lottery tickets.

Sam wouldn't even listen to the dream. Recalling the sting of her cousin's anger gave impetus to Valentine's search. Rarely had she been so sweetly vindicated. But where the hell was Sam?

"Darn it, Sam, where—Oh, good!" she gasped, spying her quarry in the yard talking to their neighbor, Mrs. Belmont.

Valentine raced outside, nearly splatting Vera's cat in her mad haste. "Sam! Sam, guess what! Hi, Mrs. Belmont! Sam—"

"Val, for heaven's sake, what are you about, leaping over logs and squashing cats?" Sam drawled. "Did you know that Mrs. Belmont's son is an archbishop?"

"No. My goodness. Really? Imagine!" Valentine replied, hard put to be courteous when she was dying to share her news.

Giving Sam a crushing hug to expend some of her inner turbulence, she rushed on, "Mrs. Belmont, that's really wonderful, your son and all, but would you please excuse us? Business. Urgent. You know how it is. Come *on*, Sam!" Grasping Sam's arm, she propelled her back across the yard.

"Val, this better be good," Sam hissed. "I'm trying to mend fences here!"

"It is, oh, it is!" Valentine opened the door and pushed Sam inside. "Remember yelling at me for blowing fifty bucks on the lottery?" she asked. "Well, hah! Just take a look at this!" Reaching into a small sack, she pulled out a sheaf of twenty dollar bills and rained them around her cousin's shoulders. "Money, Sam, we've got money!" she sang out. "And there's more where that came from!"

"What? You mean this is . . ."

"My lottery winnings, Sam!"

"Good God!" Sam whispered. "Val, is this for real? You won? How much did you win?"

"Five big ones, Sam! Five thousand dollars!" Valentine shot her fist to the sky in triumph. "Yes!"

"Five *thousand?*"

"Five thousand! A handsome return on my investment, don't you think?" Valentine crowed.

"Val, I thought sure you were nuts, blowing fifty bucks on some weird dream! But you weren't." Stunned, Sam sank down on the floor, her green eyes registering enough astonishment to gratify Valentine's ego ten times over. "You actually knew this crazy gamble would pay off?"

"Sort of. Or maybe just trusted."

Before Valentine could continue, Vera came in.

"I heard yelling. What's going on—you okay?" she asked, looking anxiously at Sam sprawled on the floor. "Good lord, what's with all this money lying around?"

"The lottery, Vera, I won the lottery!" Valentine cried.

Vera's eyes saucered.

"Not the big one, Vera. No million bucks, but enough!"

Vera spread her hands around her globe-shaped belly, a favored habit, and stared at the money scattered around Sam's prone figure. "And what did you trust to win this?"

Valentine looked at both women for a moment, then quietly related her dream. "I had to do it—what with Grandma Fiona appearing to me, saying not to worry, she'd take care of me! And then when Elisse told me to go for it, well, I had to go for it."

"Elisse? You mean the woman in the picture?" Vera asked slowly.

"Yes. She communicates with me sometimes," Valentine answered with a defiant lift of chin. "At least *I* think she does. Sam doesn't agree."

Vera nodded sagely. "It's harder for some than for others."

"Oh, good grief!" Sam groaned.

"Vera? You accept the possibility that I . . . that at times I hear a dead woman's voice?" Valentine nearly squeaked.

"Sure. She's probably acting as one of your spirit guides," Vera said matter-of-factly. "Or maybe your guardian angel. Are you aware of her presence? Enough to help you win the lottery?"

"Vera, for godsakes!" Sam tried again.

Absently Valentine patted her cousin's head. "Yes, I have

felt her presence, Vera! And now and then I smell flowers. Heavenly flowers, not earthly flowers.''

"Wow,'' Vera breathed. "You're so blessed, Valentine!''

"Blessed? She's going to be strung up as a witch if you two don't cool it!'' Sam charged. "Even I'm a little spooked by this kind of talk, and I'm used to it.'' She glanced at Vera, eyebrows slanting. "I have an open mind.''

"Of course you do, Sam,'' Valentine affirmed with ill-concealed amusement. "Doesn't she, Vera?''

Vera's eyes danced. "Wide-open,'' she solemnly agreed.

Chapter 15

That evening, Valentine shared her triumph with Jordan, an experience that was, in itself, extremely gratifying. Standing beside him, enjoying the sparkling lake view, she detailed her venture from start to finish.

"You really did this?" he marveled. "You actually acted on the whim of a dream and hit the jackpot?"

"I really did." She cut him a glance. "You think I'm a bit dippy, huh? Pixilated, at the least."

"Oh, at the least. But, hey, different strokes for different folks!" he quipped, chuckling.

Her heart lightened, and she smiled. "Ah, tolerance for another person's little eccentricities. I like that in a man."

"In my opinion, tolerance is a vastly underrated virtue." He shrugged. "Besides, what qualifies me as your judge?"

"The value I place on your good opinion, I guess." Valentine nibbled her lip, wondering if she should tell him about Elisse. She faced him. "It gets worse, Jordan. Or better, depending on how you interpret my next revelation." She took a deep breath. "Do you believe in guiding spirits or guardian angels?"

He shook his head, dislodging a lock of dark hair. "I don't guess I've ever given it much thought, honey. Do you?"

"Well, I'm getting there, with warp speed," she said wryly. "Vera says there's only a thin veil between the earth plane and the astral realm, and I'm beginning to wonder. What would you say if I told you that sometimes I feel the presence of—and hear the voice of—a woman who died years ago? Not someone like my grandmother, either: a woman I've never met." She forced a laugh. "Would you consider me delusional?"

"That would be rather arrogant of me, wouldn't it?" With exquisite care, he brushed back the tendrils clinging to her cheeks. "My sister Jacey has an IQ of one hundred fifty, so smart and bright she makes me feel like a nitwit at times, and she's a sincere believer in spiritualism, natural healing, holistic medicine, angel visitations and such. I'm not, so do I automatically classify all that as rubbish and her a crackpot simply because our beliefs differ?"

Violet eyes, grave and urgent, gazed into his. "How do your beliefs differ?"

"Ignorance mostly. Since I haven't studied any of those subjects, I can't take them seriously. But if you do . . ." His voice lowered. "Val, don't be shy about confiding in me. I respect your opinions. If you think someone is communicating with you from another realm or another world or even from a flying saucer, well, hell, that's your prerogative." He grinned. "I can see where it would make for some interesting discussions."

"So let's discuss it. What I told you is what I believe, Jordan," she said stoutly. "Every time I start to do something that requires more courage than I possess, she's there, lending much needed support. In fact, I'm pretty sure she was partly to blame for me pulling up roots and moving to Texas."

"I'll send her flowers," Jordan promptly decided. His eyes danced. "You have an address?"

"Yeah, I do, as a matter-of-fact. My house. It was once her house. In fact, I'm starting to think she led me there."

"Jesus! Are you serious?"

"Totally."

"Well, this does needs discussing . . . afterwards." He swung her up in his arms and headed for the bedroom.

"After what?" she queried.

"After this." Gently he tossed her onto the bed and came

down beside her. His big hands rid her of denim shorts and bikini panties with little regard for the fragility of the latter garment. The heat of his mouth seared her thighs, lingering in the fragrant delta, slowly, slowly moving upward, while she gave a series of little cries to urge him on. Freed of inhibitions by his boldness, she grabbed his head and pressed it down into the wildfire he had ignited.

It quickly blazed out of control. Astonished at her swift response, she stretched up to capture his rapacious tongue— and felt a resurgent wave of the hottest, sweetest, most voluptuous pleasure imaginable. "Jordan . . . Jordan, stop! No, don't stop," she begged. Then she forgot how to even form words.

"You liked that?" he murmured, his cheek on her flat little belly.

"Oh God, yes! But it was over so fast, Jordan, and now you. Well, what about you?" she fretted.

He laughed, low and husky. "Oh, baby, what on earth makes you think it's over?"

For Valentine, the week flowed by on a Krugerrand high. "So what are you gonna do with the money?" Vera asked as they enjoyed an impromptu lunch in Vera's kitchen.

"For starters, this." Valentine took a check from her pocket and laid it beside Vera's plate. "Now don't get all huffy, it's not for you, it's for your daughter. I'm sure there are things she can use, little extras you might not feel necessary. I have only two stipulations, use it unwisely and have fun doing it!"

"Val, this is so—I'm so touched. Oh, heck, I'm going to cry, sure as shootin'," Vera moaned.

"Go ahead and cry. Just take the check while you're doing it," Valentine replied. "Oh, Vera, have you noticed how Sam looks at me lately?" she exulted. "Like she's asking, who is this person? Surely not my timorous little Mouse! You can't imagine how good that feels!"

"Probably doesn't feel so good to Sam," Vera allowed.

"No, it upsets her solid perceptions of me and that's disturbing, when someone you know turns into someone you don't.'' Valentine toyed with a strand of hair. "But I don't think it's a bad thing, do you?"

"No. Sam's kind of set in her ways," Vera said tactfully. "Val, thanks for bein' so sweet to Shanna," she added, fingering the check. "It really gets to me." She cleared her throat. "What are you going to do with the rest of the money?"

"Well, I was going to use it as a down payment on this house. I was afraid of losing it, afraid Clay might decide to sell it. So yesterday I had a private talk with him and told him about my fears and asked about buying it," Valentine confided. "Luckily I was ignorant of the fact that I didn't have nearly enough money for a down payment, or I'd never have had the nerve! Anyway, he refused my offer and gave me his word he'd never sell this house out from under me.

"And I can trust him," Valentine assured herself as well as Vera. "So I'm going to get my car checked, then use the rest for Sam's birthday. It's in October, right after mine. A computer and modem, a fax—not new, of course, not enough money—but still good stuff. And also that dress at Macy's she's been drooling over!" Her eyes sparkled with visions of Sam's pleasure. "It's such fun having extra money, Vera! I'd love to be filthy rich! I'd—"

Valentine stopped with a startled gasp as foreboding, sharp and sudden, struck her with the impact of a slap in the face.

"Val? What's the matter?"

"I . . . I don't know." Valentine wet her lips. "Vera, would you excuse me, please? I have to call my mother."

Looking confused, Vera nonetheless sprang to her feet and brought her the cordless phone. "Want me to stay?"

"No, honey. But thank you." Valentine dialed as she spoke.

"Just holler if you need me," Vera said and slipped away.

Valentine nodded, her heart pounding as she listened to the unanswered rings. She hung up and promptly hit the redial button. Still no answer. Her hands shook. She had no idea why she felt so anxious. It was just there, a shadowy premonition she could neither reason with, nor subdue.

After several more futile attempts at contact, Valentine

called Sam's mother and shrank back in her chair as the older woman erupted.

"What's wrong, you ask? Valentine, honey, what isn't wrong?" she wailed. "Your mother hasn't been herself ever since you left. She's been so miserable and now that lowlife Ed has got himself in trouble again and she blames herself 'cause she kicked him out of the house—" She stopped for air.

"Why? What's Ed done, Aunt Ellen?"

"Same as always, no job, drinking like a fish. Except worse. He's been real mean to her, Valentine, real mean. It was all I could do to keep your uncle from going over there and stomping him into the ground. But she said it's her problem and she'll handle it, and you know how stubborn she can be! But after she gave him the heave-ho, he drove his truck into a pole and got banged up, not bad, but enough to get himself in the hospital. And I told her, lissen, if you let him come back home just because he needs caring for, you're a fool, Julia Rose! But everybody else was horrified; he's your husband, they said, and—well, you know the family creed. I tell you, Valentine, things haven't been good around here, not for a long time!"

"Sweet Jesus," Valentine whispered. "I didn't know, Aunt Ellen. She never said a word about any of this."

"Well, she wouldn't. But she's hurting pretty bad, honey," Ellen said.

When Sam came in a little later, she found Valentine curled up on her bedroom window seat, weeping.

"Hey, what's the matter?" Sam asked, kneeling beside her.

"It's Mom. I had a bad feeling and I tried to call her, but she didn't answer. So I called your mom and we talked, then I finally got h-hold of Mom and she—oh, Sam, I should never have left her! God, what have I done!" Valentine cried.

Sam sat down and held her cousin. "Very likely nothing," she said reasonably, "What do you think you've done?"

"Mom threw Ed out. She said after I left he kept getting more and more abusive, just downright nasty. I guess, being there alone with her, he didn't have anyone else to act as a lightning rod, draw off his anger. Anyway, then he wrecked his truck and got banged up a bit, so she let him come back. They fought, she ordered him out of her house and apparently he blew his stack." Valentine mopped her face with the tissue Sam manifested. "So she had Cousin John escort him from the house and then she had papers drawn up."

"What kind of papers?"

"A restraining order. And divorce papers. She's got a lawyer."

"Good for her! Uncle Fillard, I guess? Cops, lawyers, preachers—God, our family has all the bases covered. No need for outside help if you're a Townsend." Sam sighed. "Why a restraining order?"

Valentine lowered her gaze. "He hit her. He hit my mother, Sam. Because I wasn't there to protect her. I should have known she couldn't handle it alone, I ought to have—"

Sam's temper erupted. "Enough with the *shoulds* and *oughts*, Val. Your mother's a grown woman, and in case no one ever told you, it's the parent's job to protect the child, not the other way around!"

"In a perfect world, yes," Valentine replied stubbornly. "But she's such a delicate person, Sam, so sweet and gentle-natured. There's an innocence about her, a soulful innocence that just can't believe bad of people."

"I know," Sam said, sighing. "I see exactly the same thing every time I look at you." She ran taut fingers through her hair from brow to nape, an agitated gesture. "But that's beside the point. Getting us out of there was the smartest thing you ever did, and Aunt Julia knows it. So give her some credit, okay? Let her put her life back together in peace. That means without you weeping and wailing all over the poor woman while she's doing it." She paused, then asked abruptly, "You don't mind Ed being booted out of the family, do you?"

"Oh, Sam, I don't know," Valentine said tiredly. "I'm trying to be fair about him."

"Why?"

"Because it's owed him, Sam. Nothing is ever just black

and white, you know that. I'm sure it was tough for him, being
a father to another man's child. He was always there for me
. . . when I was little, anyway.''

Valentine stared at her oak tree as memories churned
through her mind. Ed had been such a personable man, a real
charmer, everyone said. A handsome rogue, she thought sadly.
But there'd been a time when she was proud of Ed Brady,
proud to call him Dad. Proud of how people looked at him.
Especially women.

She had trusted him. But then, what did a child know about
reliability, integrity, fidelity? It was only later that she saw his
true colors, a weak, irresponsible man incapable of fully com-
mitting himself to a woman.

Like Jordan?

No! Valentine shook her head in violent denial of even a
breath of suspicion against the man she loved. He wasn't like
Ed. He was nothing like Ed!

Okay, so he's afraid of commitment, she continued her self-
argument. *A lot of men have this problem. But the similarity
ends there*, she defied the doubt that dared taint what she so
desperately needed to believe. *Jordan is reliable. Dependable.
I'm perfectly safe—*

Looking up to find Sam watching her, she caught herself
and continued, ''Besides, Ed was a big part of my childhood.''

Green eyes flashing, Sam sprang to her feet. ''Childhood's
over, darlin','' she said crisply. ''Let the past bury the past,
or something to that effect.''

''It's 'Let the dead bury the dead.' ''

''Whatever. Why the hell are you so devastated by all this?
You knew things couldn't go on the way they were. The situation had to come to a head some time. Let Julia take her
lumps. The rest of us have to. Personally, I'm betting she'll
come out of this mess a winner.'' Sam hugged her extra hard.
''You okay, sweetie?''

Valentine blew her nose. ''I'm okay,'' she said.

But she wasn't. A sense of guilt clung to her despite her
sensible efforts to shake it off. Those *shoulds* and *oughts* had
been ingrained into her very bones.

Sam gave them both a brisk shake. "Good. That being the case, I'm going to the market. We're out of strawberries."

Valentine eyed her cousin with a trace of amusement; Sam's breakfast consisted of shredded wheat and fresh strawberries. She'd rather starve than eat one without the other. "You don't seem too bothered by this mess at home," she observed.

"Sure I'm bothered. I love her, too, Val. But I quit playing ostrich when I realized that sticking your head in the sand and pretending it'll go away doesn't actually make it go away. Even cockeyed optimists have to face facts, babe. Well, I'm off to the store. Anything you need?"

"Not from a store," Valentine murmured.

Chuckling, grateful for even the weakest sign of humor, Sam left her alone.

Valentine drew up her knees tightly as another type of awareness flowed into her mind, the deep, connecting knowing that bridged time and space and let her see, let her feel, another person's misery.

Mom's misery, Valentine realized as it spread like molasses through her own emotional system. God, it was so real! She tensed as images of long ago filtered up from the depths: her mother, huddled in her husband's big red leather chair, his pipe clenched in her hand and his old gray cardigan wrapped around her hunched shoulders.

She heard again her mother's soft voice lowered to a desolate lament as, thinking she was alone in her dark anguish, she gave vent to it. A woman devastated by the loss of the love of her life.

Valentine saw it so clearly. Lonely and needful, Julia had taken Ed as the missing part of herself. And how it hurt to know this other part was defective, an ugliness that warped her as well as him!

Tears slid down her cheeks as awareness deepened into womanly understanding. "Oh, Mama, I'm so sorry," she whispered. She laid her head down in her arms and bitterly wept.

* * *

During the next few weeks she kept in touch with her mother, a difficult situation for both in different ways. Valentine had to block the intense sensitivity that let her feel too deeply. Otherwise she couldn't have borne the hurt.

As for Julia, divorce ran counter to her belief system, which left her with her own sense of guilt, compounded by failure. When Ed was arrested on a DWI and summarily jailed, her angst increased to the point of wavering in her convictions.

Sam was infuriated. "Don't you dare bail him out, Aunt Julia! Forget your blasted duty," she mimicked. "I don't care what the family thinks. Their opinion doesn't matter a rat's ass and you know it. You hang in there, you hear?" Later, to Valentine she added defensively, "Well, you know how our precious family loves to interfere."

"They are precious, Sam," Valentine reminded her. But Sam did have a point, she admitted.

Between these trying moments and the magnificent excitement of her soulful union with Jordan, Valentine felt as though she were riding an emotional roller coaster.

Being with Jordan was a continually unfolding panorama of rapturous experiences. She loved making love: loved it slow, lazy, achingly tender; playful and fun; fast and hot and fiercely passionate. She gloried in the holding, the nuzzling, the soft, sensual strokings, the rough caresses, the gusty sighs and wordless murmurs. And the laughter, she thought, her mouth already forming a smile. The pure, simple, rollicking fun two people can make together.

To her, lovemaking was not only exhilarating physical pleasure, it was a connection to the divine, a spiritual pledge made in the passionate fusion of flesh.

She was fairly sure that Jordan felt the same way. How could he not? He was always so glad to see her, his blue eyes sparkling, that grin lighting up his entire face when they got together.

And they were together a lot, she thought smugly. Every moment possible, in fact. When they were apart, she called him for long, satisfying talks, ofttimes even at work. It was an erotic thrill to know that he had to monitor his response because he wasn't alone in the office.

"You've got to stop this, Valentine! You're ruining me. I'm not worth a damn after one of your calls," he had growled, kissing her in fierce denial. "I'm too distracted to think, much less work! We see each other every night. Must you torment me during the day, too?"

She'd laughed, delighting in his charge. She knew he didn't mean it.

He needs me as much as I need him, she thought as she dressed for another night in his arms. Of that, if nothing else, she felt absolutely certain.

Jordan hurried through his den without a glance for his splendid lake view. He'd have liked to sit in his chair and leisurely read the paper, watch the seven o'clock news, have a cold beer. But he'd come in from work and headed straight for the shower. Valentine would be arriving any minute.

Part of him couldn't wait to see her. But the other part wanted to grab his truck keys and run. Instead he stopped in front of the window and stared blindly at his splendid lake view.

She'd called him again today at work.

Twice.

Despite his request that she stop doing that.

Maybe he shouldn't have made a joke out of it. But hell, he couldn't just come right out and say it.

That was a big part of his problem, he admitted. He was a man of direct, logic-oriented, straight-line thought, yet he didn't know how to talk to her. He had no trouble playing hardball with other women. Why couldn't he with Valentine?

Because I might lose her, and I'm not ready to let her go. Stymied, Jordan shook his head. Solid truth, he admitted. In his wildest dreams he couldn't have imagined a sweeter relationship. Her very presence gladdened his heart. Even her naivete was something to be treasured; he disliked cynicism in women. But the last few weeks he'd begun feeling . . . smothered.

Or was he just using that as an excuse to run from his feelings?

The flash of insight drowned in his flood of denial. He knew what he was doing. Being realistic, that's what, hanging onto rationality in spite of the spell she'd cast. They were getting too damn close, too damn quick. Deeper involvement carried obligations that he wasn't ready to take on. Luckily he knew it.

What could be more sensible than that?

The doorbell rang and he hurried to answer. "Hello, Valentine," he said, opening the door with a smile that wouldn't be disciplined. She carried a flat, square box that smelled delicious. "You brought pizza?"

"Yep," she said, eyes crinkling. "I knew you'd be starving!" Placing it on the coffee table, she discarded her purse and flung herself into his arms.

"Whoa, you're in a good mood!" he exclaimed as she waltzed him around the room.

"A terrific mood!" She caught his face and kissed him. "Oh, Jordan, isn't it wonderful how much we enjoy being together? We just can't seem to get enough of each other!" she exulted.

His throat tightened. Placing his hands at her waist, Jordan lifted her until their eyes were level and balanced her weight against his body. "No, we can't. Speaking for myself, I have serious doubts that I'll ever get my fill of you. The time we spend in bed is out of this world. But, honey, don't you think there's such a thing as too much of a good thing?" he asked, smiling to take the sting out of his words.

Her mouth quirked. "Oh, nonsense. How on earth could there possibly be too much of a good thing?"

"Well, 'tis said that man does not live by bed alone," he replied sardonically.

Laughter spilled from her red lips. Jordan kissed them, then rested his brow against hers. He had spoken solid truth. His desire for her was constant. Yet, as soon as she'd launched herself into his arms, that smothery sensation had enveloped him like a raw-wool blanket.

Sighing, he closed his eyes and inhaled her unique scent. Wildflowers and rain, so fresh and clean, so endearingly *her*. He couldn't think of a way to tell her how he felt without hurting her, and he couldn't bring himself to do that. Besides, he thought ironically, to hurt her was to hurt himself. Strange as hell, but there it was.

Drawing back, he asked, "Why the good mood? Win the lottery again?"

"Something much better. Seeing you." She giggled. "Remember what I said on the phone this afternoon?"

"Remember what *I* said?" he countered. She just laughed. Damn, what does it take to get through to her? he wondered. Disliking his thought, he asked, "Beer with the pizza?"

"Yes, please." When he released her, she sat her pretty bottom down on his couch and crossed her legs. She wore a pink flowered dress and her hair in a topknot. She looked so appealing he ached.

"Heard from your mother?" he asked, returning with two frosted glasses of beer.

"Not lately. She's gone away for a few days."

"She'll come back," he said, sitting down in his chair. "They always do."

At first puzzled, she leaned forward and touched his hand as she deciphered his enigmatic remark. "Did your mother go away?"

Cursing his carelessness, Jordan tasted his beer. "Now and then. When things got too much for her, I guess. But I knew she'd always come home."

"And you were always waiting."

He shrugged, irritated by her compassionate tone. "Since nothing else came to mind, yes. My options were fairly limited."

She nodded. "Notifying the authorities would have been a betrayal, at least in your eyes. And, too, if it got out that you kids were left alone—"

"Social workers," he filled in. "Reminded me of buzzards circling their prey." Half of his beer disappeared in one swallow.

Nodding, she opened the pizza and offered it to him.

"In a minute." He'd lost his appetite.

She took a small slice. "How often did she go away, Jordan?"

Another shrug. "Not often. And never for long. More beer?" he asked, even though she hadn't finished this one.

"A refill would be nice," she agreed, seemingly unperturbed by his brusqueness.

Jordan walked to the kitchen castigating his loose tongue. To confide in Valentine was foolish and why in hell did he keep forgetting that? What was merely a lapse in judgment to him was another sign of intimacy to her. She'd give it far more significance than it deserved.

After pouring the beers, he lingered in the kitchen, wishing he was better at relationships.

Or at least more capable of articulating how he felt, Jordan thought grimly. Because something sure as hell had to give.

September was identical to August, miserably hot and humid. "God, no wonder Texans air-condition everything from malls to doghouses," Sam groaned. "I thought it was supposed to cool off by this time of year."

"Umm," Valentine replied, not really listening. She had an entire evening ahead of her with nothing to do and no one to do it with. Sam had a date. Vera had called, wanting to talk, but she didn't want to talk. Except to Jordan. And Jordan was busy. Homework, he said.

"I'm so far behind I'll never catch up, especially if a certain young lady shows up on my doorstep," he growled when she called to ask about seeing a movie tonight.

Graciously, she accepted that. He really didn't have much time to himself, and she'd seen all those unread periodicals stacked beside his bed.

"For heaven's sake, Valentine, you'll see him tomorrow," she chided her melancholy self. But tomorrow was such a long way off! Her need for him was insatiable. She lived, breathed and slept Jordan Wyatt. She had never felt anything remotely like it. Nothing could compare with it, she thought emphatically, nothing! She was head over round-heels in love.

And she was quite sure it was reciprocated. He sent her flowers—once even a great sheaf of white lilacs and roses and where on earth did one find lilacs in the dead of summer! He bought her darling little gifts: a golden rose with a diamond dewdrop, a fuzzy armadillo, a rhinestone pin that spelled out Texas. Then there were those bewitching endearments he lavished on her during lovemaking—they just seemed to spill out of him.

She laughed; oh, of course he felt the same way! And life, she summed up, was wonderful.

But she still yearned to see him.

Prowling around her silent house, she wandered to the kitchen, which gave birth to a terrific idea. There was plenty of Vera's marvelous manicotti casserole left over from dinner, and Jordan loved manicotti. Being so busy, very likely he'd nibble on pretzels or some such thing instead of having a nutritious meal. Whipping on an apron, she set to work.

The day's heat had abated by the time she left the house with casserole in hand. She'd made a salad and added half a loaf of French bread, then packed it in a small basket. With wine, he'd have a meal fit for a king, she thought happily.

And no hanging around, either, she warned herself. She'd simply give it to him and skedaddle.

Jordan slipped a rubber band over the roll of blueprints and slapped it on the table, then stepped out on the small balcony off his den. Dusk was gathering, the sun going down in a swirl of apricot and gold, a lovely ending for the day. He felt a singularly strong, persistent need. Like that of a plant for sunshine, he thought. But too much sun can scorch a plant.

Sighing, he massaged his shoulders. He really wanted to work, but there was too much on his mind. He'd just spent an hour on the telephone dealing with his sister's problems. Glory's indecisiveness was hard on a man's patience, he admitted.

And then there was Valentine. . . .

For an instant the two women merged into one.

Jordan blinked and the double image vanished. But a gap had inexplicably opened in his defenses, and memories, like skeletal ghosts, swarmed through his suddenly vulnerable mind. The specter of an old, recurrent nightmare became, for that brief moment, numbingly real. . . . *Hands reached for him—voices cried his name. Fear suffocated him, frustration and rage took the form of an avalanche rolling over him; the black, oily soot of guilt drove him to his knees as he tried desperately to meet the snowballing needs of his family, and failed. He raged against their expectations—He couldn't do it all, it was too much just too goddamn much and he wanted to run, run until he reached a place where no one knew his name, no one demanded anything of him, no one cried out for help he didn't know how to give. But he couldn't run because his shoelaces were knotted together, hobbling him. . . .*

Expelling a harsh breath, Jordan shook himself. God, he'd forgotten all about that dumb nightmare! Weird how it could still make his heart thud. "Kid stuff, Wyatt," he muttered, chagrined at its strong physical effect. Well, he had no tolerance for ineptness, and love did have a way of making every failure razor-edged.

Wheeling, he went back inside and headed for his bedroom. Emptiness seemed to gather like shadows in the corners. The distinct lack of warmth had nothing to do with the drawn drapes and air-conditioning. Valentine wasn't here. "Which is what you wanted, Wyatt!" he rasped as he stripped naked. His attention focused inward, he turned on the shower, stepped under the flowing water—and nearly froze his ass off. An oath split the air as he jumped back out. He'd forgotten to regulate the water temperature.

"What the bitching hell is wrong with me?" Jordan roared.

As if in reply, the telephone rang, a jangling noise that made him jump. Irritably he strode into the bedroom and picked up the receiver. Gaby's cheery voice sliced through his tension.

"Hello, Jordan! I'm ten minutes away and badly in need of food and shelter. Can you help a friend in need?"

Jordan's quick smile was genuine. Yet he found himself temporizing as a feathery unease brushed his broad shoulders.

"I'm afraid the larder is bare, Gaby," he said, sighing.

"No problem! I've brought groceries and shall prepare dinner myself. All I ask in return is a hot shower beforehand, and a comfy spot to lay my weary head afterward. Is that too much?" she asked silkily.

Jordan's split-second hesitation dissolved in a flash of undirected anger. Dammit, he wanted to see her. He'd known her for two years. Two years without the slightest hint of pressure. With Gaby, there'd be no demands he couldn't meet, and thus no culpability.

He chuckled. "For such a grand gesture? Of course not."

"Great! Meet me downstairs in eight minutes; I need help with the groceries. See you!"

Jordan hung up and stood mulling over his quick acceptance of having Gaby back in his life. An ego function? Or was he just flailing around like a man tangled up in sticky spiderwebs?

"Oh, hell," he muttered. He enjoyed Valentine immensely. When they were together he was solidly content and near to purring. So why did he feel this almost feral need to escape her? She gave so much . . .

Maybe that's it, he thought. Maybe I don't want so much. Because I can't return it. Because it costs too damn much.

Jordan didn't bother defining that cost. Ego again, he suspected, but right now he really didn't care. Gaby was exactly what he needed. She aroused no terrifying emotions, evoked no overriding needs, posed no challenges to his self-control.

She was also sexy, intelligent, beautiful. If anyone could wipe Valentine from his mind, she could. Glancing at his watch, he redressed, slipped his key in his pocket and caught the elevator down to the lobby.

Valentine was crossing the downstairs lobby when she spotted Jordan and his lady friend approaching the elevator. Instinctively she stopped behind a tall palm. She'd only seen Gaby once, but she recognized the tall, willowy blonde immediately.

Jordan carried two plastic bags of groceries. Gaby toted an expensive little overnight bag and cosmetic case. Realizing the full meaning of the little tableau, Valentine felt the first frisson

of outrage flash through her system like an electrical shock.
Switching the bags to one hand, Jordan draped an arm around
Gaby's shoulders with an easy intimacy. When she looked up
at him, that pouffy mane of bright gold hair cascaded over his
rolled-up sleeve. He leaned down to listen, then threw back
his head and laughed. "You think so?" he asked, still laughing as the elevator opened.

They stepped inside and the door slid shut, enclosing them
in their own private little world.

For a moment Valentine just stood there choking on hurt
and fury. She felt abandoned, bereft. Making a sound halfway
between a moan and a hiss, she dropped into a chair.

Jordan was cheating on her!

Everything in her wanted to deny it. But she had to believe
what she'd seen with her own two eyes. It hurt. Oh God, it
did hurt. But she couldn't think of the pain—the pain was
simply goddamn unthinkable.

Anger was what she needed. Where was this sustaining
emotion? She felt frozen.

At length she became aware of cramped muscles. She had
no idea how long she'd sat here. Maybe minutes, maybe hours.
The impact of seeing Jordan with another woman was so stunning she couldn't function intelligently. Shell-shocked war
veterans must feel like this, she reflected.

She suddenly thought of Sam and Clay. He saw no one else,
wanted no one else—how did Sam manage that? Maybe it
was just Sam, smart, sophisticated, nearly perfect. Not like
Valentine, sitting here with a manicotti casserole stinking up
the lobby.

Jordan. The beloved name burrowed under her shattered
defenses and struck her full force. A volcanic river of jealousy
washed in behind it and sent her surging to her feet in the grip
of a truly astounding rage. Oh God, yes, this was what she
needed. Never had she felt such elemental wrath! She wanted
to throw things, smash things, scratch, bite, hammer, claw! As
she strode to the elevator her temples throbbed, her blood was
molten lava hissing through her veins. She had to gulp air to
cool its fiery race from the caldera of her heart.

Valentine didn't stop to consider what she was going to do or say. She was simply mad as hell and when he opened that door, she would jump onto him with both feet. And if that . . . that *female* was still here, she'd pull out great, satisfying chunks of hair.

The elevator stopped at his floor, so she must have pushed the right button. Set-mouthed, she strode down the hall to the small, private alcove guarding his front door.

She punched the doorbell again and again, and waited with the hammer pulse of hurt and outrage boiling in her veins.

By the time he opened the door she was on the verge of detonating.

Chapter 16

"Valentine, what the devil!" Jordan began.

Gazing beyond him, Valentine needed only an instant to take in the opened luggage, the cozy spill of feminine items, the black satin panties carelessly tossed on his coffee table. The smell of pesto and garlic sauce wafting from the kitchen sickened her. She swung around to confront the cheating man who was just one step from being torn to shreds. Two steps—he backed up.

"Is she still here?" Valentine hissed.

Rattled by those blazing violet eyes, Jordan stood in the open doorway staring at her. "Is who still here?" he asked dumbly.

"That woman, that's who! Gaby! I know she's here, Jordan! Don't deny it, I saw you! I saw you coming up here. I was watching you!"

Jordan's mouth fell open. "You were watching us?" he asked incredulously. "You know what that sounds like?" He drew an explosive breath. "Dammit, Valentine! You have no right to come barreling in here like some . . . some privileged madwoman! So I have an old friend come by—what's wrong with that? Not a damned thing! Yet here you stand, screaming like a fishwife and looking like one of the Furies! Jesus! Who the hell do you think you are?"

Valentine shrank back. All of a sudden, her actions were spotlighted in a scalding flood of awareness. She saw herself as he must see her, a grotesque image. "But we . . . you and I, we're—" She gulped desperately needed air. "I do have a right. I have every right! Jordan, you were the first!" She stopped in confusion. It even sounded stupid to her own ears.

"So I was the first. That doesn't give you one single goddamn special right!" he hotly denied. "What I do is my damn business! You don't own me! So what the hell makes you think you can tell me what I can and cannot do!" Jordan stopped as he heard his words and felt their knifing impact in his own chest. "Val, I didn't mean . . . oh, Christ." He sighed as tears flooded her eyes.

Valentine didn't know what to say. She could taste the bitter truth of what he'd said. *You don't own me, you have no right . . .*

His denial of her specialness rang on and on in her ears. Waves of humiliation washed over her as she sought to explain her anger. "Please don't, Jordan! I'm sorry, I apologize. It's just that I thought . . . Because I was so happy . . ." she said in a frantic rush to make him understand. "You're the reason, you're responsible, don't you see? You hold my happiness in your hands—"

"Oh, no, I'm not playing that game," he responded, deadlevel. "Your happiness is your responsibility, not mine. I'm not in charge of your life. I'm not accountable for whether or not you're happy or sad or miserable. Don't put the burden on me, Valentine, for I tell you right now, I won't accept it."

"I didn't mean to put any kind of a burden on you, I just wanted to be close. . . ." Her plea ground to a halt as she heard a feminine voice calling his name.

"That long, hot shower really did the trick, Jordan!" Gaby sang out. "I hope you don't mind me borrowing your robe. It feels so good to get out of those tight jeans. Oh, sorry, I didn't know you were talking with someone. Oh, dammit, Jordan, the sauce is scorching, can't you smell it?" she screeched and tore past him to the kitchen.

Valentine caught a glimpse of a lithe form wrapped in the white terry cloth robe that usually hung behind Jordan's bath-

room door. Damp blond hair and bare feet added a devastating
note of intimacy.

Valentine glanced at Jordan. She was in too much turmoil
to trust herself to speak. But then, there was really nothing
else to say, she thought bleakly. That brief moment had said
it all. Turning, she flew down the hall to the elevator.

Still somewhat stunned, Jordan was a little slow in reacting.
She was out of sight before he could break his momentary
paralysis. "Valentine, come back here! Valentine? Val, will
you wait just a goddamned minute!" He got his legs moving
and raced down the corridor after her. She flung herself inside
the elevator before he could reach it.

The door closed slowly, but not slowly enough. When it
concealed her face, she was looking at the floor. "Good
God!" Jordan said in a strangled voice.

Every instinct he possessed screamed for him to go after
her. But he resisted. No, he told himself. I hate what just
happened, but the end result is exactly what I wanted. I'm a
free agent again.

Squaring his shoulders, he turned and walked back to his
own door. He could breathe easier now. Valentine was gone,
and so was that smothering hint of threat. She was out of his
life forever.

No regrets, he assured himself.

But somewhere deep inside he knew better.

Valentine's small black car raced at breakneck speed down the
highway as she reverted to her old habit of driving to calm
her raging nerves. Her mind was chaotic, replaying over and
over every word he'd said, her lame responses. Through this
mad jumble ran a desolate refrain; how could he? How *could*
he!

"Déja vu, huh, Valentine," she said with a throat-tearing
laugh. "Boy, you sure can pick 'em!"

Questions slashed at her. How often had he seen Gaby? Had
he ever stopped seeing her? Had he been sleeping with her,
too? Valentine nearly choked on that thought.

Twilight flowed into darkness without notice. A long time

later she became aware of where she was, or rather, where she wasn't. God,' how far had she driven? She recalled passing through Waco but that was a while ago. At least she still had gas, a plus in an evening of minuses. Better turn around and go home; Sam would be worried.

She made a U-turn.

Her thoughts flashed right back to Jordan's denial of wrongdoing. Well, maybe to his way of thinking, he hadn't done anything wrong. But not to hers. White-knuckled, her fingers clenched around the steering wheel, she rehashed the extent of his perfidy.

He'd lied. Cheated. Betrayed her trust.

And she'd been a fool all wrapped up in cotton-candy dreams. Nothing else would describe it: a stupid little, ignorant little, brainless little fool!

Actually she was more than a fool, but she couldn't think of any worse word than that. Mistakes didn't teach you anything, she thought bitterly. They just humiliated you, scalded you with shame, made you wish you could crawl into a hole—just pull the dirt in after you and hide!

It was fitting that the car should choose this moment to gurgle and die. Muttering furiously, she coasted to the side of the road and tried to restart the engine. A futile attempt. She swore—what was wrong with the damned thing! It couldn't be out of gas; the gauge showed over a quarter of a tank left. Except for her headlights, it was pitch-dark. Why hadn't she at least stayed on the main highway?

She ground the starter until it sounded fearfully weak. She slammed her fist against the steering wheel. God, she hated this car! Yearningly she thought of Sweet Cherry, that dear little red coupe. A person could rely on that car; Sweet Cherry would never leave her stranded on a dark, lonely road. Tears ran down her cheeks because she missed it so.

Struggling for composure, she reached for her cellular phone . . . which she'd forgotten to bring. "Hellfire and damnation!" she choked, and tried the ignition again. Hopeless. Abruptly the lights went out. "Oh jeez, oh God! Elisse? Elisse, please! Help me, please help me," she whispered and waited through a silence that stretched into forever.

At length she opened the door and wearily got out. Nothing to do but start walking. Fear gnawed at her as she looked up and down the dark road. She could get killed, could get raped . . .

"Angels, protect me," Valentine whispered as she did as a child. Fitting her keys through her fingers like brass knuckles, she started walking.

Telephone in hand, Sam paced to the window again. "No, she hasn't come in yet," she said gruffly. "Goddammit, Jordan, I know it's nearly midnight. You think I don't know how late it is?" she exploded. "Oh, shit. I'm sorry. Yeah, yeah, I'll call you when she comes in." She slammed down the receiver. Where was Valentine?

Thirty more minutes crawled by before she heard a car pull in. "Val?" she called, exploding out the front door.

"Hey, Sam," Valentine said, plodding up the steps.

Sam grabbed her arm. "Where the devil have you been! Jordan's called three times. I've been worried half to death. Where did you go after you left his place?"

Patently exhausted, Valentine replied, "I went for a drive and I ran out of gas. Two teenagers took me to a gas station and got me on the road again and if you don't mind, I'd rather not talk about it." Shaking free of Sam's grip, she ran inside and took the stairs two at a time.

Sam followed and rapped on her door, insistently. "Val? I'm sorry, I didn't mean to yell at you. I was just worried, that's all. Sweetie, please, can't we talk?"

"No, Sam. I'm too worn-out. I just need to sleep, okay?"

"Tomorrow, then," Sam reluctantly gave in. "Good night, honey." Walking back downstairs, she shoved her hands in her robe pockets. She had some news she'd wanted to share, spectacular news. But she would have to sit on it a while. Valentine's welfare came before anything else, even her own.

*   *   *

"Val, could we talk a minute?" Sam asked the next morning. They sat at the table, coffee fragrant and steaming, waffles waiting, Valentine remote and icy-eyed. Sam had never felt so helpless. "Darling, where you are, it's likely I've been there. You want to tell me about it?"

A smile of sorts twisted Valentine's mouth. It was inconceivable that beautiful, confident Samantha could ever make such a fool of herself. In the glaring light of day, the scene with Jordan was twice as ghastly. Each time her mind touched it, she swallowed bitter vetch.

Sighing, she rubbed her aching temples. She hadn't slept; hadn't even tried. By the time dawn tinted the sky she was cried out, cursed out, and wrung out, thank God. Nothing but a bleak stillness remained. Like a woods after a forest fire, she thought, just ashes and charred chunks of blackened dreams. It had all been so lovely, and to die like this . . .

"Val?" Sam persisted. "Jordan told me that you two had a disagreement. He's already called again this morning. Honey, he's so concerned about you!"

"Sure he is," Valentine snorted. But even as she denied it, she knew it was true. He would be concerned. "It was a little more than a disagreement," she said dryly. Disinclined to say more, she cut off Sam's response by standing up and walking toward the door. "I think I'll get started on my errands. You going to be here, or at Clay's office?"

"In and out." Sam held out a hand. "Valentine, wait? I love you and I want to help, sweetie. I want so much to help! Please tell me what happened, tell me how you're feeling—"

Valentine wheeled around. "Let it go, Sam, all right? I made a fool of myself; is that what you want to hear? I was totally inept, totally powerless. As for how I'm feeling . . ." She paused, checking. "On the whole I feel like I've been gutted. So go ahead, indulge in at least one little satisfying *I-told-you-so-Valentine*! Go on, Sam, enjoy!"

Catching herself up short, Valentine bowed her head. "I'm sorry, that was completely uncalled for." Tears splashed her cheeks. "God, Sam, how did you ever manage to put up with me all these years?"

"I didn't find it so hard." Sam stood up and approached her. "As I said, I love you."

"And I'm very glad you do. But this time you can't help. I got hurt. My own fault, mostly."

"No, I share some of the blame. I knew these feelings were new to you and I should have paid more attention to what was going on. But I—"

"You were going through something new to you, too," Valentine cut in. "So blaming yourself is nonsense. As I said, it's my own damn fault. But knowing that doesn't do much good." She drew a raspy breath. "All I wanted was to be special. Is that so goddamned awful?"

"No, oh no, it's not, love!" Sam responded fiercely. Anger distorted her features. "I swear, I'll kill Jordan Wyatt! I'll get a gun and shoot him right between the legs!"

Valentine gave a strangled laugh. "Just a waste of superb young manhood, Sam."

"Or good riddance to another lousy bastard," Sam grated.

Valentine grimaced. "Put away the shotgun, Cousin, I don't need defending. He didn't mislead me. I misled myself. Just plain old self-deception. No victims here, Sam," she declared with a defiant lift of chin.

Sam groaned. "Valentine, you are killing me. Please, honey, sit down and talk to me? Tell me what happened?"

"No. It's my problem, not yours," Valentine replied. "Maybe I'm growing up. About time, isn't it? Time to discard teddy bears and unicorns," she ended so forlornly that Sam swore vengeance on the whole universe.

Valentine stopped her with a sharp shake of head. "I guess growing up is something you have to do all by yourself." She sighed. "Shit, now I sound like part of the Walton family."

"You sound like a woman going through the painful process of experiencing raw new emotions," Sam corrected. "I'm always here for you, Val, you know that."

"Yes, I do. Well, guess I'll hit the road." Valentine paused, and softly confessed, "Last night, when I was waiting for help, I really longed for Sweet Cherry, Sam. She'd never run out of gas in the middle of the night."

"Of course she wouldn't. Her, a woman could trust," Sam agreed, testing out a smile.

"Yeah. Well, I'd better go. Before I start bawling again," she said, making a face. "See you later, Sam. Oh, and if Jordan calls, I'm busy. Permanently."

Valentine knew he would call, and he did, several times. But she wouldn't speak to him. She couldn't. This dismal muddle of feelings had to be sorted out and then dealt with before she saw him again. So she let the machine take his calls.

And then she played the message over and over just to hear that deep, husky voice saying her name, she acknowledged bleakly, listening to his latest message for the third time.

"Valentine? Valentine, dammit, are you there? Pick up and talk to me, please? I know you're angry, but we can't resolve this unless we talk. And I do want to resolve this, Val."

"Sure you do," she muttered with a painful new cynicism. "Guess I wasn't too bad in bed after all, huh! But then, look what an experienced teacher I had!" She gave a ragged laugh and then dissolved in a torrent of tears.

When it passed, once again Valentine dried her eyes and tried to get on with her life. It had been a week since their *misunderstanding*. Seven incredibly long days, and she ought to be over the worst of it by now. But she was totally unprepared for the difficulty of living with heartache. Not only was she miserably unhappy. To her dismay, she, who'd once found joy in the smallest things, was joyless.

The only place she felt alive was in the bright glow of anger located somewhere in her midriff. It flared up hot and intense every time she relived the devastating moment she'd become aware of Gaby's presence in Jordan's condo.

Remembering just added jealousy and mistrust to her misery. But she didn't know how to forget.

Jordan Wyatt moved his hands in his pockets and stared blindly out his bedroom window. The television blared in the background, but all he heard was the voice of his conscience. At times he thought he would gag on the bitter taste of guilt and remorse. And regret. God, such regret! Its depths continually astonished him. It seemed to reach deep inside him to the dark, subterranean levels of his soul.

He'd thought he wanted to be free of her. He'd thought wrong. Dead wrong. How was it possible to miss anyone so much?

"Face it, Wyatt, your misery is your own damn fault," he muttered with the inner rage of a man who has done something too stupid to be believed.

That he couldn't change the situation was maddening in itself. When he called, she was out. When he went by the house, she wouldn't see him. All because she'd come by his apartment—unexpectedly—and found Gaby there.

In numerous telephone messages he had told Valentine the God's honest truth. Nothing had happened between him and Gaby! She'd left shortly after dinner, which wasn't too surprising; he had been poor company, too preoccupied to even make decent conversation.

He regretted that, too, for he genuinely liked and respected Gaby. But the image of Valentine's face as the elevator door closed still haunted him. In fact, there were times when he thought he'd quietly go crazy envisioning her soft, trembling mouth and tear-sheened eyes. A mouth he had caused to tremble, tears he put there with the words hurled at her from the depths of his own fearful denial and confusion. *So I was the first, so what? That doesn't make you special!* Cruel words, he acknowledged guiltily. He'd give anything to erase them!

For the hundredth time he wondered what she thought of him. Pride instantly defied it. What did it matter what she thought of him? When had her opinion become so all-fired important? Then he had to marvel at his talent for avoiding the obvious. The way he saw himself in her eyes had always mattered, profoundly so.

She stayed on his mind in deeply felt and unexpected ways; the memory of her was inside him now, part of his very being. That astonished him, too. Good sex had always been his criteria for women. Fabulous sex, sometimes. But Valentine surpassed them all. She was totally innocent, totally naive, totally giving. Different, he summed up.

She'd stolen his heart with that enchanting difference. But he'd been too dense to realize his heart was even missing.

Or maybe just too deep in denial because he'd always equated love with responsibility, Jordan reflected. He still did. At least the boy in him did. But the man? A wry smile touched his drawn mouth. The man was not immune to fear, either. In fact, this new emotion Valentine had instilled in him was so strong and vital, so unwieldy, that it both exalted and terrified at the same time.

He vented a hard sigh. Analyzing himself cleared away some of the mists shrouding the inner man, but it didn't make him feel any better. *Got her under my skin, in my blood . . .*

His thoughts and agitated pacing came to a swift halt as Jordan glanced at the bed and saw Valentine lying there, her satiny cloud of hair spreading over his pillow. He gave himself a sharp shake, but the delectable curves of breast and hip, the dark ruffle between her thighs, the seductive smile as she stretched out her arms, were as real as the thump in his gut.

"God, now I'm hallucinating!" he said incredulously. Wheeling, he strode to the dresser. But he could still see the bed and she was still lying on it, on her belly now, that luscious rump jutting into the air like rosy hillocks. The legs bent over them were so tangible that he could count her little pink toes. To his amazement he found himself actually leaning over the bed. The fragrance of wildflowers and woman-scent coated his nostrils; the smell of Valentine just before love . . .

He dialed her number before he realized he'd picked up the telephone.

His mouth went dry when she actually answered. The sound of her voice was like a drink of cool water to a parched man. "Valentine? Thank God you finally—don't hang up! Don't you dare hang up! Please, talk to me."

"Jordan, I really have nothing to say."

"Yes, you do. Honey, we have to discuss this! Just do me the courtesy of letting me explain, if nothing else," he begged.

"No explanations are necessary," she replied, dead-level. "As you said, I don't own you."

"Oh, hell, Val, you know I didn't mean what I said—not a word of it! I was surprised, confused . . ." He drew a breath. "And I told you nothing happened."

"Unfortunately your opinion of 'nothing' and my opinion of 'nothing' are poles apart. Please don't call me again, Jordan." She hung up.

Jordan immediately redialed and got the answering machine. Slamming down the receiver, he pressed his face against the hard, metal bedpost. "Now what, Wyatt?" he mumbled.

A moment later he made his decision. Slipping his feet into leather house shoes, he headed for the door, and Valentine.

Action had a restorative effect on him. When Sam and Clay drove past him, he waved with creditable insouciance. Turning into Valentine's driveway was good for a shot of sheer exhilaration. He'd spent his young life solving problems, he could certainly solve one more. Racing up the steps, he rang the doorbell and whistled while he waited.

Rather than answering the door, Valentine opened a window above the veranda and called irritably, "Yes, what is it?"

When he stepped off the veranda, she exclaimed, "Jordan! What do you want? Sam's not here—"

"I know Sam's not here, I didn't come here to see Sam!" Jordan instantly regretted his furious response, but he'd just suffered a swift, painful loss of confidence. "Look, I want to talk with you. Like sane, mature adults, Valentine, in a quiet, reasonable manner."

"I haven't time to talk, I'm meeting someone at eight and I'm not even dressed yet. Sorry, Jordan. Another time, perhaps." She slammed down the window.

Jordan swore mightily but returned to the door. Now what? He had to see her, had to talk to her, had to make her understand! The doorknob turned under his hand. Instantly he was outraged that it wasn't locked—she was here alone, for God's sake! By the time he'd processed that thought he was taking the stairs two at a time.

Valentine was in the bathroom pinning up her hair when

she heard footsteps. She knew instantly they were Jordan's. Her mind spun, insisting, "He wouldn't! He's not the swash-buckling type!" Simultaneously a shiver shot the full length of her body. Though it wasn't justified, there was an element of pleasure in it.

She pulled on a blue satin robe and tore out of the bathroom just as Jordan strode through her open bedroom door.

His impact upon her senses made her giddy. His stormy blue eyes caught and held hers without mercy. Remembering the robe's sash, she feverishly tied it. At the same time she rediscovered her voice, but not how to use it. Her eyes asked the questions.

"I said I want to talk with you," he said evenly.

Valentine swallowed to break the deadlock in her throat. "And I said no." Outrage steadied her. "How dare you come busting in here like this!" she lashed out. "Get out of my bedroom! *Get out,* I said!"

For a moment Jordan simply stared at her. He could see every line of her body through that thin robe. Her nipples were taut peaks and the bewitching flow of hips and thighs played hell with his libido. But it was her eyes that compelled him inside the room. He had to change the way she was looking at him—he *had* to! Because there was no way in the world he could live without this woman.

"No, I'm not getting out. I said we're talking and by God we *are* talking." Hearing his commanding tone, Jordan struggled with his frustration, and lost. "Why won't you see me? Why won't you even talk to me on the goddamn telephone?"

Her chin snapped up. "Because I don't desire to see you or talk on the *goddamned* telephone," she replied quietly.

"I'm sorry, I . . . I apologize for my language." Jordan savaged his hair. "Valentine, don't do this. I've tried to explain. You're making a big something out of a nothing, can't you see that?"

"Nothing?" she echoed incredulously. "Jordan, you spent the night with another woman! That's a nothing to you?"

"No, of course it's not! But I didn't, dammit! Nothing happened, Val! We didn't make love, she didn't stay the night!"

It was a duel, fast and furious. "But she would have, had I not barged in! She's done it before, hasn't she?"

"No! Yes, but not since I met you! Honey, listen, please listen? I didn't lie to you, I didn't invite her to come by that night. I had work to do! She just dropped by!"

"But you let her stay!"

"Well, well, yes, for a little while. But she left right after dinner."

"Because my showing up spoiled it for you!"

"Because I didn't want her! Because I wanted you! Because it's you I care for, not her!"

"Yeah, sure it is." She shook her head. "Look, this is a waste of time and I'm late as it is. Good-bye, Jordan."

"No, it's not good-bye!" came Jordan's instant denial. He cradled her face, his fingers registering the exquisite delicacy of flesh and bone. So soft, he thought, so very sweet and precious. Desperately he willed her to feel this elemental need to be close again. "Never good-bye, Val," he said huskily.

Her eyes met his again, as cold as a December dusk. "You no longer have the say-so about that."

"Dammit, Val, don't look at me like that!" he said hoarsely. She was drawing away from his touch and he couldn't stand it! He caught her shoulders and was instantly overwhelmed by her nearness. The sweet, warm smell of her clogged his mind until he felt wild with the need to take her, tame her, wipe that frost from her eyes. Oblivious to the right or wrong of it, he wrapped her in his arms and kissed her with all the natural tenderness and passion of his being.

She stood unmoving, a slender blue column of ice.

Jolted, Jordan drew back. "Valentine . . ."

"Please leave, Jordan," she said tonelessly.

He stared at her, his eyes intensely blue, his features drawn with bewilderment. "But . . . but why? Sweetheart, I've told you over and over, nothing happened! There was no physical involvement between Gaby and me, no intimacy—"

"There was intimacy. Sex might not have been part of it, but something *did* happen. That you might not consider it important doesn't mean I don't."

Jordan regarded her searchingly, realizing, like a blow to the solar plexus, that he had no true conception of what that evening meant to her. "Valentine, maybe I'm dumb as hell, but I simply don't understand what you're trying to say. You know you're important to me, so naturally I care what you think, how you feel—dammit, I love you," he blurted.

Valentine froze. She wanted so much to believe him! But the wound went too deep. "You don't even know the meaning of the word," she said. She would have gone on in that bitter vein, but she saw him flinch and sadness flooded her. "Jordan, I know that part of our . . . our misunderstanding is my fault; you gave me fair warning. You can't commit and you don't know how to love. No one could put it much plainer than that. I don't deny that you care . . . in your own way. But what you give is shallow and makes no demands on you. So what's it worth, Jordan?" She shrugged, and lowered her head in a gesture of infinite weariness. "Now please go. Please. I just can't handle this . . . this affair any longer. I'm through with it. Through with you."

"Valentine—"

"It's over, Jordan!" Her voice cracked. "Now please get the hell out of my house! And don't call me anymore, either! Just leave me alone!"

Jordan stared at her for a moment of stark silence. A muscle ticked in his jaw. Then, with a brief nod, he turned on his heel and left her, as she'd requested, alone.

Chapter 17

$\mathcal{A}$ week passed, and with it went the dog-day heat that had lingered, pitiless, through September. October danced on stage with all the grace of a ballerina. Blue skies, golden days and tormentingly soft, silken nights were punctuated by tempestuous thunderstorms. Lying in her rumpled bed, caught up in the excitement of the elements, Valentine felt wild with need. Need for love, for joy, for peace of mind—anything to quell this relentless longing! Sam hadn't told her that desire could be so painful, so blazingly, independently alive . . .

Without warning, her mind flashed back to that incandescent moment when she'd stood like an icicle in Jordan's arms. Neither by look nor gesture had she betrayed her inner turmoil. But she had wanted him. She had craved every inch of the long, hard body pressing against hers!

Valentine shivered. She had literally ached to accept his explanation and melt into him. But that glimpse of Gaby in his robe, Gaby's underthings strewn across the coffee table, was all she'd needed to turn to ice!

She hadn't seen Jordan since. And dear God, she did miss seeing him! Time had taught her a harsh lesson; thoughts of Jordan unleashed almost paralyzing heartache. In its grip she couldn't function properly, couldn't reason. She told herself there was absolutely nothing to be gained from rehashing the past. Yet her mind had the aggravating habit of sliding right back into its well-worn "Jordan" groove the instant she let down her guard.

She turned over and thumped her pillow. Rain sluiced down her windows, its dark turbulence vastly increasing her loneliness. *Elisse has deserted me, too,* she thought sadly. In logic's wide-angled view, it seemed a silly misery, but still, she did feel abandoned.

Even the vibrations that came with holding Elisse's picture were missing. Why? Valentine wondered. Am I being punished? Did she leave me because I've done something bad? It was a childish thought, raked up from the residue of a child's fear of death; *is* it my fault Daddy died? "Foolish, irrational kid's stuff," she muttered, kicking off the covers. But wasn't it funny how tenaciously it clung to the adult psyche!

She got up and took an aspirin to soothe her various aches. Anyway, Elisse wasn't kid's stuff. She had been real. *Was* real. "So why did you leave me, Elisse?"

The inner silence against which she hurled her question had all the aspects of a black hole, Valentine concluded wearily. Giving up on sleep, she wandered downstairs.

Music drifted from Sam's bedroom. In dire need of companionship, Valentine called, "Sam?"

"In the bathroom. Come on in, sweetie."

Obeying, Valentine smiled with genuine pleasure. Sam had filled the huge, footed tub nearly to the brim and immersed her lovely self neck-deep in a steamy bubble bath. That firecloud of hair billowed atop her head and green eyes peeked out of a white facial mask.

Positioned within easy reach, a small tray table held flickering candles and a bottle of fine brandy. Grabbing a paper cup, Valentine poured herself some of the golden liquid. "Hey, Sam! Enjoying a romantic bath all by yourself?"

"Yeah, darn it, all alone. But I'm enjoying the hell out of it. I know I called this tub a monstrosity when I first saw it, but to tell you the truth, I love it!" she confessed.

"Me, too. I can just imagine Elisse and her beloved sharing a bath in this tub."

Sam shivered as thunder shook the windows. "A lovely

thought,'' she said dryly. ''So what's your problem? Just couldn't sleep? Or is it Jordan?''

Valentine sighed. ''You know.''

''Yeah, I do know.'' Sam shot her a quick, assessing glance. ''Sweetie, are you sure about him? We all make mistakes. Really stupid mistakes sometimes, that kill us with remorse and regret. So isn't it possible—''

''No, it isn't possible!'' Valentine retorted, then sighed. ''Sorry, I didn't mean to yell at you. But yes, I'm sure about him, so let's dispense with the subject, okay?'' She took a swig of brandy. The fiery liquid hit her empty stomach like a bomb. ''Whoa!'' she gasped.

''Watch it, Mouse,'' Sam warned. ''That stuff's potent!''

Valentine finally caught her breath. ''Potent,'' she agreed. ''You think we could dispense with the nickname, too?''

''Why, I guess so,'' Sam said, taken aback. ''You don't like it?''

''No, not anymore. It pinches, Sam. It also hurts that you can't see I've outgrown it.''

Sam's eyes widened. ''Val, I wasn't making a judgment when I called you that! It was always done with love.''

''Oh, I know that.'' Valentine perched on the tub's broad rim. ''But right now I'm so confused about things . . .''

''What things?''

''You name it, I've confused it.'' Valentine finished off her brandy in one torturous gulp and refilled her cup. ''You know what I find so funny? Not funny-ha-ha, although it is amusing, but funny in a terribly ironic way.''

''No, darlin', what do you find so funny?'' Sam asked gently.

''You won't make love with Clay because it's too important. And I made love with Jordan because it was so important. Is that not the funniest thing you ever heard?''

''Well, I'm not laughing, so I guess not,'' Sam replied. Her heart constricted at her cousin's pain. ''Babe, we all do things for different reasons. It's you doing it your way and me doing it my way, you know? Who's to say which way is right? Certainly not me. Not anymore. Not since we came to Texas.

I think you've crammed five years' growth in eight months' time. That's what's so astonishing; how much and how swiftly you've changed. It threw me at times. It still does. I don't always know how to react to this new you."

"Well, neither do I, Sam," Valentine said indignantly. "I'm having a helluva time trying to make sense of some of my more erratic behavior. When you've been as predictable as an old shoe your entire life, it's not easy not knowing what you might do next! In fact, it's downright scary."

"It is that."

There was an odd note in Sam's agreement. Valentine's quick glance evolved into a double take as psychic senses opened and suddenly expanded to blazing awareness. The many-colored wave of emotion swirled around Sam like a glorious banner.

Wondering how on earth she'd missed such a visual shout of joy, Valentine cleared her throat. "You're holding something back from me, Sam," she said softly. "Why? Because you're happy and I'm not?"

"Well, I . . . Val, I know you're suffering and I hate that!"

"I kind of hate it, too," Valentine conceded drolly. But . . ." She shrugged. "Now why are you so happy you're in danger of splitting a seam?"

Sam gave a strained laugh. "Lord, you really can see through walls and around corners!" Her gaze lowered. "I am happy, Val, happier than I ever thought possible," she confessed. Shining green eyes met Valentine's like a head-on collision. "Clay asked me to marry him and I said yes."

Valentine awoke to a morning made for lovers, soft with the cooing of turtledoves and spiderweb breezes drifting in through the open windows. Blearily she wondered why she was in Sam's bed, then remembered last night and their celebratory madness. Flinging an arm across her forehead, she began crying as she recalled why they were celebrating. Sam was getting married.

On the surface, the haunting sense of loss that plagued her was foolish—nothing had changed between them. Yet, in that brief instant everything had changed. Her cousin, her confidante and best friend, now had someone more important in her life. Once again she was alone and bereft. . . .

"You're being silly, Valentine!" she chided her tearful self. Although her relationship with Sam would never be the same, it did still exist. But the same couldn't be said of Jordan. She'd lost him, too.

Valentine sighed, exasperated at her treadmill thoughts. Regardless of who or what else she might be thinking of, they always came back to Jordan. He wasn't worthy of her love. But that didn't stop her from loving him. "Oh, damn you, Jordan Wyatt!" she whispered, wiping away tears.

Tension-tight muscles creaked a protest as she turned on her side. Her head ached with a vengeance only brandy can exact. When Sam came in with coffee, she moaned piteously. "Going to hell in a handbasket, Sam," she quipped with a valiant laugh.

"Yep. Drunk as a skunk last night," came Sam's blithe agreement. "The way you carried on, I figured I'd better keep you under surveillance lest you fall off the balcony or some such thing, so I put you in my bed. Here, sit up and drink Vera's surefire cure for overindulging. Tomato juice, herbs, a shot of this and that. Yum! Smells horrid," she said with ghastly good cheer.

Holding her nose, Valentine drank the fragrant concoction. "Ugh. It's a kill or cure thing, isn't it?" she accused.

Sam grinned, picked up the empty glass, and left.

Against all odds, Valentine managed to keep it down, and soon began feeling restored. When Sam came back with hot coffee, she smiled. "Hi, Sam. I love you. And I'm very happy for you and Clay. Regardless of what I might have said last night . . . did I say anything amiss last night?"

"No, love. In fact, you were sappy sweet. Now try the coffee." Sam chuckled. "I spoke to Clay this morning and he's delirious with relief that you're taking this so well."

Realizing that Sam and Clay had discussed her probable reaction to their marriage, Valentine averted her gaze. Then she laughed and tossed her head. "I don't know why. I told you I'm happy for you! Delighted, in fact. Have you set a date yet?"

"No, not yet. I want a long courtship. Gets a girl lots of flowers and presents," Sam said archly. "Oh, Deke called. He'll be here around five this evening to pick you up and commands you to be ready."

"For what?" Valentine sat up with only marginal discomfort.

"For your birthday present from him to you. He thinks you've been a bit frazzled lately, life being what it is and all, and you could use some alone-time. So you're being whisked off to San Antonio for the weekend. 'Quote: Leave Friday evening, return Sunday afternoon. Champagne, roses, pickup and delivery included. Happy birthday: D. Salander.' Unquote. Now isn't that nice!" Sam cooed.

"It's crazy, is what it is," Valentine said crossly. "I don't want to go off somewhere with Deke for a weekend. I have enough troubles."

"Well, of course you do," Sam agreed. "But you won't be weekending with Deke, sweetie. He'll just drop you off at his River Walk hotel and be on his way, which leaves you with a lovely, pampered span of time to yourself. I know you're too smart to turn that down."

Valentine eyed her. "I thought you considered Deke a base-hearted rogue. Why the change of heart?"

"Oh, I still think he has the hide of an armadillo," Sam said airily. "But he kind of grows on you after a while. Anyway, he's doing this lovely thing for *you*, which makes me happy, too. And Sunday, when you get back, Clay and I are teaming up with Vera and Ozell to treat you to a splendid dinner at Tony's. Now is that a birthday present or what!"

Valentine held her head and groaned. "I'd forgotten my birthday is Sunday. Great. Then I'll be a twenty-*four*-year-old idiot."

"But you'll go?"

"Of course I'll go, Sam. I'm not that much of an idiot," Valentine said.

*   *   *

Deke slipped off his boots and settled into a comfortable position for the ride to San Antonio.

Sitting quietly beside him in the limo's backseat, Valentine offered little more than a comment or two before lapsing into silence. Then, catching his eye, she smiled wryly. "I told you I wouldn't be very good company."

"You're fine company. I never was keen on chatterboxes. Anyway, I'm still recovering from that outburst you greeted me with."

She laughed. "I guess I did get a little carried away when you first arrived. But I couldn't wait to tell you my most excellent news. Admit it, you think it's wonderful, too."

"And surprising. Sam and Clay getting married . . . never thought she'd fall into that fine trap," he mused. "She always struck me as a little too hard-shelled for the love-and-romance bit."

"No one's ever too hard-shelled for love and romance," Valentine rebuked. "Besides, underneath that sophisticate's crust dwells a puffy marshmallow."

Liking his rich chuckle, Valentine looked at him and saw the subtle change that had taken place in this dear man. It finally happened, she realized, elated. Deke had made a breakthrough. Somehow he had gotten in touch with the pervasive, hard-edged loneliness that lay at the core of his being. An aloneness, she suspected, that had, for most of his life, influenced his every thought, his every act. What effect did this powerful new awareness have on him?

Rousing herself to a sparkling display of interest, she playfully inquired, "So what have you been up to lately? Or can't you tell me?"

Deke's inner smile was painfully dry as he acknowledged the raw need to boast of his feats. He wanted to lay them at her feet like trophies of the hunt. His mouth twisted with the savage irony of admission. In some way he did not yet understand, she had given him something priceless. *Awareness.* Yeah, he was beginning to realize things. Deep things, like the knowledge that a man's existence was not defined solely by this singular time and space. That how much money he'd squirreled away did not determine his intrinsic worth.

Powerful strange thoughts for an ole country boy, he mocked himself. But the mockery wouldn't hold. "For your information, I've been up to a helluva lot of good lately," he announced, twirling his mustache.

"You have? Like what?"

"Like giving away some of that money I've piled up." He mimicked the prim tone she'd once used on him. "You'll be happy to know that Sugar Lee's new catering business is set to open on the Square in another three weeks or so. Probably lose every dime I invested—who eats at a deli?" He snorted.

"Lots of people do," she retorted. "Real people, that is. And trust me, your investment will be returned tenfold, just like bread cast on the waters. I'm proud of you, Deke," she said warmly. "Now what else?"

"What else? That's not enough? Damn, Valentine, what does it take to satisfy you?" Looking pained, Deke opened another imported beer. "I'm setting up two separate endowments for that school Vera's child attends."

"Oh, Deke, that's marvelous—*you're* marvelous!" Valentine cried, kissing his cheek. "But why two endowments?"

"Because it's smarter than just handing over a wad of money," he replied gruffly. "One endowment will be used for new capital improvements. The interest on the second one will be used to help operate and maintain existing facilities. This doesn't mean everyone can lay down their tools and goof off. Hell, no! Becoming self-sustainable by creating a saleable product is still a prime objective, especially since I'm now on the board. But the endowments should ease the financial strain quite a bit, even leave funds for expansion. I trust this meets with your approval?"

"More than meets." Valentine cleared her throat. "It overwhelms, darling Deke. Thank you."

"You're welcome." Deke shifted. "I hate seeing you so unhappy. Makes me feel like taking my deer rifle after Wyatt."

"Ah, poor Jordan. Seems like half the town's gunning for him." Valentine sighed. Mimicking his drawl, she pitched her voice absurdly low. "Don't shoot him, please, Deke? The varmint's not worth you goin' to jail!"

Deke matched her jesting manner. "I reckon you're right, ma'am. But if your heart's dead set. on gettin' hitched, well, hell's bells, I'm willing."

Valentine caught her breath, and slowly released it. He was serious! "My lord, Deke, you just leave me breathless!" she charged. "I mean, you're so sweet . . ."

"I'm not sweet, I love you, Valentine," he said testily.

"And I love. But not that way, Deke. You kissed me once and it was nice. But that's all it was and you know it. There hasn't been a speck of passion between us."

"No, I guess not." Deke leaned his head back against the seat and closed his eyes. "But is passion so all-fired important?"

"Yes."

Silence. "Okay, that's settled," he growled. Another silence spun out between them. "There are just some people you want to give the whole goddamn world to, Valentine. Unfortunately, you seem to be one of those people." He opened one eye. "Are you laughing?"

"Sort of. A tiny bit. Because you consider me one of those people," Valentine said smoothly. She could see that his relief far outweighed regret. *He'd probably faint had I said yes*, she thought, hiding her smile. "We're friends, Deke. Have been from the first, will be till the last, God willing. I'll survive my sorrows, trust me. Now hush before we say something we'll both regret. Does that TV work?" she asked brightly.

Obligingly Deke turned on the small television set and they watched the six o'clock news. Traffic on Interstate 10 was sparse and the big car hummed along so smoothly that she soon nodded off. Pillowing her head on his shoulder, Deke sat tensely, contemplating the changes in his life since he'd met this enchanting creature. He still hadn't figured her out and doubted he ever would. To him, she was even more mysterious than the man Deke Salander. He'd probably bare his soul to her before the weekend was over, and who knew what lay in that nether region of self? he thought sardonically.

Sarcasm aside, he had to admit that she'd had a forceful impact on him. He had never stopped to give thanks before. Thanks for what? For all the ugly pain and hardships that had shaped his life? For his material goods, sure, but before meeting Valentine, that's all that would have merited his gratitude, and even there he was doubtful. No one gave him anything, he'd earned his good fortune the hard way.

But right now he could make a long list of things that had nothing to do with possessions. Like good friends, good health, people who were as real and honest as his treasured land. The unconditional love and loyalty of horses, deserved or not. For grass, for water: birds, flowers, trees, the singing winds of autumn. For future plans, and for even the promise of a future.

He'd always been in such a hurry. Going nowhere and running like a madman to get there. He was nearing the half-century mark and felt incredibly old. And empty. He had no one to share his accomplishments, no one to hold him and say, *well-done, Deke.* From some hidden reserve sadness welled up, and within it lay a terrible, unspoken loneliness.

Swiftly he blocked this new awareness with another rush of thought. He didn't even have anyone to leave his money to— now wasn't that the pits! It was funny in an excruciating kind of way, he mused; you spent most of your life grubbing for substance. Then you die and discover that you have to leave it all behind, because you sure as hell can't take it with you.

Maybe that's why he'd proposed to Valentine. Everybody needed someone. At this late date it wasn't likely he'd find the right kind of love—that passionate, fly-me-to-the-moon kind of love that he doubted even existed. Pragmatic most of the time, hard-nosed as always, he was resigned to that harsh fact. But half a loaf was a helluva lot better than none, he concluded, shifting again, ever so gently, to give Valentine's head more support.

Friday evening Jordan leaned against his front door and surveyed the mess his two nephews had made of his den. In truth, he quite liked the clutter they'd left behind. It added vital warmth to the silent room.

The noisy, joke-filled meal he'd shared with his sister and her two children would have been fun had he been in a better mood. But he'd carried it off, he thought. No one had an inkling of the heartache concealed under his hearty laughter.

He folded the sweater Glory had forgotten. God love her, he thought fondly. He was so damn proud of her! And proud of himself for having the good sense to take Valentine's advice.

Valentine. Funny how her name shaped his mouth into a smile.

Pensively he began clearing the coffee table of empty juice boxes and the remains of the turkey burgers he'd grilled for them. What would it be like to have kids of his own? Trouble, his mind promptly answered. But pleasure, too. With a bleak smile he loaded the dishwasher and turned it on. As soon as he'd finished his small, homey tasks, the room closed in around him like a fist.

Heartache knifed his chest again. God, he missed Valentine!

Go to her. He pushed away the tempting thought. He was a man of action and taking a passive role was tantamount to standing in a fire ant nest, but dammit, he couldn't just bully his way into her life. He'd already tried that, even told her he loved her. But she hadn't believed him.

Well, the ball was in her court now. He had too much pride to court another stinging rejection. *If she cares for me, she'll come to me*, he defied the longing tightening his lean frame. But he knew she wouldn't.

He jumped at the telephone's loud ring. His heart jumped, too. He was almost idiotically stunned to hear his father's voice.

"Well, you finally took my call," the elder Wyatt drawled.

Jordan nearly choked on the rage funneling through his throat. "Not by choice, I assure you," he said grimly. "I don't want to talk to you and I don't want your goddamned messages on my machine!"

"Hey, boy, simmer down," Chuck Wyatt advised.

"After all these years—who the hell do you think you are that you can—" Jordan's breath caught on the surprising hook of pain.

"I'm your daddy, that's who I am. Like it or not, you can't change that."

"No, I can't." Jordan's voice leveled. "What do you want from me, old man? Money?"

"All I want from you is your sisters' addresses. So I can look 'em up. Maybe just drop in on them, like a surprise. 'Cause I remember how those girls loved surprises!"

"Good God!" Jordan exclaimed, genuinely shocked by the man's effrontery. "Do you really think they want to see you?" he asked incredulously. "Or that I'll help you? I wouldn't let you within ten miles of my sisters!"

"Well, now, who died and made you boss, Jordan? My girls'll be glad to see me!"

That querulous voice set Jordan's teeth on edge. "No they won't," he responded, struggling for control. "Because you're not getting near them. And you died and made me boss."

"Huh. You're riding pretty high there, sonny," the older man drawled. "Listen, boy, you and me, we're just alike—"

"The hell we are!"

"The hell we're not! My old man took off when I was young and left me to do his dirty work. Hated ever minute of it, but like you, it made me grow up smart. Made me realize what a load families are, made me see the trap a woman sets. But unlike you, I got stupid for a minute and took that pretty bait. I got to admit you outsmarted me there."

"You're pathetic," Jordan ground out. "A miserable loser from the word go."

"I'm not a loser. A loser just sits around and whines about his screwups. Me, I did something about it."

"Yeah, you sure did. You skipped out." Jordan's laugh clawed his throat. "Tough decision, huh, Pop?"

"Hey, cut me some slack, will you?" Chuck Wyatt growled. "You have no idea what drove me away. Hell, boy, when I was your age I was running scared just like you. The difference is that I already had a shit-load of responsibilities.

Four kids, a whining wife, mortgaged to my soul and no sign of daylight. So I split.''

Jordan answered with contemptuous silence.

"I gotta look out for ole number one, Jordan. Just like you do. Judge me, you're judging yourself.''

"I'm nothing like you!'' The outraged cry was gouged from Jordan's heart.

"No?'' The older man laughed gratingly. "Who's sharing your castle, huh? Who's putting the screws to you ever day of your life? Nobody. You're a loner just like me. I'm gonna die a loner and so are you. 'Cause that's the way we are.''

"I'm not you, goddamn it!''

"No? Look in the mirror, Son. You see you, you're looking at me.''

"Bullshit! Listen, old man, and listen good. Your girls want nothing to do with you, now or ever. Neither do I. You weren't there for the first part of my life and I don't want you in the rest of it!'' Jordan slammed down the receiver.

Immediately the telephone rang again. Stiffening, he snatched it up and barked a raging hello.

It was Clay with a work-related problem.

With colossal effort, Jordan reined in his emotions and dealt with it.

Hanging up on a more congenial note, he threaded a hand through his damp hair. God, but he felt jangled. He had to get out, had to work off some of this pent-up energy, this explosive tension! He put on running shorts and shoes and headed for the lakeside jogging trail.

His familiarity with the path left his mind free to surf his stormy sea of thoughts. He tried concentrating on business, but other, far more perplexing things crowded in, all fighting for precedence.

The call from his father won out. Fragments of their conversation still stained his mind. *Look in the mirror, Son. You see you, you're looking at me. . . .*

Remembering, Jordan shuddered and sent an oath slicing through the still night. "I'm not like him," he whispered. "I'm not, dammit, I'm not!" But his denial collided head-on with his father's words. *No? Who's sharing your castle? No-body. You're a loner, just like me. . . .*

Other phrases from their conversation clung like dirt to his mind. *The trap a woman sets . . . unlike you, I took the pretty bait . . . putting the screws to your life . . .*

Such an ugly way to look at life, Jordan thought. It was the viewpoint of a frightened little man. For the first time in his life a sliver of pity penetrated the contempt that encrusted his father's image.

Troubled and confused, Jordan increased his speed and tried to set his mind on a less provocative topic. But his father's disturbing accusations kept pace with his steps. *A loner, just like me . . . Running scared, just like me . . .*

I'm nothing like him, he assured himself. But I *am* his son. Could I, too, fail to live up to the promises I make to someone I love? No, never! My sisters are testimony to that!

But I failed Valentine, didn't I? he continued his self-argument. No, dammit, I made no promises, I didn't lead her on—I was very careful not to do that. Still, she expected something from me that I didn't give her. . . .

Couldn't give her?

Running scared. . . . Just like me . . .

The eye-opening words spread like an oil slick through his mind.

Several hours later Jordan sat at the kitchen table drinking a beer he didn't remember getting, still wearing running clothes from a run he scarcely recalled. Obviously his mind had been preoccupied with something else.

"September Valentine," he murmured with caressing hunger. Had someone told him that he would ever feel this needful, he would have surely laughed, knowing that for him such a thing was impossible. He had closed himself off to love long ago, when it saddled him with so much obligation he'd staggered under its crushing weight.

But the load that grinds down a boy can be easily borne by a man.

The stunning flash of insight came out of nowhere and

floored him with its simplicity. Even given love's magic al-
chemy, he'd had trouble believing that it could transcend such
deep-based fear. But with the aid of hindsight, he saw that
love hadn't acted alone; he'd grown up.

"And dragged all that emotional baggage right along with
me," he mused, shaking his head at the sudden clarity of his
thinking. He'd been such a fool . . .

The telephone tempted with its siren call to action. He hesitated; at best Valentine thought him shallow and insensitive;
at worst, a cheating bastard. Her last question clanged through
his mind. *What's your love worth, Jordan?*

"Maybe nothing, to her," he admitted with brutal honesty.
But he had to try one more time.

He dialed her house.

Sam answered. "She's not here, Jordan."

"Well, I . . . can you . . ." He floundered, his habitual self-
assurance vanishing on the instance. Sam must think him a
bastard, too! He cleared his throat. "When she comes in tonight would you tell her I called and that I . . . I'm sorry, Sam.
So goddamned sorry!"

"Clay's already told me that." Sam sighed. "Jordan, she's
not coming in tonight. She's spending the weekend in San
Antonio. With Deke."

It was a visceral blow and it winded Jordan as effectively
as a fist. His fingers tightened around the receiver, knuckles
white from the force of his grip. So he'd been right to consider
Deke a dangerous rival! "God, I really *am* a fool," he grated.

"No," Sam said gently. "No, Jordan. Deke's just a friend."

Jordan didn't reply. Everything in him wanted to believe
her. But hurt, anger and jealousy brewed a hellish stew. He
cleared his throat. "Where's she staying in San Antonio?"

Sam hesitated, caught in her own dilemma. She had to be
wary of anyone hurting Valentine, but Clay's good opinion of
Jordan hadn't changed. And, loving Clay, she had to trust him.
Sighing, she growled the name of Valentine's hotel.

"Thanks, Sam," Jordan said. Replacing the receiver, he
sank down on the couch. His painful turmoil was unabated.

He still felt the need to pound something! But ranting and raving and cursing his fate wouldn't change the facts. The woman he loved was spending the weekend with another man—and he had no one to blame but himself.

Chapter 18

The lavishly quaint hotel in which Deke installed her over-looked San Antonio's renowned River Walk. The building's white stucco facade was embroidered with lacy, black wrought-iron balconies. Although small, they afforded a bird's-eye view of the activity taking place along the winding river below.

After Deke left for his own quarters in another hotel, Valentine sat outside for a while watching the small, open-air, bargelike boats drift along the dark green waters. Some were crowded with sightseers, some with nattily dressed diners enjoying their catered dinners despite being on public display. She felt distanced from their gaiety by the apathy that dulled her senses.

The sun went down. She ordered soup and salad from room service, and ate it without pleasure. She hated this joyless mood. How could she be here in this fascinating city, in this luxurious hotel, and feel so indifferent to her surroundings? Itchy with frustration, she decided to take a walk.

She soon discovered that the scenery was wasted on her, so she stopped looking and just walked. At some point she paused beside a sidewalk vendor specializing in fresh strawberry daiquiris, and discovered they were delicious. She drank two before moving on.

Tourist traffic thinned as she left the restaurant area, and a fresh breeze blew off the water. Feeling better, she moved faster, simply following the cracked sidewalk. Wayward thoughts stole into her mind and reactivated an ever-present ache. Wouldn't it be lovely strolling the River Walk with Jordan! They would have half a dozen strawberry daiquiris and then tumble into bed in a glorious haze of love and sex and fun. . . .

Romantic nonsense, she chided herself. But common sense was pathetically ineffective against such deep, intense desire. It went beyond a mere physical ache to something far more unmanageable: *love*. Such a small word for so much trouble, she thought with a mirthless smile.

Seeking a less painful subject for her restless mind to ponder, she examined her rejection of Deke's proposal and even wondered if she ought not reconsider. It wouldn't be difficult to live the life of an older man's pampered darling. She could have the kind of security most people only dream about. More than one woman had gladly substituted money for passion. Why not Valentine? To paraphrase Deke, was passion so allfired important? Besides, she felt the urgency again, the pressure to shape her life in the way she wanted it to go. So why *not* Deke? Why not stop dreaming and hoping, and try being practical for a change? Deke had charm and personality. He made her laugh and she considered a sense of humor vital to a man's character.

Unlike Jordan, Deke was independent without obsessing about it. Jordan hung on to his independence like a lifeline, she thought sadly. But then, Deke had never felt obligated to take care of anyone but himself.

With a sudden flash of insight she realized the point she'd just made. Somewhere she had read that psychological independence meant total freedom from all obligatory relationships. At the time she had not fully comprehended what that meant, or how it related to her situation. But now it seemed so clear. Jordan was averse to a serious relationship because, to him, independence meant being free from having to do something he might otherwise choose not to do.

"So the obligation is the problem, not the relationship!" she thought aloud. Jordan had been trying to tell her that all along, but she hadn't understood. And very likely, neither had he. He was simply trying to describe his feelings in the matter. If she had listened with her heart instead of her ego, maybe—

Insight winked out as her mental alarms went off. She had left the public part of the river walk behind and wandered into the poorly lit lower-income residential section. The path ahead wound under an ominously shadowed overpass. Simultaneous with this realization came another—she heard heavy footsteps behind her. Masculine footsteps.

Sensing negative intent, Valentine cursed her carelessness. She had no weapon, not even a purse, only this small fanny pack strapped around her waist. Nerves taut with fear, she whispered, "Angels please protect me," and whirled to confront her assailant.

The thick-set young man stopped dead and stared at her, a look of astonishment and fright stamped on his stubby features. Then he wheeled and ran back the way he'd come!

Dumbfounded, Valentine stared after him. What had spooked him? Nervously she looked around but saw no one other than her own lonely self.

Except that she *wasn't* alone!

Valentine gasped at the sudden, profound awareness of being . . . *guarded*. Yes, that was the word! Something stood beside her, protecting her. She felt its presence first. Then she saw it and her knees went weak.

Swirling light, shimmering white and silver light, brilliant sun-on-snow light. The radiant light of a thousand summer suns.

Angel light.

The formless florescence glowed like an image superimposed on the world of everyday life. Mesmerized, Valentine simply watched it. She was scared at a shallow level, scared enough to stop breathing, scared enough, she thought, to die.

But deeper down, an elegant peace was stealing in, and the name trembled on her tongue. Elisse? Was it Elisse?

"Hello, Valentine."

.The calling words were infinitely loving, the voice celestial music. Valentine let out her breath as the misty swirls of light began to coalesce. She stared, wide-eyed, at the woman materializing from the ethereal substance. Wondrously beautiful, she had golden hair and luminous amber eyes. Her attire, silver slippers and a long white gown tied at the waist with a silver cord, shimmered with its own soft brilliance.

She was perfection itself. Divine perfection, Valentine thought, awed. The woman's form was not the dense, heavy matter of Earth, but rather the stuff of clouds. A heartbeat later two great white wings outstretched, then folded back behind her slim shoulders in exquisite symmetry.

Instantly aware that the symbolic gesture was for her, Valentine smiled with sheer delight. "Behold, an angel," she said, her own voice a harsh croak in comparison. "Are you real?"

"I am real. Do you know who I am?"

"Oh, yes, yes, I know who you are," she cried softly. "You are Elisse. And this time you remembered the wings!"

Elisse's tender laughter poured through Valentine's stressed system like a balm. Tears flooded her eyes. "Oh, I'm so glad you're here!" she blurted.

"So am I." Elisse tilted her head, her smile rueful. "Although I shouldn't be; it's very much against the rules and I know I'm going to catch it from Bradley!"

"Bradley?"

"Ah, yes, you don't remember." Elisse sighed. "Maybe it's time you do. I can't bear seeing you so confused and afraid."

"God, yes, I'm afraid! Help me, please help me. Get me out of this dark place and back to the light," Valentine pleaded.

"Valentine, you are safe now," Elisse said. "You can walk back to the hotel without further danger. But I see how sad you are, and it distresses me. Don't you remember what you were thinking before that poor soul interfered?"

"No, I don't." Valentine rubbed her aching neck.

"All right, in for a penny, in for a pound—isn't that an old Earth saying?" Elisse asked, chuckling. "Let's sit down and commune with each other, shall we?"

"Sit down?" Valentine looked around the dim River Walk, at the damp embankment, the thin grass. "Where?"

Elisse gave a tinkling laugh. "Ah, I forget where we are. Well, we can easily remedy that. Give me your hands, dear one."

Without a trace of wariness, Valentine obeyed. The huge white wings enfolded her in blissful security. An instant later she was standing in a meadow at the base of a waterfall whose waters created a glistening white bridal veil.

Elisse stepped aside, smiling as Valentine looked around with childlike wonder. "My God, Elisse," she whispered reverently. The sky was heavenly blue. Impossibly delicate mosses and ferns grew among the tumbled rocks; noble trees shaded the pool and formed a green canopy over their heads. There were flowers everywhere, hyacinths, gardenias, the beloved lilacs of her youth: myriad lilies: bowers of roses of every imaginable hue. A gentle zephyr carried their sweet perfume to every corner of the world.

If this was still the world, Valentine thought shakily.

"Where is this place?" she asked.

"It is my place. I created it for the same reason I've brought you here. Even a guardian angel must now and then have a respite from earthly woes. Let us use this brief time out of time wisely, Valentine." The angel motioned to a flat, moss-cushioned rock. "Please sit down, darling. You'll find this as comfortable as a pillow, I promise."

When Valentine sank down onto the rock's cloud-soft surface, Elisse perched across from her and took her hands. "You've remembered nothing about meeting us because that was your choice. But I think the progress you've made—entirely on your own—absolves you of that decision."

"By us, you mean you and this Bradley person?"

"This Bradley Being, yes. Valentine, when your plane crashed in the wilds of Montana, you had a near-death experience."

"I did? But I don't remember anything like that!" Valentine protested. "I mean, I've read about those experiences and they all come with visions and tunnels and bright lights. I had nothing like that. We crashed, everything went black and then it became light again."

"Because you decided to block it out," Elisse explained gently. "Believe me, darling, you had a classically beautiful experience traveling into the Light. If you wish to remove the block and recall it, you have only to command it."

"But how? I don't know how!"

"You do. Just close your eyes. Desire it."

"I do desire it, I . . . Oh!" Valentine gasped as lights began gathering behind her eyelids . . . and suddenly exploded in a starburst of soft, incandescent radiance. She was utterly incapable of describing the glory of that radiance. Its sublime purity cleansed her soul and restored it to wholeness.

Like a running montage she saw her still white form lying in the snow, saw the scene growing smaller and smaller as she drifted upward, feather-light in the caressing warmth that bore her along. She still had a body, a fine body. The only difference was that it no longer encased her spirit like a heavy coat of clay. Free at last, she thought exultantly.

The montage gained speed, brush-stroking her actual conversation with the two white-robed Beings, one so merry and gentle, the other endearingly pompous and given to harrumphing whenever his good heart got the better of his brilliant mind. They radiated loving kindness. She was not afraid.

And then she was traveling back through the tunnel of her mind, her Higher Self supportive but firm as the Personality that was Valentine protested her return to Earth. And squeezing her magnificent Self back into the cold, clammy body was incredibly distasteful. She had shuddered as its icy cells enclosed her, she wriggled and squirmed trying to fit comfortably into these dank environs again. *I can tell you exactly how it feels to be inside an icicle*, she'd told Sam, and no wonder! "Ugh, I hate this," she said, opening her eyes.

"You'd hate being an infant again even more, remember?" Elisse teased.

Valentine looked puzzled.

Elisse sighed. "Oh, Valentine, you make the very stars laugh and clap their hands with joy!"

"I'm not following you," Valentine confessed.

"They rejoice because you are so strong, darling. Don't you

see? Once again you chose not to remember the conversation
that took place between you and Bradley, even though remembering would have made it so much easier for you to make
decisions. Your spiritual growth strides are spanning entire
universes!'' Elisse proclaimed jubilantly. ''Do you remember
the rest of your journey into celestial realms?''

''Yes, I do remember, Elisse. Especially the part where I
met you!'' Valentine replied with open affection. ''You've
been with me all the time, haven't you! Guiding my decisions,
steering me onto the right path—''

''No, not steering. We are not permitted to steer,'' Elisse
said sternly. ''Just guidance. Although I might have overstepped a little, depending upon who you ask,'' she added with
a charming moue. ''But you were so brave, Valentine, so resolute, so determined to find your own way! If you had kept
even a scrap of memory to lean upon—but no. You decided
to muddle through alone, learn your lessons the hard way if
need be.''

''I didn't do all that great a job,'' Valentine said sadly. ''Is
Bradley pissed at me for being such a dud at helping others?''
She gasped and flung her hand to her mouth, appalled at her
language. ''Oh jeez, I can't believe I said that! I meant offended, is Bradley *offended* is what I meant to say!''

''Valentine, Valentine,'' Elisse chided, laughing. ''You
think your Counselor is so easily shocked? I imagine he has
heard worse than that!'' Sobering, she asked softly, ''Why do
you consider yourself a failure?''

''I've let people down.'' Valentine's head lowered. ''My
mother, for one.''

Elise made a *tsk-tsk* sound. ''Yesterday is gone; examine it
for lessons, then let it go in peace. Today is all that's important. And today, Valentine, your mother is standing alone for
the first time in her life. Yes, her strength is fragile, her steps
wobbly, but still, she leans on no one for support. Applaud
her, offer a hand when she expresses a need for it. But do not
volunteer to take charge of her life. That weakens a human
being.''

Elisse waved her hand and a tray materialized from thin air.

On it were two tall, frosty beverages. "You seemed to enjoy those strawberry daiquiris so much, I thought it would be fun to try one with you!" She passed one to an amazed Valentine and took the other for herself.

"Daiquiris? Angels drink daiquiris?"

"Oh, yes. You see, here one can eat and drink whatever one likes without negative effects. And that includes calories!" Elisse said gleefully. "Umm, delicious," she decided after a delicate sip.

"Thank you!" Valentine said, laughing joyously. She didn't want this to end, ever. Just to stay here in this beautiful place with the very Spirit of love and affection shining upon her with the warmth of a thousand suns.

"Someday, darling, someday," Elisse said very softly. "Because you have chosen to resume your Earth lessons, I am going to release some insights to help you at certain times. They are your insights, not mine. They're locked within you, waiting for your permission to surface. This insightful wisdom will seep in rather than flood your mind with knowledge." Smiling, she put down her drink and touched cool fingertips to Valentine's temples. "You will not consciously remember this . . ."

Sometime later, eons or moments, Valentine knew not, she felt a gentle, forceful movement deep within her mind as Elisse's telepathic message ended. They shared a communing smile. Then they focused on the simple pleasure of enjoying excellent strawberry daiquiris.

"It is time," Elisse said reluctantly. "But before you return, I must counsel you against giving your power to another. The fear that consumes you is a thief of the worst sort. It robs you of initiative and will, of your innate ability to resolve problems, even of your common sense. Remember I told you once before that nothing—*nothing*—can harm the essential Valentine."

Elisse set aside her empty glass. "I've given you all the instruction I can without actively interfering in your life. You won't have instant recall, of course, just a glimmer now and then to help you at a crossroads."

"By crossroads, you mean Jordan?"

"That's one, yes, and a very important one. But as in every-thing else, what you decide to do about your relationship with Jordan is your decision. I can only wish you the very best and assure you that you are always loved and cherished." She stood up and unfolded her magnificent wings. "Farewell, dear one. Until we meet again, vaya con Dios."

To Valentine's surprise, returning to reality was as uneventful as rousing from a soft drowse. She knew immediately that she was back on the River Walk headed for her hotel. Tentatively she examined herself. She felt strange. Transformed. Oh, yes. And drained, she realized. Emotionally wrung out. Joyous, but touched with some indefinable pain that pulsed with the joyous proof that she was alive. Her entire being sparkled and glowed with Life!

Questions pounced with feline quickness and began to shred her lingering sense of bliss. Had it really happened? Had she actually been sitting beside a waterfall in some Edenic garden sipping strawberry daiquiris with an angel? Put into words, it sounded certifiable, she thought, chuckling. But she remem-bered it, every word, every act, every gesture. The only thing she could not recall was what Elisse said during their silent communication.

Although parts of her near-death experience were hazy, she recalled most of it with vivid clarity. She had felt so loved, so treasured, so devoid of fear and niggling anxieties. Curi-ously, she did not doubt that this mysterious event had hap-pened. She knew it had. She knew a lot of things now, a lot of answers to puzzling questions. Yet, defining these answers was impossible. It was more an instinctive knowing than a rational explanation.

She walked quickly, threading her way through the remain-ing revelers with cheerful tolerance for their various states of inebriation. When she reached her room she saw a bottle of champagne on the table in a silver bucket. The message read: *Enjoy! Yours truly, Deke*.

Beside it was a wicker basket, lined with ferns, filled with roses the icy pink of a winter dawn. "That Deke," she murmured fondly. He'd promised her roses and he'd delivered.

But they weren't from Deke. Valentine read the card with an audible catch of breath. Jordan had sent the roses! *"Tis said that a blind man will not thank you for a looking glass, but this one does."* He'd signed it simply, *Jordan.*

"What does he mean?" she wondered, groping for a chair as hope stormed in, breath-taxingly swift and strong. Reading the oblique message twice produced no answers, nor did it clear her mind. She hugged herself with a little rocking motion. I could call him, she thought. Just call him and ask, "What do you mean, Jordan?" Her nerves shrank from such an obvious solution. But her fingers reached for the telephone.

The shock of hearing his husky voice instead of a dial tone momentarily stilled hers.

"Hello?" he repeated.

"Jordan?" she asked incredulously.

"Yes," he said, a wry smile coloring his tone.

"Oh! I . . . uh . . . thank you for the flowers. They're gorgeous! But the card . . ."

He chuckled.

"Well, what does it mean, Jordan?" she demanded.

"It means I'm sorry I was so blind to the cause of your distress. That's why the reference to the looking glass. I turned the situation around, put me in your place, and finally realized what made you so mad." His words quickened. "Nothing did happen between Gaby and me, not physically, anyway. But then I thought about walking in on you and some guy in that same situation; supper cooking, you running around in his robe, barefoot and freshly showered . . ." He sighed. "I got the picture then, believe me."

"What picture was that?" she asked, carefully neutral.

"A picture of shared intimacy," he said, feeling his way. "Had the situation been reversed, very likely I'd have punched him out first and asked questions afterwards. So accusing you of going off half-cocked was way out of line. I'm sorry, Val. Forgive me?"

"You mean for being so dense." So disappointed she could

cry, Valentine dragged a laugh through her clogged throat. She wouldn't kid herself; this was just typical male bullshit! He didn't want her but he didn't want anyone else to have her. "Yes, I forgive you," she said lightly. "You know, of course, that I'm here with Deke?"

"Oh, yes, I know. And yes, I hate like hell knowing it!" Jordan replied roughly.

"Well, nothing happened, Jordan," she said slyly.

Jordan felt like he'd been rabbit-punched. At the same time, relief tumbled through him with disconcerting force. "Touché," he said gruffly. "You hit your target dead-on."

"Good."

The change in her voice hit another sensitive spot. God, I'm walking through a mine field here, Jordan thought. Hastily he sought a less provocative subject. "Glory and the boys came by this evening for dinner. My sister, remember?"

"Of course I remember."

"She was on the horns of another of her dilemmas and needed my advice; should she go to work now that both boys are in school, or return to school herself and get an accounting degree? Like you, she loves working with numbers. This time, though, instead of making the decision for her, I did what you suggested and asked, 'What do you want to do? And what's stopping you from doing it' Guess what? She worked it through to a resolution."

"That's great, Jordan. What was it?"

"School." Jordan paused invitingly.

She didn't respond.

Wanting desperately to hold even this small part of her, he cast about for something else that might intrigue her. "I talked to my father today," he blurted.

"How did it go?" she asked with genuine interest.

"About like I expected."

"Bad, huh?" Compassion laced her voice. "Why did you decide to talk with him?"

"I've been wondering the same thing," he said sardonically. "Being able to predict the outcome should give any sensible man reason to avoid making a hellish mistake. So why the devil didn't I just hang up? Maybe just plain old curiosity," he mused. "Or maybe it was you."

"Me?" she echoed, startled.

"Yeah, you. When I told you I had nothing to say to him, you said, '*How do you know unless you talk to him? You might find you do have something to say.*' " He gave a rasping laugh. "And sure enough, I did."

"I'm sorry, Jordan," Valentine said, touched in spite of herself. "I shouldn't have stuck my nose in your business."

"No, don't be sorry," he said quickly. "Actually it felt pretty good getting rid of all that hostility. To be totally honest, I was surprised as hell by my explosive reaction."

Valentine was both startled and pleased by his candor, although mystified at the reason for it. Why couldn't he have confided in her like this before, when they had been close? It was her turn to speak, but uncertain what to say, she made an encouraging sound.

Heartened, Jordan went on, "What set me off was his request to help him locate his daughters. Christ! Did he actually believe he could walk back into their lives as easily as he walked out?"

Valentine bit her lip. She wanted to agree with him just to keep him talking. Instead, she said, "That would be up to the girls, wouldn't it?"

"Why the hell would they want to see him?" Jordan countered. "Anyway, it's always been my job to make that kind of decision, protect them from making mistakes they'd regret."

"Well, everyone's entitled to regrets," Valentine said lightly. "Lord knows I've had a few. If you want my advice— and even if you don't—I'd say call your sisters and tell them what's happening. Let them decide if they want to see him." Wondering if she'd overstepped, she shifted into neutral territory. "San Antonio's really a lovely city. I can't wait to explore it tomorrow!"

"Yes, there's a lot to see and do. So you're having a good time?" he asked awkwardly.

"Yes, I am. I went out for a walk and met an angel. We

drank strawberry daiquiris and talked for a while.''

"About what?" he asked, a smile in his voice.

Valentine let out her breath. "About my near-death experience. Seems I died in that plane crash, Jordan. It was very interesting." She waited.

"I imagine so."

"You don't believe me."

"You haven't the foggiest idea whether or not I believe you." He exhaled audibly. "Unfortunately, neither do I. But I'm willing to listen."

"Well, maybe when I'm ready to talk about it . . ." She let it drop. "Deke sent me a bottle of champagne. The good stuff, too. I'm going out on my balcony and drink it. The whole darn bottle, maybe. Well, thanks for the roses. Good night, Jordan. See you around." The line went dead.

"See you," Jordan half whispered. He held the receiver as though, by this small act, he still held onto her. The twin devils of frustration and longing raged through his heart. Dear God, I do have a passion for that woman! he thought. And she's in San Antonio with another man. . . .

Jordan shook his head. Damned if he'd go that way! He'd wasted too much time already agonizing over Valentine's weekend with Deke. He didn't like it then and he didn't like it now, but how he felt about it was of no concern to anyone except himself. She had made that plain enough even for a chowderhead like Jordan Wyatt, he reflected glumly.

"But if she says nothing happened, then nothing happened," he muttered, squaring his shoulders. But he still wanted to pound on something. Or some*body*.

Chapter 19

*S*unday afternoon, Valentine settled into the limo's plush gray seat and closed her eyes. Her luxurious sigh was for Deke's benefit. They were returning to Destiny after a weekend she would never forget.

"So you enjoyed it, Valentine?" he asked gruffly.

"It was the grandest birthday present I've ever had," she replied. Saturday he had met her at the hotel for breakfast, then given her a royal tour of the city. She'd seen the Alamo, of course, as well as Sea World, the botanical gardens and the zoo. It had worn her out and enabled her to sleep that night. This morning they had breakfasted at an old flour mill that had been renovated into a charming restaurant. The staff had sung Happy Birthday to her and presented her with a candlelit muffin. She'd loved it.

But now, no longer distracted by the fun and excitement of a holiday, she felt herself sinking back into gray reality. Anger spiked her mood. Would she always be haunted by the memory of Jordan Wyatt?

As the limo rolled along down the wide, smooth highway, she lapsed into a semidrowse. Thinking her asleep, Deke tuned the television set to a stock market report.

An inner smile lit her mind as she followed his careful actions. Last night she had accepted the fact that she would not marry this beautiful man. They were not right for each other. Still, she cared for him and wanted very much for him to experience the kind of regrettably brief, but intensely satisfying bliss she'd found with Jordan. It would take a very special kind of woman to get under Deke's hard-boiled skin. She wished she knew someone, but she didn't.

As usual, her thoughts ran back to Jordan. Their phone call still tormented her. Surprised and pleased that he'd talked so freely about his personal life, her hopes had burst into bloom again. Now she derided her heart's enduring foolishness.

She had wanted so much to hear him say he loved her. But he hadn't even said he missed her.

He's not ready yet. The thought whispered through her mind and she didn't know whose it was. Her own? Or Elisse's?

Remember, it's not what happens to you that counts, but how you look at it. Would you take the risk again?

Yes! Oh, yes, I would, Valentine answered, surprising herself with her immediate, incautious response. Though she knew the consequences of loving Jordan—the wretched hurt, the river of tears she'd shed for him—she would do it all over again. Those few weeks of unparalleled happiness were worth any price.

On the heels of this decision came a strange sense of freedom, as if the band of sadness girdling her chest had suddenly snapped. Shaken by the swift, inexplicable change in her emotions, Valentine turned to the window to shield her reaction from Deke.

Cautiously she tested the new feeling by bringing to mind Jordan's handsome image, the touch of his hands, the crooked grin she loved so much. Expecting the piercing pain of memory, she was elated to discover that though it still hurt and she ached with regret for what might have been, it didn't devastate, didn't destroy.

Muscles taut with tension, Valentine examined this bold new concept of being in control of her life. It was probably deceptive, she thought, still unwilling to trust such stability to the Valentine she knew. Yet the feeling was there, imposingly strong and certain.

Pride in her femininity flowed through her like a powerful current. No longer the insecure, fearful Valentine, she was a strong, confident woman. Although possessing only the most childish notion of guardian angels, she had met hers face-to-face, heart-to-heart, Valentine thought exultantly. Her spiritual beliefs were simplistic, yet she had talked with, laughed with, and even argued with radiant Spirit-Beings from a Higher Realm. Her heart fluttered with the audacious contention. Yet she would not dilute it to make it more palatable. It had happened. She curled her arms around herself in a reassuring hug.

"You all right, Valentine?" Deke rumbled.

"I'm all right." Valentine glanced at him and felt troubled. Thus far their conversation had been pleasantly light, and she had no desire to introduce a controversial topic. But last night she'd had too much to drink and poured her heart out to him. While, womanlike, she might enjoy stirring up a bit of jealousy, she did not want enmity between him and Jordan.

She touched his hand. "Deke, don't think badly of Jordan. You two have been friends for so long, and friends give friends the benefit of the doubt. But you're feeling so protective of me that you're not being fair. Jordan has his reasons for . . . for what happened between us."

"Like what?" Deke grunted.

"I think psychologists call it burnout. Did you know that he was responsible for his whole family from the time he was twelve years old? Sometimes that's too heavy a load for grown men, much less a boy."

Relieved by Deke's courteous attention, Valentine continued her soft persuasion as the miles rolled by. He didn't say much in turn, but she thought she'd swayed him a little. At length, dispensing with the subject, they slipped back into easy silence.

It was nearly five o'clock when they entered Destiny. Eager to get home, Valentine occupied herself with spying familiar landmarks. "Stick around and go out with us tonight," she invited. "Sam and Clay are taking me to dinner . . ." She paused as they passed the Lovings' house. "My goodness, look at all the cars in Vera's driveway! I wonder what's going on?"

As soon as she asked the question, Valentine knew the answer. "Oh, good grief, it's a surprise birthday party, isn't it!"

"It is not!"

"Is, too!" Valentine shot back as they passed through her beloved brick pillars. Clay's vehicle was parked behind Sam's, but otherwise, their drive was misleadingly clear. Laughing, she hopped out as soon as the car stopped and flew up the steps.

Sam and Clay met her at the door and both caught her in an effusive hug. "Oh, Sam, Clay, thank you!" Valentine cried. "A birthday party—what a lovely thing to come home to!"

"I didn't say a word!" Deke protested Sam's glare.

"You didn't have to say anything, the woman's a sorceress!" Clay charged, hugging Valentine again.

Valentine put her arms around them both. "God, I love you guys something fierce!" she proclaimed, sniffling. And I love this house, she thought, drinking in its mellow ambiance. Fresh flowers abounded. The fine October day poured its gentle warmth through open windows and gaily colored balloons danced in the aromatic breeze created by lazily whirling ceiling fans.

"Happy birthday!" Clay shouted.

Right on cue, heads popped up, voices rang out and laughter filled the big house. Even as Valentine joined in the gaiety, her gaze swept the room.

Jordan wasn't here.

Concealing her disappointment, she hugged Dan Marshal, resplendent in his policeman's uniform: a beaming Vera and sour-faced Mrs. Belmont: Bubba with the precious pickup truck: Hank The Champion Cowboy—it said so right on his T-shirt—and a dozen or so others.

Recalling those first lonely days in Texas, Valentine looked around her home with a tinge of awe. All these friends, she thought tearfully. She had gathered them like wildflowers, picking some here, some there, until she had this lovely bouquet.

Her gaze caught on Vera's hot pink dress and stayed there

as the thin blonde turned in profile. "Vera? Oh, my God, Vera, you're not pregnant anymore!" she blurted.

"Nope." Vera grinned from ear to ear. "Last night I had a boy and girl, just like you said!"

Valentine stared at her for a frozen moment, then exhaled gustily as her own senses answered the question blazing across her mind. "They're all right," she whispered.

"They're all right," Vera confirmed. "They're still in the hospital—doc's taking no chances, but it's just a precaution, keepin' them under observation for a day or two," she babbled, torn between laughter and tears.

"Wonderful. *Wonderful!* But, my God, Vera, shouldn't you still be in the hospital, too?"

"Naw. Drive-through deliveries are all the rage these days," Vera said dryly. "I'm fine, honey. Just walkin' a little slow, that's all."

Valentine laughed, too. "I guess so! Here, sit down, darlin'," she said, helping her into a chair. "Where's Ozell?"

"He's busy right now—but don't you worry none, he'll be here," Vera assured her.

"Good grief!" Clay exclaimed, wrinkling his nose. "Is that your spaghetti, Sam?"

Sam glared at him, all outraged hauteur. "What you're smelling is Valentine's birthday present from Ozell, not my spaghetti."

Valentine's eyes widened as she, too, caught a whiff of the exceptional odor. "Oh, no, he didn't!"

"Oh, yes, he did!" Vera lilted. "Finally got you that load of chicken manure, Val. He's spreadin' it over your garden spot right now!"

Valentine ran outside to see for herself.

Ozell, incredibly grimy, stopped shoveling long enough to smile at her. "Now don't worry," he said reassuringly. "I'll put a layer of dirt on top to cut the smell."

Deeply touched, Valentine blinked back tears. "Oh, Ozell, you're beautiful, just beautiful! So are those babies, I bet. I can't wait to see them!" Barely restraining herself, she congratulated him and promised him a prodigious hug—after he'd cleaned up.

She hurried back inside, where, amidst much oohing and aahing, Vera produced pictures of her sleeping babies. Things had just quieted down when a soft, sweet feminine voice spoke from behind her and sent Valentine into joyous hysterics.

"Mom?" she asked incredulously. "Oh, Mom, *Mom!*" she cried, flinging herself into her mother's outstretched arms. "When did you get here. Why didn't you let me know! Oh God, I'm so glad you're here. I've missed you so!"

"I've missed you, too, love, more than you'll ever know," Julia replied tremulously. "I got in late last night. And it should be obvious why I didn't let you know. Surprise, darling!"

"Oh, I love surprises!" Valentine sobbed.

Luckily Sam stepped up with a tray of drinks. Dabbing at tears with a lace edged handkerchief, Julia accepted a glass of wine. "Thank you, dear heart, I need this."

"Me, too. You're better than a St. Bernard, Sam," Valentine teased, taking a glass. Using the moment to look closely at her mother, she felt a distinct shock. For far too many years she had seen only a tired-faced woman who spoke with resigned voice and smiled with lots of fortitude and very little joy. No longer the gentle gray dove, *this* Julia looked smashing in a chic ivory frock with a black patent leather belt spanning her small waist. Makeup enhanced her luminous eyes and bright red lipstick outlined her full mouth. Her hair was coiled and caught high at the back of her head with a silk flower.

Valentine marveled at the change. Her image of Julia had always been simply "Mom." Certainly she had never thought of her mother as a desirable woman. But she was! The evidence was there in Clay's eyes, in Dan's and Hank's.

And especially in Deke's, she noted with astonishment!

This time the shock streaked all the way to her toes as Valentine intercepted the glance exchanged by Deke Salander and Julia Townsend Brady. She'd seen the same blue flash of electricity when Sam and Clay had first met!

Mom and Deke? she thought wildly, then caught her breath

in dazzling realization; Deke and her mother were meant for each other all along! Deke had seen in the daughter, a small part of the mother, which is why he had proposed! It was the closest he'd ever come to recognizing a soul mate.

Overwhelmed by the beautiful rightness of it, Valentine struggled to compose herself. "Mom," she said as Deke materialized at her side, "I'd like you to meet my good friend and benefactor, Deke Salander." She grinned. "True, he's something of a scoundrel, but on the plus side, I'd trust him with my life." She stepped back, her grin helplessly spreading as Julia slipped her slender fingers into Deke's outstretched hand.

"May I get you a drink?" Deke asked Julia, apparently oblivious to the wineglass she held.

"Thank you, that would be lovely," Julia said, thrusting the glass into Valentine's hand.

Glancing at Sam, Valentine rolled her eyes. She felt alone and lonely as she saw the radiant redhead nestle against her hovering fiancé's shoulder. Beside her, Vera glowed fluorescent, and across the room, Dan Marshal's head was bent attentively to the town's newest caterer, Sugar Lee. Valentine's smile matched her poignant conclusion; being in control of one's life did not bestow immunity against pangs of the heart.

Filled with longing, she watched Sam's face turn to Clay's as naturally as a sunflower turned toward the sun. Once so aloof and correct in his presence, Sam was now openly warm and affectionate, her transformation from fearful distrust to faith in her man now complete.

But then, any romantic relationship was paradoxical simply because of that fear, Valentine realized insightfully. The more you cared, the more cautious you were. The more someone mattered, the less open you were, because opening up to someone for whom you cared desperately was dangerous and potentially hurtful. Was that why Jordan had been so averse to deepening their involvement? Because he really did care for her?

Sam's bright voice interrupted her disturbing train of

thought. "Guess how Aunt Julia got here from Ohio, Val! She didn't fly, she drove—in Sweet Cherry!"

Valentine's eyes and mouth rounded. "She *what*?"

"Drove down here in your little red Mercedes, darlin'," Sam caroled. "She put a down payment on it as your birthday present. You'll have to take up the payments, but I told her you wouldn't mind at all!"

"You're kidding!" Valentine wheeled to confront her mother, but Julia and Deke were deep in conversation on the veranda. "Oh God, Sam, all her troubles and she still—what a sweet thing to do," she said, eyes brimming with tears.

Holding herself in tight restraint, she slipped into the bathroom for a moment's respite. I've fooled them all, she thought, gazing at her image. But I can't fool myself. The question was there, in darkened violet eyes, in the down-curving mouth. Was Jordan coming to her party?

So nervous his hands shook, Jordan removed the key from the ignition of his car and sat gazing at the old white house. Though still riddled with confusion, he had managed to live through what he ironically termed his "dark night of the soul."

Irony aside, he had agonized that night. He had sweated blood and by God if he'd let anything stop him from finding his way back to the land of the living!

Bracing himself, he got out of the car and started up the cracked walk. How would Valentine react to his presence? She'd been pleasant enough on the telephone, but . . .

Standing straight and tall, he rang the doorbell.

Sam answered. "You took your sweet time getting here!" she hissed.

"I deliberately came late, Sam. I didn't want to chance spoiling her reunion with her mother," he hurriedly explained.

"Huh. So what do you plan to do when you see her?" she asked, green eyes flashing. "Play macho man again?"

"Not exactly," Jordan said with a very wry smile. "In fact, I kind of planned on crawling in on my belly and kissing her feet."

Sam's mouth twitched. "You don't have to go quite that far, Jordan." Noting the flawless red rose he carried, she sighed. "Look, I know your relationship is none of my business, but I love her, dammit. Just don't spoil her birthday, okay? Because if you do I'll have to shoot you. It's a matter of honor. Okay, join the festivities. Val? Another guest!" she called.

Jordan whisked the rose behind his back as he stepped inside. Valentine watched him approach, her face expressionless. Did she want him here? he wondered.

"Hi. You're lookin' mighty pretty, Miss Scarlett," he drawled and handed her the rose.

Startled, Valentine took it. "Why, thank you, sir," she replied in an equally absurd Southern accent, then laughed and touched the flower to her nose. "Hi, Jordan. I'm so glad you could make it to my party. I think you know everyone. . . . Except this pretty lady!" she said as her mother approached. "I'd like you to meet my mother, Julia Townsend Brady. Mom, this is Jordan Wyatt, another good friend," she said, immediately aware that her mother knew all about Jordan, courtesy of Sam.

Poker-faced, Julia replied, "Glad to meet you, Jordan."

"My pleasure," he said.

Just then someone else claimed Valentine's attention. His smile fixed, Jordan turned to chat with Clay and Ozell. But he was always aware of Valentine's position in the room. Covertly he watched her. She wore a blue dress, something soft and feminine with puffed sleeves that kept sliding off her shoulders. Long strands of hair spilled from her topknot and curled around her flushed cheeks. Such an alive little face, he thought, enchanted all over again.

Valentine was blazingly aware of his regard. As she noted his slow but steady progress across the crowded room, her erratic heartbeat kept pace with his movements. Was he making his way to *her?* Still wary and self-protective, she shivered as their eyes met. Anger strengthened her. Okay, she thought, let's have this out. I can't take another second of this nerve-jangling suspense! Holding his gaze, she tilted her head ever so slightly toward the door.

He nodded.

She slipped out the kitchen door and made her way to the gazebo. Nerves twitching, stomach fluttery with excitement, she waited for Jordan.

He appeared just moments later. His rolled-up sleeves revealed golden skin sprinkled with dark hair, and she quivered as images danced madly through her mind. God, how I want him! she thought, aflame with longing. She wanted all of him: the tousled dark hair, the crooked grin, the trim waist and those long, long legs, his thoughts, his worries, his joys and his triumphs. She wanted, ached for, needed his love. But it had to be freely given.

Swiftly he mounted the two steps leading into the airy structure and faced her. She meant to speak, to discuss their relationship in crisp, sensible words—

"Valentine, I love you. I've never said that to another woman," Jordan said roughly. "You're the most precious thing in the world to me, and I have to know you feel the same way about me—I *have* to."

He held out his arms. A mighty flood of love and longing swept her into them.

Oh God, the bliss of it, Valentine thought, the Heaven of being in his arms again! It was a homecoming in the most profound sense of the word. Closing her eyes, she stood very still and let it fill the many small cellular hungers created by his absence.

He said her name in that special way and her heart pounded. As his warm mouth touched her cheek, the elixir of life coursed wildly through her veins. Desperately she tried to withstand the demands his nearness placed upon her vulnerable self. She had something to say, something important. But it was so hard to remember when he held her like this!

Body hard, taut, trembling with passion, Jordan pulled her closer. "Darling, my darling," he murmured, trailing kisses down her neck.

Valentine quivered in response to that husky voice calling

her darling. He had not done that before. "Jordan. Jordan darling," she said, and it was her warm, throaty bedroom voice. Blindly she raised her face for his kiss. The taste and feel of his firm mouth ignited wildfires within her. Her body answered his, pure, mindless female glorying in the primal demands of the dominant male.

The word struck her pride, a tiny *ping* of resentment; but she was still responsive to it. Twisting her face aside, she slowly pulled away from his enticing magic.

"Jordan, no, this is too fast! Before we go any further, I have something to say and so do you."

"We'll go as slow as you want—God, I don't want to lose you!" he said hoarsely. "Marry me, Valentine, be my wife."

Valentine caught hold of the railing. She dreamed of this, prayed for it!

"I don't blame you for doubting me," he blurted, misreading her silence. "I haven't forgotten what I said that night on the boat. To be totally honest, I don't know why I felt that way."

"I know why. You're afraid of obligation, Jordan."

He drew back. "You can trust me, Val, I've always met my obligations."

"Precisely my point. You've met yours and everyone else's. In fact, you've spent your entire life taking care of others," she said softly. "Because you had no choice, darling. Not because of circumstance, but because your good heart wouldn't let you do otherwise."

Jordan frowned. "Valentine, I didn't martyr myself."

"No, of course you didn't. That's simply the way things were. But it's not going to be that way with us," she said firmly. "I want you to enjoy living with me, I want our relationship to be something you cherish rather than resent."

"Valentine, for God's sake," he began an angry protest.

She placed a silencing finger across his lips. "Hush, love, let me finish. It's important that I say this. I don't need you to take care of me. I'm not dependent on you for *any*thing. And I don't want you needing me, either. We're two self-reliant people . . . well, you are, anyway. But I'm learning."

She brushed back the fallen lock of hair from his brow. His regard was so intense! The sense of woman-power flooded her again like an adrenaline rush.

"This is the way I want it to be, with both of us, Jordan. I've made two resolutions for myself and I'm going to try very hard to keep them. The first is that no one is more important than I am in any of my relationships. The second is that my primary reason for not doing what another person expects of me is 'I don't want to.' I matter, darling. You matter. Our individual needs are vitally important and deserving of respect. In fact, speaking for myself, I demand it."

Yes! Yes! Yes!

As Elisse's exultant approval rang through her mind, Valentine smelled flowers again. Orange blossoms this time. She laughed aloud and wound her arms around Jordan's neck. "And yes," she mused between nibbling kisses, "I am and probably always will be a romantic. But I don't think we're ever going to merge into oneness. Nevertheless, I'm willing."

"Valentine . . ." Jordan cleared his throat. "Willing to do what?"

"To love you with all my heart." Valentine drew a quick breath. "So. Will you be my husband, to have and to hold from this day forth?"

Jordan looked stunned, then delighted, and after that Valentine lost track of the expressions flitting across his face. "Yes," he said. "Oh, hell, yes!" With a joyous laugh he scooped her up, whirled her around and kissed her half a dozen times.

Then he set her from him and assumed a serious mien. "I must warn you, though, there'll be strings attached. Demands, actually, nonnegotiable, of course: absolute commitment, trust, fidelity, eternal love, blazing passion, back rubs and warm-oil massages, the whole nine yards."

"The whole nine yards?" she echoed with a slow smile.

His crooked grin traced a well-worn trail around her heart. "I would accept nothing less."

"I would offer nothing less."

He sobered. "I doubt I've resolved all my problems, Val.

But one thing I promise you, baby, I'll always be there for you and the kids. Always," he repeated fiercely. "I'm not like my father, I swear it, my love. There'll be no running away when the going gets rough. I love you, my September Valentine. True, it's the scariest feeling in the world, but I'm a brave man. Well, with you here beside me, I am," he amended with humorous self-mockery. He pulled her back into his arms. "God, I have missed you!"

"And I've missed you. Oh, Jordan, without you I'm—" Valentine stopped. "A whole person," she asserted, "but a lonely one. How many kids?" she asked as a new thought struck her. "Two, four, five, what?"

"Valentine!" Jordan groaned and buried his face in her hair.

His laughter vibrated against her chest. Smiling, Valentine wrapped him in her arms and held him with soaring dreams of a bright future. Her gaze fell upon the old white house visible through the trees. Laughter and music emanated from its open windows. Light streamed through the panes as if to light her path home.

Feeling profoundly blessed, Valentine bowed her head. "Thank you, Elisse," she whispered soundlessly.

You're most welcome, darling, came the soft, lilting answer. But you're the one who's responsible for all this. You, Valentine, not me. I simply suggested; it is you who acted, and thus achieved your dream.

Her smile radiant, Valentine sent a questioning thought back to the angel. *After Jordan and I are married, will you still be with me?*

Oh, yes, I'll still be with you. Although not in the way you think, the angel replied with a sly, celestial laugh.

Though puzzled at that last remark, Valentine's attention was reclaimed by the man who tipped her chin and kissed her. As usual, she became lost in the joy of loving him. But this time, suffused with the certain knowledge that they truly belonged to each other, she was bathed in a sensation she'd experienced only once before—and that was not of this earth.

For a fleeting instant she saw herself in a place of swirling white mists, standing before a soft-as-rose water desk reading from the Akashic Records—her last words as the plane went down. *Please let me find bliss. . . .*

A soft laugh entwined the luminous thought arcing across her mind. *You asked for bliss, Valentine, and you found it. Love is the key. Love fills the universe, and earth is a part of it.*

Valentine's radiant smile acknowledged the message, as well as the gossamer breeze playing around her face like a felicitous blessing. She snuggled closer in Jordan's arms. "I love you," she whispered.

"I love you," Jordan murmured. He sighed, his clasp tightening. "I know we have to go back to the party, but tonight is ours, my September Valentine. And every night for the rest of our lives."

Epilogue

The Being known throughout the southeast quadrant of the sixth plane of the tenth realm as Sunbeam, put the finishing touches on a bejeweled wreath, then stepped back to assess the results of his labors.

"Beautiful!" the neophyte angel, Miriam, assured him. "Because of your loving efforts, Bradley will leave here with a song in his heart."

After judicious consideration, Sunbeam agreed. His first attempt at decorating looked pretty good if he did say so himself. He had strung rainbows from horizon to horizon, then woven baby stars through the shimmering bands of color. Butterfly streamers fluttered in the soft stellar breeze. Instead of balloons, glowing comets and a glorious version of the northern lights danced across the heavens. Later, when the party really got going, an Angelic Chorus would perform.

Divinely satisfied, Sunbeam sent Valentine a rush of good feeling in lieu of thanks. Her party had given him the charming idea. Bradley would love this oh-so-appropriate way of saying adieu. Or so he thought.

"What the blazes is all this?" the guest of honor asked, eyeing the colorful—or, in his eyes, gaudy—display.

"It's a celebration, Bradley," Sunbeam explained.

"What are you celebrating?" Bradley asked testily.

"Your leaving," Sunbeam replied. "Oh, dear, that didn't come out right," he murmured, hiding a grin as Miriam giggled. "We're just so proud of you, Bradley. It's an admirable decision you've made, certainly worthy of celebrating."

Bradley harrumphed and checked his watch. "As usual, Elisse is late. What's taking her so long? Doesn't she realize I'm on a time delay? The body has already been born and I must enter it."

"I'm sure she'll be along any minute," Sunbeam soothed. "Miriam's leaving for earth today, too, as a replacement for Jordan's current guardian angel."

Miriam nodded, her blue eyes somber. "I just hope I'll be better at this role than I was as his mother."

"You will be," Sunbeam assured her. "Ah, and here's our Elisse, lovelier than ever!" he exulted as a radiant female in full angelic regalia appeared beside him.

Elisse examined one of her wings. "A seagull." She sighed, brushing at the dingy white splotch. "Hello, Sunbeam, hello, Miriam! And darling Bradley—surprising us all with your decision to take on physical form again! Earth won't be the same after this," she predicted merrily.

"No, it most certainly won't," Sunbeam agreed. "Have you something to share with us, Elisse?" he prompted as Bradley gathered himself to speak.

"Yes, indeed I do. So before you start fussing at me, Bradley, let me tell you my news." With a little shrug, Elisse disposed of her wings. "I, too, have decided to take another turn at Earth living. And furthermore . . ." She paused for effect. "I've just come from watching Valentine fulfill the last of your conditions. She is now free to live out her natural life span!"

Bradley, deprived of the lecture already churning up his throat, stared at the radiant Being. "Excellent news, of course. But you know you transgressed, Elisse."

"Now and then we just absolutely have to break a rule," Sunbeam opined.

"The results do not absolve the misdeed," Bradley thundered.

"The ends do not justify the means," Elisse helped.

"*Precisely. You were far too familiar with your charge, much too visible—*"

"*I know I was. I should never have become so involved. That scene on the River Walk was inexcusable. But I couldn't resist,*" she said, casting Sunbeam a woeful glance. "*Which is why I, too, am reincarnating. Obviously I left some loose ends behind during my last earth-life.*" Her luminous smile showered upon Bradley. "*And why are you returning?*"

Bradley, looking uncomfortable, hemmed and hawed for a moment. "*Let's just say that I, too, left a few loose ends,*" he said dismissively.

"*Ah. Well, doubtless you'll benefit from the experience.*" Overlooking his scowl, Elisse perched on a puffy little cloud and coaxed, "*Do tell us all about the parents you've chosen, Bradley. Intellectuals, I imagine, like yourself!*"

"*In point of fact, I don't know anything about them. I've entrusted all that to Higher Counsel,*" Bradley said with lofty unconcern. "*I'm certain, however, that they've chosen an appropriate couple, and that I'll be reared in an environment tailored to my disposition and temperament.*"

Elisse smiled to herself as she imagined him in earthly garb: a portly man in a three-piece suit aptly accessorized with a watch fob and chain. She blinked, and he was Bradley the pompous seraph again.

"*You don't even know their names?*" she asked.

"*Oh, yes. A couple named Loving, a good-omen name in itself, you'll agree. They reside in an area affectionately called the Lone Star State. I'm certain my qualifications were taken into careful consideration before the selection was made on my behalf,*" he stated.

The Lovings? Elisse was taken with a fit of coughing as the name registered. Ozell and Vera? And Bradley? "*Oh my,*" she said, casting Sunbeam a wild glance.

Smiling benignly, Sunbeam's eyes met hers in a private message. He would keep his present position. Someone had to be on call for all the tribulation he sensed Bradley was in for.

A laugh tickled her throat. Clearing it, she asked brightly, "*Boy or girl, Bradley?*"

"Since this is a twin-birth, I had a choice of male or female, but I feel I can do the most good in the position of dominant male. Thus I can counsel my weaker sibling in times of feminine need." Feeling too good about his noble decision to notice Elisse's quick turn of head, Bradley asked expansively, *"And what about you, my dear?"*

"Oh, I'll be right back at the scene of the crime, so to speak," Elisse said with a leprechaun's smile. *"Firstborn daughter to Valentine and Jordan Wyatt."*

Three breathtaking novellas by these acclaimed authors celebrate the warmth of family, the challenges of the frontier and the power of love...

ROSANNE BITTNER
DENISE DOMNING
VIVIAN VAUGHAN

CHERISHED LOVE

No one believes in ghosts anymore, not even in Salem, Massachusetts. And especially not sensible Helen Evett, a widow who lives for her two teenaged kids and who runs the best preschool in town. But when little Katie Byrne enters her school, strange things begin to happen. Katie's widowed father, Nat, begins to awaken feelings in Helen that she had counted as dead. But why does Helen get the feeling that Linda, Katie's mother, is reaching beyond the grave to tell her something?

As Helen and Nat each explore the pain of their losses and the joy of their newfound love, Linda Byrne's ghost plays a bold hand, beseeching Helen to uncover the mystery of her death. But what Helen finds could make her the target of a jealous killer and a modern Salem witch-hunt that threatens her, her family...and the magical second-time-around love that's taking her and Nat by storm.

BESTSELLING, AWARD-WINNING AUTHOR

Beyond Midnight

KAT MARTIN

Award-winning author of *Creole Fires*

GYPSY LORD
_____ 92878-5 $5.99 U.S./$6.99 Can.

SWEET VENGEANCE
_____ 95095-0 $6.50 U.S./$8.50 Can.

BOLD ANGEL
_____ 95303-8 $5.99 U.S./$6.99 Can.

DEVIL'S PRIZE
_____ 95478-6 $5.99 U.S./$6.99 Can.

MIDNIGHT RIDER
_____ 95774-2 $5.99 U.S./$6.99 Can.

Publishers Book and Audio Mailing Service
P.O. Box 070059, Staten Island, NY 10307
Please send me the book(s) I have checked above. I am enclosing $_____ (please add
$1.50 for the first book, and $.50 for each additional book to cover postage and handling.
Send check or money order only—no CODs) or charge my VISA, MASTERCARD,
DISCOVER or AMERICAN EXPRESS card.

Card Number_____

Expiration date_____Signature_____

Name_____

Address_____

City_____State/Zip_____
Please allow six weeks for delivery. Prices subject to change without notice. Payment in
U.S. funds only. New York residents add applicable sales tax.   KAT 11/96